Born in the UK, **Becky Wick**[...] interminable wanderlust from[...] lived and worked all over the[...] to Dubai, Sydney, Bali, NYC and Amsterdam. She's written for the likes of *GQ*, *Hello!*, *Fabulous* and *Time Out*, a host of YA romance, plus three travel memoirs—*Burqalicious*, *Balilicious* and *Latinalicious* (HarperCollins, Australia). Now she blends travel with romance for Mills & Boon and loves every minute! Tweet her @bex_wicks and subscribe at beckywicks.com.

Lifelong romance addict **JC Harroway** took a break from her career as a junior doctor to raise a family and found her calling as a Mills & Boon author instead. She now lives in New Zealand and finds that writing feeds her very real obsession with happy endings and the endorphin rush they create. You can follow her at jcharroway.com, and on Facebook, Twitter and Instagram.

A MARRIAGE HEALED IN HAWAII

BECKY WICKS

NURSE'S SECRET ROYAL FLING

JC HARROWAY

MILLS & BOON

First published in Great Britain 2024
by Mills & Boon, an imprint of HarperCollins*Publishers* Ltd,
1 London Bridge Street, London, SE1 9GF

www.harpercollins.co.uk

HarperCollins*Publishers* Macken House, 39/40 Mayor Street Upper, Dublin 1, D01 C9W8, Ireland

A Marriage Healed in Hawaii © 2024 Becky Wicks

Nurse's Secret Royal Fling © 2024 JC Harroway

ISBN: 978-0-263-32159-3

05/24

A MARRIAGE
HEALED IN HAWAII

BECKY WICKS

MILLS & BOON

For Hawaii, with love for all who are still rebuilding
after the 2023 wildfires.

CHAPTER ONE

LANI KEKOA STEPPED onto the decking of Mermaid Cove Marine Sanctuary, and sucked in a lungful of fresh, salty air. The midday sun kissed the surface of the ocean in sparkles and high in the palms, two myna birds trilled in conversation. Crossing to Pua's tank, she ran her hand softly over the turtle's lumpy brown shell. "How are you, buddy?"

Pua wriggled his wrinkly legs in reply, and she leaned against the rail of the dock, letting the warm breeze tickle her skin. Her eyes scanned the bay, searching for the dolphins playing around the early-morning boats, but something else caught her eye. What was that in the water, floating in the white surf? A long white object, but not driftwood, and not an abandoned water toy either, she was sure. Lani stared at it for a few moments, trying to make out what it was. Then…

Oh, no.

Quick as a flash she was on her feet, racing down the steps and across the sand for the Jet Ski. Revving the engine to life, she tore across the waves toward the object, her heart pounding with dread as the shape became clearer. Cutting the engine, she drifted closer to the baby dolphin, so still and lifeless. "Oh, poor baby."

Taking a deep breath, she cast her eyes to the Hawaiian sky, trying to calm herself. Not an easy task, as her emotions were bubbling like lava inside her. They should have been able to stop this by now!

A flash of silver caught her eye. The pod of dolphins was leaping and playing in the waves, except for one. The mother of this calf no doubt. The creature swam up close, put her silver head up inches from the Jet Ski, and nudged the baby. The action brought tears to Lani's eyes; she knew what it was like to be a mother in distress, the gut-wrenching, soul-shattering pain of realizing you've lost something irreplaceable, forever.

"I'm so sorry," she whispered. "I'll figure out what's happening, what's causing this, I promise."

The dolphin met her eyes in a moment of what she swore was understanding, and Lani again felt the urge to cry. It was her duty to protect them, to always look after the ocean for them, but this felt out of her control. Why were the dolphins dying?

Reaching the shore with the lifeless calf on the back of the Jet Ski, she saw Mahina. Her assistant was walking from the back room onto the dock, carrying a white storage container full of fish.

She took one look at Lani's face and dropped the container. "No!" she wailed, speeding down the steps, dropping to her knees beside the poor, dead creature.

Lani's shoulders tensed, noting the marks on the dolphin's skin. Blemishes, almost like burns, just like the one they'd discovered just a few days ago. That one hadn't died, thank goodness, but it had been badly injured and carried the same marks.

"What is going on?" Lani whispered, forcing her emotions to stay buried as Arnie and Mo, from the conservation management program, arrived to take the calf away for an autopsy. She'd join them later—she often worked with the scientists on necropsies of marine mammals. But it was going to be beyond frustrating having to wait four to six weeks for the finalized reports.

Mahina hung her head, her face hidden behind her mass of wavy brown hair.

"We need to find out what's causing this," she said to the guys, flashing her eyes to Lani, who nodded slowly. Lani had been working with the dolphins for years and something had definitely changed recently. They were suffering some kind of skin disease—that much was clear—but even as senior vet at the marine sanctuary with over twenty years of experience dealing with every oceanic creature around Oahu, she was out of ideas as to what might be causing the strange marks to appear.

Later, as they did their rounds with the mammals in the tanks at the back of the sanctuary, Mahina shoved her hair back, looking at her with some trepidation. "Maybe you should call...you know."

Lani bristled. "Mika? No."

Mahina sighed, like she'd been storing this question up all day, and expecting this very reply, too. "But he deals with stuff like this all the time. He was the one who figured out why the sharks were getting sick in the Red Triangle, he linked it to that shipping route..."

"We don't need my ex-husband getting involved, Mahina. Just...no."

Lani huffed out a sigh as Mahina held her hands up. She didn't mean to snap, but her assistant vet nurse had struck a nerve. The last time she'd heard anything about Mika had been about a year ago, when she'd run into his mother and learned he had a serious girlfriend.

Hayley was some perky blonde thing, no more than thirty, probably, judging by the photo she'd been shown later after

Mahina had stalked him online. Older than *they* had been when they'd walked down the aisle, her own pregnant belly bulging from her white gown, her hand gripping her father's... seeing Mika, at twenty-four, two years her senior and impossibly, devastatingly handsome, waiting for her *I do* in his tux.

Catching a glimpse of herself in the window to the storage room, she puffed up her hair. At forty-seven, people said she hardly looked a day older than thirty-five, but they were probably just being kind. Her thighs weren't as firm, her belly wasn't so quick to fit so snugly into the band of her jeans, her hair was losing its luster and at times she missed the old her— the one who'd grown complacent in her smooth, taut skin, and her uniform of Daisy Dukes and bikini tops. But then, it wasn't like she was out to look sexy these days, or even lure another man! What could she have to offer a man, anyway? Her whole life was the sanctuary these days, and her foster daughter, Anela, just eight years old and already the biggest challenge she'd ever taken on, she thought, picturing Anela's mother suddenly—her good friend Sharie. Had it really been nearly a year since she'd taken on the new foster duties, after Sharie had unexpectedly passed away?

Life is just a series of challenges I'm not equipped to handle, she thought briefly, before she could bite back the surge of self-loathing.

Every bit of self-deprecation boiled down to what had happened to Iolana; she knew this, but it didn't stop her dwelling on her misgivings anyway. Or on her baby daughter, who'd be an adult by now, if she'd lived.

Did Mika still think about it all, too? Maybe he did, but he'd moved on in other ways. At least, over twenty years spent in the US, away from the island and *her*, had proved enough time for him to get the full replacement package in Hayley. Good for him, she thought. If that made him happy, good. God knows they'd only brought each other misery before he'd packed up and left for California.

You know why he left, the voice inside her head chided.

And she closed her eyes as the image of their beautiful, perfect daughter flashed into her mind's eye, faster than she could block the rush of stomach-twisting pain that followed.

No. Focus.

There was work to do, and anyway, Mika probably wouldn't come here even if she called him. He was always busy. And there were too many memories here, waiting to bite them both.

Lani was still battling with what to do as she lay in the hammock on the house porch later, listening to Anela giggling at the new batch of kittens who'd already clawed their way into their hearts. Was she being silly, not calling him? Mika knew the ocean around here better than anyone. He'd grown up in it; the waters around Oahu used to be his playground. Him and his sharks. No one could believe the way he'd actually befriended a tiger shark!

A small frown creased her brow as she looked at Anela bopping her nose to a kitten's. Anela's mother, Sharie, had lost her life just over a year ago as a result of her own too-close encounter with a great white shark. Hence Lani had put her own maternal inadequacies aside and stepped up. Sharie was her friend, so of course she'd taken Anela in; the kid had no one else! What Mika did would scare the child silly if she knew about his job, but maybe Mahina was right and he *was* the only one who could help the dolphins. If there was even the slightest glimmer of a chance he could help, it would be worth a few bad trips down memory lane.

She picked up her phone.

After a few rings, a gruff voice answered, "This is Mika."

Oh... God, he sounds the same, only more...distant.

"Hi," she said, clearing her throat. "It's Lani."

A spark ignited in his voice then. "What's wrong?"

What? Just three words from me and he knows something's wrong?

"It's the dolphins," she said, clutching the phone tight. "We found a dead calf today, and we've noticed some kind of skin disease on several others but the tests we've run so far haven't shown anything conclusive. I mean, we'll know more after this necropsy but it'll take weeks for that to happen and... I thought maybe..."

"Lani. Breathe."

She shut her mouth. His command cut straight through her rambling monologue like a knife blade, and she swallowed a giant lump from her throat that felt an awful lot like a sob being stamped out. Closing her eyes, she breathed long and hard. *In. Out.* He knew how passionate she was about the dolphins.

"They're dying, Mika," she managed to say. She was gripping the phone so hard now her palms were sweating.

"Okay," he said, after a pause. "I can probably make the 10:00 a.m. from LAX."

She sprang up in the hammock and stared at Anela, stunned. "Tomorrow? Oh...okay."

"See you tomorrow. Keep breathing, Lani." He clicked the phone off.

Lani sat back, letting out all the air she'd been storing in her lungs. Ten a.m. tomorrow? Was he serious?

Anela's head was cocked in interest now. "Who was that?"

Lani blinked. What to say...what to say. Who was Mika now? She shrugged, fighting a smile. Mika wasn't just her ex-husband, she thought, glancing at her wrist. The tattooed turtle with its geometric shell was still a jet-black inky reminder that he'd been her Honu longer than her ex. The Honu, or turtle, was a Hawaiian cultural symbol of longevity, safety, and mana, the spiritual energy that coursed through everyone's blood here. Maybe Mika thought of her, too, every time he looked at his matching tattoo. He'd had his inked on his upper arm, hers on her inner wrist.

"Someone who used to be very important to me," she replied, noting how the words *used to* from her own mouth sent her stomach into a knot. What had she just gone and done, inviting him back into her life?

CHAPTER TWO

MIKA STEPPED OFF the plane onto the sun-kissed tarmac at Daniel K. Inouye International Airport. Dragging his small case, he felt the warm Hawaiian breeze sweep over him, carrying with it the familiar earthy scent of salt water and plumeria. In arrivals, judging by the bustle of locals and tourists already draped in leis made from sweet-smelling frangipanis, Oahu was no different from his last visit several years ago. But everything *felt* different. Because last time he'd only seen family and friends, not Lani. And now, no one else knew he was even coming.

He'd taken a much-needed vacation over the month of July in order to come here, but he hadn't even told Manu yet. His brother, aka SparkyMan—the renowned island electrician— would give him no end of stick over that, no doubt, never mind his mother, but he'd only thought of Lani when he'd packed his bags. She was here. Less than twenty miles away. And she needed him.

It made him more apprehensive than it should, seeing as he'd known the woman most of his life. What on earth had propelled him to offer to fly here, mere seconds after answering the phone? He could only blame the fact that he was tired, a little bored and emotionally drained after the breakup with Hayley.

Despite it being an almost incomprehensible twenty-two

years now since his and Lani's divorce, something about hearing his ex-wife upset had always spoken to his heart. Part of that, he had to admit, was definitely due to the guilt. It weighed heavily on him like an anchor: guilt for not taking a step back from his work when it had mattered, when being there for Lani and Iolana had been more important than anything. Guilt for not realizing how badly Lani had wanted to get back to her veterinary studies and qualify, for not picking up some of the slack with the baby sooner. Guilt for not knowing the early signs of meningitis, for brushing off his daughter's cold hands and feet and sniffles as a mild cold before calling the sitter and heading out with Lani out on the dive boat that day after her dive partner had canceled at the last minute. He'd wanted to support her getting back into her research, finally, but hours later, when Iolana had been lying in hospital, surrounded by strangers, attached to tubes and drips, they'd still been out on the dive boat, making up for being so distracted in the first place. That guilt, for letting down his daughter and his wife, would follow him until the day he died.

Mika bundled his case into the rental car. No need for GPS. Driving down the island's winding roads, verdant foliage hugged every curve, and glimpses of turquoise water winked at him through the gaps in towering palm trees. He was certainly not in Pasadena anymore. He was...home?

He sniffed at himself. Oahu hadn't been his home for years, but his heart told him otherwise as he kept on driving. It was a familiar ache that he'd grown used to ignoring, but now it pulsed like an open wound. The Mermaid Cove Marine Sanctuary Lani had started and built from the ground up was near Kahala, the laid-back part of the island, famed for its tranquil solitude, limited fanfare and next to no nightlife. The best part. Far from the world-renowned surf breaks and the craziness of

Waikiki, it was where they'd grown up and fallen in love, and then fallen to pieces, he thought grimly, stopping at a light and rubbing at his temples. He wasn't here to dredge up the past.

Oahu was a magical place, the perfect blend of island paradise and urban energy—something he'd never quite managed to find in California. Vibrant flowers painted a rainbow of colors at every turn in the road. With each passing mile, the rhythmic sound of waves washing gently against the shore felt intoxicating and invigorating, waking him up despite his tiredness. How had he forgotten the way this place always made him feel? There was never any reason to be bored here; he'd never once turned to the TV for comfort at the end of a long day like he'd been doing these last few weeks, without Hayley around. The ocean was all he'd needed, living on the brink of it, immersing himself in its depths. This island had been his forever home. Before they'd lost Iolana. Before he'd also lost Lani, and part of himself, too.

A message popped up on his phone, on the dash. Hayley.

I miss you babe :-(

She's used the sad face, he thought, suddenly irritated.

Emojis were so devoid of the characteristics they were supposed to embody; they were the lazy person's language. He'd been with her for two years, delighting at first in her busy, fulfilled life; her carefree attitude. The age gap had been an issue for a while, though, at least for him. He was happy winding down the day with a book or a sunset from the veranda. She was in her thirties, and wasn't happy unless her diary was full, morning to night—bands, parties, launches, lunches, most of which she now wanted him to attend with her. "It's a couple's thing," she would say, which had eventually forced him to admit to himself that he wasn't in the right couple after all.

He still felt bad about the way he'd called it off, right before she'd left for her girls' vacation to Milan. But between his senior vet duties at the aquarium and the talk he was set to deliver at the upcoming event for global maritime professionals on the treatment he'd played a major role in implementing for gray reef sharks under threat in the Red Sea, he hadn't found time for that difficult discussion. Sure enough, he'd put his work first again.

And then you came here to another ex, he reminded himself, feeling his jaw twist. *You came the second Lani asked you to.*

Even Hayley knew he and Lani had shared something huge. Lani Kekoa had been a part of so much in his life: childhood dreams, the loss of their little one, his first and only marriage, and the end of it. They'd agreed to stop counseling just two months after Iolana had died; Lani hadn't wanted any of it, instead hiding in her shell like a hermit crab. And in truth, he'd had no interest in its merits back then either, no faith that anything could help either of them. The overpowering grief that they'd never actually addressed properly together still formed the backbone of his existence.

A man carrying a crate of pineapples waved at him from the roadside, and he waved back, wondering if he knew him, deciding he didn't. Hawaiians were just so friendly and welcoming, always willing to drop everything if it meant sharing the aloha spirit that defined their culture. A jolt of pride struck him like a lion. His people, his home. Nowhere else compared. If he was honest, he'd never stopped wondering if someday he would find the strength to move back.

He shrugged off the thought immediately. Of course, he never would. It would be too painful. Lani might need his expertise right now but she would never forget the way he'd put his new family second, back when Iolana was a newborn, or how he'd been so intent on being the breadwinner, becoming a success, that he'd missed vital moments with his daughter he would never get back.

Being two years older and already a qualified vet, even when Lani did stop being a stay-at-home mom to go back to her studies, he'd continued to work just as hard, often calling the sitter when he should have been with his daughter himself. He could still hear the tears in Lani's voice when they'd argued about his tunnel vision. Months before Iolana died she'd begged him not to do that course in disease ecology off the island, said she'd needed him with her. He'd been so sure he was doing the right thing for them all, but all he'd done was deny her the family time she'd wanted. All he'd done was prove he was a terrible husband and father.

Mika scowled. Ending things with Hayley was right, he reminded himself. And not just because she never did quite understand why, after two years together, he wasn't interested in having another child—not with her, not with anyone. He could still hardly believe Lani was fostering a kid now, either. Manu had told him. At first he'd been shocked; how could she do it? How could she put her heart out there again after what she'd been through? But that was Lani all over, forging ahead, onward and upward, offering all that room in her big heart to those who needed it. Still, it was going to be strange, seeing her caring for a child again. Everything they'd planned to do together, she'd gone and done without him.

By the time he had passed the Welcome to Kahala sign and pulled up outside the marine sanctuary, thoughts of seeing Lani again—with all of her beauty and all of their history, and all of their arguments still as fresh as the day they'd happened—made him feel far too hot and bothered. He kind of hoped she'd spare him the agony of looking into her eyes, seeing all that pain, and that a member of her staff would give him the paper file on the dolphins he'd been promised before he drove on to Mama Pip's guesthouse.

But trust his luck to run out now. The door swung open before he reached the porch, and suddenly there she was—looking a picture in denim overalls, holding a bird in her arms.

The lump rose like a stone in Lani's throat as Mika walked toward her, the morning sunlight shining like a halo behind him as he took the steps two at a time up to the porch.

"Hi," she said, her voice sounding small.

"Hi," he replied. "It's good to see you."

She stared at him as her mind spun. He was saying it, but was it true? Was he really thinking it was good to see her, when all they'd done toward the end of their marriage was argue and then avoid each other? This was awkward as hell. There was nothing good about it, she realized now.

The gray, brown and white Hawaiian petrel fidgeted in her arms, and she crossed to the cages, gently placed it inside and closed the door. Mika followed and stood behind her. His presence consumed every single one of her senses, until she forced herself to turn around, and her throat went bone-dry.

Mika was handsome as ever, sturdy and fit. The same strong jaw set in a square frame, the same wide smile that spoke of a thousand boyish secrets. It took her breath away, right before the silent acknowledgment of their shared tragic past stole his expression clean from his face. She saw it then: the deep sorrow that would always unite them, clouding his eyes. He looked like he was about to say something profoundly serious.

"This place looks great. So do you," he said instead, stepping backward, leaning on the railing with his elbow and running his eyes from hers down to the leather sandals she was wearing, then across to the beach.

"You, too," she replied, for lack of anything else to say, instantly self-conscious. "I'm not sure about that bandanna, though. You're more Californian than even I expected."

Mika smirked, touching a hand to the red bandanna tied around his forehead. It was *way* too young for him, she thought with a trace of disdain she knew instantly was just her brain's way of fighting the fact that he looked sexy as hell. Forty-nine years old, and he didn't look a day older than forty, if that.

"Well, I guess that's where I live now," he said, scuffing a boot to the decking. He wore a safari shirt, too. The collar was open and she ran her eyes along the dark hair on his chest beneath it, down to his jeans, really taking in his chunky boots. The boots were made for walking city streets, not Hawaiian beaches. He used to live in sandals, like her.

"Well, thank you for coming." She busied her hands with moving a box of fish toward the rehabilitation tanks. He moved beside her to help as she started tossing tiny fish into the tank with a recovering sea lion in it, stealing glances at him. "I wasn't sure if you would come, Mika. All things considered."

Her words hung in the salty air and he glanced at her sideways, resting both arms on the tank. Would he bring up Iolana? *Please don't... Please don't.*

"You sounded like you needed me," was his tactful reply.

"I do... We do," she corrected herself. So he *wasn't* going to bring up Iolana. Why did that worry her just as much now? Everything they'd gone through together, had it really faded so fast for him?

They fed the other animals together, her conscious of his every movement, while she explained in more detail what had happened with the dolphins. His brow furrowed as he listened and she committed this new version of her ex-husband to memory. He looked different, but better, in the way gorgeous men always did when they aged. Did Hayley know he was here? What did she think about it all? Had he ever told her about their daughter?

His hair was tight to his skull now under the bandanna, the color of a river fish, she thought: black, speckled with silver. It looked good. His years gave it a sheen that only nature's palette could create. She'd stopped the years creeping into her own hair the only way she knew how: with regular trips to the salon. What used to be long tendrils of honeyed blond was now a crop of silver-white, streaked with mahogany, which she usually wore scraped back from her face. Everyone said the color in it made her look younger. In truth she wished she could let it all go gray and be done with it. What was so wrong with ageing anyway? So many people never got the chance. Like their daughter.

Did he think she looked old? she wondered, suddenly self-conscious all over again.

Mika was tanned in the way most Californians were, like the sunshine ran through his blood and up through his skin. She'd felt the muscles underneath his clothes for the first time that day when her shoes had washed away on the tide, back when she'd first realized she had feelings for him. Big feelings. She had crushed so hard watching the then-fifteen-year-old Mika Mahoe on his surfboard, she hadn't even noticed the disappearance of her shoes. He'd given her a piggyback to the road after that, like a knight in shining armor, and she'd wished the moment could've lasted forever.

"Who's this, Lani?"

Anela's voice yanked her from her thoughts. She'd appeared

with Mele from the main building, both dressed in denim shorts, colored T-shirts and baseball hats. Seventeen-year-old Mele was her neighbor's daughter. She often collected young Anela from school when Lani was busy at the sanctuary and now the teen was looking at her with a grin on her freckled face.

"Anela, Mele, hi," she said hurriedly. "This is Mika. He's come to see if he can help figure out what's going on with the dolphins."

Little Anela took his outstretched hand with some trepidation, mouthing the name Mika. Mele did the same. Then the penny dropped for the teen, and her brown eyes widened.

"*The* Mika. As in, your ex-husband?"

"The one and only," Mika replied without missing a beat. "I see my reputation precedes me."

Mele looked him up and down, her grin widening. "I never know who is who. Lani has so many male admirers."

Lani flushed at the blatant lie. "Teenage exaggeration," she refuted.

"It's true," Mele laughed, nudging Anela. "What about Mr. Benos the other week? He was practically begging her to let him take her out after she fixed up that injured bird he brought in, right, Anela?"

"Mr. Benos is seventy-two years old," Lani reminded her.

"Yeah, but he knows a thing or two about how to treat a woman. He's been bringing you fresh fruit and flowers from his greenhouse ever since! Not like that last guy you went out with, the tourist who ghosted you after two dates. What was his name?"

"Don't you have a riding lesson to get to?" Lani replied quickly, noting with excruciating embarrassment the way Mika was observing this banter with a slight smile on his lips. She noticed part of a frown, too, as Mele bid them farewell, ruffled Anela's hair and ran down the steps to the beach.

"She's a treat," he quipped when she was gone, and Lani sighed, picking up the now-empty box of fish. "Quirky. Like you used to be." He took it from her, carrying it back to the refrigerator in the storeroom, and she watched his muscles flex as he lifted it to the top shelf. Maybe it was weird for him, seeing her around kids and teenagers. They'd been younger than Mele when they'd met, and it felt like only five minutes later she'd been pregnant, moving into his parents' annex. Her own parents had been supportive, but had moved to Maui long before that. She'd insisted on staying put, with Mika. Now she saw them twice a month, but they too had drifted from the Mahoes over the years, no thanks to her own emotional retreat after the death of their beloved granddaughter.

She couldn't help remembering the annex now, and the time Mika had bought a ton of roses, stripped them of their petals and used them to spell out Mika Loves Lani on the porch. She'd had to pause her studies for a while after she'd had Iolana, and Mika, being only newly qualified himself, had worked so hard to support them. Sometimes he'd worked so hard she'd barely seen him, which was how she'd gotten so close with his parents. He'd missed a lot, like Iolana's first tooth, but they'd seen it all. They'd loved Iolana so much.

"What's *quirky* mean?" Anela asked him now, following them with a skip in her step, then swirling a finger in the water of the turtle's tank.

"It means interesting," Lani told her, before Mika could cut in, and he raised his eyebrows at the little girl, which made her giggle and ask to borrow his bandanna. He looked confused for a moment, like he wasn't sure what to do.

"Manu told me you were fostering your friend's child," he said quietly, bobbing his head toward an engrossed Anela.

She swallowed tightly, hearing the slight uncertainty in his voice. He probably wondered what kind of foster mother she'd be, when she'd abandoned her own baby to go out in the name of her studies. She'd been so caught up in getting back on track to qualify that she hadn't seen just *how* sick Iolana really was before getting on that research dive boat...

Of course, Manu would have told Mika she was fostering now. Not that she'd seen her ex-brother-in-law lately. Sharing her grief with anyone had felt impossible for so long that she'd shut everyone out. She also couldn't help fear their judgment for her not wanting to be a stay-at-home mom anymore, for not being there when Iolana had needed her most.

Manu had done the wiring for the sanctuary before she'd opened, but it had been pretty awkward for her to say the least.

"What happened to Anela's parents?" Mika asked now.

"Her dad passed away before she was born, and her mom... died a year ago. She has no other living relatives." Lani held back the rest of the information. She debated telling him about the fatal shark attack that had taken Sharie. Mika lived and breathed sharks, while Anela understandably couldn't even stand to step foot in the ocean.

Mika was nodding at her in thought. Again, he looked like he wanted to say something. But a sudden ruckus behind them took his words away.

CHAPTER THREE

MAHINA WAS A MESS, bloodied and bruised. "I couldn't swerve in time," she managed to explain as Lani ushered her back through to the bench in the operating room. She could barely put any weight on her left leg and her left elbow was bleeding, too.

Anela was staring at the blood. Before she could order the child back outside, Mika stood in front of her, shielding her eyes from it, so Lani rushed for the first aid kit.

"Why didn't you go to the hospital?"

"This was the closest place!"

"What happened?"

"A motorcycle happened, right in front of me! Forced me off the road on my bike, then he sped off!"

Behind her, Mika had walked Anela back to the door and pulled something out of his bag. She couldn't quite make out what it was with his back to them, but thank goodness the girl was distracted. Soon they had Mahina lying flat on her back on the table they usually reserved for sea lions and injured wild birds.

"I was almost here when he hit me, so I came to you," she explained, wincing in pain as Mika rolled up her trouser leg and inspected the wound. The gash looked pretty nasty. It probably needed stitches. "Good to see you, Mika," she managed.

"Good to see you, too, not so much the blood. Last time I

used a needle it was on a shark's fin but..." Mika reached for
the gauze as Lani swabbed the wound with antiseptic. "I can
try, save you another trip to the hospital?"

"I trust you, Mika," Mahina said, gasping for breath, clutching Lani's hand.

Lani tossed her cotton swabs into the trash and stepped
between them. Sure, they all knew each other. Mahina had
been a teenager when Mika had left the island and she'd always idolized him; didn't everyone around here? But letting
him stitch up her leg?

"I think we should get her to St. Paul's," she said, and thankfully he agreed.

"We can take my car."

"I have an appointment arriving in fifteen minutes," Lani
explained apologetically, but Mika was already lifting Mahina
carefully in his big arms, heading back the way he'd come in,
where his rental car was parked on the driveway. Lani rushed
to open the door and he laid Mahina out on the back seat, then
Lani watched in bewilderment as the vehicle rumbled away in
a cloud of sand and dust. What just happened?

"Will she be okay?" Anela asked behind her. She was
clutching a book, and seemed as unsure about it as the situation with poor Mahina.

"She'll be all right... I hope," she replied, although, the
more she thought about it, it didn't seem like Mahina would be
able to put weight on her leg for a while, even after the hospital
stitched her up. She'd probably need time off, and rightly so
after what had happened, but they were already short-staffed.

"What have you got there?" she asked Anela now, taking the
book from her hands distractedly, wondering who she might
call to cover. Hilda, their Danish locum, had already left for
her annual trip home.

"Mika gave it to me but I don't like it," Anela said, walking to where the injured petrel was resting in the cage at the side of the room. Lani had saved the petrel's wing from the threat of amputation. Anela stuck her finger through the bars and stroked its soft feathers and Lani frowned as she flipped through *Anatomy of a Shark*, written by Mika himself. It was packed with incredible photos he'd taken while diving and conducting his research. Hmmm. So he'd brought it with him. And given it to Anela, without knowing it would freak her out more than seeing Mahina all bloodied and bruised.

It wasn't his fault. She sighed, realizing she was thinking more about how impressive it was, holding a book that Mika had written. After the photo book he'd self-published in his late teens he'd always said he wanted to write and publish a children's book to encourage wildlife conservation. This one wasn't exactly for kids, but then maybe that dream had died with their daughter. There was so much she didn't know about her Honu now.

Between appointments, she found herself flicking through the book on the deck, admiring the colorful photos, and wondering if the tiger shark he'd somehow befriended, Nala, was still around. Would that graceful creature recognize Mika, if the two were to meet again? Sometimes people saw Nala on dives, but it must have been years since Mika met her himself. That relationship had been such a testament to his loving soul; he loved all creatures. These days, she didn't even know if he had a dog! It was sad, not knowing him anymore, she thought despondently.

When her phone sounded out a couple hours later, it wasn't news from the hospital, like she'd been expecting. It was Mika.

Mahina would be fine but being at the hospital had drained Mika, both physically and emotionally. Hospitals for humans were the worst, never mind all those memories of being there with Lani the night they'd lost Iolana rushing back in. Still, he had to admit, there were good memories everywhere on this island, too.

Time hadn't marred Lani's looks one little bit, he thought as he steered the car back toward the sanctuary. In fact, she looked better than ever and just seeing her had his brain on rewind—all the times he'd walked behind her when they were teenagers, admiring her butt in her Daisy Dukes, before he'd even worked up the courage to kiss her.

Despite the years that had passed since they last saw each other, her beauty still took his breath away. He was just wondering about all those men that Mele had said swarmed around her, realizing a scowl had taken his face hostage, when he noticed the line of cars ahead of his had crept to a standstill. People were hurrying from their vehicles and taking the path down to the beach, one after the other. He opened his door.

"It's a humpback whale, she's stranded near the shore. We need to act fast," someone said, and he bolted from the car with his phone to his ear, a surge of adrenaline coursing through his veins. In seconds he was standing on the sand, asking *himself* how on earth a humpback whale got stuck like this.

"Don't touch it. I've just called Lani at the marine sanctuary," he heard himself say, feeling his heart clench at the sight of the majestic creature lying helpless on the damp sand. Its massive body heaved with each labored breath, and fear and pain shone in the whale's dark, gentle eyes.

In minutes, Lani had arrived and was hurrying from the rescue vehicle, her shirt flapping in the wind, her sandals clacking on the hard sand, Anela at her heels. The crowd parted as she approached, and he helped her move the gawking crowd to a reasonable distance. Anela stopped even farther back, looking on like she was afraid. An island kid, afraid of a whale? Or maybe it was the water she was scared of, he thought, which would be even stranger.

No time to think about how that could even be possible. The whale was slowly being strangled by fishing nets.

"Get some towels and blankets from the truck, keep it wet and cool," Lani instructed him. He didn't miss her eyes roving his body for a moment as his shirt flew open. "I'm going to check its vitals."

"Got it," he answered, racing to the rescue truck, quickly grabbing supplies and hurrying back again.

Mika watched Lani's slender fingers working deftly as she checked the whale's heartbeat, while he instructed two of the bystanders to gently douse the animal with water. Every now and then their eyes would meet, and he knew they were both thinking that this was just like old times. Lani was never sexier to him than when she was calling the shots.

The whale was a grayish color, so beautiful, so soft to the touch. Its fin was bent and its body covered in barnacles and scars from years of fighting off sharks, but still magnificent nonetheless. Outside of an aquarium, he hadn't seen anything quite like this for a long time.

Pulling a knife from the bag, he got to work alongside Lani, cutting and snipping and detangling, all the while noting how Lani never took her eyes off the whale, not unless she was glancing at Anela, making sure she was okay.

It was pretty impressive that she'd taken to fostering; he'd been *more* than shocked when he'd heard about it from his brother, though he'd tried not to show it, of course. It wasn't just that she could put her heart out there again for another little girl. She was risking something going wrong again, something terrible. He'd be terrified of messing up again, if he were to

ever take on a role like that. What if he missed another crucial sign, made a selfish move he couldn't undo? No. There
was just no way he'd ever do it. He didn't even know how to
react around kids now anyway, he thought, cringing as he remembered how he'd just stood there, when Anela had asked
to see his bandanna up close.

"Is it going to be okay?" Anela asked now, her voice filled
with concern as much as trepidation.

"Yes, honey, don't worry…just stay there, okay?" Lani said.

But then she looked at him and his heart contracted. He
knew what she was thinking. It wasn't good. They needed to
get this creature back into the water, and soon. He sped up
his cutting, and so did Lani, determination written all over
her face. Every second counted. Soon enough, the netting fell
away, and Lani pulled the last of it to the side while he sprinted
back to the rescue truck.

"Hurry," Lani urged through gritted teeth, her voice hoarse
from exertion.

Mika quickly grabbed the specially designed net. He
shouted to Lani to help throw it over the whale's body, securing it tightly around the gentle giant. Then, as fast as he
could, he tied the other end to the winch on the nearby rescue truck. "Ready?" he called to her, his hand hovering over
the controls.

"Ready," Lani confirmed, taking a step back and motioning for the anxious crowd to do the same.

"Here we go!" Mika held his breath as the winch whirred
to life, pulling the net taut and gently lifting the whale off the
sand. The crowd seemed to be holding their breath, too, as the
whale was lifted closer to the water. It was a slow process; he
had no choice, but with each passing second their humpback
came one millimeter closer to freedom.

"Keep going!" Lani instructed, her eyes still fixed on the whale, even as he caught a reporter speeding from the roadside down to the beach with a camera. "We're almost there!"

Mika watched as Lani walked around the whale, guiding his every movement.

"Stop!" Lani yelled suddenly as the whale released a bellowing sound, causing him to release the winch controls. "We need to check her breathing before we move any further, she's probably stressed, poor thing. She might be pregnant."

Lani pressed a stethoscope against the whale's side. After a few tense seconds, she nodded. "Okay, we're good. And she's not pregnant. Keep going."

Relief washed over him as he resumed operating the winch. Inch by inch, the creature moved closer to the water, until finally, he was able to get it submerged in the shallows.

"Well done," Lani said, her voice barely audible to him over the sound of crashing waves. His heart pounded as he watched her wade into the water, the salty sea foaming around her waist, soaking her shirt, which she'd probably been too distracted to remove.

The woman with the camera was wading in after her, but Lani ignored her, focused only on the whale. Soon it was free. He couldn't keep the grin from his face as it swam for the horizon, emitting a mighty gush of water from its blowhole. The crowd erupted into cheers and laughter and whoops of relief.

"Was she just saying thank you?" Anela asked as he met them on the sand.

"I think so," Lani said, and Mika tried not to look at the way her wet shirt was sticking to her skin, showing her bra through the fabric. "I can't believe we did that," Lani exclaimed, her eyes wide with amazement as the reporter hurried up to them. "We actually saved a humpback whale, your first day back on the island. It's almost like it knew you could help it, that you'd be there…"

She met his eyes and he felt a rare surge of pride at the way she was looking at him. It threw him right back to the night she'd told him nervously that she was pregnant. An accident. At first he'd been too stunned to speak; they were both so young. Yes, he'd wanted to be a dad, but not then—they had too much to do! Both of them were on track for successful careers, and Lani would have to postpone her studies…

But the idea of a child, *their* child, had suddenly felt so right, such a blessing, that he'd picked her up and spun her around and asked her to marry him right there and then. He knew he'd do whatever it took to make it work, to keep them safe and stable and provided for.

"Can I get an interview?" the reporter interrupted, pointing the camera at them.

Lani cleared her throat before starting to answer her questions, glancing at him even as he stepped back and let her take the helm. Usually, he was the one answering questions about marine rescues, but this was Lani's territory now, not his.

When the reporter finally left, Lani ushered Anela toward the rescue vehicle. "We'd better get back. I have an appointment with a frigate bird and it looks like it's going to be just me for a while," he heard her explain to the child.

Mika sprinted after her. "Just you?"

She bundled the scraps of netting into the back, buckling Anela into the back seat. "Yes, just me, I guess, till Mahina gets better. She's my only full-timer at the moment."

She sat in the driver's seat, and shut the door as if she suddenly couldn't wait to put some distance between them again. Mika watched her click her own seat belt into place. For a second, when she turned back to check if Anela was good to go, and told her the whale would be fine, he was moved to silence by the look of pure, maternal affection on her face. The same way she'd looked at Iolana, he thought with a pang of raw emotion.

"Well, how busy are you at the sanctuary?" he said through the window as she turned the key in the ignition. He should get back into his own car and go to Mama Pip's guesthouse before he landed himself in trouble, but already the wheels of thought were keeping him from walking away.

"Very busy," she answered. He could tell the thought was unsettling her as much as his reignited urges to fix her problems were unsettling *him*.

"Let me help you out while she's recovering," he said, before he could think too much about it.

"Thanks, Mika," Lani said with a tired smile. "But I don't think I can afford another assistant right now."

"Who said anything about paying me? Consider it my penance for being away so long. Besides, I'm pretty good at this stuff, as you know."

"I know," she said and smiled. "You're pretty good at a lot of things, Mr. Author. I saw your book on—" she lowered her voice, glancing back at Anela "—sharks," she whispered.

He felt his eyebrows shoot up. "Why are you whispering?"

"I'll tell you later," she murmured.

He shrugged, resting an arm on the open window. The engine was still running, and she still had her thinking face on.

"Just let me help you, Lani. Being around the sanctuary more might throw some extra light on what's going on with the dolphins. Maybe there's a link with some of the other sick animals..."

"We haven't found one yet." She let out a sigh and he knew he'd put her on the spot. She probably didn't want him around at all except for when he *needed* to be around her, figuring out what was affecting the dolphins, but he was damned if he'd stay here knowing she was suffering in any way. The guilt from taking his eyes off the ball when it came to Iolana still seeped into every one of his actions. The cold hands, her cold feet. His baby girl had been sick and pale, but he'd brushed it off as a minor cold. All babies got the sniffles from time to time, right? He'd chosen to go with Lani after her dive partner had canceled last minute; he'd known the research meant a lot to her. He should have just stayed with his two-year-old daughter instead of leaving her with the sitter. Would he have spotted the signs earlier if he had?

The meningitis had crept up so quickly, the hospital staff had said later. It had been too late, even as they'd rushed through the doors, panting and red-faced, beside themselves with terror and still sticky with seawater. She'd died in Lani's arms.

"Lani…"

"Okay, fine," she said abruptly, and he stepped back from the vehicle. "I guess I could do with a pair of capable hands around the place."

"My hands are your hands, until Mahina's are better," he heard himself say, and he caught a glimmer of a smile on her face as she drove off.

"My hands are your hands," he repeated, cursing himself. *Who even says that?*

After all this time, and all that was behind them, here he was, being reduced to mush again as soon as he was around her. Maybe he'd always known it would be this way, he admitted to himself with a sigh. It was probably why he'd avoided her for more than twenty years. So what on earth was he doing here now?

CHAPTER FOUR

MIKA WAS STANDING at the controls of the research boat, navigating the vessel with practiced ease, as if he'd never been away from the island. He looked so good in a loose denim shirt, unbuttoned, with the morning sun dancing across his chest in the ocean spray. A chest she'd rested her head upon a thousand times, Lani reminisced as a fresh surge of attraction threatened to throw her off-balance on the already rocking boat.

She shouldn't have come out here with him; she should have just let him do the first inspection alone, but something had compelled her; the same thing that had led her to accept his offer of standing in for Mahina the other day. The way he'd handled that whale experience had affected her more than she wanted to admit to herself. And now look at him, shirt flapping open, looking as delicious as when he'd taught her to surf all those years ago. She'd been so bad at it, at first, but then, every time she fell off and he "rescued" her it was so enjoyable, she'd kind of failed on purpose a lot of the time.

Despite the beauty of the ocean, a somber atmosphere had settled between them. She had to wonder if he was thinking about the mysterious dolphin deaths now, or was he thinking of the day they'd lost Iolana, while they were out here together on the waves?

Do not even bring that up, not even in your own head, she reminded herself sternly.

She should have been more concerned about the toddler's sniffles, but she'd been obsessed with getting out here again, back to her plants and coral. The sitter was great; she'd always been a blessing, and Lani had spent so much time with Iolana up till then that she'd decided her studies needed a swift revival if she was ever going to qualify as a vet. Little had she known she was leaving her stay-at-home mom role for good that day, and not just because of her career.

No, talking about it would turn her knees to jelly and bring it all back for him, too, how selfish of a mother she'd been.

Better to focus on their shared passion for protecting marine life, for the new hope he'd brought her by being here, she decided. The photo of her in the paper this morning had started tongues wagging all over town, because of course Mika had been captured in the background. Everyone within a fifty-mile radius knew their history and was now talking about them, which unsettled her more than the boat was doing on these waters.

She'd isolated herself from almost everyone over the years, afraid people would judge her as harshly as she'd always judged herself. Maybe that was one of the reasons she'd agreed to take on Anela, she thought now. A child wouldn't judge her. With a child, she could start afresh, and maybe be a better version of herself than she'd been for Iolana.

"Here," Mika said, turning and handing her a clipboard filled with data sheets. They were out to record any abnormalities they might find, something he intended to do every day that he was here. Apparently, it was crucial that he gather as much information as possible himself; he didn't trust pre-recorded data to be accurate.

His eyes scanned the sheets before locking onto Lani's. "What do you think is happening? You mentioned it could be pollution. Or disease. What does your heart say?"

"Hard to know," she admitted, glancing toward the circling gulls on the horizon. "I can't always trust my heart."

"You used to," he reminded her, taking the wheel again.

"That was before…" Lani swallowed back her words, but not before he drew his lips into a thin line. He knew what she meant, surely.

Before they'd lost their daughter.

Before her heart had imploded and left a gaping hole that made her feel like only half of a person, loaded with so much shame and self-blame that some days, if she thought about it too hard, she could barely breathe. She'd never openly admitted how harshly she'd blamed herself for Iolana's death, for fear that someone might agree with her, but she knew full well her own inadequacies as a mother. The shame of leaving her daughter in her hour of need was so profound, she'd never shift it completely, even if she fostered every living, impoverished, broken child in Hawaii.

"It takes up to six weeks to receive the final necropsy reports, even if I personally attend an autopsy," she said instead, hoping he wouldn't bring up anything personal related to their past. Her heart couldn't handle it if she were to hear even a trace of blame in his voice. He was hiding it well, but surely he still felt it. She'd been relieved he'd called the sitter that day so he could go with her; had barely given it a thought.

"There are so many hoops to jump through, I feel like a dolphin myself sometimes," she said distractedly.

"I can help make that go faster," he replied.

Of course he could, she thought—he'd always known how to get things done, had prided himself on it.

Still, as they collected samples and tested hypotheses and kept the focus of their conversation solely on the marine life, the weight of their past hung heavy in the air like a sail that might suddenly get caught in the wind and blow them in another direction. It had been a day just like this, when it had happened.

Finally, it seemed like Mika couldn't bear the silence any longer. "Lani," he began hesitantly, and her heart almost catapulted out of her chest.

He put the clipboard down and studied her eyes, and she braced herself for him to bring it up: all the things he'd never said, like how if she hadn't been so preoccupied with getting her damn career back on track that they might still have a daughter, *oh, God.*

"Why is Anela so afraid of the water?" he asked.

"What?" Lani released the breath she'd been holding, her hands stilling momentarily as she turned to face him.

"Yesterday," he said, adjusting his bandanna. "On the beach, she looked as if she was scared. At first I thought she was afraid of the whale but no kid in Hawaii thinks whales are anything to be afraid of."

"Anela doesn't like anything that comes from the water," she said, realizing her palms were damp. "A great white shark went for her mother just over a year ago. The poor woman didn't even make it back to shore before she bled out."

"I didn't hear about that," Mika said after a moment, his brow furrowing. "I mean, I usually hear about all shark-related incidents around here."

"They were on vacation in Australia," she explained.

"Damn."

"I know. Anela was with friends, so she didn't see it happen, but she still won't go in the water. She's convinced the same thing will happen to her the second she does."

Mika shook his head at the horizon, and before she knew it he was reaching for her hand, squeezing her fingers till the empathy and long-forgotten feel of his flesh and bone entwined with hers made her blood tingle.

"She can't live here, in a place like this, and avoid the water forever," he said.

"I've tried to coax her in so many times. We all have, but she just won't do it," she heard herself say distractedly, looking down at their hands. Why was her heart singing?

Mika's phone pinged and as he pulled his hand back she saw the name Hayley appear on the screen, along with a sad-face emoji. Gosh, what did someone like her have to be sad about? she thought unkindly, before shaking it off. It wasn't Hayley's fault she was younger and beautiful and would soon have *her* ex-husband back in her skinny yoga-toned arms.

She bristled again, imagining them together, Mika and his pretty young thing. If he still found *Lani* attractive, it was probably just muscle memory, him remembering how she *used to* look underneath her clothes. But still, the thought of him sleeping at Mama Pip's guesthouse, less than half a mile away from her house on the hill, had kept sleep beyond her grasp for most of the night. Their sex life had always been off the charts; did he even remember that? The two guys she'd slept with since their divorce had been brief flings, and neither could hold a candle up to the raging fire she and Mika had ignited.

"Maybe I can help her," he said now, breaking into her unwelcome thoughts.

"With Anela?" Lani felt her brow crease above her sunglasses. She was about to counter his words but she thought better of it. He always wanted to help; everyone had always gone to Mika when things needed to be done. Wasn't that why he was here now, for the good of the dolphins? But Anela had suffered as tragic a loss as they had, and she was only eight years old!

"If she keeps delaying going back into the water, it'll scare her her whole life. You know how those things stay with you."

"Hmmm," she replied without meeting his eyes. Then she realized he was waiting for her to agree with him. *Those things.* Those *things* he was talking about had nothing to do with Anela, not really. But they had everything to do with them.

"Maybe she's not ready yet," she said after a moment, and turned her back, refocusing on checking the map of the reef, so he couldn't press her.

"Maybe she isn't. Or maybe you're not?" he said quietly.

Lani ignored him. Her heart was suddenly pounding like high tide against the base of a cliff.

Of course, she'd only cared about the dolphins when she'd called him, but she should have known that Mika's return would bring up everything she'd tried to barricade away. What had happened to Iolana was an invisible force connecting them, even with her mouth shut and her back turned. Lani's tears, long after he'd left, had never *just* been about their daughter, either. They'd been about everything *they* had lost together, every dream they had buried and every promise that had gone unfulfilled.

Still, she would have to do her best to keep things professional, she thought, glancing back at him directing a water sample into a tube. As long as she was careful not to remind him of her misgivings, not to drag up *any* of the emotions and hardships that had no doubt contributed to his departure from the island and their marriage in the first place, maybe they had a chance at coexisting as colleagues for the few short weeks he'd be here.

Mika approached the injured seal with caution, a tranquilizer syringe at the ready. He didn't want to use the tranquilizer unless it was necessary, but the animal was in critical condition. They'd checked its vital signs. Its body was battered and bruised, and red with lacerations they were struggling to stitch back up. It was laboring for breath, but that didn't stop the muscled creature lunging at himself and Lani from the table, pulling at the straps securing it to the metal slab.

"You're just frightened, buddy, come on," he coaxed, lowering the syringe, stepping in front of Lani in concern as she narrowly avoided a heavy swipe by the creature's head.

"I'm okay," she told him breathlessly, and he nodded. His instinct to protect her had never quite gone away.

Someone had been waiting outside the sanctuary with the seal when they'd stepped off the boat. The seal had been caught in the path of a Jet Ski, which sadly, wasn't that uncommon. He and Lani had set to work quickly, lifting it to a stretcher and bringing the heavy mammal straight inside. The operation was touch and go once they'd sedated it, thankfully without the use of the tranquilizer gun. Its breathing became shallower partway through Lani's careful surgery, and its heartbeat began to slow beneath her hands. He watched her face when he wasn't jumping in to assist, and he marveled at the way she did everything with the same blend of compassion and fierce determination.

"Come on, buddy, stay with us," Lani muttered from behind her mask.

He couldn't help admiring her more and more as the minutes ticked by, her eyes locked on the animal as they had been on that whale, like half of her soul had been poured into it, blended with it. She'd always been like this, he thought, remembering the time she'd cried for an hour over a crushed crab on the beach. It was good to see she hadn't lost her touch, even with everything she'd been through, losing her daughter, losing her friend, Anela's mother. Losing him. The difference was, she'd have been glad to see the back of a man who'd let her and their daughter down so badly.

He could have said so much on that boat this morning, he thought now as his phone pinged in his pocket. It was probably Manu asking when he was free—his brother and everyone else had figured out he was on the island again, no thanks to that reporter and her story on the whale. Or it could be Hayley again, he thought in dismay. He couldn't keep up with her emojis fast enough.

No time to check his phone when Lani needed him. Lani, who he was here to help, but who he also couldn't seem to talk to.

"Oops, sorry," she said now, blushing as she accidentally bumped into him.

"Not a problem," he said, feeling his throat go scratchy.

The tension was always there between them now; it coated their every interaction. Physical, emotional, everything. He'd been wanting to talk to her on the boat, like *really* talk, so why hadn't he? He could at least have spoken their daughter's name, but it had hung like a ghost in the wind, and he'd let it go, telling himself Lani wouldn't *want* to talk about it with him, wouldn't want to face it with him, like Anela wasn't ready to face the water.

They'd grieved alone in the end, after Iolana's death, moving around each other in his parents' place like ships trying and failing to find a port in the darkness. He'd blamed himself for not insisting he stay with Iolana that day, instead of calling the sitter. He'd wanted to go out there with Lani on that boat; he'd wanted to make love to her on the waves like they used to, too. But hearing her *say* she blamed him, too, would have destroyed him, even though he knew he deserved it. So he'd never spoken about any of it, and neither had she. By the time they'd quit on the counselor it had felt a lot like she didn't want him around anymore. And he didn't have any strength left to keep fighting. Leaving here had been the hardest thing he'd ever done.

Finally, after what felt like an eternity, the seal's breathing began to stabilize. Watching Lani press the stethoscope gently to its heart, he knew from the relief on her face that its heartbeat was stronger. The heavy weight of all his thoughts lifted momentarily at the triumph in her smile.

"Close call," she said to the creature, meeting Mika's eyes.

"You're a miracle worker," he heard himself say.

"I don't believe in miracles," she retorted too quickly, her face darkening. "But we got to him just in time. Come on, help me move him. We'll need pain medication and fluids to keep him hydrated—can you get them?"

Maybe it was more skill and compassion than a miracle that had saved the seal's life, he thought, fetching the medication from her meticulously organized cabinet. He wondered what she'd meant, earlier on the boat, when she'd said she didn't trust her heart. She had such a big heart; such good instincts for when animals *and* people were in trouble, even when they weren't saying a word.

Looking up through the door, he saw Lani bustling around the seal, cooing and speaking softly to the petrel on the way past its cage. He knew she'd fixed the bird's wing up, saving it from amputation and a life in a cage just like this.

His jaw started working left to right, tighter by the second. She had put *everything* she'd had left into this place, and taken on fostering, too, *because* her heart was so big. And it all distracted her from having to think about Iolana. Maybe they weren't so different these days after all, he thought. Most of what he'd done every day since leaving here had been in an effort to forget his failures as a husband and father. More work, of course, the same as ever, but what choice did he have?

Suddenly, an idea started forming. Apart from helping out at the sanctuary in Mahina's absence, maybe there *was* another way he could help around here, while he was temporarily back in Lani's world.

CHAPTER FIVE

"YOU GOT THE results of the necropsies already?" Lani couldn't believe what she was looking at on the printed papers in front of her.

"Told you I could speed that up," Mika said, tossing another fish at their newest recovering sea lion, who was quite happily swimming in the tank out back with the other one. Anela had nicknamed them Lilo and Stitch.

"So, now we know for sure it's some kind of chemical compound that's reacting adversely with the dolphin's skin, and that it was pretty advanced in your little dead calf, but where's it coming from?"

"That's what we need to find out," she said, watching him hand a fish to Anela, who took it happily and threw it straight into Stitch's mouth.

"Have you seen any suspicious or unregistered boats around lately?" he asked.

She frowned, racking her brains. Surely she'd notice, though; she knew most people who worked out on the waters, and the tourists on their Jet Skis and banana boats couldn't have done anything so drastic as pollute the ocean—could they?

Seeing her look, Mika sighed. "We'll continue with the site analysis and sampling, from the locations where you've spotted irregularities in the dolphins. I'll have everything sent to my lab, too, see if any pathogens, bacteria, parasites or any harmful substances that may contribute to skin diseases match up with anything already discovered."

"I really appreciate your help," she said, realizing her heart was beating harder, just at the way he was looking at her while speaking with such heroic determination.

They locked eyes for what felt like an eternity, and she realized she was waiting again for him to say something about Iolana. Sometimes, she swore she could see all the things he *wasn't* saying building up in him, which was why, whenever her shift had finished this past week, she'd made an excuse to hurry away, and never initiated anything that wasn't related to their cause.

A knock at the door revealed Mr. Benos, her elderly admirer, grinning in his usual uniform of denim cutoffs and Hawaiian shirt.

"Not interrupting, I hope," he said, holding out a basket at her. "Fresh sunflowers, a bag of peaches and some plump kiwis for you, my lady," he said, beaming. "Picked just this morning."

She thanked him and took the basket gratefully. Mika was smiling behind his hand, and she tried not to do the same until Mr. Benos had gone.

"So, he does like you," he teased, and she laughed, admiring the healthy-looking fruit. Bigger than he'd grown them last season.

"No cause for jealousy, I assure you."

"Me? Jealous?" He stepped toward her, grinning that goofy yet manly grin she'd fallen for all those years ago. For a moment it felt like old times.

"Right, I think our boys have had enough fish, Anela. How

about we go down to the beach?" he said, busying his hands by wiping them with a towel.

"Why?" Anela's large brown eyes were filled with trepidation, but her curiosity seemed to overpower her fear because she didn't outwardly tell him no.

Lani kept her mouth shut. Anela always needed a valid reason to be on the beach. Usually, she only used it as a path to get to school and back.

"I need some help," Mika told her. "I need to collect some samples of the creatures, and sand and stones, so Lani and I can test them. The trouble is, I've been away from here for so long, I can't remember the names of some of them. Maybe you can help...?"

Lani raised her eyebrows and he winked at her over Anela's head. Of course, he was telling a huge fat lie; he knew every stone and tree and creature that had ever occupied this island. But to her shock, maybe feeling a sense of impending achievement, Anela agreed.

"If Lani comes, too?" she said hopefully.

They spent at least an hour on the beach. Lani couldn't help smiling every time Anela swiped up an object, explained what it was to Mika and gently placed it in her bucket. She stopped, however, the second she thought she was getting too close to the shoreline. To his credit, Mika didn't draw attention to it. He pretended not to notice, and she could tell he was concentrating on building the girl's trust. It warmed her heart, and she realized she'd clean forgotten she had promised to scrub the deck this afternoon.

Oh, well, she could do that tomorrow.

Following along quietly, she watched Mika with Anela, feeling a sense of calm washing over her for the first time since his arrival. This was a little like when they'd brought Iolana to the beach. She could still see her little fingers clutching the handle of the bucket, toddling along with intent. Okay, so they had argued a lot in the past, over him working so much instead of being there with her, but he'd only been doing his best as a young man, trying to support their surprise little family! He'd been such a gentle, encouraging father, she thought, forcing herself to remember how they'd laughed at their delightful daughter discovering shells and starfish on the sand, without letting the later tragedy overshadow what were some of her happiest memories.

She should try harder to remember the good times more often, she thought to herself. And it wasn't right that so far, she had completely failed to address with Mika the one thing they'd loved more than anything together: Iolana. The dolphins were important, and yes, that was why Mika was here but... maybe they *did* need to talk about more than work.

Ugh. Just the thought of dragging it all up made her shiver.

As they all walked along the shore, Mika showed the sweetest excitement as Anela pointed out various creatures—from crabs scuttling across the sand to a school of silvery fish she said she could see darting through the water just beneath the surface. Though she wouldn't walk to the edge with him to make sure.

"I think I know what fish they are," Mika said, crouching down next to her. "They're called mullet, and they play an important role in keeping our oceans clean. Do you know how?"

Anela looked thoughtful, then told him no.

"By feeding on algae and other underwater plants," he said. "Most fish have a job to do, you know. Every creature in the ocean plays a part in keeping it healthy and balanced. If we don't take care of them, the whole ecosystem could collapse. All of them are equally important. Even the sharks."

"I don't like sharks," she replied straightaway, making Lani's heart leap.

She half expected the girl to stomp away, but instead she adopted a small scowl directed at the ocean. Mika shot Lani a look, and she pulled an apologetic face at him. He was trying; she had to give him that. Thankfully he didn't push it. He looked around, spying a group of seagulls squawking near a tide pool. "Let's check out that pool over there. It's like a tiny underwater world, and I bet we can find some cool stuff in it!"

Soon, the smile returned to Anela's face. Lani stood back as Mika encouraged the child to touch the smooth surface of a sea anemone, explaining how its tentacles captured food.

"Isn't it incredible?" he asked, grinning as Anela's eyes lit up, feeling the anemone's tentacles brushing against her small fingers.

"You said you didn't know about the things on the beach," she accused, and Mika shrugged.

"Maybe you're jogging my memory, because you're such a great sidekick."

"Can I help again sometime?" Anela asked eagerly.

"Of course you can," Mika replied, and Lani's heart swelled with pride.

He was good with her, and even that damn bandanna on his head was growing on her, too, she thought in mild annoyance. His eyes lingered on her face for a moment longer than necessary before he shook his head at some unspoken thought, and she got the distinct impression he was trying to clear his mind of any wandering thoughts regarding her. Not that he could really still find her attractive. Could he?

Of course not, she scorned herself. What about Hayley? He was probably missing her young, lithe body and taut, perfect skin—and her lack of emotional baggage too, no doubt.

But he was in danger of melting her heart like he had when she'd been sixteen, doing all this for Anela. She'd never seen her so engaged in beach activities. Part of her had almost given up suggesting things to do on the sand, but in just a few days, Mika had shown up like foster father of the year and turned the situation around. There was still a long way to go, but something had changed in the girl already, like a light coming on, and Lani was beyond grateful.

If only she could make a habit of enjoying his company like this, she thought, instead of feeling the guilt creep back in every five minutes. She could see it all over again; the smile on his face had been just like this one right now, that day on the boat after their dive when they'd eagerly tugged off each other's wet suits and made love on the waves. They'd had no idea Iolana was being rushed to hospital with suspected meningitis. She'd frequently wondered if he blamed her, for not being more concerned that Iolana was a little sick before they'd left—she was her mother, after all. He'd never brought it up, never doled out any blame, but how could it not have dominated his mind when it was burned into her heart?

Not that it mattered now, she thought wearily. Even if Mika somehow found it in his heart to forgive her, she'd never forgive herself.

The sun had begun to set, casting a warm glow over the shoreline. As they went through the items in Anela's bucket one by one, a growing sense of purpose and connection settled in Mika's chest, taking him by surprise. A purpose, and a connection, not only with the beach and the island, he mused, but also with the little girl by his side. Okay, so he'd failed to convince her the ocean wasn't a writhing mass of unspeakable horrors, but Rome wasn't built in a day.

"Come on, let's head back," he said, standing up and brushing the sand off his shorts. "We have a lot of samples to test for tomorrow, and I think we've collected enough for now, thanks to you, young lady."

Anela looked disappointed, but Mika promised they would come back soon and explore more, and he didn't miss the warm appreciation in Lani's glance as she took the girl's hand.

The setting sun streamed onto them, heating his back with the last of its rays as they made their way back to the sanctuary. These sunsets! There were none like them anywhere else.

He couldn't help thinking back to a thousand sunsets spent with Lani. She looked pensive now, though, and lost in thought as Anela babbled about the kittens she was going to play with back at the house, and the story she was reading. Was Lani thinking about Iolana? he wondered for the thousandth time. Was having him here too weird for her? Did she feel a sense of longing for what they had lost, watching him interacting with a little girl? Having them *both* be here together, with a little girl? If she was having any of those thoughts, she clearly didn't want to open a can of worms by bringing them up but… maybe *he* should?

Iolana would have been twenty-four by now. She would have been scuba diving with him, and Lani would have had her learning multiple languages, learning how to fix a car, all the things she'd had planned for her. Maybe it would actually help clear some tension if they spoke about it all.

Yes, he decided. They had to talk, he and Lani. Alone. He wasn't letting himself get out of that. Even if she reminded him of his incompetence as an actual father, which he probably deserved to finally hear from her mouth.

Manu called him, just as they were stepping back into the sanctuary's back room by way of the beach. Mika knew what his brother was going to ask before he even asked it. The family's annual beach barbecue, aptly named Mahoe Luau, was coming up soon, and seeing as everyone in the family had RSVP'd except him, it was about time he gave a definitive answer.

He felt Lani's eyes on him the whole time he was on the phone, though when he turned to look at her, she pretended she wasn't looking at all and continued checking on the petrel with Anela. Suppressing a groan, he said he'd be there and hung up, feeling awkward. What had she heard?

"So you're going to go," she said simply, to his chagrin, picking up Anela's schoolbag and turning off the light at the main switch.

He grimaced. Of course she knew when the Mahoe Luau was; it had been held on the same day for over thirty years. She'd been the star of the show for many of those years, with her made-up songs on the ukulele, a performance which had long become part of the annual itinerary.

"I guess I'll *have* to," he said, and she smirked.

"As if they'd let you live it down if you didn't."

"Truer words have never been spoken."

The sun had fully sunk now, and he'd be driving back to the guesthouse in the darkness for another night alone. He followed Lani outside, watched as she locked the doors, and noted how Anela seemed reluctant to leave without checking on Lilo and Stitch one last time—the kid was adorable.

The question hovered on his tongue: *Do you want to come with me to the luau?*

Just ask her!

He should just ask her to the stupid event; it would be weird not to, seeing as everyone knew he was here, spending time at the sanctuary with her. And it would also be a chance to finally talk, to stop avoiding the important stuff. But she probably wouldn't want to. It would likely just be awkward for her, right?

Mika found he was still making excuses not to ask her by the time he was sitting behind the wheel of his rental car, driving back to the guesthouse, cursing his cowardly self. Why couldn't he just take her aside and talk to her? Why couldn't he so much as even ask her to a party? The woman had been the center of his world once! Until he'd run for the hills. He hadn't wanted to spend one more day knowing his presence did nothing but remind her of Iolana and his failures. He'd gone so she could heal…hoping he might heal, too, but part of him had been broken ever since.

The moon hung like a hammock in the sky as he drove on, till he was digging his nails into the steering wheel in turmoil. Talking to Lani meant leaping down a rabbit hole of misery he'd tried so hard to push deep down and bury out of existence. Only now he couldn't get his mind off it. Any of it.

He could arrange to see a friend, or another family member, and talk to them instead, he reasoned at the moon, but he hadn't done that either yet. He'd buried himself in research and work, work, work. For some reason, he realized now, even as he worked on discovering what was making the dolphins sick, he'd been making himself one hundred percent available for Lani, just in case she needed him. He hadn't even done that for Hayley. That thought only led to another memory: Hayley asking if he'd ever thought about having a child with her. Him having to explain that he hadn't. Her telling him smugly that he'd change his mind. Him assuring her he wouldn't. Her getting emotional and starting a fight. Him resuming his work away from her. So draining. He was literally always running away from emotional conflict.

It was time to stop.

He slammed on the brakes in the middle of the empty street, clenched his fists around the wheel. Then, before he could talk himself out of it, he did a U-turn and sped back toward Lani's house.

CHAPTER SIX

ANELA WAS THE cutest right now, Lani thought, all snuggled up on the couch with three of the snoozing kittens, engrossed in another chapter of *The Lion, the Witch and the Wardrobe*. Folding the last of the laundry into a pile on the back of the couch, she was about to issue a bedtime call when car lights appeared on the driveway. Her heart leaped into her throat. She knew that car.

Mika was standing on the steps already when she opened the door. "Did you forget something?" she asked him. "Do you need the keys to the sanctuary?"

"Er…no," he said, sweeping a big hand through his hair.

He looked worried, she thought as she invited him in. More intense. His eyes seemed to be on fire and Lani felt a tingle in her stomach, a familiar sensation that she hadn't felt in a very long time around anyone else, almost like her body had a totally different set of reactions in reserve, just for him. She'd had a crush on Mika since before she'd even known what a crush was. The first time they'd had sex, she'd actually cried from the intensity of her emotions, and felt like a total idiot for it.

Why are you thinking about all that now? she scolded herself, but she still couldn't keep her eyes off his backside as he walked into the lounge.

Anela looked up. "Mika!" she exclaimed. "Did you come to see the kittens?"

"I sure did," he said, sitting down on the couch next to Anela, who promptly placed one of the kittens on his lap.

Lani sat down opposite him, feeling a little breathless. "What's up?" she asked, trying to keep her voice casual. She'd known the second she saw his face that he had something important to share with her that for whatever reason, he hadn't been able to say earlier. Something beyond the small talk. Was it about Iolana? The thought still made her feel cold. Of course, they'd have to talk about her eventually. But right now?

She would never be ready.

Mika cleared his throat, and she realized she couldn't avoid it any longer. She also got the impression he hadn't expected Anela to still be up. As tactfully as she could, she ushered the girl upstairs, telling Mika to make himself at home. It sounded weird, coming from her mouth. This was not the home they'd always planned to buy together someday, the one on the beach with the yellow doors and shutters—the one Mika had been working so hard to help save up for, should it ever come onto the market. But as she tucked Anela into her bed she felt hot to her core at the thought of him downstairs among her things, in her space.

"What's going on, Mika?" she said when she came back down, resuming her position again on the little chair opposite his. He was stroking the kitten gently, and it purred in his hands just like she used to, she thought, swallowing a golf ball of grief from her throat.

"I just— I had to talk to you." He leaned a little closer, his eyes meeting hers intently. The kitten scampered from his lap down to the floor and chased a shadow. "That whole thing with the family luau felt weird. I should have asked you to come, but I assumed you wouldn't want to. There's so much we've been trying not to say, Lani."

She sucked in her breath and felt her cheeks flush as she looked away. It honestly hadn't crossed her mind that he'd ask her to the luau after all this time.

"We don't have to drag up anything painful if you're not ready," he continued as her heart started to thrum. "I know I hurt you badly…"

"And I hurt you," she said now. "I didn't mean to hurt you," she added, her voice cracking. "I felt dead inside after she died. I wasn't myself. I'm still not, Mika."

"Neither am I, but we have to at least be able to say her name."

"Oh, God." The words came out on a strangled breath and she stood up quickly, sending the pile of laundry to the floor. She made to pick it up but he was on his feet in a flash, taking her wrist. Lani froze, staring at his hand around the turtle tattoo, feeling her stomach swirl.

He closed the gap between them, his hand coming up to cup her cheek. "It's impossible not to see her everywhere," he said quietly, pressing his lips together a moment, like he was forcing down his own tidal wave of emotion. "I was a coward staying away so long, when you've done so much here, despite your grief, despite all these…memories."

"I had no choice," she whispered, feeling her hand come up to cover his, distracted by the warmth and familiarity and what it was doing to her insides. His impossibly handsome face and intense eyes had always made her heart skip a beat, but now, combined with the current topic, it was almost too much to handle.

She broke the contact, made for the kitchen and pulled the dish of homemade haupia out of the refrigerator. The creamy coconut dessert was her specialty, and she set about cutting it into squares for Anela and her classmates—anything *not* to look at Mika.

"I just wanted to remind you how strong and brave I think you are," he said, following her. "What you've done, for Anela, and at the sanctuary. You've done so much for this whole island, whereas I…" He trailed off and she dared to look at him now over her shoulder. He was pondering the magnets on the fridge like studying a complex code and she could almost see his mind working, his regrets piling up in his head like the dishes in her sink.

"You've done a lot yourself, Mika," she heard herself say, sensing he needed to hear that she recognized his achievements. "Your research and your work has—"

"Exactly. Work," he muttered, cutting her off. "I threw myself into work, like I've always done."

"Your work is important to you. To everyone! And anyway, so did I," she admitted now. She watched his eyes travel around the kitchen. It was painted the same yellow as the shutters on the beach home they'd dreamed about owning together once. Did he even notice?

Mika faced her. "I guess what I'm saying is I can see your *heart* and soul in everything you do here. I'm just following protocol, avoiding…well, you know."

"I know," she admitted, gripping the counter behind her, as if she might fall to the floor without it.

"I'd be lying if I said I don't sometimes think about what we might have done together, if I hadn't left," he said softly.

"You *had* to leave," she told him, realizing she was fighting back tears now. "You told me that. There were too many awful memories here. And yes, like you said, there still are.

But that's life, Mika. *My* life is still here, and yours isn't, but that's what you wanted."

He stepped toward her again, looking like he regretted his last words already. "It's what I *thought* I needed. It's what I thought would be best for *you*."

She gaped at him, her coconut pudding clean forgotten. "You thought leaving the island would be best for me? How?"

"I was just a reminder that I messed up, spending all that time away from you and our daughter... I should have just been a better father. I should have been *there* more."

She looked at him, incredulous. This was the first time she'd heard anything like this from his mouth. They'd barely spoken to each other after the tragedy; she'd been convinced he'd fallen out of love with her and hadn't wanted to give him a chance to actually say it. She'd also assumed that letting him go was the best thing for him—he wouldn't be able to heal with her around, a constant reminder of their failures as parents. Hearing him confirm all that would have broken the final shards of her shattered heart, so she'd gone cold, shut him out. Wallowed in the shame and blame alone. Was it possible he'd felt the same? Had he really assumed she had fallen out of love with *him*?

Lani's throat constricted as she ripped her gaze away from Mika, desperate to conceal the giant swell of emotions that were threatening to engulf her.

"I was her mother, Mika," she uttered through clenched teeth. "I should have seen how sick she really was..."

"Lani." He grasped her hands, looked deep into her eyes with the kind of unwavering conviction that stole her next protest straight from her mouth. "It wasn't your fault."

"Well, maybe we were both to blame," she muttered weakly.

He shook his head slowly, squeezed her hands. "It's not a

blame game, and it doesn't help either of us to keep thinking that way. We didn't know her cold was actually meningitis."

They stood there for a moment, their hands intertwined, their eyes locked. "Every day, I wonder what she would be like now, what she would be doing," she told him, feeling her chin wobble. "I can't help but think that if I had just been less focused on that stupid dive…"

"Stop it, Lani. That dive was important for your studies, and you spent more time with Iolana than I ever did," he said.

The warning in his voice told her he wrestled with similar guilt—of course he did. How had they managed to shut each other out so completely after it happened? She should have been there for him.

Lani felt a hot tear streak down her cheek, and she swiped it away, trying to compose herself. Mika was right: they couldn't keep living in the past, blaming themselves. She let herself indulge in the warmth of his touch, the familiar scent of him that still caused a stirring in her belly. He was studying her lips now, like he wanted to kiss her all of a sudden, and just as she found herself leaning in on instinct, she dropped his hands, stepped back to the bench and resumed cutting up her sweets.

No. Nope.

This was all kinds of weird as it was; they had different lives now, not to mention a divorce behind them! A huge, great planet-worth of pain they could still dredge up in each other with so much as a look, just like they were doing now. She would not be crossing *that* line again, not ever. Besides, what about Hayley?

Mika drummed his fingers on the bench. "Maybe we could go to the cemetery. Together," he said, carefully.

"I'll think about it," she told him, handing him a piece of

the haupia. He sniffed it, then took a small bite, and she rolled her eyes. "It's good!"

"Has your cooking improved, then?" he teased, and she pretended to swipe at him, thankful the intensity between them had finally subsided, although the thought of going to the cemetery sent her skin to goose bumps. She couldn't stand it there; she avoided it, in fact, which only made her feel even more guilty.

"I'm kidding, this *is* actually good. You should bring some to the luau."

She raised her eyebrows. "Are you serious? You think I should come?"

"Sure, bring Anela."

"She likes you a lot," she told him now, wondering if she *should* go to the luau. It would be strange, and probably a little awkward. But if he'd made the first move toward clearing the elephants from the room and finally talking about what happened, she could at least show him the same courtesy and face his wonderful family. She'd been avoiding them for such selfish reasons, she realized with shame—as if they would have judged her in any way. Not that she was about to hurry into telling him she'd attend. The thought of it, and the look on his face just now when she'd almost kissed him, sent butterflies of anxiety take flight inside her.

"I'll think about that, too," she said instead, just as the sound of little footsteps behind them made them both turn around. Anela was standing in the doorway, hair ruffled, in her pajamas.

"I had the dream again," she sniffed, and Lani's heart sank.

"What dream?" Mika asked.

"About the sharks," she replied, and he frowned in concern.

"Do you have that a lot?"

"Most nights," Lani told him on her behalf with a frown, suddenly aware that he was maybe getting a little too invested in Anela's struggle. She could handle it herself, as her foster mother. In fact, everything had been fine until he showed up... for the most part anyway.

To her relief, Mika seemed to get the message. He backed up, stayed quiet while she and Anela discussed what book they might read to take her mind off the dreams.

Good, she thought. The last thing she wanted was to make him think he had to step in as some kind of temporary foster father for the next few weeks. He had enough on his plate, what with his dolphin research and filling Mahina's shoes, not to mention Hayley. He'd moved on from her, his ex-wife. They were water under a big fat bridge. And anyway, her heart was already a mess around him, changing pace with his every word and action, like it just couldn't figure out how to beat right.

She really shouldn't go to the luau, she thought.

Maybe she should keep on staying away from him, outside of the sanctuary.

"You can see yourself out, right?" she told him, making for the stairs with Anela.

"I know exactly where the door is," he replied coolly.

Five minutes later, she felt the strangest mix of dread and relief when she heard his car pulling out of the driveway.

CHAPTER SEVEN

MIKA STEPPED BACK from the wheel of the boat and let their volunteer driver, Noa, take over. Lani was already halfway into her wet suit, rolled in a neoprene fold up to her waist, and he couldn't help admiring her in her bikini top while she wasn't looking. Maybe it was a little to do with the fact that he couldn't have her, shouldn't touch her, but God, he was still so attracted to her. It went beyond her looks; it was how she carried herself, he thought: her energy and spirit and fire, not in-your-face, or brash or loud, but stoic and quiet and burning under the surface. It was all the things that transcended her physical form and reminded him why he'd married the woman. She was in fact the total opposite of Hayley. He realized now that he'd gone for the opposite of Lani with every woman since their divorce; probably because he didn't *want* to love anyone else that much again, only to lose them.

"Let me get that zip, at the back," he said now as she caught his eye. Damn, she'd caught him looking, and was he imagining it, or did she just get a little redder in the face?

"I can manage," she muttered, wriggling the tight wet suit up faster and over her arms like she couldn't wait to cover herself suddenly. His fingers itched as she fumbled with the zip herself, insisting she was fine.

"I was only trying to help," he said, feeling snubbed.

"I know," she tutted, as if it was the last thing on earth she wanted.

Annoyed, he took over the tanks, checking the compression, attaching the regulators. She'd been distant with him for the last few days, probably because he'd insisted on opening a can of worms in her kitchen. Cute kitchen, he'd thought at the time. She had painted it the same yellow as the finishing on their dream beach house. God, he hadn't thought about that place in years. They'd always planned to buy it someday; they'd driven past so many times, even sneaked onto the private beach out front at night to imagine their lives there, as soon as they could afford it…if indeed it ever came up for sale.

As it happened, they'd never even moved out of his parents' annex. Getting pregnant when Lani was just twenty-two had changed everything. She'd stopped her studies for two years, while he'd worked stints at institutions on and off the island, determined to provide for them, to his detriment in the end; he'd missed so much. After Iolana died, the house might as well have burned down along with all their other dreams.

He cringed to himself, remembering how he'd basically admitted to her that he thought about the what-ifs all the time. She had moved on with her life after *he'd* decided to leave the island; he had no right to openly reflect on how he might regret that decision sometimes. Make that *all* the time.

Okay, so they'd both agreed to the divorce, and obviously both made mistakes in that marriage, clamming up and shutting each other out, instead of talking and sharing, but they'd been so damn young, and while their love had been undeniable, neither of them had been prepared for such intense grief to take its place so abruptly. It had torn in like a beast, and the ripple effects were almost as bad.

It killed him knowing Lani had been blaming herself instead of him all this time, and knowing she might *not* have thought him leaving was the best thing for her after all. Why had he just assumed those things? He'd been so blinded by guilt, nothing anyone could've said would have made a difference back then. Now it was far too late to mend what was broken—but perhaps at least they could try to be friends?

"Almost there," Noa told them now, as Mika pulled on his buoyancy vest, resisting the urge to help Lani with her weight belt when it slipped momentarily from her grasp. Maybe he'd overstepped before, showing up at her house, almost kissing her.

Friends—ha! He couldn't get that almost-kiss out of his head. Obviously she'd thought better of it before he had, but it was built in to him, the attraction to her mouth, even after all these years. Not that anything would happen, he reminded himself, telling her to tighten her weight belt.

She grunted in response, which irked him…but didn't make him want to kiss her any less, even now. He'd have to stop thinking about what used to be, he warned himself. Divorced couples didn't go around locking lips and besides, she couldn't have kicked him out of her kitchen fast enough the other day!

"Here we are. Are you guys ready?" Noa asked, slowing the boat till it bobbed on the surface like a slow spinning top under the sun.

They'd come out to the edge of the reef. Several scuba divers on a tour had reported seeing a white tip reef shark with a fishing hook lodged in its mouth this morning. It was his hope that he and Lani could locate it and help, and he was trying his best to focus on this mission. But it was their first dive together since that terrible day, when they should have been with Iolana. She was thinking about it, too; he could see it in her anguished glances.

Thankfully Anela had been at school when they'd received the call. Poor kid, with those nightmares. He'd offered to talk to her, but Lani had kept the girl away from him these last few days, arranging play dates and other activities to keep her busy elsewhere, even after he'd asked if he could take her to the beach outside the sanctuary again. Even if they had somewhat agreed not to play the blame game over Iolana's death anymore, he got the distinct impression Lani didn't trust him entirely around Anela.

Lani jumped into the water first, holding her regulator to her mouth. The sun was hot in the midday blue sky and the water felt cool against his face as he tumbled backward after her. It was a long shot, looking for this injured shark, but he couldn't help but wonder, too, if his old friend Nala might be around. This had been her hunting ground. Would that beautiful tiger shark even remember him?

The reef looked majestic, almost as beautiful as Lani did swimming in the blue as they made their descent together. Ocean life teemed around them; a blur of tiny silver fish swirled in a vivid tornado, and below them, a turtle eyed them with curiosity. He pulled out his navigation device, signaling to Lani to go left along the reef. She gave him the okay with her fingers, and he let her go ahead. Like him, Lani was an experienced diver.

They floated for ten minutes, maybe fifteen, with no sign of the shark. Usually he could switch his brain off but being down here with Lani, it was racing. Lani *must* still think him somewhat responsible for what happened to Iolana, even if she wasn't saying it.

Maybe she was right to step back from him like this. Part of him didn't trust himself not to mess something up, either, and until meeting Anela, he hadn't even *wanted* to hang out around children.

It always brought back too many painful memories. It still did, because of course he saw Iolana in everything, everywhere, even in the little girl. But he'd done something nice for Anela to help Lani, as much as to help the child, and in doing so something had shifted inside him. A wall was falling away. He'd never be anyone's foster father, or stepfather, or real father... He could never do what Lani did. That would mean living every day in fear of messing up again, and the thought of feeling that kind of pain again was incomprehensible. But while he was here, he wasn't going to give up on his quest to make Anela see the magic in the ocean again, he decided. He'd just have to bide his time and not tread on Lani's toes.

Suddenly, Lani pulled to a stop in front of him, so fast he almost banged into her tank. She motioned ahead of her and clutched for his hand in a cloud of bubbles. Sure enough, they'd found their reef shark. It was swimming slowly, mouthing at the coral in distress as it went round and round in circles.

The shark was around ten feet long and looked exhausted. The hook in its mouth was obvious. A bright blue nylon fishing line trailed behind it, tangled around its lower jaw. With a nod of agreement, they began to swim slowly toward it together, careful not to startle the shark.

The sight as he drew closer filled him with sadness and anger on behalf of this innocent creature—why did fishermen have to be so careless? He could tell by the look on her face that Lani was thinking the same thing.

Mika flipped his fins till he was floating ahead of Lani. She knew about his special method of calming sharks; they'd discussed it on the way out here, how it had so far never let him down. Lani's eyes were trained on him as he swam ahead, holding out his hands with his palms facing the creature. Just as he expected it would, the shark lunged forward, but Mika's hands came down firmly on its nose, batting it away until it redirected itself and eventually flipped upside down.

Lani clapped her hands in delight and swam to the other side of the shark. He took out his regulator for a second and grinned at her triumphantly, and for a moment the tension that had settled around them since that night at her house seemed to dissipate and float away on the current with their bubbles.

He'd conducted many seminars about sharks; there was nothing better than seeing kids' faces light up when he told them how flipping certain shark species upside down pretty much rendered them immobile for up to fifteen minutes. It was known to induce a trance-like state known as "tonic immobility." In this case, it meant he and Lani could work together to extract the hook from its mouth.

Once they were finished, Lani gathered the fishing line and shoved it into a bag attached to her weight belt. His heart sank for her, knowing she must witness this more and more these days in the waters around Oahu.

They dived deeper, careful to keep their distance as the shark regained its senses, righted itself with a dramatic twirl and darted away into the deep blue beyond.

Lani's smile was unmistakable; not that they weren't attuned to each other under the water already. The two of them had completed thousands of dives together till now, and he'd missed moments like this, just the two of them out here. He met her smile through the bubbles around her face, and instinct took over. He removed his regulator and blew her a kiss. She did the same, laughing now.

It was something they'd always done, a little shared ritual— the under-the-ocean kiss. Usually he pressed his lips to hers before he put his regulator back in, but this time he ignored the urge. There was no way he should be kissing Lani, or even pretending to, underwater, above water, anywhere—things were complicated enough. But he didn't miss the confusion—or was that disappointment?—in her eyes through her mask as he signaled that they should start their ascent. His heart was probably beating harder than he had enough air for.

They were just beginning their slow float upward toward the surface, Lani three feet above him already, when Mika noticed something huge and dark hovering in his periphery. His breath caught as it swam closer, gracefully sweeping through the water toward him.

"Nala?"

Excitedly he motioned to Lani that it *was* her; his tiger shark had returned! But Lani was too close to the surface already. He could tell it was Nala, he thought as he slowed his ascent, and checked his air. The shark had the same beautiful markings around her belly, and a wave of relief washed over him as he noticed she appeared healthy; there were no signs of any fishing line caught in her mouth or fins. A few more scars, yes, but that was to be expected.

He stayed calm and still now, letting her approach his mask. She paused a moment, as if studying him, figuring out if he was indeed her old friend. Thrilled, he held his hands out slowly, and sure enough she bopped her head against his palms several times, eyes rolling in delight the way they always used to do. She recognized him!

Mika laughed as she flipped over, inviting him to rub her belly. "It's so good to see you girl, how've you been?" he mouthed, and he swore she could understand; she'd loved nothing more than getting her belly rubbed, like a giant dog. Sharks loved affection, he thought, bewitched by the creature's grace and beauty.

Mika was so enchanted by this surprise encounter that he clean forgot he was supposed to be back on the boat by now. And when he finally looked up, he realized he couldn't see Lani at all.

CHAPTER EIGHT

LANI SCRAMBLED TO the edge of the boat, searching wildly for Mika. As she peered into the water, her heart started pounding out of her chest, her mind racing with terror as she yanked off her weight belt. Waves lapped around the boat and the sun was glinting on the surface like a spotlight, but she couldn't see Mika anywhere.

"He was right behind me," she told Noa as he took the tank from her back. She barely noticed him doing it. She was paranoid—of course she was—but the panic still rose like a tidal wave in her chest, threatening to overwhelm her. "Where is he?"

"He probably saw something down there. Give him a few minutes," Noa reasoned, and she bit her lip, reminding herself he was an experienced diver. He did this all the time; he was a pro!

Memories of losing Iolana flashed through her mind, and her breathing came in shallow gasps, her chest constricting with dread. It almost felt like the sea was punishing her all over again—they'd been out on a boat like this the day their daughter had died. How could she have ever expected their first dive together after that to go smoothly? It had been on her mind since she'd boarded this boat, even when she'd just been laughing underwater. It was always there.

"Where is he?"

Noa frowned now, peering overboard. His look dried her throat up on the spot.

"I'm going back in," she said, grabbing a snorkel and climbing back up to the ledge. She was just about to leap from the side and dive under when she spotted the bubbles. *Mika*.

Relief flooded her veins as his hands found the rungs of the ladder, and he pulled himself up onto the deck, grinning from ear to ear as he ripped off his mask, dripping glistening salt water all over. Tears flooded her vision as she scrambled back from the edge, but hot on their heels was pure anger, a fire inside her that had probably been smoldering ever since he'd arrived, ever since he'd ripped open old wounds and made her start facing them all over again. The second his tank was on the deck she lunged at him, wiping the grin clean from his face as she pummeled his chest.

"How could you do that to me, Mika?"

"Whoa, Lani, what?" He dodged another thump, tried to take her wrists.

Hot nausea twisted in her stomach, burning up the bile in her throat. "I thought you were gone! I thought I'd lost you, too…"

"Lani, I'm right here!" He grasped her wrists finally, and she wrestled with him, desperate to drum her fury and pain and bereavement into him, to make him feel what she'd been trying for so long *not* to feel since long before he'd even got here. He held her firmly, calmly and she realized she was sobbing, hurting, physically now, crumpling to the deck.

He sank with her as Noa rushed for towels and water. The second Mika's arms were around her she felt another surge of fury rip inside of her, but this time it seemed to burn away in seconds, leaving only exhaustion and the comfort of his closeness. He was here, and he was very much alive. She was too tired to do anything but accept his embrace and press her cheek against his chest, and cry.

"I'm sorry," he whispered, cupping her face from his place on his haunches, dripping salt water from his hair and wet suit. "I should have come up with you, I'm so sorry. I saw Nala and it distracted me."

"You can never do that to me," she told him through gritted teeth. "Never! Do you hear me?"

She was crying over more than Mika's slipup, and he knew it; she could feel it in the way he was holding her, pressing his mouth to the top of her head. They held each other like that, on the floor, for what felt like forever, until she couldn't cry anymore. She just felt numb.

"I miss her so much."

"So do I," Mika whispered, rocking her gently. Suddenly, there was no point even trying to pretend they hadn't both been bottling this up in their individual corners. But what happened now?

Late that afternoon, as the sun beat down on the porch, Lani could hardly concentrate on anything. The quick rice dinner she'd assembled for Anela was so burnt she'd wound up ordering them a pizza, and felt a little guilty at how relieved she was when it came time to drive Anela to her friend's house for a sleepover.

She drove back toward home slowly, finally pulling into the little parking lot that led to the hiking trails instead. Leaving her car beside a scuffed red bike, she set off absentmindedly toward the waterfall, sucking in lungfuls of the calming, tropical air. The birds sang a high, sweet song, their colors flashes of iridescent reds and blues in the trees, and she let her mind run over it all.

She'd left Mika after the dive, at his insistence that she rest. But now it was just mortifying, knowing she'd embarrassed herself, and him, too, probably. She'd totally overreacted! And now she just couldn't stop thinking about it. Things hadn't exactly been great since their talk the other night; she'd pushed him away, scared he might think she expected him to slip back into his old roles around her: protector, caregiver…father. Scared she might come to rely on him to be there for her again, only to have him go straight back to California, and to Hayley.

But it was more than knowing he was going back to Hayley, whom somehow he never mentioned and…urgh…as if she was going to torture herself by asking about her.

If she let him get too close again, become involved in her life, she would only disappoint him *again* somehow. She still worked as hard as ever—although admittedly, she was understaffed. If she stopped being a control freak with zero social life and hired more staff, maybe she'd free up a little more time. It wasn't like she couldn't afford it these days.

Hmmm. But she'd had her chance with Mika anyway; there would never be another one. She couldn't put her heart through losing him again—this afternoon had proved that. She'd only live in fear of him disappearing one way or another. And no matter what he said, about how she shouldn't feel so guilty for not knowing Iolana was so sick, she always would.

As she walked down the path, the grass tickled her ankles until she heard the crash of the waterfall up ahead. The air was warm and thick and she was sweating, grateful she'd kept her bikini on as she stepped across the rocks. A swim in the cool, refreshing pool at the base of the falls would be heavenly right now.

Only, she wasn't alone. Someone else was standing at the water's edge, stripping off his shirt. She gasped as she recognized the wide, broad shoulders, the tattoo on his upper arm—Mika. Her Honu! Well, ex-Honu, she reminded herself, running a finger absently across her turtle tattoo while looking at his. Trust him to come here now, at the same time. But then, this had always been their spot.

Clasping her hand over her mouth, she froze in place as he discarded his bandanna and sunglasses, watched the muscles flex in his back as he undid his belt and threw his shorts on top of the pile. Then, there he was. Naked.

Suddenly, she was even hotter. Mika was butt naked, and oh, what a butt. It hadn't changed a bit. She watched him dive gracefully from the rocks like an arrow, cutting the water as he started to swim, one arm over the other, in a direct line to the falls. Creeping closer, she shook off her flip-flops, took his place on the rocks, straining her eyes for him. The mist from the raging falls was like a cool breath against her skin and she wanted to get in so badly. But he still had no idea she was here.

Suddenly, out of nowhere, a wide grin took her mouth hostage. The carefree teenager inside her was awake and inspired now, and in that moment she knew exactly what she was going to do.

The cool waters of the waterfall were a balm to Mika's skin as he made for the rocks behind the cascade. It seemed like just yesterday that he and Lani had swum here together, chasing each other in the warm shallows, then later, when they were older, making out behind the falls.

She used to tease him about not being able to dive off the rocks like she could, how he never made a neat splash as he entered the water, not like she did. She'd cut it so clean you could barely tell she'd dived in. Lani had always been so fearless and daring, whereas he'd been, and maybe still was, more of a thinker than a doer. Holding her today, though, on the boat, she hadn't seemed so fearless.

He pressed his back to the cool rocky wall, blinded by the blur of the falls in front of him. God, his heart had shattered right there on that deck, seeing her like that, knowing what he'd put her through. It must have put her on edge, the same it had him, being out there, knowing it was a dive trip that had taken them both away from Iolana for the last time, and then he'd gone and done that to her. He'd regret it forever; no wonder she'd freaked out so badly.

She was still as feisty as ever; he had to give her that. If only he could hear more of her laughter, he thought. He'd have to stop doing such stupid things around her if that was ever going to happen.

His hands were getting wrinkled, he realized after a while. He made his way back to the shore, pondering whether to go check up on Lani after this. He probably should. Unless she didn't want to see him. He had to make up for frightening her, though; there was no question about that.

Shaking off the water from his hair, he looked around for his shirt. Frowning to himself, he spun around, searched the rocks. He'd left his clothes here...hadn't he?

There was no one else in sight, so where the hell did his shirt go? His shorts? He couldn't even see his shoes.

Perplexed he walked around the pool, turning over stones, sweeping foliage aside.

Damn, he was butt naked, a mile from the bike he'd ridden here on, and his clothes were nowhere to be seen. Then he saw it. Tucked away in the rocks, beneath a cluster of ferns, a corner of a small wooden box protruded from the sand. Its tiny hinges creaked as he lifted it out carefully and wrestled it open, hardly believing his eyes. Lani and he had buried this container here years ago, when he'd been twelve or thirteen. He'd almost forgotten about it, but here it was, right in front of him, and the items inside, while weathered, sent the memories racing back in. Inside lay two shells they'd collected together from a beach on the other side of the island, a piece of pink glass shaped like a heart that she must have given him at some point, some old coins they'd found with his uncle's metal detector and a badly written treasure map. It showed where all their adventures had taken place over the years. So many memories wrapped up in one little box!

He was just spilling the items onto the rocks for closer inspection of the map when an arm snaked around his neck from behind, making him gasp. Before he could react he was being pulled back against a body, and a pair of lips were pressed to his ear. "Say you're sorry, or you'll never see your clothes again."

Spinning around, he scrambled to his feet, meeting Lani's grinning face. She was on her feet now, holding out his shirt, dangling his shorts just out of his reach. Remembering his nakedness, he covered himself with both hands quickly, standing there like a fool, and her laughter echoed through the jungle all around them.

"I've seen it all before, remember," she laughed.

"Really? We're doing this?" he said drily, making another grab for his shorts. "What are you, *eleven years old*?"

Lani tutted and tossed him his shorts finally, and he hurried to pull them on, just as she seemed to notice the box, its contents now spilled across the rocks. Her eyes grew wide as she dropped to her knees.

"No way... I forgot about this—where did you find it?" She took the pink glass onto her palm and inspected it from all angles, while he retrieved his sunglasses, setting them atop his head.

"I was looking for my clothes," he said, crouching next to her, and she rolled her eyes, biting back another laugh. It *was* good to hear her laugh, he thought. He wasn't really mad at her for her prank—how could he be? He'd deserved it. "This isn't the first time you've stolen my clothes," he said with a pretend scowl.

"And it probably won't be the last," she retorted. Then she pulled her eyes away, as if realizing there might not be many chances, seeing as he didn't even live here anymore. He took the glass heart from her hands, determined not to make things more awkward.

"Where did you get this?" he asked her.

"The beach outside our dream house... Remember how we'd cycle past it and promise each other we'd buy it someday?"

"I do," he said quietly.

She sighed softly, turning the glass over. "I loved that house."

"So did I. Look, Lani..." He took the glass from her palm and held her hand. "I was such an idiot today, forgive me. I know why you got so angry, and scared, and I deserved to feel your wrath."

She shook her head and chewed on her lip. "I overreacted. You saw your shark—of course you had to go meet her."

"But not when I was supposed to be ascending with you. I was your dive buddy, and I broke all the rules."

"I forgive you," she said simply.

Mika tilted her chin up, searching her eyes. There were so many things he wanted to say but suddenly he was lost for words. All he could do was kiss her.

He pressed his lips to hers tenderly, asking her without

words if this was okay. Lani responded in kind, wrapping her arms around his neck, deepening their kiss till she was straddling him on the ground, her shirt open, the warmth of her flesh tight against his chest. God, he'd missed her kisses, the way she just fit with him. It was like they'd sped right back to day one of their teenage love affair, like he could feel and taste her craving all over again. Back then, she'd been wanting him for years by then, maybe more, she'd always thought, than he'd been wanting her. But she had nothing to worry about; he'd always want her.

After just a few moments, though, she pulled away breathless, covering her mouth in shock.

"I'm sorry," she said, with her back to him. "We shouldn't..."

He nodded silently in agreement, cursing himself, not wanting to ruin this moment any more than he already had. Why had he kissed her? As if things between them weren't muddied enough!

"I know that was purely muscle memory," she said now, facing him again. "Because I know you're not a cheater. It's just because of our history, we both got carried away..."

"Cheater?" He frowned, shoving his bandanna into his pocket. He could still taste her.

Lani snorted, putting her hands to her hips. "Hello, have you forgotten Hayley?"

"Oh." Mika grimaced. Of course, Lani had no idea they'd broken up. He'd been so distracted by everything since he got here, he hadn't even mentioned it, or her, probably. "About that. We...um...we ended things before I came here."

Lani fixed her eyes on his, then ran a finger over her lips. He could almost see her mind whirring. "You never said anything."

"You never asked."

She pursed her lips. "Okay…" she started. "So, you're *not* a cheater."

"I was never a cheater, Lani," he retorted, irritated now. "I never had reason to even *think* about anyone else when I was with you, and Hayley and I, we just…"

He shut his mouth as she looked to the floor. It wasn't fair to talk about Hayley, for so many reasons. Besides, he didn't want to hear himself admit he didn't want her kids, or that he had never wanted kids with anyone but Lani; they'd both moved on. Lani had a different role now, parental duties that he would never have.

He picked up the box and all its trinkets, and they walked in silence back to the parking lot, where she took it from him, to take home in the car. Neither of them said one word. Watching her drive away into the sunset, Mika couldn't help thinking he'd just solved one problem and leaped headfirst into another.

CHAPTER NINE

THIS MUST BE the sanctuary's busiest morning in a long time, Lani thought as she closed the door after Mr. Benos and yet another generous basket of fruit, only to find it opening three seconds later. Her heart lodged in her throat. Mika was here, for which she was more than grateful, even though he might just as well have injected her stomach with a set of hatching butterflies.

"Hi," he said, giving her a lingering look over the top of his sunglasses, as if waiting for her to kick him out.

"Hi," she replied, shutting the door after him, wishing she *could* just kick him out. Maybe she would if she wasn't so damn busy.

Lani couldn't get that kiss at the falls the other day out of her head. It had been her fault as much as his, a spontaneous outpouring of emotion, as was becoming her norm around him, annoyingly. But she'd made things even more complicated than they'd been before. Still, she would have to try to act like it wasn't such a big deal. It wasn't really. They used to kiss all the time, and he wasn't seeing Hayley anymore... whatever had happened there.

Considering Hayley's age, she wondered if Hayley had wanted children and for some reason Mika had been scared off. Maybe he still wanted to play the field. And why should she care if he did?

Mika's desires, or his single status, should not affect anything at all in her life right now, she reminded herself.

He looked very handsome today, she had to admit, as she tidied some papers up and he wandered over to the petrel in its cage. She studied his muscular backside in the same shorts he'd worn to the waterfall. His crisp linen shirt showed off his strong forearms; she could still feel his arms around her when she closed her eyes. The three days since she'd kissed him had felt like an eternity, but she'd have to get used to the fact that it wouldn't happen again. They were exes, they only brought up the worst kind of memories together and the past was the past, she reminded herself quickly. It was all far too complicated.

Well, okay, she reasoned, so not all the memories they shared were bad. There was the treasure box, for example. That had been fun to uncover. A nice reminder that they'd had some good times before everything fell apart. Anela had made the glass heart her own and was very invested in visiting all the places on the treasure map.

Mika turned from one of the birds and caught her looking at him, chewing the lid of her pen.

"Something on your mind?" he asked, probing her with his stare.

"No. Nope."

She panicked suddenly. Was he daring her to bring up their kiss? They'd gone on as usual ever since, casually sweeping it under the carpet. He must know she'd been thinking about it, though; damn it, was it written all over her face?

"I have the results from the samples we took from the beach," he said now, walking past her to the desk in the corner and flicking on the small light. "I cross-checked the results against the others we collected off the coast last year and it turns out I was right—we've encountered this before."

He looked around for Anela.

"She's not here," she told him, self-consciously tightening her hair in its clasp on top of her head. "They're on a school trip until tomorrow, at Rainbow Bay. So, what exactly did you find?"

He put the file down in front of her and opened it, pointing to a list of numbers, and she watched in surprise as he pulled out a pair of glasses.

"Since when do you wear glasses?" she asked, resisting the urge to tell him he looked sexy as hell in them.

"Since I got old," he deadpanned, and she smirked. "We identified the *exact* cadmium chemical compound that's causing the dolphins' skin irritation. It's a highly toxic metal that can enter water bodies through various ways. The next step is to narrow down who's using the compound around the island and run on-site tests."

"You don't think it's an illegal operation, do you?" she asked in horror.

Mika lowered his voice and leaned in so close her stomach dissolved into knots. In a flash she was reflecting on their kiss once again, that stupid mistake of a kiss. But, oh God, it was such a nice kiss.

"I really hope not," he said, making her ear tingle.

He stepped away quickly as the door opened again and a young woman appeared holding a box. Clearing her throat, Lani forced a smile to her face. Her latest sea turtle patient needed their attention; another one had been caught in fishing nets. It was still the most common cause of injury around here, even after all those campaigns by the island activists to make the fishermen well aware of the implications.

"I found him on the beach this morning. His flipper is hurt," the woman explained as Mika took it gently from her hands. "Oh, hi Mika. I heard you were back."

Lani felt her blood start to race as she noticed how this slender, blond-haired, young lady was looking at him through her fluttering eyelashes, both of their hands still on the box between them. Wasn't she the niece of one of Manu's colleagues, or something? Why did it even matter? She frowned, rolling up her sleeves.

"Let's have a look at this, shall we?" she said quickly, marching up to them and taking the box firmly. She didn't miss Mika's cocked eyebrow before he told the woman they'd take care of it and escorted her back outside. Lani kept one eye on the door as they spoke in a hushed whisper for a moment. What were they talking about? Why was she so…jealous?

No. She grimaced to herself, lifting the poor turtle from its back and putting it on the table to examine it. She was not jealous. How ridiculous—she was just busy. And Mika was supposed to be here, with her, not standing outside for like… ten whole seconds.

"Sorry," he said when he came back in.

She forced another smile to her face. "No worries."

"She was just asking me what to bring on Friday."

"Friday?"

"To the luau," he added, as if she should already know. Of course she *did* know; she just hadn't brought it up again.

Mika pulled on a pair of latex gloves and rolled the light over quickly. His face dropped when he saw the turtle's injuries.

"Don't worry, little one, we'll help fix you up," he said with confidence, reaching immediately for the medications in her carefully ordered cabinet. He knew where everything was, as if he'd always worked here at her side.

Lani clamped her mouth shut, kept her talk about the turtle. There was no point talking about the luau, because she wasn't going. Absolutely not. It would be too weird, for so many reasons, she thought, glancing at his lips. Kissing him was a silly move, so why was she even imagining doing it again?

Somehow, though, working with Mika was easy. They had a kind of rapport and instinct as to each other's methods that meant they conducted each examination and procedure like a well-oiled machine. He was warm and welcoming to every client who came in, too. Maybe they would have been running this place together if he hadn't left, if they'd stayed married… if they'd fought for it.

Maybe she should just let that water stay under its bridge. It wasn't like she didn't have enough to deal with. There was still a stack of emails to answer from the wildlife rescue organization taking Lilo and Stitch, and she had to prepare their postoperative-care instructions and…so much. As if she even had *time* to think about her husband's regrets, and how they seemed to match her own, or how the women around here reacted to him when they walked through the door. He could have anyone he wanted, she mused, wondering for the thousandth time what had happened with Hayley.

Should she have asked him? He probably thought her selfish for asking nothing at all, but why would she want to hear about her perfect size-two replacement? Or the one before that, or the one before that. No, thanks.

She was jealous, Mika realized in shock as he wheeled the little turtle into recovery. He could read her like the children's book he'd started but hadn't finished writing. She was also clearly harboring all kinds of questions about what had happened with Hayley, but after that kiss, she'd decided not to get personal.

It was probably for the best, he concluded. Whatever happened, he would always just bring up a bundle of bad memories for her in the end. And one kiss didn't exactly mean they were paving a path to a new future together. How could they? Lani was an amazing foster mother who was juggling those duties with her work like a pro. He still worked as hard as he had done back then, though, with little time for much else.

Well, okay, so he could *make* time; it wasn't like he couldn't afford more time off these days. But no. He'd been a terrible father back then and he'd be a terrible one now, too. That was just the way it was.

Out in the back, Lilo and Stitch were splashing about in their tank, like they'd become close friends, and he placed the new turtle into a separate tank, where they could monitor it. Lani was cleaning up inside, so he went about the feeding rounds, tossing small fish to the sea lions, preparing a fruit mush for their recovering petrel, who was almost ready to be released. It was so peaceful out here, just doing his thing for the animals, swinging in the hammock at night. Totally different vibe to California.

As he stood on the deck, he felt a tug of nostalgia for all the times he'd spent making plans out *here*. Funny but he didn't miss California, he thought to himself now, watching the way the sunlight danced in the palm trees over the deck. It was strange how quickly that part of his life had started to feel like a distant dream, as though the whispering palm fronds had woken him up from a deep sleep, and reminded him where... or to whom...his heart belonged.

He caught a glimpse of Lani through the doors, and she looked away quickly. Hah! She'd been watching him, as usual.

Not that he could do anything about their obvious attraction, not when their lives were on completely different trajectories. He was back to being a teenager again, trying to ignore her crush on him until she grew up a little more, knowing his infatuation was probably obvious to everyone. But if she wasn't bringing that kiss up, *he* wasn't going to, either.

When Lani stepped onto the deck, looking tired, she joined him in the feeding rounds, and they moved around each other in silence. He should ask her about the luau, he thought, because this was stupid. If she didn't go, it would make things even weirder—everyone knew they were working together, and he'd never avoid all the questions… Besides, he really wanted to hear her play her funny songs on the ukulele after all this time, if she even remembered them.

"Lani, did you think any more about—"

"Oh, no!"

The look on her face sent a bolt of dread to his core. She was staring over his shoulder at the beach. He followed her gaze, heart pounding till he saw the leaping dolphins. One… two…five of them? His mouth fell open.

"What are they doing?"

"They're calling us to help them," she told him, and raced down the steps just ahead of him. Sure enough, he could see the closest dolphin now, floundering in the shallows. He tore off his shirt and shoes and waded straight into the ocean, Lani by his side now as the water crashed around their waists. The dolphin's eyes were piercing black and shining into his, but he knew it was fighting for its life.

"Look at his skin," Lani said in dismay. "It's the same infection. Not as advanced but…"

"Help me," he said to her over the roar of the surf. "Let's get him closer to shore."

"I can do it," she said, so he raced to fetch the specially designed stretcher while she guided the creature slowly toward the shore. Hurrying back, he found Lani crouched on the wet sand, inspecting the dolphin's eyes. Her wet shirt was open, her red spotty bikini top now soaked. In the distance, the rest of the pod were still leaping and arching in the waves, as if encouraging them to help their friend. The dolphin was breathing heavily, his eyes drooping. It wasn't good—they needed to move fast if he was going to make it.

Once they had the dolphin inside the sanctuary, they could breathe a little easier. "He's showing signs of extreme weakness and dehydration," Lani said, as he gathered what they'd need to administer the intravenous fluids and stabilize the mammal.

Mika prepared the IV fluids and equipment and helped steady the dolphin, so that Lani could locate a suitable vein. As she readied the IV catheter for insertion, her face was a picture of determination, but he could almost hear her heartbeat. This was everything to her. It used to be everything to him, too, which left a bitter taste in his mouth now. Could he have done something about this sooner, if he'd been here?

"How many times have you done this procedure already, Lani?"

"Too many," she said, touching a finger to the skin around the dolphin's eyes. The white patches were the same as on the other dolphins. Whatever was in the water wasn't going away. If anything, it was getting worse. Mika found his jaw pulsing—this wasn't right.

"We'll keep an eye on his heart rate and respiration. I'll run some more tests…" He paused. "If that's okay with you?"

"Yes, please," she said, pressing a hand to his arm. A moment passed between them when helplessness flooded her eyes. It tore at his heart just seeing it. "You've done so much already, to help me. Us."

Yet it still wasn't enough, he thought grimly, though her appreciation was welcome. "We'll gather volunteers for on-site inspections. We can't handle this alone, not as quickly as we need to. Conservationists, rescue and rehabilitation organizations up the coast and beyond, we all need to be on the same page."

He had to find out what was going on before this happened again, he thought, just as Lani spoke his exact thoughts out loud. Without thinking he took her fingers and pressed his lips to her knuckles.

"We will save them," he told her resolutely. "Whatever it takes."

Lani nodded. On this matter at least, they were unwavering allies.

"Lani, come to the luau," he said next, squeezing her fingers. She studied his gaze and for a second, he saw the conflict in her eyes. "It wouldn't be the same without you there," he admitted. What a relief it was to actually admit his real feelings for once!

Finally, Lani bobbed her head, a soft smile spreading across her lips.

"Okay, Mika," she sighed. "I'll be there."

CHAPTER TEN

THE LUAU WAS in full swing when she arrived, little Anela close behind in her pink T-shirt and red flowery skirt. Lani breathed in the smoky-sweet fragrance of the kalua pig, slow-roasting away in its underground oven, but her stomach was so full of butterflies that she couldn't even feel hungry. Mika was already here.

Draped in a lei in an open floral shirt, he was bent backward under the limbo pole. His brother, Manu, cheered as Mika managed it easily. The two high-fived, then Manu said something she couldn't hear and Mika laughed, slapping his back good-naturedly before lowering the pole a notch. They'd often played limbo together, and Mika had always been better at it. Not as good as her, though.

Under the shaded palms, surrounded by twinkling fairy lights that would turn on at sunset, was the coconut bowling arena. A few kids were playing already, tossing the wiry brown coconuts across the sand with gusto. Anela watched them in interest, till Lani walked her over.

"I hope you both brought your coconut bowling skills?" came a voice from behind them before Anela could speak.

"Mika!"

Lani watched in shock as Anela wrapped her arms around his middle, like embracing an old friend. Mika looked just as surprised, like he really didn't know what to do with the child's affection, and Lani felt the strangest mix of love and nostalgia that almost made her hug them both, before she managed to rein it back. She had once loved nothing more than those little group hugs: her, Mika and Iolana. Their flawed yet untouchable unit.

"Come play with us!"

Anela was being called away now by one of the kids, and Lani leaned on the shabby palm frond fence with Mika as the girls gave Anela a coconut to roll toward a set of pins.

"I'm glad you came," he told her after a moment, nudging her shoulder. Lani swallowed her nerves. People were watching; she could literally feel their eyes on them. Adjusting the strap of her striped sundress self-consciously, she wished she didn't have to wonder what people thought about her being here.

Mika took the dish she realized she was still holding from her hands.

"She'll be fine here," he said, bobbing his head Anela's way. She was already giggling as another kid pretended to high-five her with a coconut. "Let's go put this where it belongs."

At the long trestle tables standing under the palm trees, the ocean glistened behind him as he placed her coconut haupia between a pineapple shaped like a hedgehog with sausages for spikes, and a delicious-looking salmon *lomi-lomi*. Everything looked incredible. The tables were laden with tasty Hawaiian dishes of all kinds; as usual everyone had brought something. The pineapple-and-macaroni salad used to be her favorite, and as for the poi…

"Mmmm, your mom always did make the best poi," she enthused.

"She still does!" Mika grabbed a spoon and took a scoop of the thick, purple-colored paste made from taro root. He brought it to her mouth, smiling into her eyes, and she let the tangy coolness of it run over her tongue. He watched her closely as she licked her lips and her heartbeat pulsed through to her fingers.

"It's exactly the same," she affirmed, swiping at her mouth.

She couldn't help staring at his exposed chest inches from her face, and now her mind's eye wouldn't stop showing a replay of his firm naked butt at the waterfall. She'd joked that she'd seen it all before, brushed it off like him standing there naked before her was nothing, but her heated dreams at night ever since told her it wasn't.

Manu wandered over, interrupting their small talk about the food, and promptly engulfed her in the biggest hug known to man.

"Lani, Lani, Lani, where have you been? We've missed you, lady!"

She pretended to slap him away like she'd always done, realizing she was laughing now, bundled against his huge chest. Eventually Mika stepped in. "Okay, okay, leave it, Manu. Haven't you got to start shredding?"

"Do you mean the pig, or my chest?" He puffed up his chest like a peacock in a too-big Hawaiian shirt, and Mika prodded his exposed, slightly podgy belly with the spoon.

"Hey!" Manu grabbed the utensil and pretended to stab him with it.

"Get shredding the pig, big boy," Mika cajoled, but the two continued play-fighting in front of her just like old times, and she shook her head, hiding her laugh in her shoulder.

She had almost turned down the invitation to come here again, but opening up to him a little, finally, and having him around these last few days especially—racing between the sanctuary and various other places to meet with conservation-

ists, every marine biologist on his books and experienced divers from around the island, all in an effort to speed up their
investigation—had boosted her confidence. Besides, all of
these good people had lost Iolana, too—she'd been pretty selfish, she realized, shutting them out of her life for fear they'd
judge her. No one had ever judged her, she mused now as Mika
stopped his play-fight and dragged a hand through his hair,
glancing at her as if embarrassed that he'd just been reduced
to a little boy in front of her.

God, she'd missed Mika, the boy and the man; he was, as
ever, a mix of both, still. All the little things, like the way his
laughter carried on the breeze and tickled everyone in its reach,
the camaraderie he had with his family, so different from hers.

He led her over to where another group had already started
the hula competition, and Mika's sister, Betty, sought her out,
followed by his uncle, his nephew—everyone seemed nothing
short of delighted to see her all afternoon.

"We've missed you. All you have to do is reach out. We're
always here," was the general theme. Even the woman who'd
flirted with Mika the other day came up to thank Lani for what
they'd done for the injured turtle. She'd brought her boyfriend,
too. A nice guy with big nerdy glasses. Lani felt a little silly
now, for being so paranoid back at the sanctuary.

"I'm starting to think your family might still like me," she
whispered to Mika at one point, her eyes on Anela, who was
now very much in competition with another child, swaying
her hips to keep the hula hoop high.

Mika took her elbow, led her to the side, where no one else
could hear. He stepped up closer, his expression now deadly
serious.

"They love you. They consider you family. They always
did and always will."

"Even if *you* don't," she interjected, no thanks to her nerves. His eyes were bright, brimming with all kinds of emotions she couldn't read suddenly, and the beach and everyone on it seemed to fall away.

"What do you want me to say, Lani?" His breath tickled her face before he shoved his hands into his pockets and threw his eyes up to the trees. "I thought you couldn't stand to be around me."

"When?"

"After I failed you. I should have helped with the baby more in the first place, let you go back to your studies sooner. You delayed your dream of becoming a vet to stay at home with her. I didn't have to work so hard the whole time. I should have stayed with her that day, too."

Her breath hitched. "I wanted you on the boat with me. Anyway, I thought we weren't doing regrets or guilt anymore."

He shrugged and she took his arm with a sigh. "Mika, we loved her, but we didn't know *how* to be parents—we were always making it up as we went along. We both had big plans for our careers before I got pregnant. And do you know how guilty I've felt about *that* over the years? Maybe that's a part of why I took on Anela, you know? So I could finally have both, and make it work out this time."

Her words hung in the salty air as he scanned her eyes, and she hugged her arms around herself. People were looking again now, and she watched him force a grin to his face and straighten up as someone waved him back over. He threw her a look that was half apology, half regret over his shoulder as he walked away. Unnerved, she sat on the sand, listening to the party all around her, watching the water. That last conversation wasn't over, and they both knew it.

Anela was having the time of her life, but all Lani wanted to do now was get out of here. They'd built so many walls around themselves back then that he'd actually left thinking she'd *wanted* him to go. And then, she'd pushed his family away, too. They might not be saying it, but they would always know it.

"Lani, come try this!" His mother was calling her suddenly, and she got to her feet, determined to put on a brave face.

She did love his mother, Alula, and always had. The big comforting bulk of her, the bright-patterned clothing that hung from her round frame, the easy laughing lilt to her voice, the way she somehow always smelled of baking.

Mika was watching her from the coconut bowling lane as they chatted, and she realized that some part of her was aware of where he was at all times, even when she couldn't see him. He did know how important his family had always been to her.

As the sun began to sink it came time for the tug-of-war, and Lani realized she was actually laughing more than she had in a while, watching Mika on the other end of the rope from Anela and the kids. The big Mahoes were letting the kids win, of course, pretending it was some tough, enduring battle. Then he called her over.

"Lani, we need you! Anela and her pals are smashing us!"

Breathing in the salty air, she let it fill her lungs, and gave in. She got behind him, clutched the rope and felt his shirt caress her cheeks whenever she was forced into his back in the battle. Eventually the crowd roared as they fell to the sand in stitches, the kids triumphant.

"We won, we won, we won!"

She'd never heard Anela so happy, and it made her heart swell, even as a wave of remorse flooded in. This had been here for her all this time—all this love, all around her, and she'd pushed it all away, feeling like it shouldn't be hers for the taking, like it was something she just didn't deserve. It might be too late for her and Mika, but she could start making more of an effort with the people who'd always been there for her, she decided.

Later, with the sun sinking slowly into the ocean, they sat around the campfire, listening to the comforting, crackling undercurrent as the waves lapped the shore beyond. Mika had pulled a cushion up for her, and he sat close, so close she felt forced to keep her hands in her lap while his brother and their friends roasted hot dogs and s'mores on command. What if that stupid muscle memory took over again, and she held his hand or something?

Anela giggled with a little girl, elbows in the sand, playing a game with shells and cards, and Lani watched her with a smile. This was the first time the little girl hadn't seemed cautious about being on the beach. She told Mika so.

"Okay, so she didn't paddle earlier, when the others did, but she is loving this. Look, she's not worried at all."

"Good," he said, smiling warmly, first at Anela, then at her. His eyes glowed in the firelight, so familiar, but still, he looked like a stranger, more handsome now than he had ever been. She found herself so lost in his eyes that she barely noticed when someone waved a ukulele at her.

"Come on, Lani, it's your turn."

Lani groaned and looked around. Shadows danced on their faces as they egged her on; she should have known this was coming. Even Anela stood up to clap in encouragement.

"All right, all right!"

Drawing the ukulele onto her lap, she shot one bashful glance at Mika, who just shrugged, a huge smile on his face. Her fingers worked the strings on autopilot, a Hawaiian folk tune that everyone knew the words to. Sure enough, soon their voices lit up the dusk and the sparks rose to the sky and burst there, scattering red stars above them. One song wasn't enough, it seemed.

"Play one of yours," Mika encouraged.

"One of mine?"

"You know the one I like best," he teased, and she almost refused. Except everyone was cheering for it now. Reluctantly at first, she started to play, and as Mika sung along, like he always had done to this tune, she found she had tears in her eyes suddenly, which she couldn't quite wipe away fast enough at the end.

Mika took the ukulele from her and held it high.

"Ladies and gentlemen, Lani Kekoa Mahoe!" he roared to rapturous applause.

Lani's smile faded on the spot. Lani Kekoa *Mahoe*? She wasn't a Mahoe, not anymore. Why did he say that?

He caught her look, and shrugged again, slightly apologetically after seeing her face. She got to her feet as a couple of others did the same; it was bedtime for the kids. Time for her go.

"I should take Anela home," she said as Mika stood with her.

He frowned, searching her eyes. Already someone else was playing ukulele, but she felt more than a little uncomfortable now if she was honest…maybe because he'd called her a Mahoe. Maybe because she'd been starting to feel a little too relaxed. This was too nice, too familiar, but soon Mika would be gone again, back to his high-flying Cali-career, and she didn't really know how to go about having all of this without him. She'd worked so hard for her dream job, she couldn't be anywhere else. And Mika had worked just as hard over there.

She couldn't exactly ask him to give up his whole life and move back to Oahu.

"I shouldn't still be here," she told him, calling Anela. The girl was engrossed in a card game, ignoring her.

"Yes, you should," he said firmly.

"I don't even have nightclothes for…"

"I made a bed for Anela in the red tepee. There are spare pajamas on the pillow."

They had tents set up close by for the children, same as every year. It was the annual tradition to camp on the beach on the night of the luau. Long after the kids went to bed, tucked up in their little tepees with their friends, the adults stayed up talking and playing music around the campfire. They'd slept in those tents themselves as kids and she still remembered the first time they'd been allowed to stay up and join in around the fire. It was such a great vibe, but…no.

"I can't."

"Why not? You can't drag her away now. You just said she's starting to feel okay about being by the ocean—maybe this is just what she needs."

"How do you know what she needs?" she retorted, annoyed at being put on the spot.

Mika's face fell, then grew dark as thunder.

"I'm sorry. I didn't mean it to come out like that," she said quickly, but he dug his toes into the sand and shifted on his feet, his mouth a thin line.

"Maybe I don't," he said, and his voice carried a gravitas that turned her stomach. "But you and I still need to talk about some things, don't you think?"

CHAPTER ELEVEN

MAHINA FOUND HIM as he took his place by the fire again. Lani was still putting Anela to bed. The kid had insisted on sleeping in a different teepee with her new friend Kiki, the little red-haired girl who'd taught her the coconut bowling game. He'd stopped himself from getting involved.

"So, you and Lani looked serious back there," Mahina ventured, resting her leg out on the sand in front of her.

Mika bristled, dragging a stick through the sand. His brother was making up some song on the ukulele now, which should be making him laugh but all he could think about now was how Lani had reacted just then, how he knew *nothing* about what a child might need. She was right but it had stung.

"You okay?" Mahina nudged him and he grunted.

"Sorry," he said, glancing at the tents again. He could hear giggling, a couple of kids singing, a pair of feet he guessed were Anela's sticking out of an awning. It was weird, how much he wanted to walk over there and check things were all right—none of them were his children. It was just that Lani was bustling around, scolding Anela laughingly for lying down with her shoes on…acting just like a mother. In another world, one where they hadn't lost Iolana, he'd be doing those kinds of things, too. He'd be a pro at it by now. Instead, he was pretty much redundant.

"How are your injuries now?" he heard himself say.

"Better." She nodded. "I'm more concerned about you and Lani. How is it going, working at the sanctuary…um…together?"

Mika told her about the petrel, the sea lions and the turtles, and how they were still gathering data and intel on what could be affecting the dolphins. Mahina tried to seem interested, despite the disappointment on her face. She wanted to know all the things he would not be telling her, of course.

"We're going to be fine," he said on a sigh, as if that should cover it. She pressed an empathetic hand to his arm, just as Lani appeared again.

"What's going to be fine?" she asked, adjusting the straps on her dress. She looked just as good in sundresses as she always had, better even than she had with her long lean legs on display in her Daisy Dukes.

"Everything is going to be fine," Mahina enthused with a smirk in her direction.

Mika got to his feet, and motioned for Lani to walk with him.

"What did you tell her? Did you tell her we kissed?" she said quickly, stopping him on the shoreline.

He almost laughed. "What? No, why would I do that?"

Lani shrugged, flushing. "It looked like you were talking about something… Why did she say everything is going to be fine?"

"Maybe because she picked up on…" He wiggled his finger between them. "I don't know—this! But I didn't tell her anything. That kiss was between *us*."

"Us," Lani whispered, her gaze firmly fixed on the ocean.

His heart felt heavy and his stomach churned with apprehension. Letting himself kiss her, unwrapping all those emotions they'd both tried so hard to suppress, had been a mistake. But it didn't mean he wasn't constantly thinking about it every time he saw her. In fact, the more he thought about it now, it felt kind of *good* to unwrap some of it with her, after all this time. He'd started it, back in her kitchen. Fake confidence was carrying him through.

"You were right before. Neither of us knew how to be parents back then. We didn't even really know how to be married. There was so much we could have said, but we didn't and…"

"Yet here we are now," she finished. "Saying it."

"Exactly."

Lani kept her eyes on the sea, and he reached for her hand.

"I might not know what Anela needs—you were right about that, too—but it doesn't escape my attention that you're a great mother figure, Lani. In case you ever had any doubts about that. I've said it before, but I could never do what you do, and I think we both know that."

Lani looked at him, her expression furrowed. "But you were an amazing father."

The look in her eyes made his throat contract—was she serious?

"What?" she pressed.

Conflicted, Mika dropped her hand, and continued walking along the sand. He'd openly told her not to play the blame game, but it didn't mean he didn't berate himself daily for putting his career before his family so many times.

"Mika, what?"

"I was a terrible dad. I was hardly there," he said, his voice strained.

"You did what you had to do. You were trying to provide for us, and protect me, too. I always knew you loved me."

The stars were out now, twinkling above the sparks from the fire. They said nothing for a moment as he processed her words. She always knew he loved her. It didn't mean she'd always loved him back.

"What happened with Hayley?" she asked, stopping to face him again.

He felt the folds of her sundress flit about his own ankles in the breeze as he fought for the right words. He should have known she would ask eventually.

"I thought you were happy together," she continued. "Two years, wasn't it?"

He shrugged again, frowning.

Lani sighed. "She wanted your babies, didn't she?" she said, eyeing him closely. He pulled his gaze away, then crouched to his haunches, where a tiny ghost crab was scuttling for the shoreline.

"How did you know?" he asked gruffly.

"Mika, she's only what, twenty-eight, twenty-nine…?"

"Thirty-five next week, but why does it matter?"

"I'm right, aren't I?" she said softly. "And…you said no?"

"What do you *think* I said?" He stood and this time, Lani caught his hands. "You don't even want me around Anela after what I…after what happened to our child, and I can't say I blame you."

Lani's eyes widened. "Is that what you think?"

He screwed up his nose. "It doesn't matter. I don't want *any more* kids in my life, Lani."

Lani shut her mouth, and Mika kicked himself. What he really wanted to say was that he didn't want, and had never wanted, children with anyone *except* her, and he never would, and not just because he wouldn't be able to trust himself with the responsibility a second time. She'd been the love of his life, and he'd totally screwed it all up. He wasn't there when Iolana needed him, and then he'd walked out on their marriage, scuppering the chance for them to have another baby together. How could he even think about having someone else's child after everything *they'd* been through?

Lani was talking again. "I just meant I don't want you thinking Anela's your responsibility. I know she needs a lot of energy and time, and you're busy…"

Mika barely heard the words coming from her mouth; all he heard was that he'd never really been, and never would be, a father. Not the kind Lani needed to have around for her foster kid, if she needed anyone now at all. She was filling two parental roles all by herself and she was doing just fine. More than fine.

"Mika?" she said. "Are you listening?"

He was about to respond when a scream cut through the silence like glass. They turned to each other. *Anela?*

They both rushed as fast as their feet could carry them, back to the tepee. Lani tore at the zip and stuck her head inside, and he pulled it farther open. Inside, Anela was clearly having a terrible nightmare and shouting in her sleep, her face contorted with fear and confusion, tears streaming down her cheeks. Lani shot straight to her side, stroking her hair and murmuring softly, while Mika looked on, his heart aching for them both. He wanted to go to Lani and wrap his arms around her—around both of them. It had become instinctive again now, whether it was right or not, but he held back as Lani leaned over Anela's small body and scooped her up into a hug.

"It's okay, darling," she whispered soothingly into the little girl's ear, rocking her back and forth in the darkness. "It was just a dream."

Kiki, the other child in the tent, was stirring now, sitting up in confusion. Mika turned around, ran back to the trestle tables and grabbed up his backpack, digging out the tissues as he hurried back and handed Lani the small pack. His heart went out to Anela as Lani mopped her tears, but what had him in a stranglehold now was the love emanating from Lani. He hadn't seen such love since she'd held Iolana for the first time. Without thinking, he reached into the bag again and brought out some sheets of paper. He hadn't shown anyone yet, but this was as good a time as any.

"Does anyone want to hear a little story?" he asked.

Lani looked up, still wiping away Anela's tears. Mika cleared his throat and began reading from the papers he was holding, and she could hardly believe what was coming from his mouth, or the fact that far from showing fear now, Anela's eyes had started to shine with excitement and wonder.

"The dolphin swam in circles, crying out 'Help me!'
She was stuck on a hook, and she couldn't break free.
This was no fun, and her face hurt so bad.
But with no hands to help, it just made her sad."

At that part Anela and Kiki both giggled. "Dolphins should have hands," Anela exclaimed, wiggling her fingers. Mika carried on.

"The creatures crept closer, a crab with big claws
Started pulling and tugging, and yanking her jaws.
The octopus, even with eight gentle limbs,
Could do nothing to stop the big hook digging in.
The dolphin was trembling. Was this her fate?
To be hooked like a fish, maybe served on a plate?"

"No! The poor dolphin," Kiki cried now, inching closer so she could see what was written as Mika was reading it. He shot a look at Lani and she encouraged him on. Okay, so it wasn't exactly Wordsworth or Keats, but he'd tried his best and she could almost imagine the illustrations already.

"Two divers approached her with four helpful hands.
They got to work quickly, disentangling the bands.
With steady resolve, they worked with great care,
To ease the big hook and relieve its cruel snare.
The dolphin was grateful, she stayed really still.
These humans were helping her, humans had skill!
Through their patience and smartness, they figured it out.
'Thank you, oh, thank you,' she wanted to shout.
Released from her torment, the dolphin swam free,
And went back to roaming the beautiful sea."

Mika put the notebook down. "I need another new verse. Something about how she became friends with those humans and told all the other creatures not to be afraid of them anymore." He looked tentatively at Anela, and Lani followed his eyes, realizing she'd been staring only at him the whole time, thinking what a shame it would be if they couldn't find someone to illustrate it.

"She also needs to prove that even the scariest creatures in the ocean are all just trying to live in peace," she suggested.

"Even sharks?" Kiki piped up. She was still watching and listening intently, propped up on one elbow. "My mom says you swim with sharks, Mr. Mika, and that you're friends with one."

Oh, no. Lani held her breath.

Anela shook her head and creased her forehead in disagreement, but her voice was soft as she pulled away from Lani to lie back down on the pillow. "People can't be friends with sharks."

"They can, when they understand them," Lani said tactfully, and she knew Mika could tell she was seizing the moment to make their case. How bad she felt now, knowing he'd assumed she'd been keeping him away from Anela because she didn't trust him around children.

"I know sometimes it's hard to believe, but sharks make mistakes, too," he tried, looking at her for reassurance. "Most of the time, they're trying to figure things out, just like we are," he added.

"I guess…everyone just wants to keep the ocean a safe place," Anela mumbled eventually through a yawn. "We all need to care for it, and everything in it," she added, as her eyes fluttered closed again. "My mom loved sharks."

Carefully, when both girls were silent again, Lani crept out of the teepee, Mika close behind. Halfway back to the campfire she stopped him.

"Your children's story…" she started, and he stifled a groan.

"I know, it needs work. It was just a few notes really."

"But I get what you're trying to do, Mika. This is exactly what you always said you wanted to do—educate kids about the ocean, in a way they can relate to, that connects them emotionally… Anela never told me her mother loved sharks before."

"A love that killed her," he added grimly, and she nodded, looking away.

"Probably nothing will come of the book," he said, walking on with her. At the fire, a few people without kids were getting up to leave already, including Mahina, but Lani stopped again. She felt rooted to the spot, her feet digging deeper into the sand, the moonlight dimming the color of her toenails.

"I'm happy you told them your story," she said sincerely, and he frowned into the distance.

"You don't think I was butting in?"

"Why would I think you were butting in?" She studied his face, the reflections of the firelight in his eyes, the shadows playing on his face, and her heart went out to him, remembering what he'd said earlier. He didn't think he could do what she was doing, and she knew the reasons why. She pressed a palm to his cheek without thinking, forced him to look at her.

"You were an amazing father to Iolana," she reaffirmed, in case he hadn't heard her earlier. "I was the one who…"

No. She forced her mouth shut. What was the point of blaming herself yet again? They'd covered this already, and it had gotten them nowhere. They were finally in a place where they could at least talk about the mistakes they'd both made, even if it seemed to be bringing other things back to the surface, too. Things she had no place revisiting—because his life wasn't even on the island anymore!

His hand came up over hers, and the heat made the pulsing start deep inside her, like a kettle flipped to boil.

"You might have started her thinking differently about the ocean, you know," she said, trying to keep her voice steady. "Thank you. I mean, I wouldn't give up your day job to write poetry, but at least you know your audience."

Mika huffed a laugh. His broad chest rumbled with the sound as he pulled her closer and pressed the back of her hand to his heart.

"Woman, you'll be the death of me," he growled, and for a moment the party fell away again.

Time stopped. Lani held her breath as she saw her entire childhood and young adult life flash before her eyes, a thousand memories all at once, all the nights they'd made love on the sand, and in one of those very tepees more times than once. Her cheeks turned hot as he looked at her, and her blood raced to places it hadn't been to in ages. A wild intensity shone in his eyes as he urged her hips against his and focused on her mouth, leaning closer…and closer…

"Mika! Lani! Come here!"

They sprang apart. Lani's heart beat wildly in her chest and throat, half from the urgency in Mahina's voice as they started to run and half from what just happened. What was she thinking? She'd got swept up in the memories again, in the way he'd opened up to her and then helped Anela after her nightmare. That could not happen again, no way, and anyway, he was probably just missing Hayley. Yes, that was it; he was missing the company and the attention, someone, God forbid, making love to him at night… Of course, why wouldn't he?

Well, she was not going to be sucked right back into that, only to miss him all over again when he left. He didn't want kids in his life—he'd said as much—and part of her plan had always been to have children, to foster them, nurture them, watch them grow, the way she'd never been able to witness Iolana doing. She'd even been thinking seriously about adopting Anela.

As for her, from now on, outside of work she was going to be a Mika-free zone, she decided firmly. But her heart was a wild bird in her chest as she followed him and Mahina to the parking lot.

CHAPTER TWELVE

"THAT BIKE," MAHINA SAID, pointing to a motorbike on the gravel path by the parked cars at the top end of the beach. "That's the one that forced me off the road!"

"How do you know?" Mika asked, walking over to inspect it.

"I recognize that yellow thing on the side."

He listened as Mahina explained to a few onlookers how the accident happened again, how she'd caught a glimpse of this very bike before it had torn right past her. Lani was at his side now, inspecting the yellow sticker, and he found himself stepping back, crossing his arms over himself. It was a lucky thing that Mahina had interrupted that…whatever that had been back there. A moment? He and Lani seemed to be having too many moments like that lately.

Okay, so most were probably in his head, but either way, it wasn't wise. He should not be hitting on his ex-wife! What was wrong with him? As if stirring up the past and how he'd failed her wasn't uncomfortable enough, now he was on track for rejection, too—she didn't need him anymore.

"Kalama Tours," Lani said, touching a finger to the logo on the bike. "I know of Kai Kalama. He's pretty new in town. He runs the motorized kayak company here, came over from Maui."

"Are you sure it was this bike?" she asked Mahina.

Mahina was adamant.

"I'll go around there tomorrow," Mika stated.

Lani looked as horrified as Mahina. "And say what?"

"Can I help you?" The voice, coming from behind them, made them all turn around to see a bulky guy approaching. He was tall with wild hair and the kind of wide, gym-honed chest and shoulders like spoke of hours lifting weights...or people?

It was Lani who stepped forward.

"Kai Kalama," she said, eyeing him warily.

He was wearing a wet suit, carrying a surfboard, like he'd ridden the last sunset waves and stayed out under the moon, maybe watching their party.

Mika's instincts were primed. Something about this guy set him on edge.

"We think you ran my friend here off the road," Lani said, pointing to Mahina's leg.

Kai looked down his nose at her, which annoyed Mika further, and went about strapping his board to the side of the bike.

"If I did, I'm sorry but I don't remember." He had the sort of slight half smile now that said he was both amused by and undaunted by them, which put Mika's back up more, though he said nothing. It wouldn't do to step on their toes.

"You did. It was you," Mahina insisted.

"I said I don't remember," he replied tightly.

"The least you can do is apologize," Lani said now.

Kai's jaw moved from side to side as he looked between them. "You run the Mermaid Cove Marine Sanctuary, right?" he said.

"Yes, we've met, briefly," Lani replied.

Another long silence, before Kai frowned darkly. "Someone called me about coming to collect some kind of sample tomorrow, from the beach outside my kayak warehouse. Looking for a chemical match?"

Mika explained it was probably one of his people, looking into what was harming the dolphins in the area.

Kai looked even more infuriated, and straddled his bike seat. "Tell them not to bother, I don't have time tomorrow. And I don't have anything to do with any dolphins."

Before Mika could even reply that the site checks of local businesses like Kai's were mandatory in the eyes of the marine conservation department, Kai revved up the bike and sped off without so much as a glance behind him.

"Charming," Mahina muttered, brushing the sand from her arms and clothes.

She and Lani went back to talking, and Mika watched the road after Kai, noting how he'd sped away so fast. Something told him Kai Kalama was definitely the kind of guy who'd run a woman off the road, and if he could do that unashamedly and deny it, what else was he capable of doing?

The sanctuary was strangely quiet the next afternoon when Mika walked in, trying and failing to stifle a yawn. Most of the party had stayed up till sunrise talking and playing songs, and he'd had a good time; apart from the obvious tension in the air between himself and Lani. They'd danced around the fact that they'd almost kissed again, managed to talk to everyone but each other till she'd extracted Anela from the tepee at six o'clock and taken her home with barely a wave in his direction. Awkward.

Still, he wouldn't dwell on it. He had more important things to think about, like what made Kalama Tours so special that Kai felt it should be excluded from the site checks. Every establishment in the bay had given them the okay. He had every intention of going around there himself if Kai didn't comply today. He'd also had a call from his colleague Megan back in California. They were due at a stakeholders' briefing for the SafeCoast Guardian Project, part of a global study to help track whether shark behavior was being influenced by sea surface temperatures, and he was starting to feel guilty for taking so much time out. His role was a pivotal one; there were things only he could implement and manage.

"Mika, how did you sleep after you got back?" Lani asked when he walked in, but her voice was muffled somewhat by the huge albatross she was leaning over.

"I got a few hours," he replied. "How is Anela today?" He couldn't shake the look on her face after that nightmare; his heart had broken for her.

"She's fine. She's reading the book you gave her out on the deck," she said, distractedly.

"My shark book?"

Lani shrugged. "She said she slept really well after your story last night, and then she picked your book back up."

"Wow." Mika felt the tiniest jolt of pride, which was quickly stamped out when he saw the expression on Lani's face. She'd put a wall up between them last night and she was keeping it there. He knew that look.

"I've just done the preoperative assessment," Lani told him, all business as he approached the albatross, looking for any clear signs of illness or injury. It looked a little lopsided and he suspected a wing injury. She threw him some gloves.

"It looks like he's healthy overall, but the X-rays show he does have a fractured wing. It's a clean break, but we'll need to stabilize it," she said, confirming his suspicions.

Mika set about carefully administering the anesthetic while Lani finished the surgical prep, and neither of them uttered a word as she made the incision. This one would be mostly Lani, who had mastered the specialized avian surgical techniques he himself had little experience with. The whole time he moved around her, he felt that almost-kiss hovering in the air, like the spirit of the sedated bird. She was thinking about it, too, he could tell. But she wasn't going to bring it up, which meant she wished it hadn't happened. As did he.

Didn't he? This was all messing with his head; too many emotions came tangled up in Lani.

"Right. We'll want antibiotics to prevent infection, analgesics for pain relief, and could you set up the anti-inflammatories," she said as she readied the bird for the recovery room. By the time the meds from her well-organized cabinet were administered, and the cage door was locked behind them, he couldn't stand it any longer.

"What's going on, Lani?"

"Nothing," she said too quickly, turning her back to him and checking on a couple of other patients in the cages.

Mika pressed his lips together. He couldn't read her at all. One minute she was open and warm and the Lani he used to know, and the next she was an island he couldn't reach. He watched her check on the turtle and three birds, then followed her out back to check on Lilo and Stitch, who were now coming on in leaps and bounds and were due to leave them soon, but she was refusing to look at him. Anela looked up from her place on the egg-shaped chair hanging from a chain on the ceiling. She was indeed reading his book.

"Hi," she said, looking over the pages with a frown. "Mika, was she right?"

"Who?" he asked.

"My friend Kiki, when she said you swim with sharks and that you're friends with one?"

He felt his eyebrows shoot up to his bandanna. "Er...yes? That is kind of true."

Anela looked at him a moment in interest, then promptly went back to reading. It registered suddenly that she was *still* reading a book about sharks, and asking him about them, too.

But the thought was fleeting; Lani was putting him on edge. Eventually, back inside, he caught her arm, forcing her to stop in her tracks.

"It keeps happening," he said, his words heavier than he'd intended, his mouth brushing her ear and making her freeze. "This need to kiss you."

She released the breath she'd been holding in, and her answer came out small, guarded. "I know, but it's just because it *used* to happen...and you miss Hayley."

Mika almost laughed as he released her; he hadn't been thinking about Hayley at all.

Lani tutted and walked back inside. She went about filling in some paperwork, putting the desk between them. "I don't blame you if you miss her. She's younger, she's beautiful, she's..."

"She's not in my life anymore," he interrupted, taking a stand in front of the desk. "And she has *nothing* to do with what's going on here," he said, flattening his hands on the table so hard the lamp on it shook.

"There's nothing going on here, Mika," she said carefully, still unable to meet his eyes. "You're a good man, and I appreciate what you're doing for Anela, but please...let's not confuse the situation."

Mika moved the lamp across and leaned over the desk, trying not to feel the jellyfish sting of her brush-off. "The situation, Lani, is that we are both trying to figure out how to be around each other after all this time, and it doesn't help when you shut me out."

Lani stood taller, the glint in her eyes a warning sign. "Oh, really? Well, it didn't help me much when you shut me out, either, after Iolana died, back when I *needed* you."

"We needed each other, Lani, we failed each *other*, we've been over this."

Lani shook her head vehemently now. "You were the love of my life, Mika. But I struggled so much, thinking I was a bad mother, and I was so worried that with your work and my studies, nothing would change. Even if we'd stayed together and had another baby…"

Mika stepped closer, swept her chin up and forced her to face him. "You wanted another baby, with me?"

Lani stuttered in his stare, and her eyes filled with tears. "I don't know…maybe. Eventually. It doesn't matter now, though, does it? We live different lives, in different states."

"I should have fought harder for us," he said quickly, as his heart raced. "I will regret not fighting for our marriage for the rest of my life."

Lani sank back down into the chair, her head in her hands.

"I want to go to the cemetery," he said next, watching the sun fall over her bowed head. "I think I need to, Lani." The words were out before he could even think. Just the thought of seeing that tiny gravestone, the glossy marble covered in flowers from every single member of his family who'd made a continuous effort to keep it a living shrine… "Did you make up your mind yet, to come with me?" he added hopefully.

She sniffed and shook her head. "I still don't know. It would be too hard…both of us there. It's hard enough going on my own."

Mika shut his mouth before he could tell her it might help.

It wouldn't help his case, though. Forcing her to confront it all, dredging up the past, was everything he'd sworn he wouldn't do; she had to want to do it herself.

He turned his head to the window, expecting to see the little girl still sitting on the egg chair, reading his book. But she wasn't there.

"Oh," he exclaimed now, making Lani follow his eyes.

"She's on the beach on her own," Lani said, eyes wide as she stepped back outside.

The sky was darker now, a hint of the storm they'd been warned about on the news this morning seemed to be gathering on the horizon, but the clouds weren't what Lani was looking at as she made her way down to the sand.

Anela was inches from the shoreline. Mika sat on the bottom step, watching Lani shake off her sandals and step into the frothy surf, her shapely legs still the same…maybe not quite as firm as they had been once, wrapped around him on the sand, seventeen, hungry for him.

She still looked so good like this, he mused with a sigh. They'd always said they'd grow old and gray and let it all hang out, and fill that big house out by the beach with animals and laughter. Now look at them. Worlds apart. Which reminded him, he should probably let the institute know he might need another week or two off. Had he really been out here almost three weeks already?

"Come, Mika," Anela called, and he stood as the little girl jumped up and down. "Look, Lani found a starfish!"

He stood beside her and shook off his shoes, striding out into the water next to Lani. They crouched down to where the starfish was shimmering below the surface at their feet.

"It's beautiful," Lani gushed.

"You can't see it properly from over there," he said now,

feeling Lani's eyes on his face and letting the warm water wash over his calves. Thunder rumbled ominously in the distance behind the gray clouds, but the sun was still glinting off the water and Anela peered closer, her bare feet barely skimming the shoreline. A wave threatened to wash over her toes and she stepped back, but her body arched over the water and he knew she badly wanted to see what they were looking at.

"One more step, and you'll be able to see it," he encouraged. "You don't want to miss this. The tide will take it away again in a minute."

Lani touched his arm a second and he met her eyes. Was he pushing her too hard?

"Come, Anela, quick," she encouraged next, and he could hardly believe it when Anela gave a huge, exaggerated sigh and stepped across the shoreline into the surf. He took her hand quickly, as Lani reached for the other.

"It's okay," he said as Anela studied the water swishing around her feet, as if it might re-form into a sea beast and swallow her up—who could blame her mind for taking her there?

Lani squeezed her other hand, encouraging her closer, till they were crouching in the shallows, studying the starfish together. Anela's eyes grew wide with delight as he lifted the creature gently and placed it in her hand; she seemed so fascinated by what she was looking at that she was barely registering the fact that she was standing almost knee-high in the water now.

"Thank you," Lani mouthed at him, and Mika bobbed his head. The moment of understanding between them swelled in his chest and made his heart beat faster and seemed to blow all their own problems clean away.

The wind was picking up now, though. The smell of rain

hung heavily in the atmosphere as a few drops began to fall, stinging his skin like tiny needles.

"We should go," he said, and they put the starfish back in its watery world, just as the sound of a car horn honked from the front of the sanctuary. Kiki and her mom were here to collect Anela for a play date, and he and Lani still had work to do. Hopefully this storm would blow over quick enough, he thought, as another crash of thunder made them all run faster, laughing as they sped toward the steps.

CHAPTER THIRTEEN

LANI GRIMACED, YANKING another window closed as the guy on the radio announced the latest weather report. "They've upgraded the storm to a hurricane!" she called out to Mika. He was dashing between moving the outdoor cages inside and bringing the cushions in from the deck. The humidity was intense at the best of times, but now it was stifling outside.

"Quick, we need to get everything in," she told him, and he wasted no time in his duties as the rain started pelting the windows so hard she thought they might break.

At one point they crashed into each other and a box of animal feed almost went flying before he caught it, and a loud rumble, followed by a bolt of lightning, made him rush to the window.

"It doesn't look good," he announced, adjusting his crooked bandanna as they watched a deck chair tumble down the steps and dance across the beach.

Pressed to his shoulder at the glass, she became acutely aware of his breathing, his closeness, every steady inch of him at her side as they watched the storm whipping the ocean into a fury of churning whitecaps and salty foam. The deck chair disappeared from view and she pictured the poor starfish. Hadn't it been through enough, getting picked up by curious humans, then placed back into an ocean resembling a washing machine?

Still, she would never forget that moment, watching Anela walk into the water for the first time. It would never have happened without Mika.

I will regret not fighting for our marriage for the rest of my life.

His words had struck her deeply. They'd caused each other so much turmoil, and she felt the same way exactly. But he was here now, and sometimes, she caught herself imagining him staying here.

Of course, he wasn't going to give up the life he'd cultivated over the last two decades without her, and if he didn't want kids in his life, there was no point even going down that path. But it didn't mean she wasn't thinking of a whole new bunch of what-ifs, despite their frequent blowups. He always had challenged her, and she him, and she'd missed that a lot; everything with Mika had always felt like an adventure. Much of her life had seemed pretty stagnant when he'd stopped being in it.

They went about moving what they could from the rain-lashed deck into the storeroom, but Lilo and Stitch would have to stay where they were. She kept stealing looks at Mika in his rain-soaked shirt, getting increasingly wetter. That almost-kiss the other night had thrown her. Her heart was all over the place, wanting to make up for lost time. She should at least go with him to the cemetery, she thought now, catching his eyes on her from across the room before he bolted another window behind the petrel closed. The thought of it was agonizing. She hadn't been in a long time. Too long.

"Mika, about what you said before," she started. "Maybe we *should* go…"

"Hell!" he yelled over her as the lights above them flickered and abruptly went off. "The power's out!"

Lani's heart began to race as the darkness enveloped them,

accentuated by the howl of the wind and the whiplash of rain on the deck and windows. The birds were all squawking and flapping their wings and she worried about them exacerbating their injuries, never mind overheating without the air-conditioning.

"They just said this could last all night," she said, pressing her hands to her head, trying to think. "The birds and smaller animals, we need to get them out of here. The animals in the larger tanks will be fine."

She turned to Mika, who'd taken the stressed-out petrel from its cage and was cradling it, and for a moment she was stunned into silence at the way it quietened in his gentle arms.

"We could take them to the house?" he suggested.

"Should we drive in this?" Lani gestured to the door which was all but bending inwards from the force of the wind and rain.

Mika shrugged. "Four-wheel drive," he said simply, and she bit back a laugh. "It's not far, we can manage," he assured her.

Oh, he was serious, then?

The two of them got to work, quick as they could. The storm seemed to be intensifying, and every time she raced outside with a cage and placed it carefully into the vehicle, Lani felt her heartbeat in her throat. Finally, after what felt like far too long, Mika started to drive carefully through the storm, winding up the hill to her house.

By now it was pouring heavier than ever and lightning split the sky open overhead. She gripped the dash with both hands as the birds cried out. Thunder roared above them like a stampede of wild horses. Branches snapped from trees and streetlamps seemed to sway eerily, although it was probably just her eyes, she reasoned, adjusting to the chaos. Mika was calm, and she appreciated his strength, how it calmed her.

Her heart swelled with the knowledge that he was willing to do this for her, for the birds and the other animals, despite the tension that clogged the air whenever they were alone. She'd never got to actually tell him she would go to the cemetery with him back there, and now she'd chickened out again. It would be too hard.

Gosh, what was this? One minute she felt able to face their past and their mistakes together, and the next she was drowning in a well of confusion and pain and panic; there was no set way to feel around Mika, she thought now. He was the storm. No, *they* were the storm, blowing around in a thousand directions except for the one that might just offer them the safety and comfort they needed.

Why would she not go with him to see Iolana's grave? It was all for her own selfish fears of being sucked right back into that well of grief alongside him! She owed him this much. She would tell him she would go with him...later, she decided.

When they arrived at Lani's home, thankfully the power was on and the air-conditioner was working just fine. They unloaded the cages as fast as they could, piling them into the kitchen until the counters were overloaded with birds and turtles and the place looked more like a zoo than a place for prepping Anela's dinner.

"Poor little buddy," she heard Mika say as he opened the cage to the petrel again. The bird had been healing so well that they were almost at rerelease stage but now it looked sorrowful and its wing was hanging limply again.

"She got scared, I heard her flapping about whenever the thunder struck," Mika told her, holding it still in his arms again, checking the rest of it carefully for obvious signs of injury. Outside on the porch, the hammock was swaying wildly and the door to the shed slammed the wooden wall again and again. In the distance, at the bottom of the hill, a siren wailed ominously.

"We need to stabilize her wing," Mika said, crossing to the kitchen table. Giving low hums of reassurance, they checked along the bones of its wing. The petrel was clearly in shock and Lani was moved, noting the extra care Mika took, even as the windows shook, as if trying to distract him from the task. Lani had packed supplies, so it didn't take long before a minute dose of anesthetic had stilled the bird further and she'd resecured the wing with a tiny splint.

She was just carrying it back to its cage when another sound found her ears—the tiniest meow, coming from somewhere outside.

"Did you hear that?" Mika was at the door in seconds, and she fastened the petrel's cage shut, following him outside.

Chairs were strewed all over the place and as if she wasn't wet enough already, the rain came at her in a soggy assault that almost threw her to her knees. Mika put an arm out, stepping in front of her.

"Get back inside," he instructed.

"No, I think one of the kittens is trapped somewhere," she said, grabbing his arm as another gust of wind almost lifted her off the floor. A tiny, harrowed meow came at them again, louder this time.

"She's close, Mika."

Mika's hand clamped over hers and held it tight. "I think she's under the shed!"

They followed the sound, despite every instinct in her body telling her to get back into the house. No animal would suffer, not on her watch!

Eventually, they located the kitten, but they couldn't see it. Getting to her knees, Lani peered under the shed, but the path of fallen branches and blinding rain meant she couldn't see where it was exactly in order to reach it. Mika started heaving the debris away, his clothing stuck to his skin. Her hair plastered like glue to her own face as she helped, praying no more branches would fall on them. The kitten was now meowing constantly in terror and panic.

"Hold on, little one," she urged, as they discussed how best to get it out. Then Lani spotted an old tarp that usually covered the barbecue, on the other side of the deck. "Help me," she said, but she didn't need to. Mika was already on it.

Together they draped it over the area, creating a makeshift shelter that would protect them while they focused on moving the rest of the branches away from the shed.

"We need to move faster," she urged, panting and soaked, and Mika tugged at heavy pieces of timber while she tried coaxing the kitten out with food and gentle words. It was too scared to even try.

With one last tug of effort from Mika, enough of a gap opened up for Lani to squeeze through. She was about to dive under the shed, but Mika caught her elbow.

"Be careful," he said, and his eyes blazed with caution and reluctance to let her go, so much so that a powerful surge of an emotion she couldn't define caught her completely off guard.

Before she could hold herself back, she pressed her lips to his, breathing him in and letting his warmth flood right though her, right before turning back and crawling into the tiny, suffocating space.

Her lips burned from the wind and the kiss but she kept on crawling. A tiny yelp rose in a desperate plea from the kitten. Lani scrambled closer and sorted through what remained, moving twigs and leaves with her hands, digging deeper into the mud until she could see it; a little ball of fur shaking in fear.

"Can you see it?" Mika called out behind her.

"Yes!"

The nearest branch was still trapping it beneath its weight. Carefully, Lani moved around it and scooped up the kitten in her arms. It was wet and trembling, tiny meows escaping from its mouth as it clung desperately on to her shirt for reassurance. She scrambled backward with it, putting all her weight on her knees and one arm so as not to drop it, and Mika hurried to move the last of the debris away from the entrance. When she was finally back on her knees outside, he huddled in close, wrapping them both in his arms for a moment under the tarp.

"Is she okay? Are you?"

"Everyone's good," she said with a nervous laugh, kissing the top of the kitten's damp head as Mika pressed his own lips to the top of hers.

Lani's heart raced as she turned her face to him. He scanned her eyes and for a moment she thought he was going to kiss her, but instead he urged her up to her feet and used the tarp as a sheltering cloak as he hurried them back to the house.

The other kittens pattered over playfully to check out their thankfully unharmed sibling, giving it affectionate licks before scampering away into the sitting room, and Lani shot her eyes to Mika, who was already hurrying back from the bathroom carrying towels. Just as she put her arm out to take one, she realized she was bleeding.

"What happened?" Mika was beside her in a second.

"I must have scraped it on the branches or something..." she said, trailing off as he sat her at the table on a chair and went about inspecting her arm.

The closeness of his face and his care made her blood pulse harder; the only sounds were the wind and rain and the distant sirens, and her breath, she realized as he drew her arm closer. Lifting his eyes to hers, he pressed his mouth to her arm, just above the cut, as if kissing it better, like he used to. Warmth and love seemed to fill the room and she watched in silence as he trailed more kisses up her arm. A groan rose up in her throat, the flood of desire tingled its way around her navel, the heat spread downward to between her legs… It was all too much.

"Mika…"

"I'll get you a Band-Aid," he said, breaking away and dragging his hands through his hair.

Her heart pounded with anticipation as she heard the sound of his footsteps retreating down the hall again, and back into the bathroom. She'd only kissed him outside on an impulse, ignited by pure excitement in the midst of a storm and a kitten rescue mission, but she knew better than to let her desires get ahead of her. Of course, pursuing this was a bad idea; she already knew what the outcome would be, but, oh, *look at him*.

He'd unbuttoned his wet shirt. The damp folds of it were still stuck to his skin as he crouched at her feet on the floor and went about cleaning her scrape. She said nothing as he pressed the Band-Aid gently over her skin. He was so gentle. Like he'd always been with her, as if she were the most precious treasure, something meant to cherish. Unless she'd begged him to be rougher, she remembered with another stifled groan.

"Mika," she said again, daring to touch a hand to his hair. His gaze rose from her arm to her eyes, and he brushed away a strand of her hair that had come undone from her clip.

"Are you all right?" He frowned.

She nodded, not trusting her voice to say anything else as her heart hammered in her chest. He reached out his other hand and gently cupped hers, his fingers caressing hers lightly. And then with a deep sigh that told her this was getting too much for him to handle, he got up off the floor and stood in front of her.

"I should really get going," he said, with a faint air of reluctance. She swallowed.

"You can't go yet. Look at it out there."

"But I can't stay here, Lani." The pain in his eyes seemed to scald her as his eyes roved across her face. "You know what will happen if I do."

"We said it wouldn't," she managed, closing her eyes.

"We shouldn't," he said, but his voice was strangled.

The fire in her chest made her heart ache as he rose to his feet again and a bird let out a cry from one of the cages as the thunder cracked outside. Lani panicked. It was more than not wanting him to head out into a hurricane; she didn't want him to go yet. Far from it, she realized. Instead she wanted him even closer—for him to kiss her properly this time, like he used to—but she knew she couldn't ask for that, or expect it.

He was walking across the kitchen already, heading toward the door.

"No," she called out, as logic flew out the window. "Please stay." Her voice was trembling. "It's too dangerous for you out there."

The shrill seagulls, screaming in fury at the storm outside, seemed to highlight her words. Mika stopped frozen on the spot, before he slowly turned around to face her. She saw the way his breath had caught in his chest, the way his eyes were still heavy with so many questions, and it almost broke her not to have any answers. She would never have any answers as to why she felt this way for Mika.

The room seemed to throb with tension before she stepped forward and somehow—she would never quite know how—she was pushing him up against the door with a strength and passion she never knew still existed inside her. In seconds they were melting into one another, Mika capturing her lips in a hungry kiss. Their tongues danced and explored eagerly, and Mika's hands ran feverishly all over her body. There was no going back now.

CHAPTER FOURTEEN

THE STORM HOWLED OUTSIDE like a treacherous army trying to break inside. Lani's trembling fingers brushed against Mika's cheek, tracing the contours of his face with a delicate touch as she pulled away, staring into his eyes, asking without saying a word if they should stop yet.

No, they should not stop yet, he told her in another powerful kiss, and her hands started fumbling at his shorts.

His back was pressed against the door and he locked his mouth back to hers, cupped her backside, lifted her up, feeling her legs wrap like a vise around his middle. Sending the fruit bowl, overflowing with Mr. Benos's generous offerings, flying, he swept her onto the dining table, shooting peaches and kiwis across the tiles as she breathed hot and heavy against him, half laughing, half gasping, tearing at his shirt.

Lani's breath hitched as Mika hovered over her, his head barely missing the low-hanging wicker light. He spread her arms above her head, let his lips trail down her neck, leaving heated kisses in his wake that had her tugging her hands back and fumbling to get him out of the rest of his wet clothes as fast as possible.

Seeing him naked again, a softness fell across her features and she slowed her kisses, moaning his name and other indecipherable things that made him hot, despite the fan over the table sending cold rushes of air across his bare backside.

"I told you, you'll be the death of me," he murmured and their lips crashed back together in an urgent heat that melted away the rest of his reservations.

"Ditto."

The room was alive with electricity, and neither one of them seemed able to control it, or the intense passion now melding them together like glue. How could he have forgotten this: the taste of her skin, the silky heat of her mouth, the erotic dances her tongue could perform with his.

Mika's heart raced as Lani's fingertips slid across his skin, feeling her warmth and the gentle strokes of her palm, like she was reverently retracing her steps after all this time. Her obvious desire sent shivers down his spine. He had never felt this kind of intensity with Hayley, or anyone else, and now he'd tasted it again…well, how could he ever get enough?

His head spun, then emptied altogether as she urged him inside her and waves of pleasure swept through him with every thrust until he had to stop or it would be over too soon. She barely wanted to let him.

Lani kissed him with desperate need, hands roaming down his torso, through his hair and across his jaw as if she was wanting to take away every ounce of the pain and loneliness he'd felt since he'd left her. He'd been so bereft without her, he realized now, despite Hayley. Just his ex-wife's closeness and her touch had ignited a fire that was coursing ever hotter through his veins. He knew this could all go badly wrong; they'd built two entirely different worlds by now and he'd be left missing her while she was busy mothering Anela but… let it go wrong, he thought. To hell with it.

The melody of raindrops on the windows almost drowned out her moans. Her breath caught as he held her hips and he thought how they still fit perfectly together like they always had, as if no time had passed at all. Slowing down, he let his hands wander freely along Lani's curves, and she closed her eyes, surrendering as he rediscovered the secrets of her body.

She was perfect, he thought. With each kiss, thrust, caress, the memories cascaded through his mind, all the times they'd done this, all the places they'd done this. She was thinking the same things right now, he could tell, and it only intensified their connection as he lifted her from the table and carried her easily to the couch.

The kittens scattered and Lani gasped as he resumed his place inside her, his hand behind her head, and her back to the soft cushions. The way she clasped him again with her legs took his breath away and he realized he could watch her all day; he could find new ways to pleasure her all night. It was as if their cells were singing the exact same song… Maybe they always would, whatever came to pass between them.

Their bodies moved in sync, a dance of what felt like re-kindled love and longing, and he wouldn't be able to say, later, how long they stayed there, making love. But when the storm had subsided, and he could no longer tell how many times she'd shuddered to a climax in his arms, he let her hair fall through his fingers like silk and admitted to himself that his life going forward would never be the same.

Lani almost didn't want to move when she found her eyes fluttering open on the couch. She was naked, and Mika's fingers brushed against her cheek with a tenderness that made her heart ache. If she moved, the spell would be broken. Right now, time was still frozen, and they were both still in a world where only their connection mattered, where their past wasn't ready to jump out and bite them at any moment.

The kittens were snoozing in their basket on the floor, and she sighed as Mika cupped her face and kissed her softly.

"The storm is over. You fell asleep," he murmured, and as he moved his leg over hers the electric current fizzed back into her belly and started flowing between them all over again.

Everything he did had reignited that heady, potent mix of desire and longing that had been brewing for far too long inside her, sending shivers down her spine. Clearly her body and soul wanted more. Mika's arms felt like home. Making love to him had felt like home! Her body had moved so instinctively with his she could have cried at the connection, like she had that very first time. She hadn't realized she'd missed him so much till now, but it was almost 8:00 p.m. and she had to check on Anela, and there was probably no end of damage to contend with outside.

They might have well found some kind of solace in each other's arms, but what had happened….should *not* have happened. Now she was just getting attached again when their lives were going in opposite directions. He didn't want kids, which meant he didn't want the responsibility of raising Anela with her, and she was in this for good, for as long as she was needed, she thought, picturing the adoption papers right where she'd left them.

Begrudgingly she forced herself to move, rubbing her eyes and grabbing a blanket to cover what was left of her modesty. He didn't seem to mind what she looked like now, she thought vaguely as she excused herself for the bathroom, feeling his eyes on her as she crossed the room. And she certainly did not mind what he looked like. If anything, he looked better naked now than he had before.

"Oh," she said, turning around in the doorway.

He was already walking toward her, looking for his clothes,

and he held up his hands, revealing his full naked self again and grinning.

"What?" he asked as she threw him his shorts and located his shirt from the kitchen floor.

Lani drew a deep breath. It felt like every creature they'd relocated to her kitchen was staring at them, waiting to see what happened next. A kiwi rolled across the floor when he knocked it with his foot, and she watched a kitten dart for it as he pulled on his shirt. She'd been meaning to say it, so why couldn't she say it? Chewing her lip, she almost chickened out. It would be awful, and hard, but she owed him, really, especially after they'd just connected like…that. Maybe it would help them both, if they went together.

"The cemetery. I'll go with you, Mika," she forced herself to say.

He sank to the kitchen chair, dashing his hands through his tousled hair, no bandanna in sight. Where that had gone she could only guess—she'd probably find it stuck between the sofa cushions later.

"Okay," he said after a moment, eyeing her warily. "Are you sure?"

"Maybe in a few days. I don't know what kind of damage this storm's left in its wake…"

"Whenever you want, Lani. As long as we go together, I'll let you decide when that is. But I don't have that long left here, you know that, right? I'm running out of vacation days and there are things I need to get back to… I'll have work on the dolphin case remotely."

"Okay." Lani couldn't look at him suddenly. Too many emotions were flooding her senses. With a thudding heart she closed the bathroom door behind her, and realized her hands were trembling at the thought, both of him leaving already and of going with him to Iolana's grave. She hadn't been to the cemetery in a long time and she hadn't exactly told him that. It was always too painful, always just too hard; it usually set her back on a downward spiral, doubting her abilities as a foster mother, let alone the birth mother of a toddler who'd died when she should have been there with her, watching her.

Clutching the sink, she stared at her reflection. She *would* go…but when that would be, she had no answer yet. She supposed it should be soon, though, if he was leaving them.

The weight of her choices landed like lead bars on her head. He was always going to leave; she knew that, and she'd only gone and fallen back in love with him. If she'd ever really fallen out of it.

Stepping into the shower, her mind whirled. She could spend the time they had left avoiding all her feelings, she supposed, backing away from situations that made her uncomfortable. Or she could just surrender to every last one of them—at last—and pray she made it out the other side.

"Coffee, bro?" Mika held up the pot he'd just heated on the gas-powered stove at the sanctuary and Manu, in his blue Sparky-Man work uniform, offered his cup. One thing he knew about electricians was that just like plumbers and painters and, well, marine veterinarians, they couldn't do a job without coffee. Or maybe it was just in the Mahoe blood.

"We really appreciate you getting things back up and running for us, Manu," Lani said, coming up behind him with her own cup.

Mika filled it for her and then clinked his mug to hers, resisting the urge to wrap a possessive arm around her waist.

"I know half the island lost power," she said as Manu resumed his duties with one of the units on the wall. "But the air-conditioning is vital for the animals."

"I know," Manu told her, sticking his head back out from the contraption. "Mika told me to make this one a priority."

Lani shot Mika a look of gratitude and appreciation that he tried not to overthink. Her animals were everything to her. He watched her stroke the petrel through the bars of its cage. The wing was healing nicely again, thanks to her...thanks to both of them, really. They'd been a team throughout this whole situation.

In the days since the storm, they'd been hard at work getting things back to resembling halfway normal. The sanctuary was starting to look the way it had, save for a few severed trees around the deck, which luckily had not affected Lilo and Stitch in their sea lion rehab unit. Their release had also been delayed, thanks to the storm. Most things were looking normal again...except for him and Lani.

They'd spent every night together since. Him arriving at her house after dinner, spending the night in her bed and leaving before Anela left for school. Neither had spoken much about it, or what this meant, but it had started to feel like maybe some kind of closure, before they both resumed their real lives. Even if she hadn't mentioned their visit to the cemetery since that night. He was starting to wonder if she ever would, but he wasn't about to press her.

When the phone rang, Lani was out front meeting a delivery truck, so he answered, only to find the Environment Agency rep most disgruntled over the fact that several companies on their list had now either refused their people access to their properties, or not been there when they'd called. The site tests were behind schedule anyway, no thanks to the storm and its aftermath. This was not good news.

"Surprise, surprise, your man Kai Kalama still hasn't complied," he told her when he met her in the back room, lifting heavy boxes of medical supplies and animal feed. He took a crate from her, insisting he do it himself, and she stood back, looking somewhat relieved. "How's your cut," he asked her now, motioning to the Band-Aid he'd pressed to the wound.

"Better," she said, putting a hand to it, but she looked distracted. "Why won't he let anyone in? What's he hiding? What if he's the one poisoning the dolphins?"

Mika didn't want to say it out loud, but it definitely seemed like Kai wanted to keep *something* to himself.

"Like I said before, I'm happy to go round there myself," Mika said, only for Lani to shake her head.

"Don't get involved," she said now. "We don't know him— we don't know what he might do."

Mika rolled his eyes. "You think I'm scared of some beefed-up bro in a wet suit who takes tourists out on blow-up bananas?" He flexed his muscles playfully and Lani snatched up a brochure, pretending to slap him with it. Mika laughed and grabbed her around the waist, and she mock-wrestled away from him.

"Never underestimate the power of a blow-up banana," she laughed, batting at him again, and Mika went to snatch the brochure away.

They play-fought back and forth and Lani squealed in his arms, right until he urged her up against the refrigerator and silenced her with a kiss. She groaned against his mouth, then snatched the brochure back, and it was only then that Mika realized what he was looking at. A real estate magazine. And on the front was a photo of a house he would recognize anywhere.

"What is it?"

Mika felt his stomach drop into his shoes. He stopped wrestling with Lani immediately, standing in stunned silence as he opened the brochure. His heart drummed in silence as he stared at the image of the beach house with its painted canary yellow shutters, hugged by the beach. Lani had gone still beside him, her eyes widening in surprise as she read the accompanying text regarding recent renovation works and land potential.

"It's for sale," Lani said.

Her voice was barely a whisper over his shoulder. He could hardly speak now, either. He was thinking about all the things they planned to do in that house if this should ever happen, all the times they'd sneaked onto the private beach when they knew the owners weren't home, the night they'd snuggled together drinking whisky in the hammock on the deck and wound up so drunk they'd passed out, only to find the owners had come home and were staring at them in confusion through the kitchen window. He reminded her of this now and she reminded him of another time, when she'd set up a picnic for him on the beach under the trees, and they'd been so busy having sex that he'd squished the sandwiches.

"We were terrible," she said now.

Lani seemed to sense that he was reminiscing even more in silence. She grabbed the brochure from him and spun away, walking out front and gazing at it in silence. Mika followed her outside and joined her.

"We weren't so terrible. We loved that house."

"We loved each other in what we could get of that house," she added quietly, and he took her fingers, pressing his mouth to her knuckles. "That's where I fell pregnant."

A breeze stirred up sand from the beach below them, and this time, he did wrap his arm around her, and drew her close.

"Er... Lani, Mika, sorry to interrupt. I think I'm done."

Mika released her quickly. Manu was standing behind them in the doorway, wiping his hands on a towel. His brother raised his eyebrows at them both. Lani pretended to ignore it, smoothing down her hair, thanking him for his work, telling him again how grateful she was.

They hadn't told anyone the extent of their reconnection. At least, *he* hadn't. But something else he knew about electricians, who spent their days in and out of people's homes making small talk, was that they weren't the best at keeping secrets.

CHAPTER FIFTEEN

"EVERYONE'S TALKING ABOUT IT, so what's the deal?" Mele was looking at her expectantly from the passenger seat and Lani kept her face neutral.

"I don't know what you're talking about," she said, focusing on the swaying palms through the windshield, praying for the light to change. Mele scoffed at her over the cage on her lap.

"We all have eyes, Lani."

Anela giggled from the back seat, as if she too knew what Mele was talking about. Who *didn't* know? she thought to herself, cursing the way she'd gotten careless with Mika; too comfortable. This island wasn't his home anymore. He didn't want the life she wanted... He didn't want kids around, and he had his reasons for that, she supposed, although she had to wonder how much guilt had influenced his decision—he'd been such an amazing father. But he'd backed off trying to hang out with Anela lately, too, and she knew he was probably freaking out inside, that because they were sleeping together she might also start loading parental responsibilities on him. She had vowed to have a good time while she could; that was all. That was all he wanted, too...surely?

"Let's just get this bird released, okay," she sighed, taking a left at the sign for the road to the national park. Her mind had a tendency to get all worked up about what this whole

Mika thing really meant to her, if she didn't keep it busy on other things.

The albatross was doing much better and she was determined to get it to her contact at the Division of Forestry and Wildlife in the park before sunset. Mele had a keen interest in all the local bird life, something Lani had instilled in her whenever the girl had spent time with her, and now the teen came to every single release day with her. Each experience was filmed and added to her YouTube channel for her however many thousands of followers to comment on. Lani didn't know too much about how all that worked, but Mele was certainly becoming somewhat of a conservation expert in the eyes of all those followers, and pride put a smile on Lani's face whenever she saw the way her neighbor's daughter interacted with the birds.

Just as she was about to make another turn, something caught her eye. Was that... Mika's car? It was parked haphazardly on a verge, just off the road. She pulled her car to stop and told the girls to stay put as she jumped out and sprinted toward it. It was definitely Mika's car. But why was it here? And why at this particular address?

Then she realized something else. This was Kai Kalama's warehouse. The same yellow logo screamed from the shutters across one window. Of course! She'd only seen it properly from the beach side, never paid much attention from the road.

"Mika?" She hurried up the driveway.

Everything was quiet, no sign of him or Kai, or anyone, but the damage from the storm was evident. The wind had uprooted trees, and broken branches littered the yard. The front was a mess and a downstairs window had been smashed. She stepped over a few shards of glass, still strewed across the ground, and called for Mika again. Where was he? He'd probably come here to confront Kai about dodging the site checks; that would be such a typical Mika thing to do, she thought, a little annoyed. He'd be gone soon enough, and she'd be the one left dealing with the consequences!

Creeping closer to the window, wondering how her world had got so shaken up again and admitting that it was, actually, the most alive she'd felt in years, she peered inside. The vast warehouse was all but empty, save for a few boats and what she assumed were water sports equipment locked up and covered in tarps. A light shone from beneath one of the doors off the main space. It was the only light she could see in the whole place. Then, was that…a whimpering animal? Maybe another victim of the storm!

Curiosity and fear that there might be an injured animal inside got the better of her. Lani hitched up her dress and prepared herself.

"What do you think you're doing?"

Lani sprang back from her position halfway through the window and accidentally hit her head. "Mika?"

Mika's face was a mixture of amusement and shock, his hair damp and his eyes mischievous and twinkling.

"Were you seriously about to break and enter Kai Kalama's place?" He grinned, folding his arms like a school headmaster who'd just caught a student doing something reckless.

"What are you doing here?" she accused, smoothing out her clothes and hair. "I saw your car!"

"I was on the way back from a dive with Manu and I thought…"

"I know what you thought," she snapped, aware that beneath her annoyance she was actually touched that he wanted to help her so much, and angry at herself that she was letting him in again to the point that it was going to hurt, badly, letting him go.

Mika stepped closer, leaving her breathless. "You were, weren't you? You were one step away from crawling through that window!"

He cupped her face and kissed her, and for a moment she was so thrown she kissed him back, grinning now underneath his mouth. How did he do this; make her forget why she *shouldn't* be doing this? His kiss was salty from the ocean and needy, his lips demanding and hungry. His tongue teased her mouth as if she were the most delicious thing he had ever tasted, and he hadn't eaten in days, even though he'd only left her bed at six thirty this morning, after he'd certainly had his fill.

"You're one sexy burglar," he growled, cupping her backside now and squeezing it with intent, and Lani's laugh became a groan of hot desire, right before the animal's whimpering noises stole the smile from their faces.

In one second Mika was at the window himself, looking in, and Lani was smoothing down her shirt again, flustered. Suddenly, something moved in the shadows.

Lani gasped as she saw what it was. "It's a dog, Mika."

Mika followed her eyes to the sandy-colored golden retriever lying in the shadow of a desk some ten feet away. She could see it clearly now her eyes had adjusted. Whoever's dog it was, it was likely injured, hungry and dehydrated. Lani instructed him to give her a leg up.

Mika didn't look sure. "It's not breaking and entering if we're helping an injured animal," she reasoned. "Lots of animals were displaced after the storm. Someone could be missing this one!"

Mika helped her up somewhat reluctantly, mumbling something about how he was pretty sure this was still breaking and entering, and she was just about to drop through to the other side on her feet when the golden retriever gave a gut-wrenching howl, nearly breaking her heart.

"It's okay, baby," she cooed, "we're coming!"

Mika climbed in expertly after her and the dog limped over to them, relief written all over his goofy face. Lani cradled the fluffy animal in her arms. Sure enough, the dog was injured; his left front paw was bloodied and bruised, and she supposed he'd been struck by something before jumping in here and injuring himself further.

"There's no collar, but he could be chipped. We'll have to check."

Mika offered her his shirt as a makeshift carrier for the animal, and before she could refuse he was unbuttoning it and standing shirtless in the warehouse. She couldn't help the way her eyes kept running over his impressive muscles, or how her lips kept tasting his kisses as together they carried the dog toward the window and made to lift it outside. But no sooner had they managed, than Mika turned back and scrambled in again, and made straight for the door. The one with the light underneath.

"I just have to check," he said, pulling a face and shrugging, even as she begged him not to.

"The kids are in the car!" she called out, suddenly remembering she'd left them there waiting for her, with the albatross. How was this her life now?

Lani didn't know whether to be amused as Mika's shirtless frame yanked the door open and disappeared...or horrified.

Mika still couldn't believe what he'd just discovered in the warehouse. He knew they should probably get away from the warehouse before they could see to the dog, so he'd driven behind Lani to the national park.

Mele and Anela were watching them now, Mele still clutching the albatross's cage as he and Lani carried the injured dog toward the park's medical station and set about fixing up his wounds. Thankfully the dog seemed brighter already, thanks to a generous supply of food and water, and he was chipped, too, it turned out. His owner, a lady in her late sixties, had been looking for him since the storm.

"He'll be fine, soon," he said to Lani now, glancing around the wooden shack that constituted a med facility and a meeting point for Lani and her wildlife rep pals. It was a communal space filled with an assortment of different objects. Half-filled thermoses, net baskets, car parts and a textbook about marine biology all had to be moved before they could put the animal on the table in the corner, but soon, her contact arrived and Mika took a step back, watching her and watching how the kids watched her, like they were in awe of everything she did. Even the teenager.

He went to the window, realizing he hadn't intended to be here for the albatross's release. Lani had mentioned this morning that releases were something she usually did with Mele and Anela, and he'd changed the subject before she could invite him, too.

Sensing he might be getting too close for her comfort, and for his own comfort too, he had taken a step back with Anela the past few days. There was a very high risk he was getting attached as much to the little girl as to Lani, which was ruffling his feathers; where had this come from? He'd been a terrible father once, been so sure he'd never get the chance again, been *afraid* of getting the chance again, perhaps, in case he messed up. But Lani was managing. *She* wasn't messing up, far from it…

"So are you going to tell me what was behind that door?" she said now in a hushed tone, walking with him outside with the albatross.

Behind them Mele was setting up a camera on a tripod. In the distance he could see the lighthouse, a pillar of white on the cliffs that jutted from the park out into the ocean, and the wind blew her hair from its ponytail around her face.

"I'm so curious now!" she continued.

Mika bit back a smile. "Let's just say Kai, or whoever handles that warehouse, has a very nice collection of plants."

Lani frowned at him. Then he saw the penny drop. "No way! You mean…"

"The kind of plants that could land someone in trouble, if they should be accidentally uncovered by the wrong people."

Behind them, Anela was performing a little dance so that Mele could test her camera shots for the bird's release, and he lowered his voice. "I guess we know why he didn't want that site inspection."

Lani wrinkled up her nose. "Yes. But just because he's a keen gardener, so to speak, it doesn't mean he's automatically at fault where the dolphins are concerned."

Mika nodded sagely. "You're right. We still need a sample, though, and he has to agree to it. If we go ahead and get one ourselves, it'll raise too many questions."

"At least we have some leverage," she told him.

"You've been watching too many crime shows," he chuckled, and she rolled her eyes, just as his phone rang in his pocket. He fished it out, expecting Manu to tell him to check his email for the photos he'd just uploaded from their recent dive, but it was Megan.

"Megan?" Lani had read his screen, and now she was trying not to appear too interested in who Megan was, which tickled him more than it should. He told her it was his colleague, and that she was probably checking again on when he'd be back in California.

"Oh," she said, drawing her eyes away even as he was half-way through explaining the SafeCoast Guardian project. "That sounds important. I thought you were doing something with sharks in Egypt."

"There's a *lot* going on," he explained.

"I see."

He waited, expecting her to ask when exactly he was leaving, but still, she didn't. "I suppose your life is waiting for you to get back to it," she said instead, after a moment. "Just as mine will carry on without you, like it has since we signed the divorce. Don't let us stop you, Mika."

Okay, then.

Mika felt his jaw tick. He was about to say something rather biting when a vision of the house struck him out of nowhere— that house, for sale again out on the beach, the beach they'd had their eyes on since their teenage years. He hadn't even asked her how she'd wound up with that brochure but it had felt like a sign. Was he back on the right track, finally, in a place he felt he belonged, with Lani, who he'd never stopped loving?

Mika rolled his eyes at himself. Lani had turned to Mele already. Soon all of her attention was back on the girls and some-how, the next time he tried to meet Lani's eyes, she seemed so indifferent to his presence that she might not have noticed at all if he'd strapped himself to the bird's feathery wings and flown away to the lighthouse with the albatross.

CHAPTER SIXTEEN

THE HEAVYSET LADY with graying hair and glasses opened the door a crack, as if wary of a sudden attack. Lani smiled warmly.

"Hi, Mrs. Rosenthal," she said, almost bumping into Mika as the golden retriever started yanking on his leash, desperate to get to his owner.

"Lani and Mika, together again." Mrs. Rosenthal beamed, flinging open the door and looking between them as she fussed over the dog and beckoned them inside. "I couldn't believe it when I heard you both found Bones. Come, come inside. It's been a while since I saw you two together."

Mika hadn't seemed too keen on going with her to take the dog home after they'd dropped Mele and Anela off back at the house. But the dog's owner had turned out to be Mrs. Rosenthal, their old church group tutor, and the woman had sounded so excited on the phone at the prospect of seeing him again. Rather begrudgingly he'd joined her.

Soon they were being served cold lemonade and warm, thick, chocolate cookies, as if she'd been expecting the two kids who'd once run away from her church group to play on the beach.

"You were pretty mischievous when you were kids," she teased them now, taking a seat in the chair opposite.

Lani smiled and nibbled a cookie as Mika shifted uncomfortably in the chair. Bones seemed to like him; the dog kept snuffling his shorts, but Lani knew he was only here for the dog and Mrs. Rosenthal. It felt a lot to her like he was backing away from her, one foot off the island already, his head already in his work back in California. What was the point in pretending this hadn't been going to happen? All the spontaneous hot kisses, and early-morning lovemaking in the world wouldn't change that, or the fact that their past still brought up more heartache than she cared to try to handle.

Lani made polite small talk with the older woman, and tried to act like everything with Mika was fine, even though it wasn't. She wasn't about to *present* as if his approaching departure was bothering her, even though it was. Ugh. His kisses were addictive; they'd fired her up and had her thinking things she hadn't dared to think in ages. That house, too…the one for sale. Last night, she'd had a dream that he'd bought it, and told her he wanted her to live in it with him.

So strange!

Mrs. Rosenthal suddenly paused midsentence and reached for a box on the side table. The woman's lined face broke into another broad smile as she passed them both a photo each.

"I dug these out when I knew you were coming. Look at you two, all those years ago!"

Lani felt her pulse start to throb through her smile at the photo of her and Mika. He was around thirteen years old, she no more than eleven, their arms slung around each other's shoulders, sand in their hair from another day spent running wild on the beach when they should have been brushing up on the Bible with Mrs. Rosenthal.

"Wow," she heard herself murmur, as Mika studied his own photo next to her.

His picture had them both side by side in the classroom,

seemingly oblivious to everyone else. She was staring at him with a goofy look on her face while he was grinning straight at the camera. Her crush was achingly obvious here. Mika could see it now. She could literally see him processing it.

"You were cute," he said to her without looking away from the photo.

"Yeah, well, everything changes," she muttered, and tried to change the subject.

The older woman shook her head fondly. "I remember thinking you'd go far," she said softly. "When I heard about what happened with your little girl, I was so worried for you both, but here you are now, taking everything in anew with open hearts... I'm not the only one around here who's proud of how far you've come."

Lani swallowed. Who else had been talking about them behind their backs? Everyone, probably.

"It was a long time ago," she said, hearing how choked her voice was coming out.

Mrs. Rosenthal pressed her hand to Mika's arm, then to Lani's over the table. "But you never really heal, do you, from something like that?" she said kindly, before getting up to fetch more lemonade.

"Life has moved on," Mika said carefully. "Lani and I have both managed to keep on moving forward."

"He's going back to California soon," she added, hoping her disappointment didn't show; maybe he'd counter her statement with some kind of new development, she thought, while guilt crashed over her yet again. Mrs. Rosenthal was right: you never could heal from something like that. In more than twenty years she had only been to Iolana's grave maybe three or four god-awful times.

When Mika said nothing, she felt the stone sinking further

in her stomach, weighting her shoulders. Mika's eyes roved over her face but she refused to meet his gaze as she put her photo down.

"Shame you're leaving us again, Mika. This place always was better for having you around. You Mahoes," she laughed, before continuing to reminisce about the past with stories about their shenanigans, including when they'd sneaked off to go swimming against her orders one day and come home with an injured red-crested cardinal. "You nursed that bird back to health together," she said and smiled. "It's hardly surprising you went on to make healing animals your profession. Individually, of course. How is life in California, compared to here, Mika?"

Individually, of course.

Lani could barely look at Mika as he talked about his projects. This was excruciating: hearing someone who'd known them bringing up all these happy times, while simultaneously reminding them of everything they no longer had together.

Lani was shocked to feel Mika's hand clasp hers suddenly underneath the table, but as he continued talking about his work in California, the people he'd met and what he was learning about the sharks, Lani couldn't stop the panic rising inside her. There had never been anyone else for her but him, never, and maybe there never would be. She'd grown to be okay with that, but now she'd been reminded what it was like to be loved by him, it was going to be so much harder when he left again.

Think of Anela, she told herself, untangling her fingers from him, remembering the adoption pack at the house.

She hadn't told anyone about it yet, but the thought of Anela going anywhere else didn't sit right with her at all. She and Anela could have an amazing future together…if only she could forget the way *Mika* had always made—and *would* always make—her feel. Mika, who seemed so dead set on a life without children in it.

The sun was setting as they left Mrs. Rosenthal's. Mika was about to take the road back to Lani's house in his car, but she knew she couldn't escape the part of their past she'd been avoiding for much longer.

"We're so close, from here," she said, realizing her voice was as shaky as her hands had been, holding those photographs just now, reliving all those memories.

Mika glanced at her sideways and slowed the car. She knew he knew what she meant.

"You want to stop at the cemetery now?" he said, softly.

Lani nodded mutely, feeling her heart about to burst. "It's time."

Mika nodded and slowly turned onto a road lined with trees, glancing over at her biting her nails before parking outside the wrought iron gates. She took in the worn expression on his face as they sat there quietly for a moment in the car, listening to the birds. Eventually, Lani broke the silence.

"I guess we should go in."

Opening the gates slowly, she let him take her hand again as they stepped inside, just for a moment, as though they were both drawing strength from the other. She held her breath as they walked the single path together past row after row of tidy gravesites, wildflowers blooming around the headstones. Soon, she saw it. The small marble headstone glinting in the late-evening sun. She heaved a breath, which promptly lodged in her throat.

"It's so hard to imagine her in there," she said to him, her voice strangled even more by the overwhelming emotions.

A single rose lay on the marble slab; from someone in Mika's family, probably. Mika walked up close, taking her with him, and she found herself leaning into him, holding his entire arm for strength now as she took in the shiny headstone. The inscription on the marble read Iolana Mahoe. Forever in our Hearts. Lani felt the tears well up. Inescapable.

She flinched as Mika ran his fingers over the words, then cast his eyes up to the granite angel perched on the top. It had been a gift from the community, a sign that the angels were watching over their daughter. It should have been comforting to Lani, but it wasn't. She looked around at all the other graves nearby; different stories of grief and tragedy were etched into every single headstone, like chapters in an unfinished book. Iolana's was just one of many. There were people in the town who'd never remember she'd so much as existed, and she, Iolana's own mother, hadn't even been here often enough to remind anyone. Where were *her* flowers, even now?

"How are you, little one?" Mika whispered to the marble slab, and his words, so full of remorse, were like knives that slashed what was left of Lani's strength. With a sob, her knees turned to jelly and she stumbled, almost falling to the mossy ground.

Mika caught her, put his arm around her shoulders and held her close as she cried.

"It's okay," he said, pressing a kiss to her temple as if it alone might stop her reeling, but she could feel his chest contracting now, as if her sobs had penetrated his hardened exterior and were threatening to break him, too.

"I never come here," she said now, sniffing, dragging a hand across her eyes. He pulled her closer as the guilt crashed over her. "I haven't been here in forever, Mika. I just… I can't do it. I should be the one putting roses on her grave…"

"It's okay," he said again, turning her to face him. He took her face in her hands and tilted it up to his, wiping away her tears with his thumbs. "We're here now for Iolana. That's all that matters. And you know she's not really *here*, right? She's somewhere else, somewhere better—you know that."

Lani watched as a single tear slipped from his eye and threatened to travel down the side of his face. She made to wipe it away as he'd done hers, but his fingers stopped her hand. He pulled her against his chest, breathing into her hair.

The sun had dipped low now, casting an orange hue over the cemetery, and the birdsong seemed even louder than before. Lani felt her heart ache as she held him, and felt his heart beating against hers like a drum. Then she felt the warmth of his words through her tears as he sat with her and began to tell her stories about Iolana, like he'd been bottling it all up and only now was able to speak out loud about their daughter's life and all the memories they'd made together. This was just as important to him as it was to her, she realized suddenly with a flicker of shame. She'd been so selfish, refusing to come with him till now.

"What about that time when we were camping out by the lake?" he said, recalling the night they'd all spent under the stars, telling Iolana stories of Hawaiian legends around a small campfire. "She just wanted to stay up all night and watch for shooting stars. We must have seen dozens that night."

"Remember when she saw the deer?" Lani followed, smiling now at the memories and resting her head on his shoulder. "We had to get her a stuffed one, right after that."

It was still so hard to accept that she was gone, but the longer they stayed there talking, letting the grief consume them and wash through them and out of them, the more at peace she started to feel.

Next time, even if she'd be thinking of Mika in California, thousands of miles away again, wishing more than anything that he were here, Lani knew she'd have the strength to come alone.

CHAPTER SEVENTEEN

"WELL, WHAT DO you know? Kai Kalama finally agreed to the site test," Mika said, putting the phone back down. He couldn't help but feel victorious, although Lani, who was perched on the edge of the desk with the bird she was holding, looked like she was biting her tongue.

"What?" he laughed.

She shook her head. "I know you told him we were driving past when we heard that injured dog, and 'accidentally' discovered his secret garden while we were looking for it."

"I did what I had to do." He shrugged, running a gentle hand across the bird's soft head, then pressing his lips to hers over it.

"He's probably clearing up that garden as we speak—the inspectors will be there this afternoon."

She laughed softly as he turned his attention back to the baby seal in its small tank. The poor little thing had been brought to them severely dehydrated after being caught up in some sea trash. It was halfway through a course of fluid therapy. Lani's eyes felt like burning lasers on him as he checked the catheter and tried not to think about what he'd do if they *didn't* locate the source of these chemical nasties before he was due to return to California. Not that he wanted Kai Kalama, or anyone on the island, to be found guilty of intentionally putting marine life in danger, but he'd exhausted almost all sources already and time was ticking.

He couldn't hold off on getting back to the stakeholders about the briefing much longer, but it was more than the dolphins here that was causing him to stall.

"Mika!" Anela came bounding into the sanctuary with Kiki close behind. They'd been inseparable since the luau. "Look what we found in the school library!" she said excitedly, thrusting a book at him. *A Life in the Eye of Nature.*

"That was my favorite," Lani said, peering at the pages over his shoulder, so close he could smell the honeysuckle in her shampoo. "You put your whole heart into that."

For a moment the four of them were silent, admiring the glossy black-and-white and color photos of nature that he'd taken almost three whole decades ago: delicate images with his new zoom lens, focused in on birds with wings spread wide, bumblebees at rest, blossoms in full bloom and wildflowers swaying in the breeze. He'd self-published the book, just to distribute around the community.

"Look, it's for you," Kiki said to Lani, jabbing a finger at the dedication. "'To my Beloved Lani.'"

Anela clapped her hands and prodded them both, reciting "Beloved, beloved, beloved..." But Mika bristled. So did Lani. His throat tightened tenfold at the look on her face: one of pride, but also apprehension. When Anela asked if he would come play ball with her and Kiki out on the beach, he made his excuses and left the sanctuary altogether.

Driving in his car toward the lighthouse he let his thoughts run wild. Anela was starting to want him around, requesting his presence more often, and he found himself wanting it, too...but what kind of a father figure would he be? Not a great one!

Dropping to the rocks outside the towering lighthouse, he let the wind tousle his hair and fixed his eyes on the swirling gulls searching for fish. But he saw only Lani, crying in his arms the other day at the cemetery, breaking down in her grief. Then, miraculously, laughing, reciting long-forgotten stories of things she'd done with Iolana. Things they had both done with their daughter. They had actually laughed, right there, sitting beside her grave together. He didn't think in a million years he'd ever be doing that…or any of this.

Something had changed irrevocably in that cemetery; a load had been lifted from his back, and maybe from hers, too. She'd been right, he supposed, the other week, when she'd reminded him that they hadn't really known how to be parents back then, back when he'd been working so damn hard, thinking it was what they'd all needed, instead of giving his presence and time. Later he'd felt so guilty, thinking maybe she didn't know how much he'd loved her and Iolana. Those precious moments when he hadn't been working had been some of the best of his whole life.

Mika was so lost in thought out on the cliffs that he barely heard his phone. Pulling it from his pocket, he sprang to his feet.

"Meet me at Hook's Bay. As soon as you can," Lani said. Then she promptly hung up.

The little boat sped over the waves with intent and Lani watched Mika's face, etched with determination as he steered it expertly, his eyes scanning the horizon over their heads. His shirt was half-undone again, the sun glinting off the top of his exposed chest, revealing a few inches of sun-kissed skin. Skin she had spent far too much time pressed up against recently, imprinting on…reclaiming.

Ugh. She was getting in far too deep, and neither had brought up what all of this really meant. Coward. She was a coward. She should just ask him to stay, but he'd already left her once, and it would be unbearable hearing him say he was choosing another life a second time. And why wouldn't he, when he didn't want to be a dad, a foster dad or any kind of dad? He'd barely spent three seconds with Anela lately.

"Where is the whale?" Anela said beside her on the back seat now, and Lani tore her eyes away, realizing her heart was acting crazy again.

"We're not there yet," she told her, pulling her arm around her tighter, and double-checking the straps on her lifejacket for the thousandth time.

She still couldn't believe the girl had asked to come out on the boat, but looking at her now, watching Mika at the wheel, she knew the child was entranced by him. She'd go wherever he went at this point. Anela pretty much worshipped the ground he walked on, no thanks to him making her face her fears in a way Lani herself hadn't ever been able to do. If he still thought he wasn't good father material, he was crazy. She'd told him he'd been an amazing father to Iolana, but now…maybe he still didn't believe it. He'd been withdrawing from any group activities as fast as they'd been making progress with Anela and earlier on today, he hadn't been able to get out of the sanctuary fast enough. Her foster daughter would be gutted when he left. She had to protect her—she'd already lost her mother! This reunion, or fling, whatever it was, had been fun but…

But…

God, she should never have started this, even if being at the cemetery with him had changed things for the better somehow. Falling back into bed after that, back at her place, had seemed inevitable. Healing, maybe.

Lani furrowed her brow under her sunglasses. There it was

again, the rickety old roller coaster of thoughts about Mika taking her up, down and sideways. It just wouldn't stop!

Suddenly, Anela's excited cries brought her back to the moment. She was pointing out into the distance, past Mika at the wheel. Lani followed her finger. The giant whale's head was sticking out of the water near the fishing boat they were approaching, and the people on board were waving them over urgently. It was just as they'd described on the phone.

"Wow!" Anela stood excitedly, but Lani pulled her down again quickly as Mika powered up their engine. They moved closer cautiously toward it, and the fishermen beckoned them in.

"She's been nudging the boat wherever we've gone for the last hour," one of the burly guys called out to them over the side.

Mika lowered the anchor carefully. Lani didn't let go of Anela's hand. Her heart was in her throat already.

"Stay there, sit still, don't move," Mika told the girl now, and Anela nodded mutely.

By the look on his face, Lani was getting the distinct impression that she probably shouldn't have given in and let the girl come. But it was so momentous that she'd even asked, Lani had felt compelled to encourage her any way she could!

In the water, the whale's head went for the fishing boat again, then turned to them. Lani held her breath and held on to Anela, waiting for impact, but Mika was zipping up his wet suit already, pulling a snorkel over his head. It dangled about his neck as he leaned over the edge. Tentatively, when the whale didn't hit their boat, Lani followed, never letting go of Anela. Together they took in what they could see of the gray pilot whale.

"I think it requires our assistance," she said now.

"I think you're right." Mika frowned.

"How do you know?" Anela asked curiously.

"See those things on its head and back?" she said now, pointing over the side.

"They're called cyamids, or whale lice," Mika followed, motioning to the pale creatures that looked a bit like crabs, which were crawling about on the animal's giant head like strange little white aliens with claws.

Lani listened as he explained how they could be beneficial for the whales by feeding on all the other nasties on their bodies, like healing wounds and algae, but he guessed the whale was uncomfortable, having so many of them clinging on.

"She's probably itchy. We'll have to lend a hand, or the whale will just keep asking humans for help," he said, reaching for a set of fins.

Anela looked fascinated, Lani thought, watching as she stuck a tentative hand out toward the gentle creature. To her surprise, the whale lifted its head to her, and blew air around her face. Mika dived in front of her like lightning, even as Anela squealed in delight.

"It's okay," Anela told him, promptly moving him aside with her little hands. "I think she likes me," she beamed, and Lani couldn't help laughing. Then she noticed the look of apprehension on Mika's face, the way he wrung his hands and turned away. Her stomach churned at his distress, but she wouldn't show it; Anele deserved this moment.

The whale did indeed seem to show a special interest in her. Lani dared to reach out to it, too, and in seconds, she had plucked a cyamid from the creature's head. Quickly, Anela followed, giggling in joy. The whale stayed close and still, as if this grooming session was indeed what it had been begging for, and soon, all three of them were peeling the critters away and dropping them back into the ocean, and there wasn't a hint of the girl who'd been so terrified of the ocean just a few short weeks ago.

Mika however, still looked agitated. He kept glancing at her and Anela, as if he expected a giant octopus to emerge and curl its giant tentacles around them and drag them both to the ocean floor.

"See how far she's come," she whispered proudly to Mika, just as Anela leaned a little too far and almost toppled overboard.

Lani's grip on the lifejacket was strong, but Mika lunged for the girl again. With one swift move, he grabbed her shoulders and pulled her to safety on the deck, leaving Lani feeling useless. She hovered behind him as he dropped to his knees in front of Anela.

"You have to be more careful," he scolded.

Anela bit her lip. "Sorry, Mika."

"I'm serious, Anela, you shouldn't even be out here!"

Lani covered her mouth. "Mika!"

Anela crossed her arms and looked at him defiantly. "Why not? You wanted me to go in the water."

He turned to Lani now. "She shouldn't be here!"

Silence.

Lani pursed her lips. She wanted to defend the young girl's exuberance, and her own decision for bringing her, but she knew he was reacting this way for the same reason she'd lost her cool that time he'd stayed down in the water with Nala during their dive. He was frightened of losing someone else he cared about.

She stayed quiet as Mika turned away from them both, adjusting his snorkel, preparing to jump into the water. A palpable tension radiated from him like heat from a fire, but she bit her tongue and counted to ten in her head. He was just being protective. She could see what a good father figure he could be to Anela if only that was what he wanted. Judging by his face now, though, he didn't. He wanted to get away from them both again. But when was he leaving?

"Let's keep going—you just have to be more careful," she warned Anela now, determined not to let their own issues ruin the girl's day. This was a breakthrough for her.

Anela continued peeling the critters from the whale, albeit with a bit less excitement than before. Mika was silent for the rest of the mission. And he didn't speak during the whole ride back, either.

Maybe, Lani decided, it was time for a real talk—one that did not just end up back in the bedroom, burying their issues under their prominent sexual attraction. Even if there *were* admittedly moments of healing now, when the shadows seemed fewer and the burden lighter, it seemed he'd never be ready to take on the kind of parental responsibilities she was ready for. All the more ready, perhaps, because of him? He'd helped Anela more than she ever had!

"Dinner tonight?" she braved when they pulled the boat up, looking at him hopefully. Regardless of their relationship, whatever that was, he meant something special to Anela now. She'd make his old favorite, lasagna, maybe with a salad and some wine, and she would tell him about her plans to adopt Anela. He deserved to hear it from her, instead of later down the line, through someone else. She also needed to ask if he'd consider visiting her ever. Anela would like that, too. Maybe he wouldn't be opposed to doing that, once in a while.

"I'm making lasagna. Anela's doing the sauce."

"I can't tonight," he said abruptly. "I said I'd have dinner with my family."

Oh.

Mika was coiling up the ropes now, wet suit down around his waist, and he was not looking at her. Time to try a new tactic—honesty. Lani instructed Anela to go wait by the car, then the words stumbled out.

"Mika… I just thought we could talk."

He sighed heavily, refusing to meet her gaze. "This isn't working, Lani."

Lani balked inside. She opened her mouth to reply but one look at his hardened expression destroyed the words on her lips. He stepped closer.

"This was always going to end badly. I can't seem to ever do the right thing around you or Anela. I completely overreacted in the boat."

She hung her head. "I know why you overreacted, Mika, I know. But—"

"I'm just not cut out for this dad stuff," he interrupted. "It wasn't anything I asked for, Lani. Besides, I have a life somewhere else now. I think we've been getting carried away."

Digging her teeth into her cheeks, she curled her fingers up hard into her palms. They just got carried away? It was true, they had, but there was love here, too. Love that was pointless fighting for if he didn't want to be a father, her internal voice warned her.

Think of Anela. It's your job to protect her now; she's already lost her parents!

"I need you to tell her that you're leaving, Mika," she said, fighting back her tears—no, she would not cry right now. "Tell her now, so the news doesn't come as a shock," she demanded, straightening her back defiantly.

Mika glared directly into her eyes. His face was a mask of anger, and it looked like a hurricane had taken up residence inside his brain.

"Just tell us both *when*," she insisted, before she could chicken out. "So I can make arrangements."

He snorted and tossed the rope back into the boat hard, and her heart pounded at her from the inside… Why was she practically ordering him away when all she wanted to do was beg him never to leave her again?

"I'll let you know as soon as I can," he said with an intensity that could shatter glass. "Then you can make all the arrangements you like, without me messing things up for you. Again."

Lani watched in stunned silence as he grabbed his hat and pulled it down over his face. Each step he took toward his car seemed to rip her heart in two, but somehow she managed to stop herself chasing after him.

CHAPTER EIGHTEEN

ANELA SHOULDN'T HAVE been on the boat; she could have been hurt, or even killed, Mika thought for the thousandth time as he flipped his fins below the surface, trying to make his swirling thoughts slow down to the point that they'd disappear. Today, even diving wasn't helping. Even seeing Nala gliding gracefully toward him, looking as happy as a toothy shark could look, didn't altogether push the thoughts of that last altercation with Lani from his head.

He'd messed up with Anela and it was nothing to be proud of, but he'd acted so defensively…so self-righteously…no wonder he wasn't the most popular person right now.

"What's going on?" Manu asked when they were lying on the deck of the boat drying off in the sun. Trust his brother to bring it up instead of just letting him stew.

Mika told him how he'd overreacted to Anela being on the boat, how awful he'd felt about it for the last two days, how he and Lani had argued and how she'd demanded he tell Anela when he was leaving. Probably because she wanted to know herself and who could blame her? All he'd done was make her life even more complicated.

"You're too hard on yourself, but then you always were," was Manu's reply.

"It's better this way, I guess," he sniffed, ignoring his brother and swigging from his water bottle. "Best that we both know where we stand. She pretty much told me she can't wait for me to leave."

As he said it, he grimaced at the horizon. It wasn't entirely true. He'd twisted it all up inside his head so he could feel angry at Lani instead of himself; so he wouldn't have to feel the sting of her rejection, or even more guilt about how he'd overreacted.

Manu said all the things a brother should say: that Lani obviously cared a lot about him; that she was simply worried that Anela was getting too attached to him; that she probably didn't *really* want him to leave at all. Then, seeing his face, he delivered the real kicker:

"Brother, you do know you were always a great dad to Iolana, right?" The look on his face was almost one of pity. It turned his stomach.

Mika turned away. "Lani said that, too, but I don't think I was," he admitted.

"Because she died? That wasn't your fault. She was sick, and you couldn't have known that, neither of you could. Even if you'd been with her, you couldn't have saved her. But if you use it as an excuse to shut your heart down around this kid, you're going to lose them both. Her and Lani."

Manu's brow creased above his sunglasses now. "Tell Lani you still love her, because I know you do. You can still make this work."

"Yeah right, like divorced guys go around saying they're in love with their ex-wives."

"Like divorced guys go around sleeping with their ex-wives," Manu countered. "Mika, you and Lani have never been ordinary, admit it!"

Mika stewed over it all afternoon, which he'd taken off to catch up on paperwork and prepare for his return trip, meetings with Megan, a call with the temporary tenant living in his apartment in Pasadena. As he tidied his things into piles, without managing to actually pack anything at all, Manu's words kept coming back to bite him. He'd said what a great dad he'd been, just like Lani had insisted. He so desperately wanted to believe them both.

And his brother was right about something else, too: he and Lani had never been ordinary. They had been shaking each other's lives up since the moment they'd locked eyes all those years ago. He'd been irrevocably in love with her since the day he'd carried her up that beach, after her shoes washed away on the tide, since she'd looked deep into his eyes and told him jokingly, in the corniest way possible, "You're my hero!" That day, he'd resolved to always be her hero. His world only had one axis from that point on—Lani—and in his grief he'd given up on her, way too soon.

Later, as dinnertime approached, he was still turning things over in his mind, and he still hadn't packed a damn thing or organized a ticket home, when the phone call about the samples came. He didn't pick up at first. As soon as the guys at the lab confirmed the chemical compounds did indeed match the sample they'd finally managed to get from Kai Kalama, he would officially have no reason to be here any longer. The case would be closed, and he'd be free to leave and never get in Lani's way again.

But when he finally did answer, what they ended up telling him was not what Mika had expected at all. The sample didn't match the compounds after all; instead, it pointed to something beyond what any of them could have imagined. He had to go and tell Lani in person. And maybe he should tell her how much he loved her, too, he thought, a new way of living suddenly panning out in his mind. Maybe they *could* try again.

They'd had significant barriers to hurdle but they'd come so far these past few weeks, further than they ever had before, in finally talking about what actually went wrong between them. Maybe Lani and Manu were right, and he had been a pretty good dad once. He'd just forgotten, so caught up in grief and guilt over what had never been his fault—or Lani's, either.

As for Anela... It wasn't what he'd expected at all; he'd pushed it away as far as he could, but the truth kept springing back at him like a persistent palm frond—he loved her too. As much as his Honu. Those matching tattoos stood for a lot more than either of them had been putting into their relationship for a long time, but things could change, he thought, grabbing up his car keys. They *would* change...

Mika could hear Anela singing softly on the porch as he walked up the drive. She was playing with the kittens, so he stood quietly for a moment just listening to her voice. It reminded him of Iolana singing nursery rhymes, a sweet little bird, chirping away without any worries in the world. Funny, he thought, feeling a wide smile cross his lips, how often now he could think of his daughter without the tight knot of dread constricting his mind, body and soul.

"Hi, Mika," she called out happily when he walked up the steps.

An open book was still resting on the hammock and he looked around for Lani. Then he saw her shadow through the window, puttering in the kitchen, and his heart lodged in his throat like a wrecking ball at just the thought of telling her how he really felt about her. And that if she wanted him to, he'd go back to California, quit his job, pack his things up and then come straight back to Oahu so they could run the sanctuary together like they'd always planned, and care for Anela, if only Lani wanted all that with him.

"Hi," he said, squatting down next to Anela and smiling gently at her inquisitive face before handing over a small bag full of treats for the kittens. "Thought they might like these."

The little one they'd rescued in the storm scampered over and he scooped it up. Soon the kittens were clambering over them both and Anela was laughing...and Mika knew he had to say something to her, too.

"Hey, Anela, you know the other day, when you got too close to that whale on the boat?"

Anela cocked her head at him over a kitten's head. "Why didn't you want me on the boat? Don't you like me?" she asked.

"It's *because* I like you so much," he said quickly, drawing a deep breath through his teeth. Where to start? "Anela, Lani and I had a daughter once, did she tell you that?"

Anela grew quiet. Her eyes narrowed as she shook her head. "Where is she?"

Mika ran a hand over the mother cat as she purred around his legs. "She died when she was little," he told her, forcing himself to meet her eyes.

"Like my mom did?" Anela said, sadly.

Lani had appeared in the doorway behind Anela now. Strands of her hair fell from her ponytail and framed her face as she took a step forward and put a hand to Anela's head.

"Yes, sweetie, like your mom did," she added softly, throwing him a look he couldn't read. He hoped it was okay, suddenly telling Anela this. "We loved her very much."

Mika's heart was threatening to explode in his chest as Lani lowered herself to her knees beside him and scooped up a kitten. "So, that's kind of why we both get a little nervous when someone we love is in a potentially dangerous situation, but that doesn't mean we don't think you're very brave, or that you should stop coming out on the boat with..." Lani paused, flashed her eyes to Mika and back to Anela. "With *me*," she finished. "You can come out on the boat with me, anytime."

"And Mika?" Anela asked hopefully.

Both of them fixed their eyes on him, and Mika struggled for the words as his heart sank. What was he supposed to say? Lani had just openly stated she expected him to be leaving, and any future boat trips would most definitely not include him. But then, it wasn't like he could blame her for keeping him at arm's length after their spat the other day.

Lani got to her feet and fetched the book from the hammock, and he squeezed Anela's hand a moment. "I need to talk to Lani for a moment," he told her gently. "Do you want to go play inside, and we'll come find you after?"

Lani let him lead her past the shed with its neat pile of swept-up branches, remnants of the storm that were perfect for firewood, and through the little gate to the lookout spot. As soon as she'd seen him just now on her porch with Anela, she'd had the distinct gut feeling he had come to tell them both exactly when he was leaving and she had needed a moment to actually process it.

She wrapped her arms around herself now and watched him frown, as the dread built up in her belly. Of course, he was always going to leave. She had to be strong, even if watching him with Anela just now had yet again given her reason to think their love could overcome anything…if only he didn't have such an aversion to being a father again.

"I never had that conversation with her, about Iolana," she said, taking the stone steps up to the circular lookout platform beside him. He cast his eyes out to the twinkling ocean alongside her, ran a hand across his jaw.

"I'm sorry. I just thought I owed her a truthful explanation for the other day—"

"No, you were right," she cut in. "She's old enough to know. I just never knew how to bring it up. To be honest, I never wanted to talk about it before because... You know."

"I know," he said gently.

"She hasn't had a nightmare in a while now." Lani glanced at him sideways, surprised to feel the love building tenfold inside her. Whenever they'd had an argument before, it had only made her want to cling to him more, and something about him in this light, too, standing here...she wished she could kiss him and make up. The last thing she wanted him to do was fix a one-way trip back to California. Now her mind was spinning with all the what-ifs again. Seeing him with Anela, watching her respond and open up to him over these last few weeks had given her the warm glowing feeling she'd had, watching him hold Iolana. She almost said it now.

Why don't you just stay? Because we both love you, Mika.

But if he didn't want what she did, despite how good he was with Anela, her heart would shatter.

"So, did you come to tell us when you're leaving?" The words were out before she had a chance to rein them back in.

Above them the palms ruffled in the breeze and he averted his gaze again. "I came to tell you we have a development," he said, shoving his hands into his shorts pockets. "The compound matched a sample from a different facility. It wasn't Kai Kalama poisoning the dolphins."

Lani struggled to process what he was telling her. "It wasn't Kai?"

Mika explained that it was actually the run-off from Mr. Benos's greenhouses that had contaminated the ocean—an unfortunate oversight from him, as well as his producers. He'd been using the chemicals quite innocently to boost the growth of his fruit and vegetables, without knowing they were toxic to marine life.

She shook her head, aghast. "Mr. Benos? It can't be… He's…so old! And his peaches…"

Lani was aghast. She could barely believe it when Mika told her the chemicals had probably been seeping into the ocean for months, and it was only now that they, and the government, had been alerted to it.

"The officials have no choice but to shut down Mr. Benos's business," Mika told her.

Lani took a breath, overwhelmed by the news. Poor Mr. Benos, he'd probably had no idea what he was doing; he was probably as devastated as they were. And to think about all those produce parcels she had gratefully accepted…

"Ugh, what a disaster," she groaned, and Mika nodded in sympathy. They stood in silence for a moment, her thoughts whirring.

He hadn't uttered a word about his plans for departure yet, and as they made their way back along the path to the house, the tension between them seemed to rise with each step. Part of her wanted to ask him to stay, while another part of her wished he would just leave already so she wouldn't have to wait any longer to feel the heartache that always came back to bite her somehow, when she put her heart in his hands. Best to just have him go and let her get on with things, she thought.

Unless she was being a total coward.

She stopped him on the porch, her heart thumping. "I'm so sorry for what happened the other day, Mika…" she started, her stomach churning with anticipation as she traced the outline of his mouth with her eyes. So many thoughts were swirling in her head now, she could hardly get any of them to make sense. "The thing is, I'm thinking about Anela and how our future looks. I swore nothing would get in the way of that, and you and I have so much history—"

The scream from inside the house cut her off midsentence. *Anela?*

CHAPTER NINETEEN

MIKA'S STOMACH DROPPED as they raced inside, his thoughts of what Lani had been about to tell him clean forgotten.

"She sounds hurt," Lani panted as they rushed upstairs together.

Anela was sprawled on the floor in her bedroom, clutching her wrist, her dress all bunched up around her, the kittens scampering around like nothing had happened.

"What happened?" Lani cried, moving the kittens away.

"I fell off the bunk bed, but I was trying to stop the kitten from falling first!"

Mika took charge of the situation, all while his heart raced. They should have been watching her! Anger at himself boiled up inside him as he gently inspected Anela's arm, reassuring her that it wasn't broken but that she would need some ice on it.

"It's just bruised," he said as Lani gathered the sheets that had tumbled from the top bunk with Anela. He could tell from her face, and by the way she was grabbing at the sheets, that she was mad at herself, too; this had been entirely preventable.

"I should have been watching her," she mumbled to herself when they'd gotten Anela back downstairs.

Mika had carried the girl in his arms, and to be fair, she seemed more shocked than hurt, but from his place on the sofa, he heard Lani's anguished sighs as she fumbled around in the freezer for the ice. She was mumbling again, and he knew she was blaming herself, just as he was.

"What if something worse had happened?" she hissed at him, turning as he entered the kitchen. "I wasn't watching her!"

"Neither was I," he said, as calmly as his voice would allow.

"It's not your *job* to watch her, it's mine!" Her words came out as a strangled sound and it froze him to the spot. She dashed her hands through her hair, and resumed her mission in the freezer, as he stood there, feeling the helplessness mount in his heart.

"Lani…" he started. "I'm here to help you."

"Well, it's too late now, the damage is done."

"She's totally fine," he reasoned.

"But she was hurt on my watch. You distracted me, and I let you."

Mika felt his fists ball, but he wouldn't take the bait and play the blame game again. He wouldn't let her panic override his common sense. She was bound to be mad under the circumstances and blame herself, and so was he, but this couldn't be the case forever.

"You have to forgive yourself, for this, and for what happened to Iolana." He took the ice from her gently and told her to sit at the dining table, but she hugged her arms around herself instead. "Lani, we can't let what happened to Iolana rule everything we do. We were finally doing better, moving on…"

"I will *never* move on," she spit, pressing her palms to her eyes, but her breathing wasn't as labored now and her hands had stopped shaking. He put a hand gently to her shoulder, said nothing. Soon, her fingers came up over his, holding him there, like she was steadying herself. This was how she had to handle it, he thought as she apologized softly, pressing her cheek to his hand. She had to let the fury wash through her, not bottle it up. She'd been teaching him the same thing ever since he got back here.

Lani followed him to the living room and watched as he sat with Anela, pressing the ice to her wrist. Soon, though, Lani took over.

"I want my book," Anela said. "Can Mika read to me?"

"Mika has things to do, honey," Lani said.

"Please!" Anela looked between them hopefully, and Mika stalled, conflicted.

His pride and dignity told him to go, to leave them both, because they didn't need him. But he'd come here to talk to Lani, to tell her he would stay if she felt anything remotely the same as he did. His cowardice would haunt him forever if he didn't.

"Where's the book?" he asked.

"Upstairs in the study," Lani replied.

Mika climbed the stairs, a million emotions running through him like liquid fire. He knew Lani was feeling guilty and needed time to process it, but he also knew she was tough and resilient and had come further than even she realized over the last few weeks. Still, his heart ached for her as he headed into the study.

He took in the bookshelves full of hardbacks along one wall and an ancient teak desk at the far end near the window. Her mother's desk—he recognized it. He ran his hands over it softly for a second, surprised as the image of that beach house flashed into his head again. Lani had talked about putting this desk in there if they ever bought it, how she'd do her work overlooking the ocean. Sighing, Mika located Anela's book on a chair by the window, but something else caught his eye, right underneath. Anela's full name on the first sheet of a stack of papers—adoption papers.

His stomach lurched as he picked them up and took in their contents—they were one hundred percent adoption papers for Anela. Lani had been planning to adopt her all along, and hadn't said a word to him. Probably because she didn't think he was ready for anything like this.

A sound from downstairs brought him back to the moment, and quickly he put everything back in place before anyone noticed he'd been snooping around. But he couldn't unsee this now. How could he?

Making his way back downstairs with the book, his head reeled. He couldn't help but feel touched. Lani had really bonded with Anela. She loved her like her own child…but then, she hadn't always been so eager to have *him* involved. She'd been protecting her future with Anela so vehemently, which was admirable, but where did that leave him? Them?

Handing the book over, he stood there a moment, watching as Lani scooped the girl closer under one arm. She clearly wasn't over *his* part of what had happened after Iolana died. She never would be. Him walking away from their marriage would always come back to bite them.

"I should go," he said now, inching backward toward the door.

"Stay," Anela demanded, patting the chair at the other side of her.

"You can stay," Lani offered, but he shook his head, trying desperately to process what he had just discovered. It was clearly no concern of his, or she would have mentioned it sooner. She was already planning a life for both of them without him around. Of course she was; he'd been kidding himself, thinking they could ever make something work a second time, with their history! She would be much better off without him.

Telling them both he really had to go, he made for the hallway. Lani followed him outside and shut the door softly behind her. Apprehension was written all over her face.

"Mika—"

"I'll be leaving within the next day or two," he said, cutting her off. "I came here to tell you, now we know what's been going on with the dolphins, that I've got to get back. I'll say goodbye to Anela before I do, but…" he trailed off.

Lani had drawn her lips together, and was seething inwardly, he could tell. Suddenly he regretted the lie.

"I knew it," she said, clicking her tongue.

"Knew what?"

"You can't wait to leave again, can you?"

"Again? Lani, you've made it quite clear you don't want me here," he retaliated, stepping up closer to her. "I just saw the adoption papers. You didn't even tell me you were thinking of adopting Anela, all this time!"

Lani looked stunned. Stepping backward, she stared at the ground. "But you don't want another child in your life," she said eventually, shaking her head. "You've made *that* perfectly clear. So it doesn't affect you, does it?"

Mika stared at her, grappling for words, his brain whirling frantically. He had said that numerous times, yes. He had even believed it. But now…now he didn't know *what* to think. He did love Lani, he wanted to fight for her, but could he ever really trust himself not to let her, or Anela, down again? He had as much work going on now as he had back then. What if he wasn't able to split his time the way she'd need him to? He'd live his whole life worrying about not being enough, and missing things that he should be paying more attention to, like Anela's accident just now.

Lani threw her hands in the air. "You know what, you were right before when you said you were just messing things up," she said now. "Anela and I will be fine, so you can go now, Mika. Go live your life."

"This isn't what I wanted—" he started to say, staring deeply into her eyes as he held her wrists. Her expression had melted into a look of longing and for a moment, he thought she was about to kiss him. But as he spoke, her expression clouded over with grief and sadness till she was shoving at his chest.

"Go!"

Mika staggered backward.

"Get it over with, Mika. If you're going to go, just go. It's what you're good at, after all."

Everywhere Lani looked over the course of the next few weeks, there were reminders of Mika, absolutely everywhere. He was in the sanctuary, in his books, which Anela had taken to reading relentlessly, and he was in her dreams. Every single night.

On the last night before his departure, she had sent Anela with Mele to say goodbye to him, but she herself had bowed out, citing too much work. Instead, she had listened to another of Mr. Benos's profuse in-person apologies, then driven across town and sat on a bench at the cemetery, talking to Iolana, trying not to think that she was potentially letting her own stubborn streak and fear of a second rejection get in the way of her own happiness.

She could have just asked him to stay; wasn't that what she'd been wishing for, and denying, and finding excuse after excuse not to say in case he refused? Now she'd never know.

She found herself talking about Mika to Iolana again today, on—what was it?—the eighth or ninth time she'd visited their daughter's grave since he'd left.

"I do miss your daddy," she admitted now, placing the small bunch of yellow flowers she'd brought beside the candle. No matter how much she tried not to talk about him, how could she *stop* thinking about the laughter they'd enjoyed, even in *this* very place, and all the love they had made, despite their past, and their differences? How had it happened, that they had actually started to heal together, after all this time, only for her to watch him leave again?

"Okay, so I practically marched him off the island," she said out loud, making a sweet old woman at the next gravesite turn in surprise and start looking around for a person. "That was not my finest hour," she continued, with a wave at her.

She'd been consumed by so much emotion, after Anela was hurt on her watch, then discovering Mika had found the adoption papers. She'd just leaped into self-defense mode, then freak-out mode! All she had been thinking about was protecting Anela, doing the right thing by her. After all, he'd mentioned more than once that he didn't want another kid in his life. He'd had every opportunity to tell her that wasn't the case, or that he'd changed his mind, but he'd said nothing. So clearly, this was for the best.

Yes, she decided, yet again. "It's for the best, Iolana. Not that I won't miss him."

Dejectedly she made her way home alone again. She'd felt more alone than ever since his departure. If this was really for the best, why did she feel even more lost than when he'd left the first time?

CHAPTER TWENTY

MANU FOUND LANI one afternoon in the sanctuary. She'd just finished surgery on another turtle victim, and literally just shooed a still-apologetic Mr. Benos out the door—he just wouldn't stop coming over to say sorry, poor guy. She had vowed to make it clear to everyone that he hadn't been causing intentional harm to the dolphins, but she felt so bad for him.

"Lani, I thought I'd find you here," Manu said, closing the door behind him.

A fully recovered Mahina smiled and played with her hair, and the two said a brief hi that made Lani think there was something going on with them that she'd been too caught up in her own thoughts to notice since Mahina had started back at the sanctuary. Interesting.

Lani tore her gloves off and perched on the desk, giving Manu her full attention. Oh, God, had he come with news of Mika? The thought made her cold suddenly. She hadn't heard from him for weeks, not since he'd left, and she was starting to think she never would again.

"What's up?" she asked him, bracing herself.

"I need you," he said, casting Mahina a surreptitious look that set another spark of intrigue aflame. "I was hoping you could come with me? There's an injured animal of some kind around the bay, by the beach…"

"Okay, what kind of animal?" she asked, wondering how

the heck he would have found it all the way around the bay, and then come here without even bringing it with him.

"You should go. I'll be fine handling the checkups and feeding," Mahina said, ushering her out the door before she could even so much as remove her white coat.

"I guess I'm coming with you, then," Lani said distractedly, picking up a cage and a blanket for whatever animal he'd found.

Manu was quiet on the drive, and she resisted the urge to ask about Mika. Had he heard anything? Had Mika mentioned them to him at all? Ugh, she scolded herself for even wondering. She had slammed that door shut and now she just had to deal with the consequences.

Soon enough, Manu slowed the car on the roadside and left the engine running as he opened her door. Lani turned to him in confusion, but he told her to get out. "It's down there, on the beach," he said, pointing through the gap in the trees.

Lani climbed out, realizing now where she was. She was right by the house that she and Mika had always talked about buying. And the For Sale sign was nowhere in sight. What a cruel twist of fate, she thought to herself, that the animal should be found here, in a place that would only serve to rub salt in her wounds.

"I'll wait here," Manu said, keeping the engine idling.

Begrudgingly she made her way through the trees adjacent to the house, craning her neck to try to see through the windows on the side. Whoever had bought this place had something truly special on their hands, and she would not be jealous, she decided.

Oh, who was she kidding? This was her dream house! Jealous didn't cover it.

As she made her way down to the beach, the palms seemed

to whisper at her; this was private property. But she had to get to this animal…wherever it was. Turning around, she couldn't see anything.

And then, she spotted something moving inside the house. So, there *was* someone there? Maybe they'd already rescued the animal and taken it inside, she thought. Lani approached the house, its beautiful porch spilling right onto the beach. The hot tub was all covered up, the barbecue draped with a tarp, but the plants blooming in their pots carried the scent of jasmine and orchids straight to her nose. She breathed in, wishing she could bottle it, then to her surprise, noticed a trail of flowers up the steps to the yellow-painted back door. It was a path of petals!

What…?

The door was ajar. "Hello?" she called out, making her way tentatively to the top step.

Then she looked down. More petals. These ones spelled out the words Mika Loves Lani.

Lani held her breath in disbelief. Was this real? Mika had done this years ago, too…

"Mika…" she whispered, the word barely leaving her lips as she felt the tears welling up in her eyes.

She stepped over the flowery message, realizing she was shaking. Then, there he was, standing at the bottom of the stairs, a faint smile playing on his lips as he watched her take it all in. He was dressed in khaki shorts, a crisp white shirt, no sign of the bandanna, which she'd actually grown to quite like. For a moment she just stared at him through the blur. Mika stepped toward her and took her hands.

"I'm sorry, false alarm. There is no injured animal," he told her, just as she heard Manu's car speeding off. They'd set her up.

Lani half laughed. "They were in on this, your brother and Mahina. Mika, what is going on, and why are you in this house?"

"It's my house now," he said, sweeping her hair back and cradling her face. "And yours and Anela's, too. I mean, you can take all the time you need. I know I messed up. But this island is my home, *you* are my home. I did a lot of thinking after I left. My work is not the most important thing to me, Lani, you are. And I know what happened to Iolana shouldn't stop me from at least trying to be the best dad I can for Anela."

Lani could barely believe what she was hearing. Tears streamed down her cheeks, faster than he or she could wipe them away. It felt like that dream she'd had, being here with him, surrounded by all these petals and the sound of the waves crashing on the beach, hearing him say *she* was his home.

"I'm so sorry I pushed you away, Mika. I was just scared in case you did it first. In case you don't want what I want for Anela…"

"I want to look after both of you," he said now. "That's all I want, Lani. I thought I didn't want any more children in my life, but my God, I have missed that little girl. I was thinking…" He glanced at her sheepishly. "We could get married, again, better this time, and we could adopt her. Together."

"Are you serious?" Lani was so stunned she laughed and threw her arms around him impulsively.

"Is that a yes?" Mika picked her up, and he spun her around so many times she was dizzy by the time her feet touched the ground.

"Yes, I want that," she managed, just as Mika got to his knee and kneeled before her, a box suddenly in his hand. Her heart raced as he opened it up, revealing an exquisite diamond ring that caught the sun streaming in over the ocean through the open back door.

"Lani," he said softly, "my Honu, for life. Will you do me the honour of becoming my wife? Again?"

Lani gasped, not quite believing what was happening. First the house of their dreams, which he'd only gone and bought for them, and now this. She nodded fervently, barely able to contain her joy as she told him yes, yes, yes! Mika slipped the ring onto her finger and she stared at it in shock and delight, imagining showing Anela. How on earth was this even happening?

He rose to embrace her and they clung together for what felt like an eternity, kissing passionately, until eventually, Mika stepped back and grinned. "Should we explore our new house? I know you've always had plans for it."

"Oh, I have so many plans," she said now, laughing into her hand and catching sight of the ring again. How did she get so lucky?

As they climbed the stairs and marked out what would be their room, and which would be Anela's room and which would be the study overlooking the ocean, she still felt like she was dreaming, and was possibly going to wake up and find this was all just a cruel act of her own imagination.

But later, when they drove to Mika's parents' place with the news, they organized an impromptu beach party that same night, and with all the congratulations coming at them, she had no choice but to believe this was her new reality. Her, and the only man she'd ever loved, and the little girl they both loved.

Anela was so happy to have Mika back. Just the look on her face as Mika swung her around on the beach and waded into the surf with her was enough to bring the tears right back to Lani's eyes. Tears of total happiness, she realized, wondering when exactly the cloud of pain and grief had stopped following them around. She couldn't quite put her finger on it, she thought, watching them splashing each other and laughing with the sun sinking into the water on the horizon. All she knew was that somewhere along the line, in ways she'd never dreamed possible, she had found the healing she'd needed in the last place she'd expected to find it. And so had Mika.

One year later

Mika couldn't even hide his grin right now. He wrapped his arms around Lani from behind, resting his chin on her shoulder as they both watched Anela take the microphone on the stage. The children's corner of the library was packed; she'd invited all her friends and even some of her schoolteachers were present.

So was Mr. Benos, he noticed now. The elderly man was sitting right at the front, applauding her already. To his credit, he'd done his best to redeem himself for his negligence regarding the chemicals and was now a fervent marine life ambassador in the community, offering his old greenhouse space for officials to host workshops on caring for wildlife and sustainable fishing practices.

They were nothing compared to the parties he and Lani threw, however. The big new house had become a real home, especially since Anela's adoption papers had been completed, and she was now officially their daughter. Their private beach had seen many a get-together by now, lots of singing, dancing, laughing. Sometimes he wondered why he'd stayed away so long, but it was possible that he and Lani were even closer now because of it. They visited Iolana a lot, told her everything that was happening, told her they missed and loved her. But they didn't let the grief darken their days anymore. And while his work was still important, he'd learned to say no when it mattered, to focus on his family, making more precious memories together.

"I don't know how she finds the confidence," Lani whispered now as Anela, dressed in jeans and her dolphin-patterned shirt, tapped the mic and took the small plastic chair, laying Mika's book out on her lap.

"This is my dad Mika's new book," she explained now, picking it up again and flashing the cartoon-like cover at the audience. "He self-published it, like his last book, only this one's for kids."

Mika smiled, as proud of himself and Lani as Anela went on to explain how the proceeds from the book were going to provide educational resources for local schools, teaching them about the importance of looking after the oceans, sharks, dolphins and other marine life.

Anela had become a real ocean ambassador in the last year. Her story about her mother had given her reason to learn more about shark behavior, and to his relief she had only grown to respect and appreciate them more. Sometimes she talked about becoming a marine scientist. Next month she'd learn to dive, and soon… Well, maybe someday she'd meet Nala.

Sure, his book gave her leverage to make regular visits to libraries, schools and even the other beachside towns along the coast, impressing everyone she met, but the thought of having his daughter at his side, spreading his message for a long time to come, made him happier than he'd ever thought possible. Her bubbly enthusiasm and her fantastic imagination were a joy, and a credit to Lani, too, he thought now, hugging Lani tighter.

"Did I tell you I love you yet today, wife?" he whispered, nuzzling on her ear. She turned in his arms, smiling.

"I don't believe you did."

"Well, I love you," he said, whispering now, so no one else in the audience could hear. "And when we get home, I plan to show you just how much."

"I'll hold you to that," she told him.

Sadly, they would have to wait a few hours, he thought. After Anela finished her reading, they had another bird release planned, then his and Lani's parents were coming over—something that was now a pretty regular occasion. The two families loved being reunited, and they all adored Anela, who was always the center of attention.

Whatever happened next in their much-loved, slightly unconventional family unit, he thought, they would take it in their stride. Somehow he had gotten the family he never thought he deserved. But now he had it, Mika was never going to let it go.

* * * * *

NURSE'S SECRET ROYAL FLING

JC HARROWAY

MILLS & BOON

To the wonderful and talented editors
who helped create this story.

To Jo Grant, who believed that Andreas and Clara's
story deserved to be told, and to Charlotte Ellis,
who encouraged me to take my characters
on an emotion-packed journey to their HEA.

CHAPTER ONE

CLARA LUND NEEDED this prestigious job. However *delicate* the situation awaiting her behind the intimidatingly vast timber door in the guest wing of Varborg's winter palace, she could handle it.

Straightening her crisply ironed nurse's uniform, she pressed the intercom button beside the door. Talk about being thrown in at the deep end on her first shift: no welcome tour of the palace; no explanation of her night-nurse duties; no pointers on royal protocol for when she finally did meet her patient, Prince Henrik, Varborg's ruler. When the intercom remained silent, Clara pressed the button again, for longer this time.

'Yes, yes. Please enter,' a disembodied male voice, deep and cultured, barked brusquely.

Rude... But at least he'd said 'please'.

The automatic locking system disarmed with a click. Clara pushed her way inside the suite and closed the door, focussed on her salary rather than the occupant's apparent sense of entitlement. It seemed, by working for Varborg's royal family, she'd have to get used to demanding VIPs. But this second salary would increase Clara's contribution to paying off the mortgage on her family's home and hopefully ease the perpetual worry lines around her mother's eyes.

Bypassing the ridiculously opulent fresh flower arrangement on the reception table, Clara set off in search of the grumpy-sounding guest. The suite boasted wall-to-wall luxury disguised beneath understated Scandinavian elegance. Were her feet not so deeply embedded in the concrete of reality, she might have spared a moment to be impressed.

Except each room was empty.

'Hello…?' she called out as she stepped into the deserted bedroom.

A splash of water sounded from the *en suite* bathroom.

'In here,' the owner of the rich baritone said from behind the half-open door.

'Are you okay, sir?' she asked, mostly keeping the exasperation from her voice. The guest sounded younger than she'd first assumed—and mildly irritated, as if she'd kept him waiting. 'I was led to believe that there was some sort of emergency.'

If his 'delicate situation' had been that urgent, someone would have called an ambulance.

The stranger sighed. 'The situation *is* urgent to me.'

'I did buzz. *Twice*,' she pointed out, his manner ruffling her usually unflappable feathers. He sounded perfectly healthy.

'I'm aware,' he said. 'Look, I'm sort of…stuck.'

Clara rolled her eyes. She wasn't a maid. An experienced nurse with her training—which included a Master's degree in Advanced Clinical Practice—was surely above reaching for the soap for some entitled visiting dignitary or foreign ambassador? Except patients, like customers, were always right.

Think about the money… Think about the money…

'I have no desire to waste your time,' he continued in that commanding voice she found both objectionable and inconveniently appealing. 'Could you please enter so we can get this…*situation* over with?'

'Okay—are you decent?' While she'd seen it all before, she didn't want to barge in and embarrass the owner of that attractive voice.

'I'm naked, if that's what you mean,' he replied, his voice

now tinged with amused challenge. 'But, rest assured, I have no immediate plans to flash you.'

Clara stifled a snigger. A sense of humour helped when patients were forced to concede their dignity and ask for assistance.

'That's good,' she quipped, pressing her lips together to contain her smile. 'We don't want a sexual harassment incident on my first night, do we?'

When her only reply was a dry chuckle that filled her belly with inexplicable flutters of excitement, Clara pushed the door fully open and poked her head inside.

Any trace of humour drained from her like water down a gold-plated plughole. There was nothing laughable about the modern-day Viking reclining regally in the generous bath, which looked as if it could happily accommodate two adults with ample room for fun and games.

Clara's mouth instantly turned dry, her pulse speeding as he arched one golden brow, his bold blue-grey stare defiant and full of questions.

'Um...hello,' she croaked, stepping from behind the door.

To her utter alarm, her face warmed. Every spirited retort deserted her, while the shocking heat of instant attraction set her entire body aflame, as if she'd rolled naked in a bed of nettles.

'You're a nurse,' he said with surprise, a frown slashing his outrageously handsome face as he looked her up and down.

Her body heated in every place his eyes landed. How could he do that? And was it her imagination, or was he vaguely familiar? She rarely watched TV, was too busy for social media and had no time for VIP-spotting.

'Well observed,' she said dryly, looking away. Not because he was naked, concealed only from the waist down by what she suspected was a dwindling foam of bubbles, but because, trapped or not, he dominated the luxurious marble bathroom like some sort of powerfully virile mountain-man.

She exhaled slowly, grateful for that modesty layer of suds. His voice alone was sexy in a bossy kind of way, but the entire package seemed to have triggered a rush of hormones—no mean feat considering that Clara deliberately avoided noticing members of the opposite sex. Relationships weren't worth her while. Even sex, the one time she'd done it, had been under-whelming, leaving her vulnerable and humiliated.

But she'd have to be anaesthetised not to notice *this* man.

'The east wing steward sent me,' she said, casually scan-ning the room for signs of blood or trauma, while she willed her body to revert to normal. 'But I'll happily leave again if you were expecting someone else. A plumber, perhaps...?'

He laughed, another dry chuckle that rumbled up from that deliciously broad chest. She couldn't remember the last time someone had found her funny or made her laugh in return. Absurdly, Clara searched for other amusing things to say.

Except this was work. She was a professional. She wasn't here to spar with him, no matter how carefree and giggly he made her feel.

'*Are* you hurt?' she asked sharply, pointedly glancing at the watch pinned to her pocket before scrutinising his well-defined chest, which was covered in manly hair with the barest hint of reddish gold. His shoulders were wide, his upper body ripped and bronzed. While she desperately tried not to envision her-self as the second occupant of that giant bath, Clara's gaze skimmed the ladder of his abs until she reached the modesty layer of suds, frustrated to have her view cruelly interrupted.

'Don't mind me,' he drawled, snapping her to her senses. 'Have a good, long look.' He relaxed his arms on the edge of the bath as if in invitation.

'As you pointed out,' she blustered, mortified to be caught

ogling the sexy, naked VIP, 'I'm a medical professional—I was assessing you for injuries.'

'Is that right?' He raised his eyebrows, a knowing smile tugging at one corner of his sensual mouth, which was surrounded by a close-cropped beard of dark facial hair flecked with similar golden tones to his body hair.

'Indeed.' Clara tilted her chin, hot shame in her veins that she'd temporarily forgotten she was there to help him; that it was her *job*, one she couldn't afford to mess up. 'And I'm pleased to find that you seem fine.'

If 'fine' denoted the kind of wildly rugged male beauty that brought to mind log cabins in the snowy mountains, fur pelts on the floor, a crackling fire…

Where the hell had that ridiculous and unwarranted fantasy come from? His raw, edgy sex appeal was as irrelevant as his VIP status. She wasn't about to undo the past eight years of struggle and heartache for something as frivolous as sexual chemistry.

From the age of sixteen, when her father had left his wife and two daughters and done a runner, Clara, the eldest, had worked part-time to contribute to the family income. At nineteen, while Clara had also been studying for her nursing degree, her mother, Alma, had developed breast cancer and hadn't been able to work for months on end while undergoing treatment. Clara's income had kept the roof over their heads and the bills paid with no help from her absent father. The emotional toll of caring for Alma, while also taking on financial responsibility for her family, had cured teenaged Clara of the foolish romantic aspirations of most of her peers.

Especially after Alma discovered her father, Lars, had remortgaged the house to fund one of his get-rich-quick schemes and had then ended up in prison for fraud. Now, at twenty-four, with her parents' unequal marriage as a warning, Clara's only goal was lifelong financial and emotional independence.

She'd never be *any* man's puppet, wild mountain-men and Vikings included.

'I need to get back to work,' she said in her haughtiest voice, willing her eyes to steer clear of his ripped physique. 'So unless you're bleeding to death…'

She paused expectantly, faking indifference to the inconvenient attraction that, for a moment, had caught her off-guard.

'No blood. Sorry to disappoint you.' His lips twitched with playful amusement other women might have found charming.

No doubt he was used to the effect he had on poor unsuspecting women. Only, Clara had seen how love could make one partner, usually the woman, vulnerable. Her mother had excused and forgiven Lars time and time again in the name of love.

Ignoring the heat and speculation in his stare, she smiled sweetly. 'What a shame.'

'Next time, I'll try to provide you with a little more drama,' he said, his silvery blue eyes sparkling flirtatiously.

'Let's hope there'll be no next time,' she shot back, unable to resist. Was this the flirty fun she'd missed out on as a teenager because of Lars's irresponsible approach to raising his daughters?

At that he only stared, amused and revoltingly confident in his nudity.

'So, what can I do for you?' She folded her arms across her chest, keeping her eyes on his face and not a millimetre lower. Now that he seemed to have awoken a previously dormant aspect of her womanhood, all she could think about was escape. *He* was the naked one, but she felt horribly exposed, imagining wildly romantic scenarios when, before meeting him, she'd have sworn that there wasn't a fanciful bone in her body.

'While that's normally the kind of offer I'd love to hear from a beautiful woman,' he said, his stare playfully daring, 'We've already vetoed sexual harassment, although you might need to stop looking at me as if you've been denied the last cookie in the jar.'

His comment drew another uncontrollable blush from Clara. A trickle of fear chilled her blood as if by ignoring the demands of her femininity up to now something vital might be missing from her life and somehow he could tell.

'You said you were stuck. And I'm not interested in cookies,' she lied, dragging her eyes away from his chest.

How had they got there again? Was he some sort of sickeningly handsome sorcerer, bewitching her with his hot bod, his sparkly eyes and the sheer force of his unapologetic masculinity?

'In that case,' he said, seeming to drop the cocky attitude, 'I won't keep you from your other duties any longer.'

'How generous,' she snapped, the testosterone fog around him the only excuse for her uncharacteristic attitude. 'I'd hate to have to attend to a *real* emergency and leave you…indisposed. I'm sure that bath is getting cold.'

She just couldn't seem to bite her tongue around him.

He laughed, something like respect flickering in his eyes. Validation shot excitement along Clara's nerves, lighting her up inside like the million stars in the night sky. She fisted her hands on her hips, furious at her rebellious body's response to him. If circumstances had been different, if they'd been equals, if she hadn't needed this lucrative job, she would have turned tail and left him to shiver in his cooling bathwater.

Instead, she clamped her lips together. Her family was one defaulted mortgage repayment away from losing their home.

As if finally done toying with her, the infuriating man sat up. The water swirled around his lean hips in tantalisingly hypnotic currents.

'Before you leave,' he said, the amused lilt lingering in his voice telling her he'd caught her watching those currents for a glimpse of what lay beneath. 'I wonder if you would save me an undignified crawl across the tiles and be so kind as to pass me my leg?'

CHAPTER TWO

CROWN PRINCE ANDREAS CRONSTEDT, heir to the Varborg throne, was rarely surprised by the many people he met. But the enchanting beauty who'd marched into his bathroom with her no-nonsense attitude didn't bat an eyelid at his rather unusual request.

'Of course,' she said, casting big, blue eyes around the bathroom. 'Your leg; where might I find that?'

Satisfaction spread through the ancient Viking blood in Andreas's veins like lava. She was spectacular. And obviously had no idea that he descended from a long, ancient line of Scandinavian princes.

'Try behind you, in the bedroom. Under the curtains, perhaps?' Andreas indicated the doorway, through which this fascinating and forthright woman had come. 'I'm quite impressed with myself for making such an improbable shot.'

'What is it doing all the way over there, when you're stuck in your *cold* bath?' she asked, casting him an unsympathetic look he found thrilling.

Rather than having the desired effect, her taunting reprimand, and the way she looked at him with both interest and astonishment at his stupidity, flooded his groin with heat. Too bad she was a palace employee, one of the round-the-clock nurses employed to keep Prince Henrik in excellent health, and therefore strictly off-limits.

'I'm afraid I hurled it away, unthinkingly, in a rare fit of frustration,' he said, gleefully admitting to this intriguing stranger that his current predicament was totally self-inflicted.

'So you only have yourself to blame,' she pointed out, one hand on her hip.

Had anyone ever before found him ridiculous? Had a woman ever stirred his curiosity so…intensely? Right then he couldn't recall a single time.

'I'm afraid so.' He smiled, noticing how her lips twitched, as if she was trying not to laugh.

'Interesting…' she said and turned away.

As Prince Henrik's second, less important son, Andreas had been allowed to pursue a career of his choosing. As a doctor, he met a lot of nurses, but none as unique, strikingly beautiful or unapologetically herself as this one. Where on Earth had the palace found such a refreshingly candid character?

Through the open door, he watched her stoop in search of his leg. As she looked behind the heavy curtains, Andreas willed his eager anatomy into submission. But he was only a man, not super-human. He couldn't have stopped his stare sliding to the curve of her hips and derrière as she bent over if his life had depended upon it. Perhaps he should turn on the cold tap, shock his libido into behaving, but where was the fun in that?

And tonight, after having been rudely summoned home, his locum position in Stockholm cut short by his father's personal secretary with only the briefest of explanations—Prince Henrik was fatigued following a short illness and needed time to recover—Andreas deserved a little flirtatious interlude with a woman for whom he was just an ordinary man.

Excitement buzzed through his nervous system at the heady freedom this encounter offered. Most people recognised Varborg's physically challenged prince, a man who was not meant to rule and could never replace his late older brother, the popular Oscar. But, with *this* woman, he had the opportunity for complete anonymity; to be no one but himself for a moment.

He'd never met anyone like her, least of all in his royal life, in which women were cookie-cutter sophisticates who fitted into two categories: those who fawned and flattered him and those too intimidated by his title to utter a single word. Even the women he bedded were careful to avoid any verbal display beyond voicing their delight between the sheets, should it somehow lose them his royal favour.

On discovering he was an amputee, some went overboard on the sympathy, infantilised him. He might have lost a leg, but the rest of him worked just fine, as proved by the very functional stirring in his groin that this delightful stranger had provoked the minute she peered into the room with her cutting remarks and her prim and proper hairdo.

'Found it,' she said, returning to the bathroom, flushed and slightly breathless in a way that made him think of kissing. 'Luckily for you.'

He was lucky that she'd been the one sent to his aid. If he'd known that *she* awaited him, he might not have been so reluctant to return to the oppressive confines of the palace, all be it to the guest wing he'd insisted upon. He wasn't ready to sleep in the suite that had once belonged to Oscar. Nor did he intend to be solely at the crown's beck and call just because he'd returned to help out Prince Henrik with royal engagements. He'd taken a locum position at the local private medical clinic, his work the one thing in his life that filled him with uncomplicated pride.

'Thank you,' he said, savouring her striking face, her hair the colour of burnt caramel and the playful glint in her blue eyes. 'What's your name?'

He swept his gaze from her exquisite features down the length of her body, tracing her blistering figure underneath the nurse's uniform, in the way she'd blatantly appraised him earlier. 'I should have asked before, given the circumstances.'

'Circumstances,' she scoffed, holding out the prosthesis. 'Is that what we're calling a fit of leg-hurling impatience? I thought it was a self-inflicted situation.'

He grinned, waiting patiently for her answer, while her stare once more dipped to his torso in obvious admiration. She couldn't seem to stop checking him out.

When he made no move to take the leg, she huffed. 'My name is Clara. Clara Lund.'

A small smile tugged at his mouth—captivating, candid Clara. 'Pleased to meet you, Clara.'

Her name caressed his tongue the way he imagined her kiss would taste: breathy, bold, undaunted: like the woman herself. A woman who clearly didn't care one jot that he was someone important enough to stay at one of the Cronstedt palaces.

She frowned and shuddered a little, as if his speaking her name gave her a thrill of pleasure that was inconvenient. He understood her dilemma. Regardless of the sparks between them, he couldn't bed this woman whom the universe had delivered as if to soothe his grieving soul. Because being back home resurfaced complex emotions.

'Thank you for finding it.' He took the prosthesis, noting with satisfaction the way her eyes were averted from the layer of thinning suds that, just about, still concealed his lower half. 'You should know that not many people surprise me, Clara.'

'Well, I'm glad I could save you that undignified crawl across the tiles.'

Andreas's smile widened. The more they talked, the better he felt about being here, a place of bittersweet memories. She'd helped him forget that, one day, be it in five years or fifteen, he would have to abandon the medical career he loved and succeed his father. It wouldn't matter that, as the spare who'd been left to his own devices, he was unqualified for the role. Nor would it matter that the nation, who still referred to Andreas as 'the party prince' he'd been in his twenties, had adored Oscar, just like Prince Henrik—just like Andreas himself, in fact. He would have no choice but to turn his back on the life he'd built for himself and step into his brother's shoes.

'I'll be going, then, if that's everything…?' She glanced at the door, as if she was dying to escape.

He should let her go, but not yet.

'Yes, time to get out, I think.' Andreas propped his prosthesis against the side of the bath and pulled the plug. He braced his hands on the bath's edge as if to lever his body from the water, unable to resist one final flirtation, if only to see the censure once more sparking in her pretty eyes.

Right on cue, she flushed. 'Right… I'll…um…leave you to it.'

She cast one last look down his chest to the waterline and scurried from the room.

'I'd appreciate it if you could wait,' he called after her, a rumble of amusement trapped in his throat. 'I'd like to thank you properly—face to face, as it were. When I'm no longer naked.'

He heard a nervous squawk from the bedroom, neither a refusal nor acceptance, but some instinct told him that she'd wait.

Andreas used his upper-body strength to haul himself from the bath. He reached for a towel, impatient now to know everything there was to know about the palace's newest nurse, perhaps the only woman on the planet who'd failed to recognise him; a woman with whom he would be free simply to be an ordinary man—not Andreas, the second-choice heir.

He attached his below-knee prosthesis to his left leg and wrapped a fresh towel around his waist, swallowing down the sour taste of failure that being back here had caused to resurface. Judgement seemed to seep from the ancient palace walls. He wasn't meant to have been the one. It should have been Oscar in line to the throne.

If only Andreas had been able to save him. The defeat and guilt brought jarring flashes of his worst memory—a crumpled vehicle wreck, the smell of hot metal and petrol, the urgency to save his unconscious brother and his attempts at CPR. And then nothing but blackness until he'd woken up in hospital.

Why hadn't he died in that accident instead of Oscar? With the ruler who'd trained for the role from birth, the future of Varborg would have been secure. Whereas Andreas knew more about the human body than being a statesman.

He found Clara in the suite's living room, her back to the fire while she looked out at the shadowy, mountainous view beyond the windows. He clung to the distracting sight of her wonderful ordinariness. It made him want to be an ordinary man, not a last-resort prince. To shrug off the sense of being second best and feel invincible, the way he had when she'd moved her eyes over his nakedness. To be himself, the man she'd seen when she'd challenged him so unflinchingly.

'Beautiful, isn't it?' he said, entranced by the angles of her profile as he flicked on the lamps.

Clara turned to face him and gaped. Her throat moved on a pained-looking swallow that fanned his ego. 'You're still naked.' Her gobsmacked stare travelled down his bare torso, which was dotted with the droplets of water he'd missed in his haste to prolong their thrilling interaction.

'Not quite.' He shrugged, unabashed. 'Would you like a drink?' He poured himself a nightcap.

'No, thank you. I'm *supposed* to be working.' She fidgeted with her hair, pushing some unruly strands of honeyed gold behind her ear, while she tried valiantly to keep her eyes averted from his bare chest and the towel slung low on his hips.

Oh, yes, she felt this primal attraction as strongly as him, and the intense chemistry neither of them could dismiss, no matter how inconvenient or ill-judged.

'Well, I need to warm up after that tepid bath.' He joined her before the fire.

Something about her made him feel less alone, as if the ferocity of their attraction proved they were humans first, all other expectations second.

'You could always put some clothes on,' she snapped.

'I could.' Grateful to have their playful banter back, he made no move to oblige her. 'But then I'd miss the way you're looking at me.'

'I'm not looking at you. I'm wondering how soon I can return to my proper job.'

'Point taken. But, before you leave, tell me, do you work here full-time?' he asked, already looking forward to their next meeting.

'*Part*-time,' she stressed. 'I have another full-time job at a local hospital.'

'You work *two* jobs?' he asked, astonished by her impressive dedication.

'Some people must if they want a roof over their heads.' She cast him another of those challenging looks and then glanced around the immaculately elegant room, a barely concealed sneer on her lips.

Of course; the palace was completely over the top compared to how most normal people lived.

'Forgive me.' Andreas frowned, appalled by the arrogant assumptions he'd made about this intriguing woman's life. 'I've detained you long enough.'

But now he wanted to know everything about Clara Lund. To understand what had shaped her, what drove her, what dreams she held. Meeting her tonight had been a welcome-home gift he could never have anticipated. Knowing she worked in a place where he should feel at ease to be himself but instead felt like an imposter gave him the strength to face all that this place represented: memories, good and bad; expectations of duty and obligation at odds with his dreams; the disappointment in people's eyes, his father's included.

He placed his barely touched Scotch on the table and held out his hand, wishing he didn't have to let her go. 'It was a pleasure to meet you, Clara. Thank you for your help.'

She took his hand, her grip firm and her fingers warm, her touch calling to that part of him that was, first and foremost, a man.

'Perhaps you'll be more careful where you throw your prosthesis in future,' she said, those big, intelligent eyes teasing.

What did she see when she looked at him? Suddenly, he wanted to know.

'You haven't asked—about how I lost my leg.' He kept hold of her hand, hoping she couldn't feel the rapid acceleration of his pulse. 'Most people can't help their curiosity.'

But he'd already established this woman wasn't most people.

If she *did* ask, he'd have to confess his true identity, explain the accident and voice his worst failing to this extraordinary, ordinary woman. Would she view him differently if she knew how he'd failed his brother, his family, his nation? Would she too find him somehow lacking?

Could he stand to find out?

Her stare clung to his. 'If you wanted me to know, a complete stranger, you'd have told me.'

Andreas's breath caught in his chest, her answer more perfect than he could ever have imagined.

'And why does it matter?' she asked, her pupils dilating in the dim lighting. 'Our scars don't define us, do they?'

Her astonishing reply sliced through him like a blade. She couldn't possibly know he struggled with imposter syndrome, not because he'd lost a limb, but because he'd been raised from birth to know that he wasn't quite as important as his older brother, a brother who had then died on Andreas's watch.

'No, I suppose they don't,' he said, as fresh heat boiled inside him.

What scars had shaped beguiling, hard-working and independent Clara?

For Andreas, his injury represented what might have been, what *should* have been, if Oscar had survived the accident instead. His scars were a daily reminder of the brother he'd failed to save. And more—with Oscar dead, and his father growing older, Andreas would one day need to forgo his career and his freedom.

But she was right: there *was* more to him than his scars, his past mistakes and the future role he would one day inherit. In that moment, he was desperate to be nothing more than an ordinary man.

'May I?' he asked, slowly lifting his hand to an escaped lock of hair on her cheek.

She nodded, her eyes dipping to his mouth for a revealing second as her breathing accelerated.

This close, he could see a tiny hole in her nose from a piercing. It made him smile and strengthened his resolve to stand up to the palace's demands for his time, to cling to the medical career he loved, until he was finally forced to stop. He tucked the silky strand behind her ear, his fingers lingering over that soft golden hair.

Oh, Clara, Clara, Clara... Why is it so hard to let you walk away?

As if she'd read his mind, she gripped his wrist, holding his hand in place.

His pulse spiked. He should tell her to leave. Except her warm, feminine scent lured him as she swayed closer and wet her lips with the tip of her tongue, her hungry stare latched to his, as if she saw deep inside his soul.

'You should go,' he said in one last ditch attempt to do the right thing, to resist the madness engulfing him like a rogue wave sucking him under.

'I should.' She nodded, swallowed and inched closer.

Damn it, just one taste.

Crushing her to his bare chest, he covered her mouth with his, pressing her pliant body close, from breasts to hips. Need roared through his blood, powerful and inescapable, setting off a chain reaction of desire so intense, he lost his mind. Her lips were soft, her whimper a moan of desperation that echoed so deeply inside him he struggled to recall if he'd ever wanted a woman more.

She parted her lips and touched her tongue to his, twisting his hair in her greedy hands. He tasted sweet triumph. He wasn't alone. She felt this uncontrollable chemistry too.

Her body writhed against his as their kiss deepened. His towel loosened and slid from his hips to the floor. But he was too far gone to care, too intent on the thrilling duel of tongue against tongue, too aroused by the intense flare of mutual passion as they kissed.

With a sudden gasp, she broke free. She pushed at him, so he stepped back, releasing her at once.

Her hand flew to cover her mouth, but not before Andreas saw the evidence of her kiss-swollen lips. 'I'm sorry. I shouldn't have done that.' She looked down at his nakedness—he was hard—and stepped back towards the exit. 'You're a guest here.'

'No, I'm…here on business.' He speared his fingers through his hair, lingering arousal and fresh guilt shredding his composure. '*I'm* the one who's sorry. It was my fault.'

'Please don't have me fired,' she whispered, backing further away as if he was some sort of lecherous creep. 'I need this job.'

Fired? Guilt rattled his bones. 'There's no question that you'll lose your job.'

He'd taken advantage of the situation, kept his identity secret and indulged himself with a beautiful woman in his father's employment. Yes, she'd kissed him back, her passion as desperate as his, but he should have controlled himself. He knew better and held himself to higher standards than other men.

'Wait,' he said, reaching for his towel as she turned and headed for the exit.

He strode after her, tucking his towel around his waist. For a wild and irresponsible moment, he'd relished the freedom to be the anonymous man Clara saw, flirted with and found attractive. He would make this right and tell her his name, hope she didn't curtsey or something equally hideous, and perhaps they could laugh about the situation.

Except, by the time he reached the corridor, she'd disappeared. Andreas cursed under his breath. He closed the suite door and retraced his footsteps. The room seemed to have shrunk, the walls pressing in on him with the heavy weight of regret. He touched his lips, the lingering taste of Clara soured by the bitter taste of what might have been if he were any other man.

CHAPTER THREE

IF CLARA HAD hoped for a quiet moment the following day to analyse why she'd acted so completely out of character, flirting with and then kissing a gloriously naked stranger, she was to be sorely disappointed. No sooner had she met her newest patient at Nordic Care, a private hospital an hour's drive from the palace, than the poor elderly man collapsed and went into cardiac arrest right before her eyes.

Shocked into action, Clara hit the alarm on the wall above the patient's bed and instantly began chest compressions. The crash team arrived within seconds—two other nurses and a female registrar. The doctor began manually bagging the patient, inflating his lungs with air, while Clara gave the team a brief synopsis of the patient's medical problems.

'This is Mr Engman, a seventy-three-year-old diabetic admitted overnight with dizzy spells.'

Clara snatched a breath, the exertion of performing CPR talking all her energy. 'We'd been monitoring him for cardiac arrhythmias. I'd just taken over his care when he collapsed and lost consciousness.'

She didn't want to tell the doctor her job, but the heart monitor seemed to show ventricular fibrillation, an abnormal rhythm where the heart's ventricles quivered in an irregular and uncoordinated manner. Other staff arrived, bodies jostling in the cramped space around the bed. Emergencies like this prompted a kind of controlled, co-ordinated chaos that ensured there were enough hands on board to do everything they could to revive their patient.

Clara focussed on timing the cardiac compressions, willing Mr Engman to respond. But her stomach tightened with fear, given his frail condition and multiple comorbidities.

'Looks like ventricular fibrillation,' a male voice said from behind Clara, confirming her diagnosis.

She was too focussed on the CPR to wonder where she'd heard the vaguely familiar voice before.

'Check for a pulse, please,' the commanding voice ordered.

There was a pause while they checked if Mr Engman's heart had spontaneously restarted. Clara caught her breath, looking up at the man running the arrest protocol.

She froze, her jaw dropping.

It was *him*—from last night—the naked VIP. The man with the body of a Greek god and haunted eyes. And he was looking at her without a trace of surprise, as if he'd expected their paths to cross.

Last night, after they'd kissed as if competing for the Olympic gold medal in kissing, Clara had met others from the team of palace nursing staff who cared for Prince Henrik, praying she'd never need to see her sexy but confusing stranger again.

Except there he was—a sexy mountain-man in scrubs.

Clara snatched her gaze away from his, fury and humiliation turning her stomach. While she'd been high from the kiss and begging for her job, he'd secretively held on to some pretty pertinent information. So this was the *business* he'd vaguely referred to. He was a *doctor*. Why hadn't he just come out and said that last night? She'd assumed he was a diplomat or a visiting ambassador, and he'd said nothing to the contrary. He'd commented on her uniform but had failed to declare that they worked in the same field. She'd even told him she had a second job at a nearby hospital, just before he'd lured her with his vulnerable stare and his talk of scars into that disastrous kiss which might have cost her a lucrative and prestigious job at the palace.

'No pulse,' Naked VIP said. 'Are you okay to continue compressions, Nurse Lund?'

Mortified that she'd lusted after and kissed someone so apparently shifty, Clara nodded and restarted the chest compressions. This was why she couldn't trust men. The last time she'd been intimate with a guy, he'd slept with her and then avoided her. Ever since, she'd resolutely refused to give anyone the power to hurt and humiliate her. Until last night...

She should have known better. After all, she'd learned to rely only on herself after her father, the one man who should have offered unconditional emotional and financial support, had repeatedly let her down. Growing up, she'd never known from one day to the next if Lars would come through the door at the end of the day, if the bills she knew worried her hardworking mother would be paid or if her father's latest dodgy deal would topple, plunging the entire family into a deeper pit of debt and despair.

One of Clara's nurse colleagues stuck gel pads to Mr Engman's chest and Naked VIP—she really needed to discover his name—positioned the defibrillator paddles in place.

'Stand clear. Defibrillating—two hundred joules,' he said, delivering the shock to the man's failing heart in line with the Advanced Cardiac Life Support protocol.

Clara couldn't bear to look at him. He looked far too gorgeous in the hospital's navy-blue scrubs, and being lured by his irrelevant good looks was how she'd found herself in this embarrassing situation in the first place.

'Nothing,' her stranger said, watching the erratic trace on the cardiac monitor.

'It's been three minutes,' Clara told him, resuming the chest compressions, glad to have an excuse to look away from his annoyingly riveting lips.

He nodded, taking a vial of adrenaline from the trolley and administering it intravenously in an attempt to normalise the heart's rhythm.

Why had she kissed him? She'd allowed him to get under her skin, weakened by desire stronger than anything she'd ever known. Flirting with him had felt carefree, whereas growing up with her unreliable father and having to care for her mother had given Clara an over-inflated sense of responsibility. They'd talked about scars and he'd seemed momentarily lost, a feeling she'd understood well as a bewildered teenager.

Until that unexpected interlude in the palace's guest suite, she hadn't realised that Lars Lund's selfish actions meant that she'd missed out on a wild and misspent youth. But with *him*, a sexy, naked stranger, she'd felt young and vibrantly alive.

She'd have to stop thinking of him naked. It was foolish to think about him in any state given that he was just another man she couldn't trust.

'Pause please,' the man in question said. All eyes settled on the heart monitor, every member of staff awaiting Naked VIP's next instruction with bated breath.

'He's still in VF,' he said. 'Stand clear—defibrillating again.'

With the second shock delivered, Mr Engman's heart stuttered back into sinus rhythm, the patient breathing again of his own accord. There was a collective sigh of relief. Clara sagged, her head woozy from the physical exertion and the adrenaline rush.

'Okay, we'll be moving Mr Engman around to ICU,' her midnight mystery man said. 'Nurse Lund, can you please call Mr Engman's next of kin?'

'Of course.' Clara nodded and placed a high-flow oxygen

mask on their still groggy patient. This necessitated stepping closer to *Dr* Naked VIP.

Big mistake. He smelled delicious, reminding her of how it had felt to be held in those strong arms last night: safe, protected, desired.

The wild desperation of that kiss—his big body engulfing hers, each of their lips chasing the other's, demanding and sensual—had surely ruined her for all future kisses. For a second, before she'd pushed him away, Clara hadn't been able to come up with a single reason she shouldn't sleep with him right there and then.

Swallowing hard, Clara fought off visions of him naked and proud, a spectacular specimen of manhood. The magnificence of his manhood was of no consequence whatsoever. And, more importantly, Clara wasn't interested in kissing, naked or otherwise. His deception made her realise just how out of her depth she was when it came to relationships.

She reattached an electrode that had come loose during CPR to Mr Engman's chest. The mystery doctor drew some blood from the patient's arm, thrusting the vials at the registrar.

'Check his cardiac enzymes and do an ECG, please. We need to exclude a myocardial infarction or cardiomyopathy.'

'I can do the ECG, if you want,' Clara said to the harassed-looking registrar, who gave a grateful nod and hurried away to order the blood work, leaving Clara alone with the patient and *him*.

An awkward silence descended.

Clara felt his observation like sun on her face as she tucked in the blanket on Mr Engman's bed. The patient was obliviously out of it, but this wasn't the time or the place for a personal conversation.

She looked up, their stares locking. 'Any other tests you'd like, *doctor*?'

She emphasised his title, showing him, and more importantly herself, that whatever had happened during last night's moment of insanity wouldn't be happening again. She couldn't trust one glorious hair on his devious head.

An image of Alma Lund, weary, sick and scared, flashed behind her eyes. Her mother had been through so much, and had always worked hard to provide a stable and comfortable home for Clara and her younger sister Freja, latterly with no help from her husband.

Clara wanted to slap herself; she knew better than to risk anything for a man, especially the income that kept them in their family home.

'No thank you, Nurse Lund.' Curiosity flickered over his expression, his blue eyes impressed and carrying the same hint of vulnerability that, last night, had made her lose her mind.

Well, in the cold light of day, her head was back in charge. She didn't need his admiration. She didn't need to know his name. She didn't need him at all, not even for phenomenal naked kissing. What she needed were her two jobs, her peace of mind and her self-reliance.

'We need to talk,' he said, pausing at the gap in the curtains around Mr Engman's bed.

'Didn't we have that opportunity last night?' she shot back, feeling decidedly uncharitable, given that she'd allowed herself to be duped by a charming smile, some witty repartee and a hot body.

'Last night, I was…distracted,' he admitted, pressing his lips together grimly as he continued to stare.

And just like that Clara's body returned to the scene of the crime—her pulse going crazy, her blood so hot she must surely have given off steam and the taste of him fresh on her lips.

A wave of fear and foolishness whipped through her chest. Even now—with every reason in the world not to; when last night's rash and unprecedented impulse to kiss a fellow lost soul might have cost her the job at the palace; when he held all of the power—she craved another kiss.

'Well, today I have my head screwed on correctly,' she said, willing it to be true.

It was only when he'd finally exited the ward moments later that Clara could finally breathe easy. Whatever he had to say, whatever his real name and his reasons for being secretive, he was just another man showing her the only person she could truly rely on was herself.

CHAPTER FOUR

LATER THAT MORNING, Andreas waited outside the acute medical ward for Clara Lund to emerge. She pushed through the doors and headed for the lifts, an assault to every one of his heightened senses. Today's uniform was navy, the fitted cut reminding Andreas how it had felt to have that insanely gorgeous body pressed against him last night while their tongues had duelled for dominance of their kiss.

He approached, his heart knocking at his ribs at the sight of her hair pulled back into a tight bun, leaving her slender neck exposed. Heaven help him; even now, when he had a whole heap of explaining to do, he wanted to remove the clips and tunnel his hands in all of that silkiness as he kissed her again and again until her eyes glazed with arousal once more.

'Clara,' he said, intercepting her outside the lift. 'Is now a good time to talk?'

If she remained ignorant of his identity after their reunion over this morning's crash call, it was time he filled in the blanks.

She glanced up, her expression carefully neutral. 'I'm on my lunch break, doctor.'

Her voice was deservedly dismissive; he missed her playfulness. 'I appreciate that,' he said, regretting that he hadn't warned her about them working at the same hospital the moment he'd discovered the fact from palace security last night after she'd left. 'But what I have to say won't take long. I'll accompany you to the canteen. It will give me a chance to explain a few things.'

'Like how you're a doctor, not a diplomat?' Suspicion narrowed her eyes. 'I've already figured that out all by myself, thanks. The scrubs and white coat kind of give it away.'

She jabbed at the already lit up call button, as if desperate to escape.

Andreas winced with remorse but he was so glad to see her feisty side. Her anger was better than her indifference.

'It's…complicated,' he said, wishing he'd explained himself last night, in private.

Technically a prince *was* a diplomat, a representative of the nation he served.

'I'm kind of both, for the time being,' he added, frustrated by the thought that, given its way, Prince Henrik's office would have him abandon his career now and commit fully to royal duties. If he capitulated to the palace's demands, he would have to give up treating patients, give up his freedom to flirt with fascinating women like Clara and give up everything he'd known his entire adult life.

A dull throb of resentment tightened his chest. He loved his job and had worked hard for his career. He was good at being a doctor. Being back in Varborg meant readjusting to the demands of his two personas: Andreas the man, free to do what he liked, and Andreas the prince.

'Great,' she scoffed, shaking her head with disbelief. 'That's cleared everything up.'

Andreas smiled to himself, his spirits already roused by a moment of her company. He had no idea if she was still upset by the kiss or because he'd concealed his profession, and he really had no time for complications of the fiery, blue-eyed variety. Except, the part of him that was just a man demanded that, for this particular woman, he *make* time.

'I know I should have mentioned that I'm a doctor last night,' he said as the lift arrived and the doors opened. 'I've just started a locum geriatrician position here.'

'Yes, you should.' She stepped inside. 'But, now that you've explained, I'll wish you a good day, doctor.'

Ducking inside the lift before the doors closed, Andreas continued, 'Listen, Clara, now that we're alone, I want to apologise again for last night.'

'Oh?' Completely unfazed, she glanced down her pert little nose at him, impressive given their height difference. It made him think of the Swedish term of endearment *sötnos*, the literal translation of which was 'sweet nose'.

'Don't worry.' She huffed, stabbing once more at the second-floor button as if her impatience alone could make the lift ascend faster. '*I* regret it too.'

She was so desperate to get away from him now.

Andreas inched closer and rested his gaze on that kissable mouth, now pinched with irritation. 'Oh, I don't regret the kissing for one second, *sötnos*.'

Alone with her in this confined space, there was no avoiding her bewitching scent or the erotic memories blasting him from all angles.

'I'm not your sweetie,' she snapped, flinging the endearment back in his face as if it were poison.

But her pupils dilated, her pulse flickered in her neck and her eyes dipped to his mouth every few seconds as if she too could remember every steamy detail of the night before.

'You might regret it now,' he taunted, 'But last night you enjoyed kissing me. I was there. I felt your body against mine, your fingers tugging at my hair…heard your sexy little whimpers.'

They had unfinished business.

'Maybe I did,' she admitted, planting her hands on her hips and leaning closer. 'But so did *you*.'

Andreas held up his hands in surrender. 'You'll get no argument from me. I wanted to kiss you the minute you laughed at me for hurling my leg.'

She huffed again, frustrated. 'But I didn't enjoy it enough to lose my job over or do it again.'

She was breathless now, her eyes ablaze with challenge and something else—something wild, reckless and needy that helped him to see the last lie for what it was.

But enough games; she might want nothing more to do with him when he told her his other secret. Being a public figure came with complications that some people couldn't tolerate.

'And *that's* why I'm apologising,' he said, turning serious as guilt at his abuse of power sent chills down his spine. 'That you felt your job was at risk is unforgivable. I would never allow you to face repercussions when the kiss was fully my responsibility.'

Now he had her attention. She blinked, as if she was momentarily confused, then her stare hardened.

'Well, I hope you don't expect me to be grateful.' Her lip curled in distaste. 'Just because I've seen the goods…' her stare dipped to his groin '…doesn't mean I'm interested in making a purchase.'

When their eyes met again, he unleashed a victorious grin. If only she'd resisted checking him out last night when his towel had slipped, he might believe her now.

'I'd rather be homeless,' she continued, her colour high, her voice breathy. 'So, if you think I somehow owe you for your discretion, you can think again.'

Adrenaline rushed his system, urgent and fiery, compelling him to act. 'Exactly what kind of man do you think I am?' he asked, his voice deceptively calm despite the accusations she was hurling his way.

She obviously didn't trust him, but did she truly think him capable of blackmailing her into sex?

'I don't know you.' She raised her chin in defiance. 'So far, you've proved yourself utterly untrustworthy. You had a perfect opportunity to tell me you were a doctor last night, but you didn't. Even now when you've *come to explain*—' she made finger quotes '—you're being vague. Maybe you enjoyed misleading me. Maybe you're used to getting your own way and manipulating people. Maybe you expected a whole lot more than a kiss.'

At her goading, all his good intentions to make amends and come clean evaporated. If only she knew what he'd wanted in the moment when their tongues had been duelling, her luscious body restless against his, craving more. And, for all her denial, their undeniable magnetism was generating enough sparks to set the lift alight.

But maybe he'd been wrong about her; maybe he couldn't be the real Andreas with her after all.

'You're right—you *don't* know me,' he said, catching the sound of her sharply inhaled breath as his stare raked her features, from the icy chips in her irises to the plump fullness of those lovely lips. 'So let me enlighten you. I don't need to bribe or manipulate women into my bed. They come eagerly and leave satisfied.'

His heartbeat raced, thick arousal boiling in his belly.

'Oh, I bet they do.' She snorted in disgust. 'Well, *I* have no intention of being one of those women.'

But she was panting hard and had stepped up close, raising her face to his so one mutual move would send them back into each other's arms.

'Are you sure about that, *sötnos*?' he asked lazily. 'Because you're looking at me like I'm the last cookie in the jar again.'

But he needed to master their chemistry, and fast. With her two jobs, she'd be everywhere he looked. Just as she knew nothing about him, he knew little about her beyond her education and employment history. Nothing about the things that counted: her integrity, her moral compass, her loyalty.

His public position necessitated discretion in the people he invited into his life, even casually. And, while it was perfectly acceptable for hospital staff to fraternise, he still hadn't explained the small detail of his royal life. Would she treat him differently when she knew that he was Varborg's heir that should never have been?

Just then, while they faced each other, eyes locked in challenge, the lift arrived on the staff-only floor.

The doors slid open, breaking the sexually charged impasse.

Andreas stepped back, breathing through the wild thudding of his heart. How had the conversation veered in a completely tangential direction from the one he'd planned? What was it about this woman that left him struggling to walk away? And what had caused her distrust and general cynicism towards men, when it was obvious to anyone with eyes how hot they were for each other?

Waiting outside the lift slightly out of breath, as if he'd taken the stairs at full pelt, was Andreas's bodyguard, Nils.

'Your Highness, there's been a security breach in the emergency department.' Nils flicked a brief look at Clara who, as a staff member both at Nordic Care and at the palace, would be well known to the security team that monitored Andreas's every move. 'You need to come with me now, sir.'

Defeat rumbled in Andreas's chest. He winced as he took in Clara's stunned confusion.

'Who's this?' she asked, her jaw dropping. 'And what did he just call you?'

She'd made it perfectly clear today that she had little trust for him, and now he'd missed the opportunity to have her hear the news from him direct.

'Give me a moment,' Andreas instructed Nils, who dutifully stepped aside out of earshot.

Andreas turned to Clara, his control of the situation now tugged like a rug from under his feet. If she'd wanted nothing more to do with him when she'd thought he was just a man who'd failed to declare his profession, his royal baggage, the ultimate complication, would likely be the final straw. It shouldn't matter. He'd come back to Varborg for family reasons, not for fun. Except that addictive lure of being just himself with this woman was hard to fight.

Taking Clara's elbow, he led her into an alcove beside the lifts. 'This is why I wanted to speak with you. I intended to explain my…heritage, my role at the palace…but then we got side-tracked again.'

He dropped his hand, instantly missing the feel of her silky skin beneath his fingertips, more off-kilter than ever with her this close physically, while emotionally he could literally see her slipping further away.

As if she'd finally pieced the jigsaw together, her hand covered her mouth, horrified. 'This isn't a joke. You're really a prince…?'

'I'm afraid so.'

What he wouldn't give to be just a doctor in that moment, to have her look at him the way she had last night, right before that kiss. He could escape for ever in eyes like hers. But escape wasn't an option.

'I thought you were familiar… But you're a doctor,' she said, clearly trying to make sense of the scattered pieces of information, the panicked tone of her voice telling him all he needed to know about her current regrets. 'You were staying in the guest wing.'

Andreas sighed, resigned. 'I refused to occupy the suite prepared for me in the family wing.' He swallowed, forcing himself to continue. 'It once belonged to my brother.'

Andreas had a hard enough time with his grief, and unfavourably comparing himself to Oscar, without occupying his rooms.

'And I've grown used to sparse but comfortable doctor's digs at hospitals,' he finished, braced for her transformation as reality sunk in.

Last night, when she'd blasted into his predictable, privileged life like a tornado—and again this morning, while they'd worked together to treat their patient—he'd foolishly clung to the hope of something real and unguarded with this exceptional woman he couldn't seem to forget.

But, now that she knew the truth, he would no longer be just Andreas the man and doctor, in her eyes. He would be something else—something two-dimensional, a caricature.

'You let me believe you were a nobody...' She scowled and shook her head, as if dazed. 'I kissed a prince...?'

She might as well have said she'd kissed a frog for all the contempt with which she spoke his title.

'Oh, don't worry.' Desire heated his blood as he stepped closer and watched her eyes widen, her breath catch and arousal flush her skin. 'Prince or not, I remember every second of our kiss and, what's more, so do you.'

'I do...' She blinked up at him, clearly stunned into an honest admission. 'But I'm sorry—it won't happen again.'

Hot, sharp jealousy sliced through him. 'So you were willing to flirt with me and kiss me when you assumed me to be a guest of the royal family but, now you know I'm Prince Henrik's son, you want nothing more to do with me—is that it?'

Futility stiffened his muscles. Part of him, the same part that refused to give up his career until he had no choice, refused to accept that the fantasy of this woman was over. He wanted to remind her of the inferno they'd generated when they'd been in each other's arms, him naked and her wild for him.

'I...' Her mortified stare darted to Nils. 'Can't we just forget it happened?' she snapped.

Andreas raised his brows dubiously. 'We could try and forget, if that's what you want.'

Ever since Oscar's death, what Andreas wanted, be it his medical career or the woman who now seemed horrified by his true identity, hadn't been his choice to make. And, when it came to this woman and the kind of chemistry they shared, forgetting the way she'd looked at him with heat and desire would be an uphill challenge.

But he would have to find a way to work alongside her until it was time for him to hang up his stethoscope for good.

Sensing Nils' urgency, he tilted his head with regret, his duty to his family tugging him away.

'Either way, we'll need to talk about the kissing some other time,' he said. 'I must go.'

Taking one last look at her, he took out his frustration on the stairs as he headed for the armoured vehicle awaiting him outside.

CHAPTER FIVE

Two days later, Clara returned to the palace for her next night shift, her stomach twisted into knots of dread and humiliation. Half of her was desperate to avoid seeing Andreas again—*Prince* Andreas—the other half had no idea what she wanted, beyond wishing she could turn back time and never have met him in the first place. How dared he flirt with her twice, but keep such an important identity a secret?

Following the footman to Prince Henrik's private rooms, her face heated with the memory of how she'd snogged, ogled and then insulted the heir to the throne. She stifled a snort of disbelief. Her actions had been bad enough when she'd assumed Andreas was a hunky diplomat and then a doctor.

Now, she was so confused, because Andreas was right— she *did* recall every thrilling second of that kiss and she had no hope of forgetting. She might not trust him, but her body didn't seem to care that, for a woman like Clara, an ordinary nobody with financial woes and a notorious convicted conman for a father, he was the most ridiculously out-of-reach man in the universe.

She had such little experience with relationships, thanks to Lars and those lost teenage years and thanks to the guy who'd taken her virginity and then acted as if they were strangers. Her attraction to Andreas of all men was…laughable.

The only sensible course of action was to keep her distance.

No more lusting after him, no more bickering and no more reliving his look of defeat when he'd accused her of wanting nothing more to do with him.

Resolved, Clara waited while the footman tapped quietly on the door. She dragged in a shaky breath, preparing herself to finally meet her patient, Andreas's father. After signing her confidentiality agreement on the first night, she'd been given the prince's medical records.

The prognosis wasn't good. After a short battle with prostate cancer, Prince Henrik had recently been diagnosed with stage four disease and was currently undergoing a course of radiotherapy for painful bone metastases.

Clara's heart ached for the older man, and for Andreas. Having nursed her mother through breast cancer treatment a few years ago, she knew exactly what the family was going through—although Andreas had shown no obvious signs that he was even aware that his father's disease was terminal, beyond stating that he was both a doctor and a diplomat *for the time being*.

Had that cryptic reference been because he knew he would soon need to forgo his medical career and succeed his father? Compassion clenched her heart. She understood how it felt to be tugged in all directions. She'd just started her nursing degree when Alma Lund had been diagnosed. Clara had considered dropping out to care for her mother full time, but fortunately her mother wouldn't hear of it. At least Clara had been able to continue with her career, her independence invaluable, whereas Andreas would likely have no choice but to give up medicine. He couldn't rule Varborg *and* work at the hospital.

The door opened. Prince Henrik's private butler appeared and quietly ushered Clara inside.

'His majesty is uncomfortable tonight and cannot sleep,' the man she'd been informed was named Møller said, his face etched in concern. 'I believe his pain management requires addressing.'

Clara nodded, trying to shove her patient's son from her mind. But she couldn't seem to block out the vulnerability she'd seen in his eyes when he'd accused her of treating him differently because he'd grown up here, surrounded by wealth and privilege.

Why had that look of defeat in Andreas's eyes called to her on such a profound level? Was it just that, for all their differences, she could empathise with him both about his father's illness and the loss of his career? Or was the idea he might be torn between his two roles deeply unsettling? She shook her head, disgusted with herself. How did all roads lead back to Andreas?

She followed Møller's stiff gait through a series of ante rooms, her nerves growing with every step. But the prince was a patient like any other; all Clara needed to do was her job.

They arrived outside another door and the butler knocked, waiting to be admitted into what Clara soon saw was the prince's private sitting room.

The man sat in an arm chair before a sleek contemporary fireplace built into a marble surround. Clara approached and curtseyed, as she'd been taught, waiting for Prince Henrik to address her first.

'Your name is Clara?' he asked, his face pale, his eyes red with fatigue.

'Yes, Your Highness.'

She'd seen him a handful of times in the media. His head was on Varborg's stamps and coins. But in person it was the likeness to his virile, handsome son that made Clara's heart gallop with longing to see Andreas again.

Huh! Her resolve clearly meant nothing…

But how could she ignore the prince she'd kissed—the man to whom, for all her denials, she was obviously still drawn—

when his life was about to change irrevocably because his father was terminally ill?

'Can I help you, sir?' Clara stepped closer, urged by the butler, who then discreetly left the room.

'I'm in pain,' the prince said. 'My bones ache and this blasted thing isn't working.'

He indicated the syringe driver strapped to his arm, which had been prescribed to administer analgesia while he was undergoing treatment.

'Can I examine your arm, sir?' Empathy for the older man, a man from whom Andreas had inherited his grey-blue eyes, tugged at her heartstrings.

Varborg's ruler was beloved by the nation. For fifty years he'd ruled with diligence and dignity, despite his share of adversity—losing his wife when his sons had been teenagers and, more recently, his oldest son, Oscar. If only she'd done her homework on her patient's past sooner, she might have recognised Andreas.

Prince Henrik nodded and slipped his arm free of his blue velvet dressing gown. Focussed on her work, and not the tragic losses of Varborg's royal family, Clara peeled away the dressing from the needle site, finding an angry red patch of skin where the cannula had extravasated.

'I'm afraid it's slipped out.' She disposed of the cannula in the nearby sharps bin. 'I'll need to re-site the needle, if that's okay.'

'Of course, dear. I'm pretty much a pin cushion at this stage,' he said with a sad smile that gave his stare the same aching vulnerability she'd witnessed in Andreas. Did these two proud men know how similar they were?

Trying not to think about his deceptive son, Clara pulled on gloves and grabbed a fresh subcutaneous cannula, some antiseptic wipes and a new adhesive dressing.

'I hear you've met my son,' the prince said, watching her

with shrewd eyes that spoke of sharp intelligence and an ability to read people easily.

'I have. We work together at Nordic Care.' Clara willed herself not to blush.

While she held this prestigious position she couldn't expect to have any secrets. She only hoped that the prince was unaware of her late-night antics with his naked son.

In the days since she'd discovered Andreas's true identity, she'd scoured the Internet for any information she could find on Europe's most eligible and unusual prince. There'd been tales of his military career, his work as a doctor and photographs of his playboy antics—an immaculately dressed Andreas attending various glitzy functions accompanied by a string of beautiful society women. The latter had caused such searing jealousy, she'd had to slam closed her laptop in disgust.

'Ah, yes, the day job...' Prince Henrik sighed and closed his eyes as Clara cleaned a patch of skin on his arm with the antiseptic wipes. 'Tell me, is he a good doctor?'

'Yes,' she said simply, recalling the way they'd worked together to revive Mr Engman. 'He's very well respected. A favourite with the patients, I'm told.' Many of whom had volunteered to Clara what a compassionate and caring man they found the heir to the throne; how natural and grounded he appeared to his patients, treating them with empathy and respect.

But why was the prince asking *her*, the palace's newest member of staff? Surely he and Andreas spoke about his work?

'Just a small scratch now, sir,' she said, burning up with questions about their relationship she would never dare to ask. At Prince Henrik's silent nod, Clara inserted the subcutaneous needle just beneath the skin, securing it with the dressing. Then she reattached the syringe driver and adjusted the dose of pain killers.

She shouldn't care what kind of relationship Andreas had with his dying father *or* whom he dated. He was handsome, intelligent and a *prince*: of course he was a catch for any woman willing to forgo her independence and put *his* life first.

Intense chemistry or not, that woman wasn't Clara.

For all her father's faults, Alma had loved Lars Lund. Young Clara had loved him too, craving his attention. But, where her mother had forgiven him countless times for his erratic employment history and excused his unreliability, teenaged Clara had grown more and more wary with each disappointment. She'd seen the fallout and had witnessed Alma struggling to put on a brave face when Lars had lost yet another job, or pretend all was well when the electricity had been cut off. Clara had been the one taking care of Freja after school while Alma had worked longer hours. She'd understood that her parents' marriage was unequal; that loving the wrong man, having his children, had left Alma vulnerable.

Even after her father had left for good to pursue his dubious, get-rich-quick schemes, the final one sending him to prison, he'd burdened the family with deeper debt. It wasn't until after his death that Clara's mother had discovered he'd re-mortgaged the house.

'We don't get on terribly well, my son and I,' Prince Henrik said, taking her by surprise.

He opened his shrewd eyes and Clara froze, uncertain how to reply. But her curiosity for Andreas went wild. The more she learned about the man behind the headlines, the harder it was to ignore him the way she wanted to.

'He resents me, you see,' the older man said, as if to himself, his stare far away. 'I've reminded him of his birth right and his responsibilities to the crown.'

Without comment, Clara silently disposed of her gloves.

She had no idea how Andreas felt about anything, his relationship with his father and his crown prince duties included. They were virtual strangers.

She understood complex relationships, having experienced

years of rejection and disappointment with her own untrustworthy father. But, whereas Lars had passed away while serving his sentence for fraud before Clara had had a chance to face him with some home truths, at least *this* father and son still had time to air their grievances and reconcile their differences.

But not much time.

'Are you feeling more comfortable now, sir?' Clara stooped at the prince's side, adjusting the blanket across his knees. His eyes had fallen closed once more, the tension around his mouth easing as the pain medication began to work.

'I gave him too much freedom when he was younger, you see...' he continued. 'I allowed the boy to choose a career for himself, when perhaps I should have had greater expectations of him as a prince.'

Clara's skin prickled with discomfort, as if she were eavesdropping. Patients voiced all sorts of things in their most vulnerable moments. Part of her wanted to leave the prince to his privacy but, if he wanted to talk as her patient, she would listen.

'I promised his mother before she died that I would allow the boys to have as normal a life as possible...' He was slurring now, obviously on the cusp of sleep. 'It wasn't always possible for Oscar, but with Andreas... I tried my best, but I missed their mother, so very much...'

Compassion squeezed Clara's heart. She blinked away the sting in her eyes, recalling the stark terror she'd experienced on more than one occasion when she imagined losing her mother. Prince Henrik was a man like any other. He was still grieving for his wife and wondering if he'd been a good enough father to his sons. Like many families, Varborg's first family had their issues, for all their power and privilege.

In desperation, Clara cast around for sight of the butler lurking in a doorway. Perhaps together they could encourage the prince back to bed. Spying a call button next to the prince's arm chair, Clara gave it the briefest of pushes, hoping it wouldn't sound in the room and wake the dozing man.

Within seconds, the butler appeared. Clara explained the issue with the syringe driver, keeping the man's privileged confessions to herself. But, as she made her way back to the staff sitting-room, her feet dragged, her heart heavy.

The more she learned about Andreas, the murkier the picture that emerged. Did he resent his father for calling him back to Varborg? Did he know the prince was terminally ill? That would surely devastate him; and how would he feel, having to give up his career as a doctor?

But the hardest question of all to answer was why she cared so much when she'd vowed to keep him at arm's length.

CHAPTER SIX

THE EMBOSSED AND gilded envelope had arrived the following day—an invitation to Prince Henrik's private Jubilee Banquet, an intimate celebration of his fifty years on the throne.

When the gown box had been delivered shortly afterwards,
she'd assumed that the formal wear was part of the clothing
allowance that came with her salary. She hadn't been able to
resist peeling back the layers of gossamer tissue paper and
trying on the most extravagant garment she'd ever handled...
just once.

And now, three days later, she was wearing the gown for
real—a black, lace beaded sheath that clung to her body and
flared at her feet, her heart beating into her throat with awe
as she was ushered inside an opulent banquet hall in the formal and ceremonial wing of the palace.

Clara swallowed, any ridiculous fantasy that she and Andreas might have anything in common, or that he needed *her*
concern, crushed into the plush carpet so thick she could have
been walking on a cloud.

This part of the winter residence was often open to the public, but tonight it glittered in celebration. The cold marble of the
columns and ornate cornices was warmed by the six enormous
chandeliers that hung from the ceiling, as well as a million
twinkling lights strung like a net of stars across the night sky.
To one side, row after row of banquet tables were precisely laid

with glittering crystal glassware, ornate gilded centrepieces and cascading fresh flower arrangements. A chamber orchestra occupied a raised dais, where guests danced to ballroom versions of popular Scandinavian folk songs.

Utterly overwhelmed, Clara slipped discreetly around the edge of the room, hoping to blend into the gold-edged midnight-blue drapes that lined the walls, stretching from the floor to the vaulted ceiling.

She scanned the room, casually searching out her nursing colleagues among the Varborg elite. Her pulse fluttered frantically, her body hopeful, her mind full of dread.

Was *he* there—Prince Andreas?

She hadn't seen him since the day she'd discovered his identity. That had left plenty of time to promise that, next time they met, she would keep things strictly professional and properly deferential.

She'd just spied her nursing colleagues on the other side of the dance floor when her stare landed on the hottest man in any room.

Andreas.

She froze. Her mouth dried. She couldn't look away as euphoria spiked her blood. How had she ever once mistaken him for an ordinary man? He'd been utterly spectacular naked, seriously sexy in his hospital scrubs but, dressed in his formal attire, he looked every inch an untouchable heartthrob prince.

Desire, thick, hot and confusing, pounded through her veins.

An impressive row of medals adorned the lapel of his dark tailcoat, the breast pocket bearing the Cronstedt royal coat of arms. His crisp white dress-shirt and waistcoat contrasted with the midnight-blue sash worn across his broad chest, the colour complementing his mesmerising eyes. Nearly every other man there was clean-shaven but, unlike them, he wore his beard, neatly trimmed short, and his golden hair swept back from his aristocratic face, just an inch too long so the ends curled above his collar.

A true, unapologetic Viking.

Horribly turned on, Clara sank deeper into the shadows. Why did her treacherous body hate her so much, when her head had already made all the decisions? She gripped the folds of velvet, wishing she could disappear into the curtains so she wouldn't have to witness him sharing that dazzling smile of his with the stunning and elegant society women who, unlike Clara, were a part of his world.

Moving on from one conversation, Andreas addressed the mountain of a man at his side—Nils, the bodyguard from the hospital—before conversing with a regal blonde wearing a tiara made of diamonds that Clara would bet a year's salary were real.

Clara's skin prickled with humiliation. Here, in Andreas's world, she was so utterly and obviously out of her depth, an imposter in a hired gown.

Nils spoke into a discreet microphone attached to the earpiece he was wearing, his stare landing on Clara across the vast room, as if he'd just been informed of her precise location.

Clara froze. Would she be told to leave in front of all these important people? In front of *him*? Perhaps it wasn't too late to duck out before Andreas saw her. She should never have come. She couldn't face him. He would surely see through her disguise to the scared little girl inside who'd been abandoned by one parent and forced to grow up fast to help care for the other. What would Crown Prince Andreas Cronstedt need with a woman like that when he could kiss any woman he chose?

The bodyguard whispered to Andreas. With a charming smile, Andreas concluded his conversation with a portly man in his sixties, turned and stared straight at Clara.

A soft gasp left her dry throat.

He'd asked Nils about *her*; the room was obviously awash with his spies.

From so far away, she couldn't read his expression. Was he annoyed to see her there after their childish squabble in the lift? What on earth did it matter who regretted the kiss, who'd enjoyed it, who recalled every detail when it was unlikely ever to happen again?

Desperately clinging to the indifference she'd spent days perfecting, Clara raised her chin and gripped her clutch, which contained her embossed invitation, like a shield.

Without taking his eyes off hers for one second, Andreas marched her way.

Her palms began to sweat.

His long strides sliced through the parting crowd.

Her ears buzzed with tinnitus.

Still he descended, full of purpose and so achingly beautiful, looking at him stung Clara's eyes.

People had started to notice his determined trajectory. Clara grew hot under their curious stares. Whispers began to spread from person to person like a highly contagious virus. Clara's pulse throbbed frantically in her fingertips and toes. Her head grew light from lack of oxygen. She gulped down a few breaths, trying to look away from his intense eye contact, but she couldn't make her body obey her commands. Was this what a stroke felt like? She could only stand and wait for him to arrive, her only armour her determination to stay immune to his overwhelming magnetism.

'You made it,' he said with a small, restrained smile.

He seemed taller and broader in his exquisitely tailored attire, every inch the regal, self-assured leader he was born to be.

Ignoring his devastating hotness, Clara lowered her gaze. 'Your Royal Highness.'

Her voice croaked as she bent her knees in the deep curtsey she'd been practising in her heels and gown all afternoon.

All around them, people were staring, likely thinking who exactly could have inspired Prince Andreas's inexhaustible pursuit across a room full of important people who, like him, belonged there.

When she looked up, Andreas's mouth wore a tight smile and his eyes were grey and stormy with what looked like fury.

'Please *never* do that again,' he said, his voice low for her ears only.

Clara blinked up at him, a barrage of questions and comments dying on her tongue. How did he expect her to act? She hadn't been trained on the proper etiquette for addressing a prince you'd kissed, seen naked and then tried to ignore. But there was no time to wonder what social *faux pas* she'd made.

He held out his hand. 'Ms Lund, would you do me the honour of a dance?'

Clara quailed inside, dread freezing her diamanté-clad feet to the lush carpet. She had no idea how to dance to this kind of music. She'd make a fool of herself and, worse, a fool of him in a room full of his snobby, aristocratic peers.

She opened her mouth, praying that it wouldn't be considered an act of high treason to politely refuse a crown prince a dance, when Andreas spoke again.

'Before you decline...' he angled his head closer '...shall I remind you that we agreed to talk about a certain, very pressing matter?'

He was so calm, so composed, they might have been discussing the weather. But surely they couldn't settle their unfinished business, *the kissing*, in front of all these people?

Clara's entire body burned hot, her skin hyper-sensitised under his observation. She could barely stand upright just thinking about the heat, fizz and excitement of that kiss. Just looking at him all dressed up made that reckless, carefree part of her that felt alive every time she talked to him ache to do it again.

'Your Royal Highness,' she said, placing her hand in his, 'I merely hoped to spare you the public spectacle of me treading on your toes. I have no idea how to dance like this.'

'I'll lead you,' he said, self-assured, smiling at several of the gawking crowd. 'Just keep your eyes on mine.'

The onlookers parted for them as, unconcerned, Andreas led her to the dance floor. He executed a short bow, gripped her hand and placed his other hand between her shoulder blades. 'Allow me to worry what your feet are doing.'

'That's easy for you to say,' Clara muttered, her body melting under his touch. 'But I much prefer to rely on my own two feet.'

Before she could make further complaints, he swept her along into the dancing crowd. Clara gasped, the thrill of once more being this close to him rendering her speechless. The warmth of his body seeped into her palm where it rested on his shoulder. The spicy scent of his cologne, delicious notes of pine forest and wood smoke, sent her head swimming back to fantasy land. The all-consuming focus of his eye contact made her forget that she was being watched by hundreds of onlookers as he effortlessly spun her in time to the music, his strong arms and skilled dance moves preventing her from taking a wrong step.

She laughed, the thrilling abandon of dancing with so expert a partner suppressing her reservations and insecurities. She might as well have been flying. Andreas grinned at her delight, spinning her a little faster so the hem of her dress fanned out, holding her a little closer so she was forced to surrender her body and dignity to him entirely, the way she'd surrendered to that kiss.

Alive once more, all she could do was smile. But this wasn't reality. Reality was her bank balance; the shameful online headlines bearing her family name; the sting of humiliation she'd experienced outside the hospital lift, when she'd realised with a sinking stomach that, no matter what her body craved, him and her could never be.

As the tempo of the music slowed, she felt Andreas's body stiffen a little, as if he was aware of the change in her mood.

'I want to apologise for rushing off that day at the hospital. I'm afraid that, no matter how much I value my work, I must put my family first.'

Clara gave a small sharp shake of her head, stunned by the regret in his voice, the implication that Prince Henrik was right—their relationship was strained. 'There's no need to apologise, Your Royal Highness. I'm embarrassed that I didn't know you straight away when you're so...famous.'

His fingers flexed against her bare back, or she might have imagined it, because he looked perfectly polite, no hint of the heat from that first night.

But what did she expect—that she, ordinary Clara Lund, was special? Maybe he wanted to explain that, given his wild and notorious past, he kissed everyone he met that way...

'You accused me of manipulation.' His jaw clenched. 'But the truth is, when you didn't recognise me, I found the anonymity liberating. You fascinated me, with your hair primly pinned back but with your bold and spunky attitude on display.'

Clara exhaled a sound of disbelief as shameful prickles of heat danced over her skin. 'I'm outspoken. The way I spoke to you must be an act of treason. Not to mention the...kissing.' She hissed the last word. 'Two hundred years ago I'd have probably been imprisoned or sent to the guillotine.'

He smiled, a glimmer of playfulness in his eyes that unfurled something deep inside her—that longing to be the young woman she was in years. Clara wished they were at work, where at least she could pretend they were equals, but here, among the glitz and glamour, the titles and ceremony, it was obvious that they had nothing in common.

'You weren't outspoken, you were honest. That hardly ever

happens to me. I've never met a woman like you.' He sobered. 'In truth, I was struggling to be back here that night. Just for a few moments, I wanted to just be myself with you. Selfish, I know.'

Why was he struggling to be home? Was it the prince's diagnosis and his regrets over his career? And couldn't he be himself with everyone? Hadn't she felt the same? For a few moments in his company, she'd felt more vibrantly alive than she'd ever felt before.

'And I guarantee that, these days...' his lips twitched with amusement '...kissing a prince carries no such penalty.'

In spite of the confusing mix of desire and unease swirling inside her, Clara laughed. If only they were alone, they could have a candid conversation and get to know each other better. Discover if they had other things in common.

Ridiculous! He was a prince. They weren't on a date. He probably had official duties tonight, given that Prince Henrik was, as yet, nowhere to be seen. And she was out of her depth. Feeling foolish at how easily she'd been seduced to feel emotionally close to a man who was from another world, Clara changed the subject.

'You look very...regal. Did you earn all those medals?'

'Yes,' he stated simply, obviously reluctant to talk about his military service. 'You look beautiful in that dress,' he said instead. 'I knew it would suit you.'

Clara stiffened, her confusion growing. '*You* picked out this dress?'

He gave a half-shrug, as if the gesture was no big deal.

'Why?' Something spiky and hard settled in her stomach. She was so naïve.

'I thought you'd like it.' A frown tugged down his beautiful mouth. 'Consider it a gift—an apology for making you feel that your job here was compromised by my actions.'

Clara's throat burned with humiliation. Of course he

wouldn't understand the symbolism of what for him was a seemingly innocent gesture.

Seeing red, Clara hardened her stare. 'Well, then, I insist on paying you back.'

As if the dress was tainted, her skin began to chafe and itch underneath.

He maintained his bland smile but a muscle ticked in his jaw. 'That's not necessary.'

'It's necessary to *me*.' A flush crept up her neck. 'I don't like to be beholden to anyone. I pay my own way in the world.'

Chills rattled her bones. She shouldn't have come tonight. She didn't belong here, not like this: pretending to fit in, wearing a borrowed dress, playing Cinderella in his arms when any second now the clock would strike midnight and he'd see how implausible their flirtation was.

'Why so independent, *sötnos*?' He gripped her waist a little tighter, as if he could literally repair the damage he would never understand by holding onto her. 'I simply assumed you might find the gift welcome. After all, you work so hard.'

Shaking her head with disbelief, Clara forced her feet to remember that they were under her own control, not his. 'That's an easy thing for you to ask when you grew up here. But seeing as you appreciate my candour, Your Royal Highness, know this: I've been contributing to my family's income since I was sixteen and my father upped and left us with nothing but his debts, never to return.'

Stricken, Andreas appeared instantly contrite, but it was little comfort.

'I'm sorry,' he said, a flicker of panic in his stare. 'Please accept my apologies for the dress. It won't happen again.'

Appalled by the burn of irrational tears behind her eyes, Clara tried to remove her hand from his.

She *never* cried.

'I should have known,' she said, shaking her head when

he refused to relinquish his grip, the panic in his eyes now full-blown.

She wouldn't make a scene, but nor would she play his puppet, regardless of their audience.

'For a minute there,' she continued, 'I'd almost convinced myself that we were, in some ways, equals. That we had something important in common. But the cold hard reality is that I was fooling myself.'

His stare turned steely, the muscles of his clenched jaw standing out beneath his facial hair. 'We *are* equals. Two human beings drawn to each other.'

Clara scoffed at his naïvety.

'Are we?' She fought to keep her voice as calm and quiet as she could, given the humiliation pounding in her head. 'In that case, what's it to be? Repayment for the dress? Or do you prefer I return the garment? I can take it off right now, in fact.'

Indignant, she skidded her feet to a halt and reached for the side zip under her arm.

Andreas's eyes blazed with an inferno of heat.

'Don't you dare,' he growled, taking her arm.

With a benign smile on his face, he guided her from the dance floor and through an inconspicuous door tucked into the corner, manned by two liveried footmen.

Awash with shame for her outburst—and spitting mad that, for all her independence and distrust, she'd been naïve enough to fall under his spell out there on the dance floor—Clara accepted her fate. She'd done it now; he would kick her out and wash his hands of her.

And it would be for the best. She was so laughably out of her depth in his world. Their stark differences had only been highlighted by the extravagance of the stupidly beautiful dress that now felt like a prison straitjacket.

But, for one heady moment out there in his arms, as he'd twirled her round and round, nothing else had seemed to matter—not his title, or her family debts, or even the misguided attraction she just couldn't seem to fight. He'd been just a man, and she a woman.

Except when the dancing had stopped, and her feet were firmly back on the ground, reality had struck. They came from impossibly different worlds: his full of glitter and magic, and hers the real world.

CHAPTER SEVEN

LENGTHENING HIS STRIDE, Andreas ducked into the nearby Blue Room, his blood on fire. From the minute he'd spied Clara from across the ballroom, the sophisticated black lace gown he'd chosen hugging the curves of her sensational body like a glove, he'd been deafened by a roar of desire. As he'd crossed the endless-seeming distance between them, urgency had pounded through his head. He'd wanted to blindfold every other man present. Better still, he should have called off the banquet, sent everyone home and selfishly had her to himself.

Except she didn't want him…

The door closed behind them—no doubt Nils's doing, so he could stand sentry.

Clara tugged her hand from his. Reeling from the loss of her touch and the tightness gripping his insides like a fist, he scrubbed a hand through his hair.

'What are you trying to do to me?' His breathing turned harsh as he fought for the control that had seemed second nature to him until he'd met this woman. 'Threatening to take off that dress?'

As if of its own accord, his frantic stare traced her lush curves, the cascading lace no barrier to his vivid and debauched imagination about what delights lay underneath.

'You should have asked someone else to dance,' she

snapped, ignoring the reference to their chemistry. 'I told you I couldn't do it.'

'You did it just fine, until you stopped trusting me. And I wanted to dance with you, *sötnos*.'

He paced closer, catching the sparks of hurt in her eyes. 'This isn't about dancing or dresses,' he said, shame thickening his voice. 'I hurt you.'

She pressed her lovely lips together and hid her eyes from him by looking down.

'I'm sorry,' he said. 'I hate that I let you down over something that looks so beautiful. If I'd known how...insulting you would find the gesture, I never would have done it.'

Guilt punched him in the gut, its force no match for the arousal coiled in his belly because she was close, so close, her scent bewitching.

'All I seem to do is apologise.' He scrubbed a hand down his face. He'd crossed the line and been selfish and entitled. He should never have asked her to dance, because the minute he'd taken her in his arms he'd no longer been able to pretend that he had their chemistry under control. When she'd talked about removing the dress, vulnerable but defiant before him, he'd almost fallen to his knees.

But he needed to grapple back control. He didn't want to hurt her more than he had already. He didn't want to let her down the way she'd obviously been let down before by her father.

'It doesn't matter.' She looked down and Andreas wanted to punch something—preferably himself.

'It matters to *me*.' He paced away in frustration, spinning to face her once more. 'I got carried away. I thought we made a connection. But then you seemed disgusted by my title. I told myself I would leave you alone, but then I learned you'd been invited tonight. I saw that dress and imagined you in it and then you came, wearing it, looking stunning, the only person in the room I genuinely wanted to see.'

She frowned, confused.

'Why me?' she asked, as fearless as ever. 'When you had that entire room to choose from, every other woman more on your level than I will ever be, no matter how fancy you dress me up?'

She was right: they were from different backgrounds. She had her own demons—financial strains and trust issues he knew nothing about. By asking her to dance, by dragging her into the goldfish bowl of his life, he'd surely exposed her to the rife speculation that would follow—the last thing she deserved. He'd have to spend the remainder of the evening running damage limitation—playing the playboy prince of old, dancing with every single woman in the room in order to head off the gossips and society bloodhounds who always seemed to bay for his blood. Andreas the stand-in—never more so than tonight, when his father, the man they'd all assembled to celebrate, was indisposed with a bad headache.

His first public appearance for his father and he'd messed up. But, as long as he lived, he would never regret it fully. For a brief time, when she'd trusted him on the dance floor, he'd felt invincible with her in his arms.

'Because I'm selfish, okay?' Andreas winced, hating that he'd made her feel so small. 'The fact that you're different, that you don't seem to care about all of this—' he waved his arm to encompass the ornate room in which they stood, the vast banquet hall beyond, the very palace itself '—is what I like about you. I wanted you, grounding me the way you did that first night when you reminded me that—away from perceptions and duty to my family, away from the shoes of my dead brother that I must one day fill—sometimes I can just be myself: the real Andreas.'

Clara hesitated, her stare softening. 'And who is the real

Andreas? The compassionate doctor taking the frail hand of an elderly patient? Or is he the party prince in those pictures on the Internet, invited to all the best gatherings, usually with some glamorous woman on his arm?'

'I admit, I've been both in my time.' Fascinated by her thrilling jealousy, he stepped closer and watched her breathing speed up, caught the enticing waft of her perfume that almost made his eyes roll closed in ecstasy. 'Are you jealous, *sötnos*?'

His blood surged at her sense of possession. She might feel that they came from different worlds, but she couldn't conceal how she felt physically. She wanted him in return—man, doctor and prince.

'Not at all,' she bluffed, clearing her throat in a nervous gesture. 'I'm just disorientated, wondering what I'm doing here, how I should address you—or if I should even acknowledge you at all, given that we're from such starkly different worlds and clearly have *nothing* in common.'

'You can call me Andreas,' he said, ignoring the parts of her argument he deemed irrelevant as he focussed on her parted lips, slicked by some berry-coloured gloss he wanted more than anything to taste.

Oh, how he wanted to hear his name on her lips—preferably cried out in passion. But, now that she knew his true identity, would she give him her honest desire, as she had that first night? Or would she demure like a timid mouse simply because he'd been born into an historic family, something over which he'd had no control?

Clara licked her lips, as if aware of his observation and the direction of his thoughts. 'That hardly seems reverential enough, given the circumstances.'

Stepping closer, he drew her stare back to his, finding it full of her signature defiance. Triumph electrified his nerve endings at the resolute tilt of her chin. Clara was no mouse.

'That is exactly why I insist on it. When I'm with you, I'm

just me. *You* are the one person I can rely on to treat me with brutal honesty. Don't turn on me now, *sötnos*, when I need an ally within these walls more than ever.'

He caught her soft gasp of astonishment and watched as her pupils dilated and compassion replaced all that fire in her eyes.

'Why do you need an ally in your family home?' she asked in a confused whisper, voicing the one question designed to strip him bare of his layers of armour. '*You* belong here.'

Andreas swallowed and tugged at the hem of his waistcoat, a reminder that he at least looked the part he'd been born to play. Except he'd spent most of his adult life free to live another role, to forge his own path, to just be a man who belonged in Clara's world.

'I do,' he agreed, desperate to talk about anything other than his royal life with this woman he wanted so badly, he could taste it. 'But I wasn't born the heir, wasn't raised for the position. So you see there are many out there, perhaps my father included, who believe I'm not fit to follow him to the throne. That it should have been my elder brother Oscar standing here today, charming the crowds and dancing with the most beautiful woman in the room.'

As the ugly truth spilled free, he glanced away from her frowning face, jealousy a hot slash through his chest at the idea of Clara dancing with the brother he'd loved. Should he also spill at her feet his guilt and regrets over Oscar's death? His secret fear that those with no confidence in him were right because, as a doctor and brother, he'd failed Oscar so completely?

No; he wanted her too much to risk it.

'That's not true,' she whispered, horrified.

'Isn't it?' he asked. 'I'm the spare, don't forget. My father certainly made that clear while I was growing up.'

'Is that why you refused your brother's rooms—why you're still in the guest wing? Perhaps you should talk to your father about this. Perhaps you're wrong about his reasons and how he feels.'

She reached for his arm, bringing him back from a dark place with her touch. But it was too much; it caught him off-guard, the desire that was never far away since that first night a roar in his head.

'While I appreciate your directness, *sötnos*, and your suggestions, do we know each other well enough for such advice? Because I might be prompted to ask why you work two jobs when one is all anyone could expect, or why you insist on paying your father's debts.'

She flushed but held her ground. 'Helping out my family financially is *my* choice.'

'As is choosing to forge my own path rather than stepping into my dead brother's shoes. But we don't always get what we want, do we? Sometimes, we must be something others need us to be.'

Clara's eyes widened, as if his words resonated deeply.

'Still think we have little in common?' he asked while they faced each other at an impasse, equals with, he suspected, more similarities than they had differences. Except, unlike him, she was free to choose how to live her life. He'd long ago come to terms with his...mostly.

Sighing with defeat, Andreas again rubbed a hand down his face.

'I asked you to dance so I could clear the air,' he said, his hands itching to touch her once more. 'Except, yet again, I underestimated the impact of our chemistry.'

Her jaw dropped, the arousal shining in her eyes urging him to lay his cards on the table.

'Even here when I must be on show, play this role that feels...borrowed, it's inescapable.' That simmer of heat in his blood he felt around her boiled over. 'That day at Nordic

Care, you said we should forget our attraction. Do you still feel the same?'

'I'm certainly trying to forget it.' Colour flushed her chest and neck. 'But… I… I don't know.'

'Whereas I feel the opposite,' he admitted, a sting of disappointment in his throat. '*You* are all I can think about, even when my priority should be temporarily standing in for my father.'

Her eyes shot to his.

'I've shocked you with my own directness,' he continued, determined now to lay his feelings out. 'Would you prefer that I lie to you? That I conceal how much I want you? Deceive and manipulate you into my bed instead, as you once accused me?'

She shook her head with conviction, her stare bold on his. 'No. But—'

'Be honest with me, *sötnos*,' he urged. 'The way you've always been. Because, whatever our other differences, our bodies don't seem to care. In this—' he pointed between them, illustrating the sexual tension coiling between them like smoke '—we are absolute equals.'

She dragged in a ragged breath, as if resolved. 'I want you too.'

The sweet-sounding words left her in a rush.

'But I can't lose my job and it feels…dangerous.' Her breath came faster, her breasts rising and falling.

'I guarantee your job will be safe.' He stepped closer, taking her hand and placing it over the medals she'd admired on his chest to show his sincerity. 'You have my word—as a prince, as a Knight of Varborg and a string of other titles.'

She regarded him silently and thoughtfully for long seconds, her lip snagged under teeth. Then she rolled back her shoulders. 'No one can know.'

Andreas nodded solemnly, his pulse pounding with excitement at this negotiation of terms. 'I never again want to hurt you as I did tonight—I hate letting people down. So, tell me what you need for this to work.'

She tilted her face up so her breath brushed his lips. 'I'm not interested in relationships, so it can only be a physical thing,' she said, adding another condition of her own.

'Agreed.' Curiosity shoved a list of questions to the forefront of his mind as he inched closer, his body restless with desire. 'At present, I have more than enough to consider without... romantic complications.'

At some point in the future, he would need to address his marital state, settle down, find a wife, produce an heir and put the needs of the principality first. But for now he could focus on pleasure and freedom—focus on Clara.

'A fling, then,' he said. Satisfaction bloomed in his chest.

'A brief fling,' she countered, her eyes swimming with need as she stared up at him.

He nodded, already forming a plan to safeguard her privacy. He didn't want his public prominence to scare her off before they'd even begun.

'I have one final condition,' he said, tugging her hand so their bodies were almost touching. 'And this one is non-negotiable, I'm afraid.'

'Oh?' A playful glint shone in her eyes. 'How very bossy of you.'

Andreas smiled. As he had that first night, he reached for a strand of her hair and eased it behind her ear, allowing his fingertips slowly to trace the curve of her cheek and down to the tip of her earlobe, where a tiny pearl earring dangled.

She shuddered and need rumbled in his chest on a stifled groan.

He stared into her eyes and rested his hand on her waist, the very air in the room seeming to crackle and hiss with electricity.

'No more curtseys. No more "Your Royal Highness",' he

stated, his gaze falling to the soft excited pant of her breath over those gloss-slicked lips he wanted so badly to taste.

'It's only proper,' she said, one corner of her mouth tugged in a knowing and defiant smile. 'After all, I *am* one of your subjects.'

His fingers curled into the fabric of her dress, an animal-istic growl sounding in his head. 'Not when I'm inside you, making you come.'

Galvanised by her low moan, he hauled her close, crushing her to his chest. Their lips found the others in a rush of des-peration and mutual, almost palpable, relief as they kissed. Her curves moulded to his chest and hips in all the right places, the heat of her fanning the inferno in his veins, the scent of her a dizzying cloud that made time recede. Andreas cupped the back of her head, directing her mouth, their tongues meeting and surging wildly, so nothing else seemed to matter. There was just this moment: just a man and woman; just passion and need.

Her fingers twisted in his hair, tugging, greedy to have him where she wanted him. Andreas paced forward, pressing her against the back of a sofa, his mind and body consumed by her, as he'd been since that first meeting in the guest suite when she'd effortlessly blown him away. He fisted the fabric of her dress over her hip, hoisting the dress up high enough to slide his hand around one silky bare thigh.

'Andreas,' she moaned, just as he'd hoped, dropping her head back to expose her neck to his ravaging mouth.

The sound of his name on her lips was more rewarding than anything he'd imagined. Cupping one cheek of her backside, he lifted her, depositing her bottom on the edge of the furni-ture so he could slot himself between her parted thighs.

He grew hard between her legs as he ran his lips over her jaw, up to her earlobe and down the silky column of her neck, sucking in her scent, filling his senses with her taste, licking and nibbling her satin-like skin. He couldn't get enough. It was as if her skin was laced with some sort of potent aphrodisiac. He'd walk away smelling of her, the scent of her torturing him for the rest of the night.

Her hands were inside his waistcoat, her touch through his shirt hot like a brand. He kissed her again, his tongue in her mouth as she dipped her hands lower to cup his buttocks, drawing his hips to hers, massaging his arousal between their bodies so Andreas almost lost his mind. This was insane. He needed to stop. But his fingers swiped the lacy edge of her underwear over her backside and sanity fled.

'Andreas…please…' she whispered, her eyes closed and her head back so her throat was exposed to him, already pink from the scrape of his facial hair and ferocity of his desire.

Her beauty was a painful throb beneath his ribs. The marks he'd left on her skin called to the primitive part of his brain, the part acting on instinct alone. If she kept calling his name in that breathy voice, he feared what he'd do next. Indulging in one last kiss, he ripped his mouth from hers, his breathing wild and painful.

'Look at me, *sötnos*,' he demanded, sliding his fingers under the lace of her underwear to stroke the molten heat between her legs. 'Open your eyes.'

She obeyed, blinking up at him, her lips parted on a series of soft gasps as he stroked her over and over.

With his other hand, he reached for her wrist and pressed her palm over his erection, steely hard behind his fly.

'Tell me we're equals now, when I'm so hard for you it hurts and you're wet for me. Tell me. I need to hear you say it. I need to know you believe it. I don't want a puppet in my bed. I want you.'

She gripped his arm, her stare slumberous with arousal but alive with the sparks of fire that were pure Clara.

'We're equals,' she said on a ragged breath, dragging his mouth back to hers as her hips bucked against his hand.

'That's right, we are,' he murmured against her lips, against the wild kisses she snatched from him in between moans. Andreas kissed her back, the taste of triumph sweet and satisfying as he stroked her faster, sliding a finger inside her core.

'Except,' he said, rearing back to gaze into her eyes, 'I've never wanted anyone as much as I want you.'

His words seemed to tip her over the edge into bliss. She climaxed, shuddering in his arms as he kissed her through the spasms with slow thrusts of his tongue. When she was spent, she leaned her weight against him, her face buried against his neck while she caught her breath.

Andreas's heart thundered in his chest, his arm holding her tight. He slid his hand from between her legs and brushed down the hem of her dress, literally blocking out the sight of temptation. One glimpse of her naked thigh, a flash of black lace, and he might not make it back to the banquet where he was to give an after-dinner tribute to his father.

Just then, there was an insistent rap of knuckles on the door. Nils had been instructed to give him as much time as possible.

'Just a moment,' Andreas called, frustration a tight knot under his ribs.

Clara deserved more than a quick clandestine fumble. She deserved seduction and satin sheets, romance and adoration. Especially after the way he'd inadvertently hurt her over the dress. But his time with her was up. His absence at the banquet must have been noticed, and his official duties called.

'I have to get back,' he said, his hands reluctant to leave Clara's waist. He tilted up her chin and pressed a soft kiss to her lovely lips. 'I have people to schmooze, an after-dinner speech to give. Hopefully my father will be recovered from his headache and join us for the rest of the night.'

How had he completely blanked out the visiting dignitaries awaiting an audience with him as a stand-in for his father? With Clara in his arms, he'd forget his own name...

She nodded, stood and looked up at him. 'Of course. You should go.'

She was flushed from her orgasm, more beautiful than ever. She cast her eyes over him and then straightened the row of medals on his lapel, which had gone awry during their passionate tryst. 'There—perfect.'

He reached for her hand, raised it to his lips and pressed a lingering kiss over her knuckles. 'It was a pleasure negotiating with you, Ms Lund. I look forward to our next meeting, more than you could ever imagine.'

She smiled, her eyelids heavy, and his breath caught. How he wished he could whisk her away somewhere private, just the two of them.

But Clara's cold, hard reality was calling to them both. Taking once last glance at her breath-taking image, committing how she looked to memory, he tugged his jacket into place, ran a hand through his hair and left the room, pulling on his persona as he re-joined the evening's festivities.

She was right: they *were* from different worlds. Hers was less privileged, but she had greater freedom. But as long as he was careful with her feelings—as long as he never again let her down, as long as he protected her from speculation, from the royal-watchers and press critics who judged his every move— they could meet on common ground as equals.

CHAPTER EIGHT

THREE NIGHTS AFTER the banquet, Andreas was enjoying a highly erotic dream featuring his favourite nurse when he was roughly awoken by the intercom buzzer.

'Andreas, it's Clara. I need to speak to you.' The urgency of her voice shot panic through his system.

He jolted into a sitting position. 'Come in.'

He disarmed the door lock and reached for his prosthesis. His pulse bounded with surges of familiar adrenaline. He was used to being woken in the middle of the night by a pager, but never here, at home.

'What's wrong?' he asked as she appeared in his bedroom seconds later. He moved his eyes over her from head to toe. 'Are you hurt?' Why else would she come to him in the middle of the night, her voice carrying a desperate edge that made his teeth grind?

She shook her head. 'I'm concerned for Prince Henrik. I need a second opinion. It's snowing a blizzard outside, and the prince's personal physician is stuck in a snow drift.' She wrung her hands, wearing a deep frown of worry. 'I've left the prince with the other nurse on duty tonight because I wanted to be the one to wake you.'

Andreas stood and shrugged on his robe, too distracted by concern for his father to enjoy the way Clara flicked her stare over his nakedness before he tied the belt.

'You did the right thing in coming to me, *sötnos*.' He gripped her upper arms, deeply touched that she'd sought out his help. 'I'll come right away.'

He scrubbed a hand over his face to clear the last fog of sleep and reached for the medical bag he kept on hand at all times. What could be wrong with his father?

He recalled the last conversation he'd had with the prince. His father had been a little tired, but otherwise seemed in good health. They'd talked mainly of business: the upcoming visit of the Swedish prime minister; the plans for the annual staff Christmas party; the list of new charities seeking royal patronage. But Andreas trusted Clara's clinical judgement and she wouldn't have woken him lightly.

'Tell me what your concerns are,' he said as they left the suite.

'Prince Henrik became acutely breathless a short while ago,' Clara said. 'His temperature is normal, pulse and blood pressure elevated. No history of chest pain, but obviously I'm worried about pneumonia or a pulmonary embolus, although I've listened to his chest and can't hear any evidence of consolidation.'

Concealing his own concern, Andreas placed his hand on her shoulder, squeezing for both their comfort.

'What are his oxygen saturations?' he asked as they rushed from the guest wing towards his father's suite, fear now a metallic taste in his mouth.

'Ninety-seven,' she answered.

Andreas breathed a small sigh of relief.

'Someone has taken a motor sled to fetch the doctor,' Clara said, keeping pace with his longer strides. 'But it could take an hour. I know it's not strictly ethical for you to treat your father,' she continued as they entered the family wing of the palace, 'But I figured it was okay in such urgent and unusual circumstances.'

Andreas sent her a grateful smile, wishing he could drag

her into his arms, but his father needed help. 'Thank you for taking such good care of the prince.'

There would be time later to tell her how he valued her inspiring dedication. How humbled he was that she'd come to him for advice. How privileged he felt because Clara was so fiercely independent, she demanded nothing from him.

Outside the prince's suite, Clara rested her hand on his arm. 'Andreas, are you sure you are okay to see Prince Henrik like this? He's quite distressed.'

For a second, she looked as if she might say more, but then she blinked and the moment passed.

'I appreciate your consideration of my feelings. Thank you.'

Of course she saw and understood him. Of course a nurse of her calibre would grasp the complex emotions pounding through him. Seeing a parent incapacitated was upsetting for anyone, even more so when that man was also your ruler, someone Andreas had always seen as a larger-than-life figure.

What she couldn't know was how the fear for his father chilling him to the bone was amplified by what had happened to Oscar. The last time Andreas had tried to medically help a family member, he'd failed, with devastating consequences for him, his family and the nation. He'd tried everything he could to treat and then revive his brother, but his efforts hadn't been enough.

But he couldn't think about his failings now. He needed to stay calm and objective. He rapped on the door once out of observance of royal protocol, urgency driving him to enter the suite of rooms without waiting to be admitted.

The prince's butler greeted them, the older man's face stricken and pale. 'The doctor is still thirty minutes away, Your Royal Highness. Should I call for the helicopter, sir?'

'Of course not, Møller. There's a blizzard raging outside,' Andreas said, fighting the sickening trepidation twisting his gut. 'I will assess the prince so we know what we're dealing with.'

The butler stood aside and Andreas and Clara entered his father's bedroom, a room he hadn't been in since he'd been a young boy.

No matter how hard he'd tried to prepare, given his training and Clara's words of warning, shock lashed at Andreas like the icy rain pelting the windows outside. His father was seated on the edge of the bed, another nurse at his side. He wore an oxygen mask, but his hands were braced on his thighs and his breathing was fast and laboured.

Fear and compassion tugged at Andreas's heart as he approached. 'Pappa, I need to listen to your chest.'

If he focussed on his training, treated the man before him like any other patient, he could keep the waves of panic at bay. Only this wasn't *any* patient. This was his father, his ruler, a proud and unemotional man much beloved by their nation, and something was wrong.

He reached for his father's radial pulse, noting it was elevated but regular.

'Do you have any chest pain?' His mind trawled the same differential diagnoses for acute shortness of breath that Clara had considered.

Prince Henrik shook his head, his eyes wild with distress, sweat beading on his forehead.

'Dizzy,' he gasped, gripping Andreas's hand with vice-like force.

Clara handed Andreas a stethoscope. He listened to the breath sounds, searching Clara's concerned expression for clues, because something was off. He felt as if he was the last person to know some sort of well-kept secret, his sense of isolation flaring anew. Yes, he belonged here, as Clara had pointed out, but he'd spent so long away pursuing his career that there was no one at the palace he could confide in.

Only Clara.

He focussed on the whoosh of air transmitted through the

stethoscope, swallowing down his rising sense of apprehension. His father's office had given little away when it came to the 'brief illness' rendering the normally fit and active prince indisposed. But was there something more medically sinister going on than Andreas had been led to believe?

He should have pushed for more information on the prince's health when he'd returned. He didn't blame Clara, or any of the medical staff who were loyal to the prince, respectful of his privacy and duty-bound to keep his medical information confidential. But had Andreas, a doctor, failed to see something that had been right under his nose? And, if there was something serious going on, why hadn't his father confided in him?

That familiar feeling of inadequacy settled like a stone in his stomach. Would he ever be good enough in his father's eyes or would he always be the less important son? They hadn't been close for years, but they were the only family each other had left. Except now it seemed that Prince Henrik couldn't even trust his doctor son with potentially important information.

Something in Clara's stare, something she could no longer hide from him because of their growing emotional closeness, told Andreas that, unlike him, she knew the full story.

Guilt lashed him. Since his return to Varborg, he'd been self-absorbed with his struggles to reconcile the demands of his two roles, doctor and heir, because being Prince Andreas had forced him to confront his greatest failure—losing Oscar. But instinct told him this was more than a 'brief illness'. As his son and as his heir, Andreas had a right to know if his father's health was in danger.

'You're right,' he said to Clara, removing the earpieces of the stethoscope. 'Breath sounds are completely normal.'

He beckoned her a short distance away so they could talk. 'There's no sign of infection or acute heart failure. No obvious pneumothorax or pleural effusion. But without a chest X-ray or a scan to exclude anything more subtle but sinister our diagnostic abilities are limited.'

Clara frowned, glancing at Prince Henrik. 'So what do we do?' she whispered, looking up at him with absolute faith.

At least *she* believed in him, even if no one else did.

Remembering that he was good at his job, Andreas dragged in a shuddering breath, grateful for Clara's presence.

'I think the most likely diagnosis of exclusion is a panic attack,' he said, hoping for his father's sake that he was right, because they could easily treat that here and now. 'It's worth a shot; if we can slow down his breathing, then we'll know.'

She nodded, her expression staying impressively neutral. Andreas wasn't the prince's doctor. It wasn't Clara's place to inform him of his father's medical history. But none of that helped with his feelings of inadequacy.

Andreas sat on the bed at his father's side and took the older man's warm and capable hand. 'Pappa, you're breathing too fast. We need to slow that down. Purse your lips like you're going to blow out a candle...that's it. Now breathe nice and slowly. In, two, three and out, two, three, four, five.'

While Andreas repeated the instructions in as calm a voice as he could muster, given the sickening, doubt-fuelled lurch of his stomach, Clara stooped in front of the prince and pursed her lips, demonstrating the slower breathing technique in time to Andreas's voice.

It took a few minutes of synchronised breathing, but eventually his father calmed, his grip on Andreas's hand reassuringly strong and unwavering, reminding Andreas of the proud statesman who'd ruled Varborg steadfastly for fifty years.

Hot with shame, he wondered how they'd ended up so estranged. The chasm between them had been so wide for so long, they knew little about each other's personal lives, fears and dreams.

'Give the prince some privacy, please.' Andreas instructed

the butler and other nurse to vacate the room. 'Would you like Clara to stay so we can make you comfortable, Pappa?'

Taking some slow, shuddering breaths, his father nodded, slowly recovering his strength and composure.

Clara plumped the pillows and together they repositioned Prince Henrik back into bed.

'I think you had a panic attack, Pappa,' Andreas said, the doctor in him needing to understand why just as much as the son. 'Your physician is on his way, and I'm sure he'll organise some tests, in case we're missing something.'

'Thank you, son,' Prince Henrik said, shakily. 'That was… alarming. I'm grateful that you were here. I'm not sure what came over me.'

Andreas startled, glancing away from the man he'd looked up to his whole life. He couldn't recall a single time when Prince Henrik had relied on him emotionally. Not after Andreas's mother had died, when Prince Henrik had become focussed on Oscar as the heir, nor after the accident that had stolen the life of his eldest son. They'd grieved differently, separately, never seeing eye to eye.

'No need to thank me, Pappa. I'm always here for you. I'll stay until your doctor arrives.' He needed to understand what might have caused his father's acute distress tonight.

Clara placed a fresh glass of water next to the bed. 'Can I get you anything else, sir?'

'No, thank you, dear,' his father said with a fond smile that spoke not only of his immediate recovery, but also their close relationship. Of course Prince Henrik respected Clara. She was an exceptional nurse: gifted and smart, humble and empathetic. And, maybe most importantly, loyal.

Clara glanced at Andreas. 'I'll leave you two alone. Call if you need me.'

Her stare brimmed with empathy that filled Andreas with fresh dread. Before she could leave the room, he caught up with her, resting his hand on her arm. 'Thank you for coming to me for help,' he said, wishing he could crush her in his arms and escape into their passion. 'The prince is lucky to have you on his staff.'

'He's lucky to have *you* as a son,' she replied, her compassionate stare leaving him exposed and raw, feelings he would prefer to conceal from the woman he was trying to seduce. 'Why don't you sit with him a while, perhaps talk?'

With his throat tight with confusion and fear, Andreas nodded and re-joined his father. The alarming realisations of tonight proved that there were conversations long overdue. Seeing his father incapacitated had brought home the reality of Andreas's situation. Even if there was no sinister explanation for his father's current state of health, no one lived for ever. Like Andreas, the prince was human, as vulnerable to illness, weakness and scars, both physical and emotional, as the next man.

Prince Henrik would one day die, as was the natural order of the world, and Andreas would take his place on Varborg's throne. His days of freedom to pursue the career he loved, a career that gave him a deep sense of pride, achievement and validation, were numbered. His personal freedoms too, such as his fling with Clara. Like it or not, prepared or not, Andreas would one day need to make these sacrifices and commit fully to the role he would inherit.

It might even be sooner than he'd imagined.

CHAPTER NINE

CLARA OPENED HER EYES the next morning, disorientated after only a couple of hours' sleep. She glanced around her bedroom in the staff quarters at the palace, her first thought of Andreas.

Last night, it had been obvious that her suspicions were correct: he *was* unaware of Prince Henrik's diagnosis and terminal prognosis. She'd witnessed the moment he'd figured out something serious was going on. She'd had to look away from the pain and confusion dulling his stare, her loyalties so horribly torn between father and son.

Only now, off-duty at the palace, could she be there for Andreas. She reached for her phone and sent him a text, asking after both men. On her way to the shower, she opened the curtains. The snow drift outside the window reached halfway up the pane. There was no way her little car would make it to the main roads. It looked as if she was snowed in. She made the call to Nordic Care, informing them she wouldn't make her late shift.

Under the spray of hot water, Clara tried to process everything that had happened since the Jubilee Banquet. After they'd agreed to have a secret fling that night in the Blue Room, she'd vowed to hold herself emotionally distant, and she'd tried her best.

But the blizzard had brought about exceptional and unforeseen circumstances. Her professional reliance on him was only natural—Andreas was a geriatrician. But now, faced with the evidence that Clara knew more about the prince's medical condition than his own son, a doctor, the thrilling affair they'd negotiated seemed almost trivial.

Don't turn on me now...when I need an ally...

His heartfelt plea from the night of the banquet twisted her stomach. He had so much weight on his shoulders: the imminent loss of his father; the enforced end of his medical career; the transition to the most important role of his life, as ruler. How would he deal with all of that? How could she help him adjust?

Her phone was stubbornly silent as she dressed in her everyday clothes—jeans and a beautiful jumper hand-knitted by Alma. She'd just applied moisturiser, mascara and lip gloss and fitted her nose stud when there was a tap at the door. Expecting another of the nurses, or the staffing manager with an update on the conditions on the roads, she pulled open the door.

Andreas stood on the threshold, his eyes haunted and fatigued. He'd come to *her* of all people. Did he have no one else he trusted to talk to?

Clara's heart cracked open for him. 'I'm so sorry.'

'You know his prognosis, of course,' he said, shock etched into his haggard expression.

Even grieving, he was unbearably beautiful, dressed in a forest-green sweater and dark jeans, his hair carelessly pushed back from his face. She wanted to hold him, her protective urges on high alert. Instead, she glanced along the deserted corridor and then, when she saw that they were alone, reached for his hand.

'I'm sorry. He's my patient,' she whispered.

Andreas of all people would understand that she had a professional duty of confidentiality, but she hated that he seemed to have been the last to know.

'I'm not blaming you,' he said, flatly, 'But he's *my* father. *Someone* should have told me. *He* should have told me.'

She nodded, stunned speechless by his understandable pain and confusion.

'He trusts me to rule Varborg because he has no choice,' he continued, his voice gruff with bitterness. 'But he doesn't trust me, his heir, his son, a *doctor*, with his confidences, even when I'm the person this impacts the most.'

Of course he would hate to stop practising medicine. Sick to her stomach with wretchedness, Clara inched closer and took his other hand. 'It's a shock.'

'I should have seen the signs,' he said, briefly closing his eyes.

She wanted to be there for Andreas, but she was trapped in an impossible position of torn loyalties, already too close to this family to be totally objective.

'You can't blame yourself. And maybe *because* you're his son,' she continued cautiously, '*Because* he loves you, he's tried to spare you the distressing news.'

Andreas frowned, unconvinced.

His relationship with his father was none of her business. They weren't friends. They weren't even properly lovers. But she understood exactly what he was going through. Clara's mother had tried to spare her daughters from worry in the beginning, before she'd faced surgery and had no longer been able to hide the symptoms.

A door slammed somewhere overhead. Clara forced herself to step back. Someone might see them or overhear their conversation. They'd agreed to be discreet about their relationship.

'How *is* the prince this morning?' she asked, to cover up her caution.

'He's feeling much better, enough to refuse me the minute details of his medical records.' His voice was bitter, his expression disbelieving. 'It's as if he doesn't understand me at all. I'm a doctor; maybe I could…help.'

Clara winced in empathy. She understood his feelings of futility, but beyond supporting his father there was nothing else he could do. And she couldn't blame Prince Henrik for not wanting to rake over it all again.

'Is there anything I can do for you?' she asked. Maybe sharing her own experiences would make him feel less alone.

He looked away, clearly struggling with complex emotions. When he looked back, his stare was imploring. 'I'm…over-whelmed by it all. Powerless. I can't think straight. I need to get away from here, clear my head. Will you come?'

Clara swallowed her immediate 'yes'. She'd promised to guard her feelings, but how could she deny him a single thing when she understood his current vulnerability? Someone he loved, his *parent*, had cancer. Whereas Clara's mother had been given the all-clear, Prince Henrik had been told to put his affairs in order. And for Andreas the news carried another layer of devastation. His birth right meant he would soon have to choose: his career or the crown.

Except, he had no real choice.

'I'll go anywhere with you,' Clara said, deciding she would double her efforts to protect herself while also being there for Andreas. 'But have you seen the snow?'

'Trust me,' he said, his stare both pleading and hopeful.

'I do.' she said.

'Grab your boots,' he instructed, some of the tension leaving his body.

Clara hurried into her room to snatch them up, along with her phone.

He led her to a part of the palace she'd never visited before. There, in a large boot room, he shrugged on a fur-lined parka emblazoned with the palace crest from a selection of sizes hanging along the wall, and then passed one to Clara, along with some mittens and a hat.

Despite the sadness in the air, excitement fizzed in her veins. Would they be digging snow? Cross-country skiing? It didn't matter. He'd come to her in his hour of need. She'd do anything to help him process the news he'd received last night, including escape with him.

Outside, the snow in the courtyard had been shovelled away and there at the top of the driveway sat a gleaming, royal-blue snow-mobile bearing the royal crest and the words House of Cronstedt.

'Can you drive that?' Clara asked, hesitating for a second as she pulled on the hat. She didn't want the heir to the throne to be injured on her watch.

Andreas smiled broadly for the first time, his eyes bright with confidence and excitement. 'Of course I can. You can't get anywhere in winter up here without one.' He took her gloved hand, leading her towards the machine. 'Oscar and I used to have races.'

'Of course you did.' She laughed, picturing the scene. 'That sounds terrifying.'

'Jump on,' he said with a sexy wink that snatched her breath away.

She hadn't imagined exactly how they would implement their secret affair, but she'd guessed it would involve late-night texts and clandestine meetings in discreet hotels. This, on the other hand—spending time with the *real* Andreas, getting to know him better, understanding his passions and doubts—was way more dangerous to Clara.

She sat at the back. Andreas swung his leg over the seat in front and started the ignition.

'Hold tight,' he called over the hum of the engine.

Clara scooted forward to encircle his waist with her arms and his hips with her thighs so she felt the thud of his heart under her cheek. The engine revved beneath her, setting them in motion, and Clara squealed, gripping him tighter.

Then they were off, skimming the undisturbed snow which glittered in the sun like a sheet of diamonds, and headed for the native forest at the perimeter of the landscaped palace grounds. Andreas drove the snow-mobile with impressive skill, weaving them with ease over the bumpy landscape and between the tall pine trees.

The wind whipped at Clara's cheeks and hair. Her smile was so wide, her teeth were cold. This reminded her of the night of the Jubilee Banquet, when she'd danced in his arms and felt as if she were flying. The wild sense of freedom was back—the heady abandon she'd experienced far too infrequently, thanks to Lars Lund's irresponsible approach to caring for his family and raising his daughters. How many more experiences had she passed up during her teens and early twenties, time she would never get back?

She gripped Andreas's waist tighter and rested her face against his shoulder, protected from the bitter wind by the imposing breadth of his chest. Other women might get carried away by the absurd romance of this situation but Clara was weighed down by reality, even as she sped along with the sun on her back and Andreas's solid warmth seeping into her front.

Ever since they'd danced together, when she'd come alive in his arms both on the dance floor and later in the Blue Room, she'd told herself that their fling didn't make him hers. He'd said they were equals that night, when he'd forced her to admit how badly she wanted him, but deep down world-weary Clara knew better. In all the areas that mattered—their upbringings, their expectations, their priorities—they were worlds apart.

And, even if she wanted him, he belonged to Varborg first and foremost and to his future princess second. That woman would be content to walk at his side, stand in his shadow, give Varborg and him an heir and never question the inherent power imbalance of their relationship. That didn't stop Clara wanting the only thing she could allow herself—a temporary interlude in his bed, freshly stamped with an expiry date.

Finally, they emerged from the trees into a clearing. Andreas slowed the snow-mobile, bringing it to a halt and killed the engine. Clara raised her face from his shoulder and gasped with awe at the sight of a picture-perfect log cabin nestled among the fir trees with a backdrop of Varborg's northern mountain range.

'Oh… It's so beautiful,' Clara said, mesmerised. 'Who lives here?'

Like the surrounding forest, the cabin was dressed in a thick layer of snow, glittering in the sunshine like a scene from a winter wonderland.

'No one.' Andreas held out his hand, helping her from the back of the snow-mobile with a more carefree smile on his face. 'It's a hunting lodge built by one of my Cronstedt ancestors.'

Already he seemed less tense, as if he felt more at home here than among the grandeur and ceremony of the palace.

'Oscar and I came here all the time as boys,' he continued, confirming her suspicion. 'It was the only place we could be free to play—build bonfires and tree houses and camp out in the summer. There's a lake over that ridge where we'd go ice-fishing in winter.'

She could envision the young prince he must have been so clearly in her mind's eye—scampering around after his big brother, away from the strict protocol and public gaze of his royal life. No wonder he chose to hide out here when he needed space.

The barest flicker of pain crossed his eyes as he tugged her close. 'Now I'm the only person who spends time here.'

She blinked up at him, her heart beating wildly at the power of the cabin's solitude and the positive change already evident in Andreas.

'It's idyllic,' she said with wonder in her voice, touched that he'd brought her to this special place—a place clearly dear to him, a place linked to his fondest childhood memories of his brother.

Clara's eyes burned, close to tears for his losses. But she *never* cried—not even when Alma Lund had haltingly confessed her cancer diagnosis to her daughters. Nor when, weeks later, nineteen-year-old Clara had swallowed her pride and called her father, begging him to come home and support his wife, the mother of his daughters, during her treatment. Of course, Lars hadn't even done it for Clara and Freja. He'd made excuses and let them down once more. She should have known better than to rely on him.

'Can we go inside?' she asked, glancing at the charming cabin, the windows of which glowed with warm, orange light, hoping to escape the humiliating rejection of that final conversation with her father.

'Of course. I asked the housekeeper to start the fires and stock the fridge.' He took her hand and led her up the steps of the covered veranda, which housed outdoor seating carved from old tree trunks and covered with reindeer pelts.

'Are you hungry?' he asked when they were inside, taking her coat and hanging it next to his on wooden pegs beside the door.

Clara stilled, overwhelmed by the sumptuous interior. The fire was roaring, warming the entire living space which boasted high-vaulted ceilings crossed with wooden beams, massive picture windows framing the views and luxurious furniture. Breakfast was laid out, the dining table romantically set for two.

She shivered, in spite of the warmth and the cosy décor. Thinking about her father reminded her how out of her depth

she was when it came to relationships. She wasn't a sophisticated seductress. After her one intimate relationship with
a man who'd never called her again—proof that she'd been
wasting her time with men—it had been easier to avoid disappointment than to give anyone else the power to hurt her
again. And she'd been preoccupied, too busy with studying,
working and helping out with her mother to devote the time
to the kind of relationship *she* wanted—one on equal terms.

But Andreas wasn't just any man. She trusted him.

As if he could read the turmoil in her mind, Andreas stared
down at her, his eyes dark with emotions, his expression turning serious.

'I've never brought anyone here before.' He brushed some
hair from her cheek, the way he had the first night they'd
kissed.

It made her feel precious. His words felt like a promise,
an acknowledgement that he trusted her with his private life;
that, despite his playboy past, Clara was different...for now.
It sounded naïve, except she *was* different. She wasn't planning to fall in love with him, so her heart was safe. She wanted
nothing from him, beyond them being equals, and perhaps
more of that reckless, carefree feeling he brought out in her.

'In that case, thank you for bringing me here.' With her
heart galloping, she stood on tip toes and pressed her cold lips
to his warm ones, sucking in the crisp scent of snow and pine
forest that seemed to cling to his skin.

She pulled back and he cupped her cheek in his palm, his
earnest stare searching hers. 'No, thank *you*—for trusting me,
for blindly following me, for escaping with me.'

Clara released a soft, shuddering sigh, his touch filling her
body with enough heat to melt the snow outside. A part of
her—a deep-seated part, home to her deepest fears—understood
his need to flee reality. How many times had she experienced
the same shameful urge in the middle of a long, dark night of

worrying about her mother? She'd been too young to shoulder such responsibility alone, but with her father's refusal to come home there had been no one else to care for Alma.

'I wanted to tell you at the palace,' she whispered, that lost and scared part of her exposed, 'That I understand what you're going through today. My mother was diagnosed with breast cancer when I was nineteen.'

His lips flattened, his brows pinched together. 'I'm so sorry, *sötnos*.'

Clara shook her head, rushing on. 'She's fine now, but at the time there was only me and my fifteen-year-old sister to care for her. I helped out at home, drove her to her chemotherapy appointments, sat awake on her worst nights, willing her to get better.'

Clara's voice broke. Speaking about her beloved mother's illness brought those painful memories back, along with resentment at Lars for heaping too much on his daughter's shoulders. But Alma Lund had been one of the lucky ones.

'It's not the same as your situation,' she said, 'But you're not alone, Andreas. Your confusion and hurt and anger are all normal reactions.'

He cupped her face with both hands. 'Thank you for confiding that in me. That you understand, that I can talk to you, helps more than you'll ever know. Your inner strength is truly inspiring, Clara.'

'So is yours.' She couldn't seem to catch her breath, as if the air in her lungs were frozen. 'You've been through so much.'

How was she expected to keep her distance when he trusted her, had opened up to *her*, of all the people he must have in his life? But maybe he had few people with whom he felt truly understood and seen for himself. Maybe he had few people who expected nothing from him. Maybe he too was weighed down by responsibility.

'Right now, strong is the last thing I feel,' he admitted, taking her hand and holding it to his chest over the wild thump of his heart while his hungry stare traced her mouth. 'It's taking every shred of restraint I possess not to kiss you and touch you and bury myself so deep inside you that I lose myself in you, just for a few moments.'

Clara dragged in a ragged breath, recognising the same urgent needs in herself. This craving for him was building out of control. It was as if their chemistry was being fanned hotter by the fact that time was running out. Reality was chasing their tails.

Soon, when Andreas was forced to give up his career, they would no longer work together at Nordic Care. Clara's nursing position at the palace would end with Prince Henrik's death. They would have no excuse to see each other. And, while she could sleep with a prince—especially when, to her, he was simply Andreas—she couldn't sleep with Varborg's ruler, an altogether more serious and intimidating man.

'Then do it,' she said boldly, her body an inferno from the fire he'd lit inside her with that first sexy smile, when he'd been resplendent in his bath like a marauding Viking. 'It's the only thing I want from you.'

For a moment he froze, frowned, as if her words were too good to be true.

'Except,' she said, before she threw herself into his arms, 'We said we'd be equals in this. And, the thing is, I'm nowhere near as experienced as you. In fact, I've only done this once, with a guy I met at college. He pursued me, took me on romantic dates, bought me flowers, made me feel special…and then, the minute I slept with him, he lost interest. I found out he'd done that to lots of girls in my year, which was…humiliating. So I just gave up on men after that. It was easier to avoid disappointment than to risk being hurt and let down. Not to mention that it wasn't even very good and…'

His fingers landed on her lips, his eyes blazing into hers.

'I don't care about your inexperience. It doesn't matter. That guy is an idiot.'

'It matters to *me*. I vowed that the next time I was intimate with someone it would be on equal terms and with honest expectations. That *I'd* be in control.'

He nodded, taking her seriously.

'The way you made me feel the night of the banquet,' she ploughed on, 'Alive, joyous, powerful. I've never experienced that with anyone else. I want to make you feel the same way.'

This complex, hurting man standing before her was everything; the sight, scent and feel of him filled her senses, making her feel alive again. She wanted to rock his world. She wanted to help him lose himself. They could escape the sometimes cold, harsh and cruel reality of life together.

'So, will you show me what you like?' she finished.

His pupils dilated, his jaw flexing as he took a pained-looking swallow. With a growl that Clara felt resonate throughout every inch of her body, Andreas hauled her close, crushing her mouth to his.

For a few moments, she lost herself in the fiery passion of their kiss. Andreas made it easy, holding her so tight her feet barely touched the floor; kissing her with such domination she forgot to breathe and turned dizzy; pressing her so close, she wasn't sure where her body ended and his began.

'You might kill me…' He groaned against her lips, pulling back to stare hard into her eyes. 'Just when I thought you couldn't be more perfect.'

Clara snorted, almost euphoric with desire. 'I'm very far from that. And I'm certain killing the heir to the throne *is* a punishable offence.'

'Then,' he said, cupping her face and kissing her once more, 'It's a good thing that right now, with you, I'm just Andreas.'

Then he took her hand and led her through the lodge to the master bedroom.

CHAPTER TEN

CLARA GLANCED AROUND the luxurious room, her body burning with need. Fur pelts covered the hardwood floor in front of the fire, which crackled and flickered, casting a warm glow. A massive carved timber bed covered with snowy white linen dominated the room.

She spun to face Andreas, reached up on tip toes and pressed her lips to his, blocking her mind to everything but the way he made her feel. She didn't want to think about the risks she was taking by allowing him this close, or reality awaiting them beyond this room. She just wanted the promise they'd negotiated: the two of them together, just a man and a woman as equals.

'I want you,' she said, slipping her hands under his jumper, seeking out his warm, golden skin, tracing every dip and bulge of the muscles she remembered from the bath. Impatient, she broke free of his kiss and pushed up his sweater so she could see his magnificent body once more, confirmation that, in this moment, he was real and he was hers.

'There's no rush,' he said, tugging his sweater over his head and tossing it to the chair beside the bed before dragging her into his arms, where the heat of him nearly burned her alive.

'I can't help myself.' She sighed. 'I've seen you naked, don't forget—*twice*.'

Clara moved her stare over the breadth of his bare chest,

her hands skimming warm flesh as she went. He was beautiful, so masculine the woman in her trembled with longing for the empowering connection they shared.

'I thought I caught you checking me out last night.' A satisfied smiled kicked up his mouth. He raised her chin, his breath whispering over her lips. 'So it's only fair if I now feast my eyes on every inch of this body that has tortured me night and day since we met.'

His warm hands slid under her jumper, deftly freeing the clasp of her bra with one flick of his fingers. He kissed her in a long and thorough exploration that left her shifting restlessly against him to appease the molten ache between her legs.

How had this man, unlike any other, inspired such desperate need? Was it just the way he looked at her, the way he'd always looked at her, as if to him she was…exceptional and unique? Had she spent too long shutting down this side of herself, so one look at him had sent her hormones into revolt?

They reached for the hem of her sweater in unison, Andreas removing both it and her bra in one swift move so she shivered before him, not with nerves but with delicious anticipation. Goose pimples rose on her skin, but she was burning up. Chest to chest with Andreas, naked skin to naked skin, she felt as if she might incinerate to ash.

'Touch me,' she begged when he only stared at her nakedness.

His eyes blazed as he raised his hands to caress her bare breasts. 'You are breathtakingly beautiful.' His voice was gruff with desire.

Clara gasped but it wasn't enough. It was nowhere near enough for that reckless part of her that craved the life-affirming freedom of his touch.

'I wanted you that first time I saw you,' he said, his thumbs toying her nipples to taut peaks. 'With your hair all prim and proper and your uniform fuelling some pretty raunchy nurse fantasies I never knew I had.'

Clara laughed and bit down on her lower lip to try and contain the swell of pleasure weakening her legs, but languid heat radiated out from his expert touch, infecting her entire body.

'I wanted you too,' she said, dropping her head back so her throat was exposed to his kisses. 'You looked so rugged and wild; I was tempted to join you in that giant bath.'

Her hands roamed his shoulders, his back and arms, the sheer strength of him. She couldn't seem to touch him enough.

'I knew it would be like this between us,' he said, pressing her erect nipples between his fingers so darts of pleasure arced to her pelvis. 'I felt the sparks the first time you looked at me as if you wanted to roll your eyes, as if you didn't care *who* I was.'

Clara moaned at his words and the pleasure he was wreaking with just his fingers and thumbs. She was already lost, whereas he seemed far too in control. Raising on tip toes to kiss him, she slid one hand down his body, his skin scalding her palm until she reached the impressive hard length of him pressing at the front of his jeans. He groaned into their kiss, gripping her tighter so she was crushed against the fiery heat of him, enclosed in his powerful arms.

But she felt powerful too, the knowledge that she could affect him as much as he affected her almost as drugging as his heated kisses.

He walked her back towards the bed. 'Lie back,' he ordered, as her thighs hit the edge of the bed. 'I want to see all of you.'

Leaning over her, he pressed kisses over her neck and chest, taking one nipple into his mouth and sucking until Clara's head spun with thick, paralysing desire. Why had she never prioritised this exploration of passion before? Surely she'd been denying herself something as essential as breathing? But would it be like this with anyone else? Her one fumbling foray into sex had been underwhelmingly brief and disappointing.

Perhaps this magic was down to Andreas. Because she'd yet to render him anywhere near as helpless as he was making her, she reached for the fly of his jeans.

His hips jerked and he took her hand, pinning her wrist to the bed. 'I believe there is a nudity imbalance to redress,' he said, smiling wickedly as he captured the other nipple with his lips, laving it with the flat of his tongue. 'You've seen me naked twice, after all.'

'Andreas…' Clara moaned, writhing beneath him on the bed as he continued to torture her breasts with the sensual pleasure of his mouth. She wasn't even naked and he'd driven her so close to the edge.

'Keep calling me that, *sötnos*,' he ordered, keeping his mouth on her breast.

He undid her jeans and together they shimmied them off with increasingly frantic tugs and shoves. Clara wanted him naked again, his weight on top of her, the heat of him scalding her, the feel of him inside her.

'Almost good enough,' he said, leaning back to move his eyes over her body from head to toe. 'But not quite perfect.'

Taking hold of her underwear, he peeled it off so slowly, so intently, with his stare scouring her nudity, Clara thought she might explode from longing.

'Don't mind me,' she whispered, her voice hoarse with want even as she tried to lighten the moment with humour. 'Have a good look.'

Andreas's eyes blazed in the firelight, showing her that he recalled the reference from the first night they'd met when *he'd* been the naked one and she'd ogled him shamelessly.

'Oh, I will, don't worry. You asked me to show you what I like and it's this—you. I intend to see and kiss and pleasure every inch of you until you sob my name. Until you never think to call me anything else but Andreas. Until to you I'm just the man who wants you so badly, he's struggling to draw breath right now.'

Everything in Clara clenched hard. How was she supposed to stay immune when he said things like that? When he looked down at her as if she was something rare, to be valued? When he made her feel as if this connection of theirs was as important to him as it was to her?

True to his word, he kissed a path across her ribs, to her belly button and lower. Clara gasped as he covered her sex with his mouth, sending fiery darts of pleasure through her every nerve. Reflexively, her fingers speared through his hair and she held on tight, her body tossed from pleasure to ecstasy to want in a cycle that happened again and again, until she was certain there was nowhere left to climb. Until she was indeed sobbing his name, as he wanted. Until she burned in white-hot fire.

Then he stopped. 'I want to be inside you when you come.' He reared back to remove his jeans and underwear so his erection sprang free, prouder and impossibly bigger than the last time she'd seen him aroused.

Aware that, for all her talk of equality and control she'd yet to do one thing to turn him on, Clara sat up and reached for him, encircling his hard length with her hand, then leaning forward to kiss him in return.

'Clara…' Andreas groaned, his stare fierce on hers as his fingers slid through her hair, holding her to him.

'Don't you like it?' she asked, stroking the silky soft and steely hardness of him with her fingers, thumb and the tip of her tongue.

'I like it too much.' He hissed through his teeth as she took him inside her mouth, his stare glitteringly hard while he cupped her face and watched.

She'd barely taken two or three swipes of him with her tongue when he yanked her away and pulled open the bedside drawer for a condom.

'I was enjoying myself,' Clara said, pouting as he tore into the condom and stretched it on.

'So was I.' Following her down onto the bed, Andreas removed his prosthesis and tossed it to the floor.

'Come here,' he said, reaching for her, his strong arms rolling her on top. 'I love the smell of your hair,' he said as it fell around them like two curtains. 'Like spring meadows.'

Gripping the back of her neck, he dragged her lips down to his, groaning when she pushed her tongue into his mouth, the way she'd licked him seconds ago. He cupped her buttocks in his hands where she sat astride his hips, pressing her close so her sensitised core met his hard length and stars danced behind her eyes as she forgot to breathe.

'Andreas,' she pleaded, looking down at him while he commanded her hips to a torturous rhythm, up and down, over and over, sliding them together so they gasped in unison. Then, with a deft and speedy roll, he switched their positions so that he was now on top, his expression harsh with desire. Cupping her breast, he sucked the nipple to a hard peak.

'You make me so hard,' he said, his thumb rubbing the sensitive nipple he'd primed with his mouth as he watched her pleasured cries.

'I want to make you feel good,' she said, feeling him between her legs, nudging at her entrance so she spread her legs wider in invitation. 'I want you to lose yourself.'

He brushed her lips with his in a series of slow, sensual kisses. 'I like who I am when I'm with you. I like how you see me. How you're not afraid to challenge me. You make me feel as if I can be myself.'

'You can,' Clara whispered, watching arousal and vulnerability cross his beautiful stare, certain that this moment couldn't be any more perfect. Then he pushed inside her, inch by inch, until they were one.

Every muscle in Andreas's body pulled taut as though he might explode and cease to exist. Clara gasped her pleasure against his lips, staring up at him as if he was the answer to prayers, she hadn't even known she had.

Holding himself still because she felt too good, he kissed her with languid swipes of his tongue against hers, coaxing out her moans, his whispered name, her pleading expression.

But still he held them both suspended. A connection like theirs deserved savouring. If he could have kept her here indefinitely in his favourite place, he would have, slaking his uncontrollable hunger for her over and over until his world made crystal-clear sense. Until he'd garnered the strength to face everything he must.

'Thank you for escaping with me,' he said, entwining his fingers through hers as he slowly thrust inside her.

He wanted to pleasure her to the point of exhaustion. His selfish need for her shocked him. She gave so much of herself, met him fearlessly, even in moments when their differences outweighed their similarities. And he couldn't seem to get enough.

'I'm so glad I met you.' He reared back and stared into her intensely vulnerable eyes, wondering how, when she'd claimed to being the less experienced, he'd ended up feeling so moved, humbled and entranced by her responsiveness and her honest passion.

'Don't stop,' she pleaded, her hands in his hair, stroking his shoulders, his back, her nails a gentle scrape that made every nerve in his body sing. It was taking every scrap of self-control he possessed not to rush to the finish. But he'd exhaust himself to make this good for her, after she'd not only trusted him with her body and her pleasure but had also opened herself to him emotionally, telling him about her mother and had been there for him when he'd needed her most.

'You're amazing,' he said, refusing to think what he'd have done if she hadn't been snowed in at the palace. He'd known it from the start when she'd strode into his bathroom and jolted his world off its axis. Shifting his weight, he rocked his hips, watching her arousal streak across her beautiful face, the flames between them fanning higher.

'Andreas!' she cried, her stare clinging to his, giving him everything he could possibly need: connection; acceptance; unity. But that was Clara: fiercely loyal; inspiringly compassionate; unflinchingly brave. He moved inside her, his kisses as wild as the beat of his heart. Every part of him coalesced, mind, body and soul, to this one moment where he truly was lost in Clara.

'Andreas… Andreas,' she said his name, calling to that inner part of him that, for some reason, with her had always found peace. Maybe because she took him at face value. Because, as she'd said, she wanted nothing from him but this.

Because he didn't want to think about tomorrow, or how long they'd have to enjoy each other as lovers, he drove himself harder. 'Lose yourself with me, Clara,' he groaned against her neck, sweat breaking out and slicking their bodies even closer together.

Temperatures soared. Hearts thudded. Stares were locked and vulnerable.

Another cry was snatched from her throat. He dived to swallow it up, thrusting his tongue into her mouth as she climaxed, her nails digging into his back, her muffled sobs sweet music to his ears.

She was his—perfection.

He followed her, the powerful spasms of his orgasm endlessly racking his body as they clung to each other, panting and sweaty and equally laid bare.

'I didn't know it could be like that,' she said breathlessly a few minutes later, wonder in her voice. 'I've heard the myths, read it in romance novels, but…wow.'

'Wow indeed, *sötnos*,' Andreas said, pressing kisses to her smiling lips, her flushed cheeks, her closed eyelids while his heart fought to get back inside his chest. 'It's not always like that, but I'd say that definitely makes us equals.'

He rolled over, scooping an arm around her shoulders to hold her close while his awareness sharpened at the periphery, the intrusion of reality returning. He clung to Clara, clung to her uncomplicated company and the relentless attraction that had helped him to escape his troubles for a while.

But he couldn't escape with Clara for ever. He couldn't even stay at the lodge with her indefinitely, no matter how sorely he was tempted. He'd have to return to the palace and be there for his father, plan an exit strategy for his career.

His throat tightened with grief—for his father, the man, the ruler; the only family Andreas had left. And for himself: for that part of him that was proud of what he'd achieved; for the loss of the life he'd assumed he'd have for many years to come; for the demise of his freedom.

Clara rested her head on his chest, her hand stroking his abdomen in a way that would soon make him hard again. Andreas focussed on breathing, on the feel of her body against his, of the scent of her all over his skin. Considering today had begun with the devastating news of his father's diagnosis—and the bitter taste of failure that he'd not only missed the signs, but had also been the last person to know—that he could feel anything like the kind of pleasure and contentment that had just ripped through him was a testament to how badly he wanted this woman. Right now, she was the only thing keeping him grounded.

Except he'd also have to sacrifice even Clara.

'Do you think your Cronstedt ancestor, the one who built this place, brought his mistress here?' she asked sleepily, her lips pressing against his chest.

'Prince Erno, my great-great-grandfather? Probably. He did have a mistress, a famously beautiful one.' Had Erno Cronstedt sought solace from the demands of his position in the arms of a woman? 'Except, you're not my mistress.'

'No,' she stated simply, leaning up on her hand to peer down at him curiously, a small smile on her lips.

'I should be so lucky,' he said, stealing a kiss, because she was too far away and he already ached for her again.

Clara laughed, glancing at the fire in the hearth. 'It's dying down; I'll throw on another couple of logs.'

Before he could stop her, she slid from the bed and crossed the room, completely naked and completely comfortable.

Andreas folded one arm behind his head, propping himself up for a better view, his mouth dry with lust and longing. How could she do that to him, turn him on and make him ravenous, within minutes of great sex? Was it some sort of power she had over him? Or was it that their connection was deeper because they worked together and because Clara also cared for his dying father? Because she saw him like no other and understood his feelings?

Every other thought in his head evaporated as she stooped and placed two more logs on the embers and then returned to the bedside, her stunning naked body cast with an orange glow from the fire.

'If this hadn't already been my favourite place in the whole world,' he said, his voice gruff with thick desire, 'It would definitely be now. I'll never be able to look at that fire again without seeing your glorious body.'

She smiled. 'I am your eternal servant, Your Royal Highness.' She gave a mock curtsey and then joined him under the sheets.

'Don't,' he said, clasping her chin, directing her mouth to his. 'We made a deal: no more curtseys.'

He kissed her, pushing his tongue against hers to try and calm the wild need uncurling in him once more. But her careless reminder had broken the spell. No matter how good it had felt to flee the palace with Clara, no matter how thoroughly he'd lost himself inside the warm haven of her body, he couldn't hide for ever from his life, his responsibilities and the difficult days ahead.

Prince Henrik needed him—the nation, too. But could he bear to lose everything in one fell swoop: his father, his career *and* Clara?

'I'm sorry,' she whispered, the playfulness draining from her eyes. 'It's too soon to joke about that, right?'

Andreas sighed, reaching for her and sliding her body under his so their rapid heartbeats aligned. 'I would normally have a sense of humour. It's just that this is the one place I've always felt I can be myself.'

He touched the glinting green gemstone in her nose, one of many facets that made Clara unique. 'And I want to be myself with you. Always.'

She nodded, regarding him thoughtfully, her stare filled with compassion when he'd rather see it burn with desire. How could she make him feel more naked than he'd ever felt in his life? He was supposed to be the one in control of this rampant attraction, he was supposed to be the one with more experience, but instead he was close to unravelling, his need for her unstoppable.

'I'm glad that you have somewhere you feel safe and free.' Her stare flicked between his eyes, as if she saw him deep to the centre of his damaged soul. 'You feel close to Oscar here too, don't you?'

He pressed a kiss to her lips. 'You have a gift for seeing people clearly, did you know that?'

He'd always appreciated her directness. But now that he'd faced the reality his father was terminal—now that he'd escaped with Clara to this magical and unique place; now that they'd finally surrendered to their desires—his past mistakes were the last thing he wanted to discuss.

Except Clara had been there for him this morning when he'd needed someone like he'd never needed anyone before. She understood what he was going through because of her experiences with her mother. His world was on its head, the sands of time slipping through his fingers, and no amount of holding on would slow the inevitable. Discovering his father's prognosis had changed *everything*.

'I do feel close to Oscar here,' he said with a small sigh of surrender. 'We had the best times growing up.'

'You must miss him terribly,' she whispered, her fingers stroking his back hypnotically.

Andreas watched Clara's parted lips, craving a distraction from the shame, guilt and pain of remembering. It would be so easy to kiss her again, to refocus on their passion, to seduce her into silence and get lost once more. But his recent experience with his father had taught him that he couldn't hide from his feelings for ever. They caught up with him one way or another, often when he was most vulnerable and least expecting it.

'We were so close as boys,' he said. 'Not so much as teens, but then close again as adults before he died.'

He rolled onto his back, tucking Clara against his side so he could stare blindly at the ceiling. He didn't want to see her reaction if he had to talk about this. He wanted her to look at him with arousal, need and desperation, not pity and blame.

'Lots of siblings drift apart as teenagers,' she said, resting her cheek on his chest. 'My sister and I used to fight all the time.'

'Now, why is that so easy to imagine?' he teased, stealing another kiss for strength. 'The truth is, I hero-worshipped Oscar. He was smart and funny and always won the snow-mobile races.'

Clara smiled indulgently, her eyes bright with empathy. 'What happened to change that?'

'Nothing *he* did.' Andreas stroked his fingers up and down her back, from her nape to the top of her buttocks, her warm, silky skin comforting even as he stepped out of the shameful shadows and into the harsh light. Would she change towards him once she knew all the ugliness of his past? Could he bear that now that he'd found something real with her?

'I was fourteen and Oscar was sixteen when our mother died,' he said, because she'd always been easy to confide in. 'It seemed that, overnight, we stopped doing everything together. Oscar was suddenly too busy for races. He was always squir-relled away in Pappa's study or attending statesman classes or meeting with important dignitaries.'

'And you felt left out,' she whispered. 'That's understand-able.'

Her statement jabbed at his ribs like a blow, the emotions too complex for a simple yes or no answer. He clenched his jaw, debating whether to share more. He didn't want her to see him this way—hung up on the past, a man who'd failed and let down his loved ones, at odds with his dying father.

He craved the way she'd looked at him in the bath that first day; the way she'd looked at him as he'd twirled her around the ballroom; the way she'd looked at him when she'd asked him to show her his desires.

'I didn't understand it fully at the time,' he continued, the inexplicable urge to be honest burning in his throat. 'But of course Oscar was in training to rule. I didn't blame him, after

all; it was his birth right. But I was a kid, and a relatively shel-
tered one at that. There was a part of me that couldn't help but
vie for a little of our father's attention.'

'Of course not. You were grieving for your mother. A part
of you must have felt as if you'd lost your father and brother
too,' Clara said simply, pressing her lips to his chest so he felt
raw inside.

Was that true? It seemed obvious now.

Andreas stared hard into her eyes, as if he could draw on
Clara's innate strength and intuition. 'After a while I gave up
that fight. Oscar was focussed on the role he'd been born for
and Prince Henrik threw himself into preparing his heir.'

'Perhaps your father was grieving too,' she said quietly.

'Perhaps. For a while, I acted out, frequented wild parties, saw the sense of freedom as a green light for anything I
chose to do.'

'I've seen the pictures on the Internet.' Clara smiled sadly
in understanding.

He nodded. 'Then I got wise and realised that, while I might
not be as important as Oscar, I had freedom. I could choose
how to fill my time and live my life. So I knuckled down,
went to university, earned a medical degree and then joined
the armed forces.'

'You are just as important as the next person,' she said,
pushing up onto her elbows, her stare glittering with sincerity. 'Even if you'd chosen to simply be that playboy version of
yourself and nothing more.'

Andreas hauled her closer and kissed her again, part of him
splintering apart that she understood his motivations when
he'd been blind to them, perhaps until this very second. 'And
you are wise beyond your years, Nurse Lund.'

'We both had to grow up fast,' she said, her insight slicing
through him like a blade.

He'd never thought of it that way, but of course losing his

mother and effectively losing his brother and father to more important duties had left his teenage self lonely and confused. No wonder he'd acted out. No wonder he'd pushed himself into a medical career he could be proud of, as if he'd had something to prove to the father and older brother he loved.

And it had worked—right up to the moment when he'd been unable to save Oscar.

'And now you must soon give up all of your hard work,' she said hesitantly. 'It must be difficult. I can't imagine ever giving up nursing.'

Something rumbled in his chest, an unsettled gnaw of uncertainty, as if her statement was another blow to the convictions that had seen him through his adult life to date. But of course Clara fiercely valued her independence, another of her attractive qualities.

'I've always known that my family must come first,' he said, dejected because, whereas Clara could continue with her career, he would be taking another path. Their worlds, the common ground they'd shared as medical colleagues, would diverge.

He continued, refusing to think about him and Clara parting ways. 'But naïvely I never truly thought about what it would mean for the career I love and take pride in until the accident that killed Oscar. I was there when he died. I tried to save him. That's how I lost my leg.'

And now, with his father's news, he had even less time left as a doctor than he'd hoped. He would have to step into Oscar's shoes, final confirmation that his brother was gone for ever…

'I'm so sorry.' She pressed her lips to his neck.

'The palace wanted me to give up medicine immediately after Oscar's funeral,' he said, recalling the rows that had driven the wedge deeper between he and his father. 'I woke up in hospital to discover my brother hadn't made it, that my leg had to be amputated; that I had to set all of that aside, put on my uniform and attend his televised state funeral. I refused to even consider giving up my career on top of everything else. And I'm glad I didn't succumb to pressure. I needed to heal and recover. I needed a reason to strap on that prosthesis every day, to do my exercises, to learn to walk again. In a way, the drive to get back to work saved me.'

Clara stroked her fingers through his hair. 'A strong motivation to recover helps. It must have been a horrendous time for you.'

'Of course, now I'm going to lose my father too. None of our past issues matter.'

He swallowed, the sense of failure intensifying. 'Not our mutual stubbornness that used to drive my mother mad, or our differences of opinion on how to rule the principality or our inability to even discuss what happened to Oscar—none of it matters.'

Defeated, he clamped his lips together, sickened by his pity party. Giving up his career, while regrettable, wasn't the end of the world. He'd adapt; he'd adapted before, to losing a limb. He could pour all his energy into his royal role. He'd do it for Oscar and try to be as good a ruler as his brother would have been.

'I'm so sorry, Andreas.' Clara wrapped her arms around his shoulders and held him tight. 'But I think you're wrong. I think that stuff with your father *does* matter. You have an opportunity not many people get, to talk about the things that have impacted your relationship before it's too late.'

Andreas stiffened. 'The men of this family don't really talk about their feelings. It's an unspoken rule to suck it up and get on with it. Even when Prince Henrik told me his diagnosis, he showed no emotion, and when I pressed for more information he as good as told me to mind my own business.'

He didn't need verbal confirmation from Prince Henrik that, as the second son, he wasn't the heir his father had hoped for.

He carried enough self-doubt. If he messed up as heir, he'd not only be letting down his father and the nation, he'd also be failing the brother he hadn't been able to save in life.

'I appreciate your opinion.' He tried to keep his voice even. 'But some things are best left alone. My father is a proud man who's used to being in charge. He won't tolerate being questioned, and I've no desire to upset him during whatever time he has left. And besides, every time we do speak on an emotive subject, a part of me seems to revert to being that young boy so eager for his approval.'

He was done with that.

'We have a complex relationship, *sötnos*.' He pressed a kiss to her forehead to lessen the sting of his words, part of him regretting that he'd opened himself up quite so much.

'Don't do that.' She pulled away, drawing the sheet higher to cover her breasts. 'Don't patronise me. I know all about complex parental relationships.'

'I didn't mean to upset you,' he said, contrite. 'Will you tell me about it?'

Her frown deepened, pain in her eyes. 'By the time my father left us—I was sixteen—he'd already let me down one time too many. For three years I survived without him. Yes, I worked hard to help out Mum, but we were happier somehow, just the three of us. When my mother got sick, I was so scared. One day, I swallowed my pride and called him. I begged him to come home and help care for his wife and to support Freja, who was only fifteen. Do you know what he did? He made excuses, dismissed my concerns, said he'd try, but he had a big deal on the horizon. It was so humiliating. Before I'd even hung up the phone I knew he wouldn't come back. He didn't care about any of us. He chose his own selfish pursuits over his wife and daughters.'

'I'm sorry.' How he wished he could brush away her sadness and wished he'd been more careful with his words, or simply seduced her again rather than talking.

'I got smart—got on with my life,' she continued as if he hadn't interrupted. 'I never relied on him again, never needed him. I stopped presenting myself for his rejection.'

She turned to face him. 'But, by cutting myself off, I never had the chance to tell him how badly he'd let me down, how much he'd hurt me…and I never had the opportunity to work through forgiving him. He died two years ago. I hadn't seen him or spoken to him since that last phone call.'

He took her hand and raised it to his lips, lingering over the kiss he placed on her knuckles to show her the depth of his regret. 'If you could confront him today, what would you say?'

Clara raised her chin. 'That I no longer need him for anything. That he can't hurt or disappoint me any more. That I'm sorry he couldn't be a better man.'

Andreas's heart ached for this beautiful woman who gave so much of herself to others and somehow, intuitively, saw what they needed. His protective urges flared. He wanted to take care of her, to give her as much as she'd given him. To protect her from ever again feeling that degree of hurt and disappointment. But, of course, he *would* react that way to a wonderful woman he was not only sleeping with, but working with while she cared for his terminally ill father. Their lives were repeatedly entwined.

'I think you're wrong, too, *sötnos*,' he said. 'A while ago, you said we're from different worlds, but I think we're more similar than either of us realise.'

They'd faced similar emotional issues, dealing with them differently.

'Maybe,' she said, kissing him so he started to lose track of his thoughts. 'And maybe we should be doing other things than talking before we have to go back to reality.'

Relief washed over him as they retreated to their passion.

'I like the way you think.' In fact, he liked everything about Clara—*everything*. He rolled her underneath him, pressing his lips to hers to block out the doubts and the pain, the past and the future.

But her confessions tumbled through his mind. Bringing her here, to a place he cherished, he felt closer to her than ever. Hearing how badly she'd been hurt by her father, he vowed to take special care of her until he had to give her up.

Because he never wanted to be the one to let her down.

CHAPTER ELEVEN

A WEEK LATER, Clara was working a shift at Nordic Care, well and truly thrust back into reality. She checked the vital signs of her frail, elderly patient, Mrs Kaase, noting her most recent blood pressure on the chart. Needing a second opinion on the case, she'd summoned the registrar for advice.

Despite speaking to Andreas daily, she hadn't seen him since that magical day at the hunting lodge. They'd worked opposite shifts at the hospital, and whenever she'd worked at the palace he'd been busy with his increasing workload of royal engagements. He'd been furious over a leak to the press on the state of Prince Henrik's health, warning Clara that the palace had been forced to issue a public statement announcing his diagnosis. The story, complete with a video clip of Andreas arriving at a prominent children's charity for which he was patron, flooded the media.

Clara had watched it a hundred times just to see a glimpse of his dazzling smile. But watching his life unfold from afar, like the rest of the nation, made him seem so untouchable, they might as well have been strangers again. The absence of him served as a timely reminder: no matter how close she felt to Varborg's heir, he didn't belong to her.

Just then, the door to Mrs Kaase's room opened. Clara looked up, expecting the new registrar, Dr Nilsen.

But it was Andreas.

Their eyes met. Clara's skin tingled, as if imprinted with his every touch. If she'd known he was working today, she'd have applied mascara and the perfume he liked. Before she could fully register the heat and hunger in his stare, she realised he wasn't alone. Sister stood possessively at his side, casting Clara a disapproving look.

Clara forced her expression into something appropriate. 'I called Dr Nilsen.'

Ignoring her body's instant response to the sight of Andreas, she glanced nervously at Sister.

'Dr Cronstedt is very busy, Nurse,' Sister said, as if protecting him from predatory females. 'There's a film crew arriving soon to interview him.'

'Yes, thank you, Sister,' Andreas interjected. 'I have plenty of time to review Nurse Lund's patient.' He held Clara's stare, as if conveying a secret message with his eyes. 'I'm not supposed to be working today, but I was missing my favourite nurses here at Nordic Care.'

He winked at Sister, who flushed with delight. When he looked back at Clara, his expression innocent, his sinful lips twitched.

She swallowed, lightheaded with lust. She recalled the feel of those lips against every inch of her skin, especially between her legs. Disgusted by her weakness for him, she looked away. One day in his bed, and she was ready to forget her professionalism and hurl herself at him at work. But her need for him was a choice, not a necessity. She could kick the habit any time.

'So, what's bothering you, Clara?' He glanced at sleeping Mrs Kaase and stepped closer, reaching for her chart.

Desperation to touch him curled tightly inside Clara like an over-wound spring. Okay, maybe for now she was hooked, but just because he'd taught her that sex could be phenomenal when it was with the right person didn't mean she should act all starry-eyed. Even if they'd been alone, they had work to do.

'I'm concerned about Mrs Kaase's increasing breathlessness,' Clara said, conscious that Andreas most likely had a hundred other things to do rather than investigate her clinical hunch.

'Is that all?' Sister asked. 'Maybe you should have run this past me before calling the doctor.'

'I'm here now, Sister.' Andreas said, staring at Clara encouragingly. 'Go on.'

His observation lit her up as if she were made of electric currents, every one of them connected to the pleasure centres in her brain. But on closer inspection there was a tightness around his mouth, fatigue in his eyes. He seemed…distracted. He had so much going on. *She* was the least of his priorities, and that was fine with her.

Except this was about their patient. 'She's seven days' post-right ventricular myocardial infarction,' she continued, undaunted.

'So you're thinking right heart failure?' he asked, his confidence in her clinical acumen obvious from the impressed approval shining in his eyes. Most doctors wouldn't have asked for her opinion.

'Yes…' she said, hating the hesitation in her voice.

She shouldn't doubt herself or her powers of observation and critical thinking just because they'd slept together. Was it just the presence of the sour-faced sister, who assumed Andreas the heir was too busy to care about his patients, when Clara knew better because she knew *him*? Or was it the things they'd shared about their respective fathers? He'd pretty quickly shut down her suggestion that he speak to Prince Henrik, letting her know when she'd crossed the line, and she'd had to pull him up on his thoughtless assumption that he was the only one with a complex father-child relationship.

But Clara didn't need his approval to do her job.

'She has worsening peripheral oedema and weight gain,'

she continued, pressing home her argument. 'She's also complaining of non-specific abdominal pain.'

'I agree. It sounds like right-sided failure,' he said. 'Let's examine Mrs Kaase.'

He gently placed a hand on the patient's shoulder to wake her. 'Mrs Kaase, I need to have a listen to your heart and lungs, okay?'

The patient nodded sleepily, and Clara helped her into a sitting position. With his auscultation complete, Andreas looped his stethoscope around his neck and palpated the patient's abdomen, encouraging Clara to do the same, particularly focussing on the right-upper quadrant, where she felt an unmistakeable liver edge that indicated hepatomegaly.

'The jugular venous pressure is elevated,' he said to Clara, indicating the distended vein in the woman's neck. 'I'll site a central line to monitor the central venous pressure and order an echo.'

He addressed the patient. 'Nurse Lund and I are a little concerned that your heart isn't pumping very effectively.'

The elderly lady reached for his hand. Andreas wrapped his large, capable hands around Mrs Kaase's frail one and something in Clara's chest jolted. The medical profession would lose a great doctor when Varborg's heir became ruler. But the hospital's loss would be the nation's gain. Just like the older brother he admired so much, Andreas would excel at anything.

If only he could resolve his issues with Prince Henrik. If only he'd talk to the man before it was too late. If he fully embraced the role that was his by birth, rather than seeing himself second choice, he'd not only be good, he'd be incredible.

Her stomach swooped with the realisation that soon they'd no longer be working together. It shouldn't bother her, but maybe she was getting too close. Maybe that was why she was so invested in his happiness, why his praise and collaboration affected her so deeply... But she couldn't become reliant on him.

'I'll speak to the High Dependency Unit and organise her transfer,' he said. 'Is she on diuretics?'

Clara nodded, handing him Mrs Kaase's drug chart. 'I'll set up a central line tray.'

Grateful to escape for a moment, she left Andreas to explain the minimally invasive procedure to the patient, while she collected the portable ultrasound machine and the equipment he would need to site the central venous catheter. Her hands trembled as she gathered wrapped sterile syringes and dressings. Just because professionally and intimately Andreas treated her as his equal didn't mean she should forget her hard-won autonomy. If she wasn't careful, if she confused amazing sex and professional camaraderie for other feelings, she could so easily be hurt, given her lack of experience with relationships.

Feelings made a person vulnerable. She'd seen that in her parents' marriage; had seen her mother's tendency to forgive her neglectful husband again and again in the name of love. Clara had no intention of falling into the same trap.

Assisted by Clara, Andreas skilfully sited the central line in the internal jugular vein in Mrs Kaase's neck before accompanying Clara and the patient to the HDU. After handing over their patient, they left the ward together, an awkward silence descending.

'I've missed you,' he said finally.

The stark need, heat and restraint in his eyes all but sent Clara bursting into flames. Gone was the dedicated doctor and the regal prince. In his place stood the stripped-back man—a complex and flawed man she now knew intimately. But she needed to be careful.

'Me too,' she whispered, her entire body molten-hot.

His eyes sparked with triumph, his sexy mouth tugged in a knowing smile. Despite her warnings to herself, she ached for him. She'd do almost anything to feel his lips on her skin, to hear him groan her name, to feel him fill that empty place deep in her core. But this physical dependency to him was linked to Andreas's skills as a lover. It certainly didn't mean that she was *emotionally* dependent.

'Come to me—tonight.' It was an order, pure and simple, filled with sensual assurance.

She dragged in a breath, desperate to agree, every inch of her clamouring for the pleasure behind the promise. But she hesitated. They paused outside Clara's ward. He leaned against the wall, his head cocked in challenge, awaiting her answer. They stood a perfectly professional distance apart, but the air between them was thick with pheromones. She might as well be naked and wrapped around him, so intense was his invisible force field drawing her in.

Clara glanced down the corridor, horribly torn. Her body was fully on board but her head couldn't shake off the words of caution. Maybe it was the ticking clock. Maybe it was Sister's reminder of his importance, of how he was regarded public property, how he would soon be promoted to the 'top job'. Maybe it was that pesky reality of hers.

'What if someone sees me at the palace when I'm off-duty?' No one could know.

'We'll meet somewhere after dark,' he said, his eyes sparkling with excitement, making a pulse thrum between her legs. 'We'll leave your car and I'll smuggle you into the palace in mine. I'll text you an out-of-the-way meeting place.'

Clara swallowed, adrenaline a wild rush in her veins, her stare obsessively glued to his sexy mouth. She wanted him too much, the longing also a reason for hesitation.

Being smuggled into the palace on her night off seemed way riskier than that day at the lodge, when she'd already had a legitimate work-related reason to be at the palace. What if she was caught in his suite? She wasn't one of his society so-phisticates; she was a normal woman.

With Prince Henrik's diagnosis public knowledge, media speculation and interest in Andreas had sky-rocketed. If any-one got wind of their…affair…if her family shame of her fa-ther's notoriety, debts and prison sentence came out, not only would she have to relive the humiliation but Andreas would be tainted by association.

She should tell him, before he found out some other way. But not here. Not now.

'It feels…risky.' She should return to the ward and her du-ties. Except he was looking at her the way he'd done when she'd been naked, when he'd moved inside her, when he'd watched her climax…triumphantly confident.

As if tired of her caution, Andreas glanced along the corri-dor and then sprang into action, taking her hand and dragging her into a vacant treatment room. The minute the door closed, she was in his arms, their lips crashing together, their tongues thrusting, their hands restlessly fisting each other's clothes.

His powerful body pinned her to the back of the door, the heat of him a stifling inferno. She rubbed her body against his, seeking the friction that would help quench the fire, but her uniform was too tight; she couldn't open her legs wide enough to have him where she wanted. She clung to him, kiss-ing him back with so much pent-up desire, she would surely leave scorch marks on his white coat.

He growled, pulling back while his greedy hands caressed her hips, her waist, her breasts. 'Please, *sötnos*. I can't spend another night without you. I'm going out of my mind. *You* are the real reason I came in today.'

Before she could answer, he kissed her fiercely once more, his lips then sliding down her neck, hitting all her sensitive spots, coiling the desire between her legs tighter. Clara tried to cling to the elusive threads of her argument, but her brain was paralysed with pleasure. It was as if that day at the cabin had primed her body to respond to him, only him, on reflex. She was panting, slick heat in her pelvis, her drugged-up mind ready to agree to any liaison he suggested.

'I can't think straight for wanting you.' He stroked her nipple through her clothes and she dropped her head back against the door, exposing her neck to his open-mouthed kisses.

This was crazy. They were at work; this room was regularly used. But she couldn't seem to stop kissing him, the thrill of his need for her, of finding him hard, making her bold and, oh, so reckless.

She cupped his erection through his scrubs. He groaned against her skin, the scrape of his facial hair sending shivers through her every nerve. But she couldn't go back to work with stubble rash from his beard. Somehow that thought gave her the strength to shove him back a pace.

'Okay. I'll meet you later,' she said. 'But the location has to be absolutely safe. If I think there's a chance we'll be seen together, I won't stop.'

He braced his hand on the door over her head, and stared down at her with hooded eyes. 'Bring your toothbrush; you'll be staying the night. I need to get my fill of you in case we are forced to spend another week like the last.'

At the thought of spending the entire night in his bed, trickles of elation zapped along her nerves, setting off a series of shudders. 'I can't wait. But now I have to go.'

Yanking his neck, she pressed one last kiss to his lips, which were curled in a self-satisfied smile. She ducked away and checked her reflection in the mirror over the sink. Debauched: there was no other way to describe the flush to her skin, the excitement in her eyes and the kiss-swollen state of her lips.

'Don't you have somewhere to be?' she asked, flicking him an accusing stare in the mirror before splashing her face with cold water.

He leaned against the door they'd just utilised, his arms crossed over his chest while he watched her smugly.

'The interview is in an hour,' he said, looking as if he might reach for her again. 'A public relations exercise dreamt up by the palace—let's show the nation a candid glimpse of the heir doing his day job while he still has it…'

At the defeat in his muttered words, Clara turned to face him. 'I'm sorry.'

'It's fine.' He shrugged, his stare vulnerable, bewildered by the sacrifices he had to make. 'But our secret rendezvous will be the only thing getting me through this afternoon.'

Clara nodded, uncertain what to say. Andreas didn't have to trust her with his feelings on giving up medicine. He'd made it clear at the cabin that her advice that he should talk to Prince Henrik was unwelcome.

'I'll let you get back to work,' he said, carelessly swiping his fingers through his hair. 'Until tonight.'

He opened the door, turning to wink at Clara before he ducked outside.

Clara rushed back to the ward, her stomach knotted with excitement for tonight which, with everything that was going on for him, could be their last. Either way, he deserved to know her most shameful secret. He deserved to know the risks they were taking with their affair.

She would tell him tonight.

CHAPTER TWELVE

ANDREAS PULLED THE CAR into the underground garage at the palace, his excited pulse a deafening rage in his ears. He was only flesh and blood, and having Clara close enough to touch but still out of reach while he drove had tested his limits to the max.

'Are you sure no one saw me?' she asked from the passenger seat, still ducked down, out of sight.

'Positive,' he said, turning off the engine. 'The windows are tinted.'

He didn't add that he'd asked Nils to do a dry run of their route to ensure there'd be no hidden surprises. Clara was skittish enough without knowing that, since the press release confirming his father's diagnosis, media interest in Andreas had tripled. There was nothing like bad news to fuel speculation about Varborg's future ruler. He'd resolutely avoided watching the news, but he'd been told that several international newspapers were running stories on the tragedy-struck Cronstedt family, rehashing the death of Andreas's mother and Oscar as entertainment for the masses.

He understood Clara's caution. The idea of her facing the kind of public and media interest he'd experienced these past few days, left him chilled to the bone. He'd do everything in his power to safeguard her privacy. He'd vowed to protect her and he wouldn't let her down.

Andreas unclipped his seatbelt. 'Come here.'

He leaned over the centre console, cupping Clara's face to give her the proper kiss he'd had to hold inside for eight endless days. He pressed kisses to her closed eyelids, the tip of her nose, the angle of her jaw and that sensitive place on her neck.

'I missed you so much,' he mumbled against her soft lips, his heart thudding with urgency.

Why had he ever taken his previous freedom and relative privacy for granted? Soon his life would be unrecognisable—every second of his time scheduled, people constantly surrounding him, public appearances and interviews to be done, like this afternoon's. His grip on his old life was slipping, and Clara was the one thing that made his situation tolerable.

He held her tighter. 'I'm adding a new condition—we can't leave it that long again.'

His time for indulging in flings, his time for working alongside Clara, was running out. Every second with her felt precious.

'We've been busy,' she said, pulling him closer so the gear stick jabbed his ribs. 'And we need to be careful at the hospital. No more steamy gropes in the treatment room, although Sister might not let anyone else near you.'

'Right now, I can't think of anything more important than kissing you.' Andreas groaned; she was too far away, had too many clothes on, was talking too much.

But Clara's words had struck a nerve. Constitutionally, he belonged to Varborg. He was obliged to marry, produce an heir, and secure the next generation of Cronstedt princes and princesses. He'd always known it would take an exceptional woman to walk at his side through the circus that would be his life from here on out. But, since meeting Clara, his desires had solidified. He didn't want a cardboard cut-out for a wife. He wanted something real with someone who understood him beyond the public role he played. Someone to grow at his side. Someone he could respect, love and care for.

But right now he only cared about one woman. He breathed in the scent of her skin and slid his hand along her thigh, which was covered in thick black stockings that disappeared under a tight woollen skirt.

She gripped his tie, pulling his mouth back to hers.

'I like you all dressed up,' she said. 'You look extremely hot in an untouchable kind of way. Is this what you wore for the interview?'

'You can touch all you want, *sötnos*.' Andreas grinned, his hand locating an inch of bare skin at her waist. 'But, yes, I wore this for part of the filming. They also had me dress in scrubs and examine a few people at the hospital—make Varborg's heir relatable to the masses.'

Clara slid her fingers through his hair, pushing it back from his face, staring up at him thoughtfully. 'You are relatable; you don't have to try.'

'Maybe you should be on my PR team.' Andreas gripped her hand and kissed her knuckles one by one. She saw things in him no one else saw; believed in him without agenda.

'If we don't move right now,' he said, reaching for the door handle at his back, 'You'll be riding me in this seat with the steering wheel at your back.'

Spurred into action by Clara's nervous squawk and the desire pounding through his blood, Andreas exited the vehicle and rushed her towards the lift to the guest suite he was still using.

She kissed him again, driving him wild with delicate darts of her tongue against his. 'You won't be able to smuggle me in like this much longer,' she said as they tumbled out of the lift, tugging at each other's clothes, pausing every few steps to kiss. 'Especially when you move into your own suite.'

She shoved at his suit jacket and he tossed it on the floor.

'I'll build a secret tunnel from your house to mine,' he said, only half-joking, 'So you can come to me any time you want.'

He refused to think of them ending when every other aspect of his life was so uncertain.

He *needed* her. She laughed but a shadow crossed her eyes. There was something hesitant about her tonight, more than her fear of discovery. It was making him jittery.

'Why are we wasting time talking,' he said, 'When that's been all we could do for eight excruciating days?'

He reached for her, losing himself in her kisses, gripping her waist and guiding her into the bedroom. Clara pulled the hem of his shirt free of his trousers and slid her hands up his back, restlessly pressing her body against his. He removed her sweater and popped open her bra, his hands greedily caressing her beautiful breasts as they spilled free.

'Because I've missed you,' she said simply, honestly, perfectly.

That was his Clara…

The possessive direction of his thoughts caught him off-guard. She wasn't his. This was a fling; even if he wanted something more permanent, that wasn't what *she* wanted. He didn't want to hurt her, disappoint her or let her down, and his father's diagnosis had curtailed his freedoms. Just as Oscar had done, he must put duty first. He couldn't drag someone as unique and guileless as Clara into his world of ancient protocol and public service. She cherished her independence and her career. He wouldn't change a single thing about her.

Right here, right now, this was all they had because he couldn't fail another person he cared about.

Unease compounded his desperation for her. He quickly peeled the remaining clothes from her body, taking one indulgent second to rake his gaze over her nakedness, his hands skimming her skin as if committing the softness, every dip and swell to memory.

'You're so beautiful; you steal my breath.' He tugged her close, the heat of her burning through his clothes. 'Later, I'm taking you in my giant bath, the scene of our first meeting. But first… I need you.'

He thumbed her nipples erect, smiling when she moaned his name and dropped her head back so he could ravage her neck with kisses.

'I need you too,' she said on a sigh, taking hold of his tie once more and tugging him by the neck towards the bed. She sat down and hurriedly undid his belt and fly, looking up at him with wicked intent. He'd barely survived the last time she put her gorgeous mouth on him. And he was strung so taut, the tick-tock of the clock flooding his body with a sense of panic, that this time he might actually fracture apart.

With a look of thrilling determination, Clara encircled his erection, licked up the length of him and then took him inside her mouth. She hummed a satisfied sound of delight. He closed his eyes, a surge of arousal filling him to bursting point. How could she do this to him—render him unstable with her touch and that look that said she saw him exactly as he was? Just a man.

But there was something wild about her tonight. Had she reached her limit in the eight days they'd been forced apart by work schedules and life? Or was she too hungrily preparing for future famine when they'd be once more forced apart, maybe for good. No; he couldn't think about that.

Spurred into action, he yanked back his hips. He tossed off his clothes and prosthesis and prowled over her naked body. He kissed her lips, her breasts, her stomach and then dived between her legs to kiss and lick her into a sobbing frenzy. He was addicted to her taste. Addicted to everything, from the stud in her nose to the sharp wit of her tongue and the sound of her moans when she climaxed.

She cried out his name now, her hands twisting in his hair.

He teased her sensitive nipples to hard peaks so she was writhing, needy for him, her hands restless and grabby.

'We won't be sleeping tonight,' he said, settling his weight over her. 'I want to make up for those eight days with as many orgasms as is humanly possible.'

He slid his hand to the slick heat between her legs, watching her eyes darken with need.

'Yes…' She dug her nails into his shoulders and spread her thighs wide so their hips aligned.

On fire from within, his heartbeat banged, dangerously high.

'I can't get enough of you,' he panted, tearing his mouth away from her kisses. He cupped her thigh, his hips grinding between her parted legs as if out of his control. He'd never been this hot for a woman. The deprivation had sharpened the ache for her, only her, and one look at her passion-dazed expression told him she felt the same way.

Clara held his face and brought their lips back together in a rush of frantic and deep kisses. She cupped his buttocks, urging him closer, tilting her hips to meet him and shrouding him in her scalding heat as he pushed inside her with a groan of profound relief.

'Andreas!' she cried.

He reared up on his elbows and captured one nipple with his mouth. She crossed her ankles in the small of his back so he sank deeper inside her. Their bodies moved together in a frenzied rhythm as they tried to quench the need riding them both so hard.

How would he ever find the strength to let her go, having taken his entire adult life to find someone so remarkable? In that moment, he could have sworn that Clara was as essential as the very air he breathed.

He rolled them, holding her hips so they stayed locked together. She sat astride him and rode him, her hair a wild tumble around her flushed face. He cupped her pert breasts and stroked her nipples with his thumbs. She shattered, her stare locked to his, her cries ringing out around the room, until he jack-knifed into a sitting position and kissed them up.

With one final roar, he crushed her to his chest and spilled himself inside her, a part of his soul surely branded hers for all eternity.

Clara relaxed back against Andreas's hard chest, so languid in the warm scented bubble bath that she might have fallen asleep if she hadn't been so attuned to every subtle shift of Andreas's touch. They'd lit what seemed like a hundred candles around the bath and left the blinds open so they could look out at the view of the snow-capped mountains and inky night sky.

Her skin tingled with awareness, the throbbing pulse between her legs barely satiated, even after that incredible orgasm. How would she survive the loss of such pleasure when this fling came to an end? And end it must. Clara was an ordinary woman, too cynical for relationships. Even if she'd wanted more from Andreas, it would be an impossible fairy tale. He would rule Varborg, marry his princess and produce his own heirs, and Clara would watch from the side-lines. Although, she had no clue how she would see pictures of him in the media and not want him with this all-encompassing need...

'I'm sorry about the condom, *sötnos*,' he said, pressing his lips to the side of her neck so she shivered with delight.

'I'm sorry too. But, despite having only one previous partner, I'm still on birth control.'

They'd been so wild for each other after their eight days apart, they'd forgotten all about protection.

'I'm normally very sexually responsible,' he said, his hands sliding up and down her thighs under the water. 'You just make me...insatiable.'

'Insatiable, huh?' Clara smiled like the cat that had stolen the cream, the flutters in her chest telling her just how much she trusted Andreas.

Now that they were finally alone, she should tell him about her father's prison sentence. But she was so relaxed, his touch so hypnotic, it was hard to think about anything but him. And, once her secret was out, she'd have nowhere left to hide. That most vulnerable part of herself, the part she'd always protected from hurt by avoiding relationships, would be exposed. He'd know *everything*.

His lips skimmed the sensitive place on her neck, distracting her once more. 'Will you watch my interview when it airs? Let me know how badly it comes across?'

'Of course, but I doubt it will be bad. You're a prince and a doctor, and you're single. Half of Varborg will be in love with you before the show ends.'

Now it was his turn to chuckle, while spikes of jealousy pricked Clara's skin. But he didn't belong to her.

'Did they ask you any questions you didn't want to answer?' she asked to detract from the helpless, jittery feeling in the pit of her stomach.

'I'd already vetoed any questions relating to Oscar's death,' he said. 'But they asked if I'm currently seeking a princess to marry—only to be expected in my position. My personal life is considered public property.'

Clara flinched. Wasn't she temporarily part of his personal life? Because she'd rather have run naked out into the snow than know if Andreas was officially courting some foreign princess or lucky aristocrat closer to home, she latched onto another topic.

'Will you tell me about Oscar?' she whispered, resting her head on his shoulder so his next kiss landed on her cheek. 'I'd love to know what he was like.'

Andreas took a deep breath, his chest expanding at her back.

'It's so hard to paint one picture,' he said on a sigh. 'He was so many things.'

'Like you, then,' Clara said, lifting his hand to press a kiss to his fingers.

'He was good at everything.' His voice lightened with admiration. 'But somehow humble too. He could ski like a champion, speak five languages and he always had a joke up his sleeve, ready to drop it into conversation if and when appropriate.'

Clara smiled, pressing a breathy kiss to his lips. 'Very useful skills for a statesman. How many languages do *you* speak?'

'Only three, I'm afraid.'

'What a dreadful under-achiever,' she teased, and he laughed. 'Hot and intelligent and kind—the palace may need to ramp up security once that interview airs.' But her teasing cost her another jealous roll of her stomach.

He chuckled. After a few seconds, he stiffened. 'Oscar's death was a great loss for the future of Varborg. He had big plans to modernise the principality. We discussed it often— how things would be different for our children.'

'What kind of plans?' Clara didn't want to imagine Andreas's fair-haired children.

He shrugged, sending out ripples of bathwater. 'Ways to challenge the old guard traditionalists, a more equal distribution of duties between royal siblings, that kind of thing.'

'Things you can still implement yourself, if you choose.' She entwined her fingers with his, cautious of making him withdraw, the way he had at the cabin when she'd pushed too hard.

'I guess. We didn't discuss it until we were adults, but we were both lonely growing up so…segregated. We needed to develop our own interests and be independent, but when it came to our royal life we could have acted as a team rather than being divided. Not that it matters now.'

Clara stilled, aware of the thud of his heart at her back and the matching rhythm in her chest. Every second of their time was precious, but Andreas's past issues with his place in the Cronstedt family were holding him back from being his wonderfully authentic self. He'd made it clear that he wouldn't be addressing those issues with his father. But, if she could get him talking, maybe it would help him to believe in his ability to rule.

'Will you tell me about the accident?' she whispered. 'I promise I'll never speak of it to another soul.'

'I know you won't, *sötnos*.' Andreas pressed his lips to her temple. 'You and I share a sense of loyalty. I trust you.'

Clara swallowed, her eyes stinging with longing. He trusted her but she was hiding something from him: her most shameful family secret. She needed to tell him, and soon.

'Oscar and I were both in the army, in different regiments,' he said, staring ahead as if staring into the past. 'We were attending the same training exercise. It was all perfectly standard until it wasn't. Oscar was in a vehicle crossing rough terrain when it hit a concealed ditch and rolled.'

Clara sat frozen, a shiver running through her, although the water was still warm.

'I heard it on the radio,' he continued. 'The medical corps were training nearby, so we rushed to help. We managed to free the driver, but Oscar was unconscious in the passenger seat, the crushed cab of the vehicle trapping him.'

His heart thudded against her back and Clara gripped his hand tighter, wishing she could undo his pain and loss.

'We cleared the shattered windscreen,' he continued, 'And I half-climbed in so I could preserve Oscar's airway while we waited for the cutting crew. I could tell it looked bad for him. He had an obvious head injury, and a scalp wound that was bleeding profusely, but all I could do in that position was stabilise his neck, pressure-dress the wound and protect his airway.'

Tears tracked down Clara's cheeks. He must have felt so scared and helpless.

'I was too emotionally attached to be objective,' Andreas said. 'But I refused to leave him, even when he went into cardiac arrest. I performed CPR, even when I was ordered to step down by my superior officer so someone else could take over. Even when someone noticed the petrol leaking, I refused to leave my brother.'

Clara turned to face him, the full horror of what must have happened hitting her like a blow.

He nodded, his face pale with grief, as if he was reliving the accident. 'The wreck burst into flames. I was thrown clear, but I broke both my legs.'

'I'm so sorry,' she whispered, pressing her lips to his in silent apology. Why had she asked him? Because she just selfishly wanted to know everything about him, for her own insatiable needs.

'They saved the right leg, but the left was fractured and badly burned, and became infected. They had to amputate three days before Oscar's funeral.'

'Andreas…' She sat astride his lap, holding onto both his hands as if she'd never let go. 'You could have died too.'

He shook his head, dismissing her concern. 'He was my brother, my senior in rank, my country's heir to the throne and I couldn't save him.'

Clara's vision blurred with sadness. She gripped his face. '*No one* could have saved him. You did everything humanly possible. It was a terrible accident.'

'A part of me knows that.' A sad smile tugged his lips; he didn't believe her. 'But the rest of me just feels guilty. I'm a *doctor*. I let him down. And why was it me to survive and not him?'

'You know why.' Clara rested her forehead against his. 'Life is random and sometimes unfair.'

She didn't need to tell Andreas that. He was an intelligent man of the world, a leader, who'd had more than his fair share of family tragedy.

'*He* should be here now,' Andreas said as if he hadn't heard, as he gripped her upper arms so they were locked together in this horrible moment of grief and heartache. 'He was meant to be the one to succeed Prince Henrik.'

Clara shook her head violently. The idea of never having met Andreas was too horrible to contemplate.

'You feel responsible because of your profession,' she said passionately. 'Because he was your big brother, a man you loved and respected; because the family you were born into has a hereditary hierarchy most families don't have. But it wasn't your fault.'

He stared up at her, pain shifting across his beautiful eyes. And something else—need. His arms came around her waist and he held her so close, burying his face against the erratic thud of her heart. It was as if their connection, this wild storm of desire that never seemed to lessen, went way beyond physical in that moment.

But it couldn't. She wouldn't let it mean more. She was strong. She would be there for him, embrace their intimacies until it was time for them to part and then she'd deal with the fallout once it was over.

Clara stroked his hair and held him to her heart as if she could fix the broken pieces of him. His life was in turmoil. He was grieving for the past and the future. He was hurting, carrying unnecessary guilt over Oscar's death and feeling that he was second best to a dead man because of his family's succession, and because he had unresolved issues with Prince Henrik. If what he'd told her the day at the cabin was true, he and Prince Henrik had never really spoken about Oscar's death. Perhaps if Andreas knew that no one else blamed him, including his father, he could start to forgive himself. It might ease his struggles with the royal role he felt he didn't deserve.

But, just like Andreas hadn't been able to save Oscar, Clara couldn't save Andreas. He needed to do that himself.

'What can I do to help you?' she asked, aching for him.

His arms tightened around her waist. 'You help me simply by being here. Things make sense when I'm with you. You understand me. You see me, the real me. You always have.'

Clara held him while he crushed her to him.

Right now, while the rest of his life was tugging him in all directions, he might feel as if he needed her, but she couldn't forget her reality. Her valued independence, her own shameful past and her determination for equality in any future relationship.

'I know you think I should talk to the prince about the past, about Oscar,' he continued. 'And maybe you're right. But, what with my crash course on ruling Varborg, stepping in to fulfil most of my father's engagements and planning a state funeral in minute detail, the prince and I already have many things on our minds.'

'I'm sorry. I didn't mean to pry.' Her voice sounded sickeningly small, the feeling she'd been dismissed once more causing a hot ache in her throat. It made memories of her final phone call to her father resurface, when he'd trivialised her concerns and refused to make her any promises.

But she didn't need promises from Andreas. This was just sex.

'And I didn't mean to offload.' He dragged her lips to his. 'Let's forgive each other.'

Clara nodded and smiled, because he'd done nothing wrong. He was just dealing with his lot in life in the best way he knew how. It wasn't Andreas's fault that she'd learned from her own regrets or that she would hate to see him miss his chance to heal some of the scars holding him back before his father died.

But she needed to accept that sometimes she just couldn't fix what was broken.

'I've handed in my notice at Nordic Care,' he said, looking up at her with such grief and vulnerability, she shoved aside her selfish thoughts on what that would mean for her.

'That's good.' She pressed her lips to his. 'You have a lot going on.'

But she understood his reluctance to end his locum job. He was clinging to the one thing he could control, the one thing he could ensure he was good at—his career.

But he had so much more to give.

'You're like your brother, Andreas,' she said imploringly. 'You'll be good at anything you set your mind to, including ruling this nation of ours.'

His expression shifted from despair to bewilderment. 'You asked how you could help…and my answer is just be yourself. Don't ever change, *sötnos*.'

He brushed her lips with his on a ragged sigh, pulling back to search her stare. 'You are the only good thing I can hold onto right now.' His hands restlessly skimmed her back and her shoulders, his fingers tunnelling into her hair. 'I need you, Clara. I want you.'

Gripping the back of her neck, he dragged her mouth back to his. His kiss grew deeper, his hands roaming her body as if he was committing the shape of her to memory.

Clara surrendered, kissing him back, losing herself again. Every time she veered away from the passion and connection they found in each other's arms, she came unstuck, her mind spinning out, searching for answers and solutions that were right there in front of her.

For, however long they had left, *this* was all that mattered.

His hands gripped her hips under the water, drawing her close. He was hard between her legs. Rising up on her knees, she guided him inside her body, each of them sighing with relief as they stared into each other's eyes.

For now, he was hers—her wild mountain-man, her Viking.

As she rocked above him and he moved inside her, passion spiralling as they clung to each other, and Clara clinging to the only part of him she could have, she promised herself she would hold something back.

She would protect her heart the way she'd always done because, of all men, Andreas had the power to do the most damage.

CHAPTER THIRTEEN

THREE DAYS LATER, Clara was just about to leave the palace after her night shift when she received a text from her sister, Freja.

Have you seen this?

The message accompanied a link to a celebrity news site. The main article featured a grainy picture of Andreas and Clara kissing goodbye at her car the morning after she'd spent the night in his bed at the palace.

Her stomach dropped at the sickening headline: *How Much Longer Can the Heir Play the Field?*

Horrified, her pulse went through the roof. She could almost taste the public's rejection, hear their judgement and contempt that she wasn't good enough for Varborg's heir. But, worse, if her identity was revealed, if the connection between Lars Lund and her got out, her family's humiliating past might hurt Andreas at a time when he must feel as if his life was falling apart.

Tears pricked her eyes. Her father's disgrace shouldn't be her burden to bear, but she'd been hard-wired most of her life to feel the sting of rejection. And that guilty part of her, that should have already come clean to Andreas, now had nowhere left to hide.

It was time to face him.

Willing herself to calm down, Clara texted Andreas.

We need to talk.

Against her better judgement, she scoured the picture again. The photographer had clearly been hiding some distance away, using a telephoto lens. Clara was only visible from behind, but her parked car was in the background. The registration number had been blurred out, but it would only take some nosy journalist a few seconds of sleuthing to find out her identity and the paper trail of shame that would lead to her door.

Andreas's reply was swift.

Come to the green sitting room in the family wing. Sorry, I can't get away.

With acid burning her throat, Clara hurried to the room she knew of but had never been inside, grateful for the sense of legitimacy her uniform provided.

Her rapid steps matched the panicked bounding of her heart. What if poor Prince Henrik had seen the photo? What if the palace press office was aware of the identity of Andreas's unsuitable mystery woman? Would she be fired or banned from seeing Andreas?

An ache settled under her ribs, its potency suspicious of grief. But she'd always known this day would come, that she'd have to give him up; she'd just hoped for a little more time. Knocking on the door, she waited for the call to enter and then ducked quickly inside.

He wasn't alone.

Even with a firestorm of fear in her veins, her heart lurched at the arresting sight of Andreas. His immaculately tailored navy suit caressed his lean and sculpted body to perfection. He looked up from adjusting his crisp white cuffs, which glinted with onyx cuff links, his stare burning into hers from across the room.

Taking one look at Clara's face, Andreas stiffened.

'Leave us,' he instructed the valet, who ceased his efforts brushing invisible specks of lint from Andreas's suit and hastily fled.

'What is it, *sötnos*?' A small frown tugged down his mouth as he crossed the room.

Clara rested her eyes on his, her heart actually stuttering to a stop. The flood of desire for him was almost strong enough to dispel her profound embarrassment—almost.

Last night, snuggled on the sofa with her mum and Freja, with mugs of hot chocolate, she'd watched Andreas's interview. She'd sat spellbound, her eyes glued to the screen as the skilled programmers painted a portrait of Andreas the doctor, Andreas the veteran, Andreas the heir.

Now, chilled to the bone, she was fooling herself to think she could have any part of such a magnificent man. He was wildly dashing, every inch the eligible prince and commanding statesman he feared he might never be. But he couldn't fight his upbringing, his genetics and the historic breeding of his family line. He was a prince. He always had been, from the day he'd been born. Clara had just forgotten that, allowing herself to be swept along by lust, by her professional regard and the way he'd made her feel special. But *he* was the special one.

'You're scaring me, Clara.' He gripped her upper arms. 'Are you hurt? Is it Prince Henrik?'

Clara shook her head and blurted out her reason for disturbing him. 'There's a photo of us together online.'

She blinked to stave off tears; her revelation would be final confirmation that this was over. Had she already tarnished his reputation by association? And at a time when he had so much else going on.

A muscle clenched in his jaw, but he didn't seem surprised. 'I've been made aware.' He reached for her hands. 'I'm sorry. The announcement of Prince Henrik's state of health has, I'm afraid, caused an increased interest in my personal life.'

She frowned, her head foggy with desire, confusion and guilt. Could she blame the public? She too had watched the candid thirty-minute interview of Varborg's heir with rapt fascination bordering on obsession, her hot drink forgotten.

'No, *I'm* sorry.' She tugged her hands from his, feeling shabby and creased in her uniform, more aware than ever before of their massive differences.

With his face cloaked in his signature close-cropped beard, he was more handsome rogue than prince of the realm, but of course that was a massive part of his Viking appeal.

He frowned. 'Why are *you* apologising? It's me they were after, not you.' He ran a hand through his tamed hair. '*I* should be the one apologising for not protecting you better, for exposing you to the seedier side of life in the public gaze. I know you wanted to keep us a secret. For now, they don't seem to know who you are.'

His hands gripped her elbows and he pressed a desperate kiss to her lips. Clara's body reacted, as always, to his kiss.

'You don't understand,' she said, extricating herself from his touch. She wanted nothing more than to curl up in his arms and hide from her past, from the ugliness and risk she'd exposed him to. But shame was a painful gripe in her belly.

'I understand all too well.' His voice rose, fury sparking in his grey stare. 'It's an invasion of my privacy and yours. *I* expect it, but they have no right to target you. I won't let that happen. I swear to you, Clara. I'll protect you.'

'I need to tell you something.' Clara shook her head, trying to stay on track, but shock and desire threatened to derail her thoughts. She could no longer deny that her need for this man was now a full-blown addiction. She'd realised that last night, watching him on the screen.

'*Sötnos...*' He stepped closer and wrapped her in his arms so she was engulfed by his warmth and the scent of his cologne. 'Please don't distress yourself over this. Let me deal with it. I have people. I'll ensure that you remain anonymous.'

He tilted her chin, brushing his thumb over her bottom lip, his stare dipping there. 'It's just a fishing expedition—social commentary from strangers who don't know me but think I should be married by now, or some such rubbish.'

Clara recoiled from his touch, turning her head away. The idea of Andreas with another woman hit her like a slap to the face. But of course there would be other women after her, until finally his princess: a sophisticated beauty with the appropriate pedigree, well-schooled in dealing with press intrusion, her closet devoid of tawdry family skeletons. The kind of woman who would look at home on the arm of the immaculate and urbane prince before her.

Hating her own weakness, her self-doubt-fuelled envy, Clara snapped, 'I don't need you to rescue me or protect me; I can take care of myself.'

Andreas frowned, his gaze flicking to the clock on the wall. 'So it's okay for you to want to help me, but not for me to help you?'

Clara dragged in a calming breath. He clearly had places to be, important people to see. Her sad family drama would be swiftly passed to some lackey in the palace press office.

'I won't keep you,' Clara said, rolling back her shoulders, 'But I need you to listen. I told you about my father running out on us, but the bit I left out was that he was something of a swindler. Not only did he get into all kinds of debt while my parents were together, he also re-mortgaged our family home behind my mother's back. But the worst thing he did was defraud a bunch of people in some sort of pyramid scheme. He went to prison, Andreas. He died in prison. That's why I never had the chance to confront him, because I refused to visit.'

'Clara—'

'I know I should have told you before.' She blinked, refusing to cry for the father who'd let her down so badly. 'But I'm not exactly proud of the fact. I thought, if we were careful, it never needed to come out.'

'It doesn't matter,' he stated flatly, moving towards her and then stopping, presumably in response to her expression.

'Of course it matters,' she snapped, her fears spilling free. 'We promised we'd be careful, but now look what's happened. I'm…news. I never wanted any of this. I just wanted *you*.'

'I'm right here.' He gripped her cold hand and rested it over his chest where his heart thudded against her palm, vibrant and steady.

Clara looked away from his impeccable appearance; he felt more out of reach than ever. 'And you may as well be on the moon, don't you see?' she cried. 'We've always been too different and now the whole world will see that. You'll be embarrassed. Prince Henrik will be embarrassed. Neither of you need a scandal right now.'

She tugged her hand free and backed away from him. She couldn't think when he touched her—that was how they'd ended up in this mess.

'I'll probably lose my job,' she continued, 'And my mother has been through enough without having the whole sordid story regurgitated.'

Tension built in the silence as she finally faced him.

'Are you ending this?' A fierce scowl slashed his handsome face. 'Because I know what I need, and I told you, it's you.'

Confused, Clara shook her head. For a brief moment, him, their connection had been the one easy thing she'd wanted. But it was no longer easy.

'I'm not sure we ever really got started,' she said sadly. She didn't want to leave him, not yet. 'But this photograph certainly complicates things.'

'I told you, I'll take care of it,' he said.

'How? You're royalty,' she argued, deaf to his promises. In Clara's experience, believing in those only made you more vulnerable. 'If people find out you're fraternising with the penniless daughter of a convicted criminal, it could damage your reputation!'

'Don't do this.' He gripped her face, staring at her with panic in his eyes. 'Don't let strangers come between us.'

Tilting her mouth up, he delivered a crushing kiss as if he could make her believe in him, that he'd deal with the issue.

Her lips parted on a shocked gasp. His tongue surged into her mouth, coaxing. Because she'd always been helpless to their desire for each other, Clara's brain shut down, her body clinging to the pleasure of his kiss to block out all the ugliness in which she felt coated.

This beautiful man, who could have any woman, wanted *her*. The power of it surged through her. *This*, them together, made sense and blocked out reality.

His fingers tangled in her hair, spilling it loose from its bun. His body heat scorched her. His hard chest brushed her sensitive nipples, his thigh pressing between her legs as he backed her up against a table. There was an ominous rattle of something heavy, perhaps a lamp, but Clara was too inflamed to care. She clung to him, drowning, so far out of her depth with this man that her only certainty was that she should walk away. But it was as if her heart knew best and wanted him, no matter what.

'Andreas,' she moaned, spearing her fingers through his hair as he trailed kisses down her neck and slid one hand up her thigh, under her uniform and into her underwear. 'You have to go,' she gasped, palming his erection through his trousers, aware that she was holding him up for whatever important princely engagement he was immaculately dressed.

'I don't care.' He shoved down her underwear and unbuckled his belt. 'I only care about you. About this. About us.'

Frantic now with desire, Clara tackled his fly, freeing him from the confines of his suit.

'You can't leave me, not yet.' With a grunt, he hauled her around the waist and deposited her backside on the edge of the table. He kissed her again, his fingers working her nipple through her uniform and bra.

'I won't,' she cried as they broke free of their kisses to fumble together.

Clara hiked up her skirt and spread her thighs. Andreas shoved down his trousers, just enough to free him from his underwear.

'Soon. I'll let you go soon,' he said, staring into her eyes as he pushed inside her. A low growl rumbled in the back of his throat. His hands clutched at her waist, hips and breasts with thrilling heated possession.

'I want you, Clara…' He groaned against her neck, thrusting inside her. 'You asked me what I needed and the answer is *this. You.*'

He pulled back, stark need in his eyes.

'I want you too.' Clara sighed and shuddered, gripping his hips with her thighs and clinging to him as they rode this storm of need together.

'Tell me you're still mine, *sötnos*,' he muttered between kisses, his hands holding her hips so tightly, she wondered if he'd leave marks. 'Tell me we're still in this together—different but equals. Tell me.'

His thrusts grew more frantic, his kisses deep and demanding, his eye contact so intense, Clara could only hold on and give him her all in return.

'I'm yours,' Clara said, stifling her cries against his lips as pleasure shook her from head to toe, heightened by the glitter of triumph and possession in his stare.

Andreas gave a rough cry and crushed her in his arms as they climaxed together, the furious need finally abating. For long seconds they stayed locked together, hearts thudding, breaths panting.

He moved first, slipping from her body. He stepped back, helping her slide from the table. He buttoned up and Clara shakily scooped her underwear from the floor, stepping inside the garment while her mind raced and her body tried to recover.

What was she doing? She was out of control for this man: risking her emotions; making him promises she might not have the strength to keep; giving him everything when she'd vowed to hold something back as a shield around her inexperienced heart.

He touched her hand and she looked up. Apart from slightly dishevelled hair and a bit of colour on his cheekbones, he was still perfect, still achingly beautiful, still a prince. Sadness, maybe even pity, touched his eyes. 'I've always known about your father, Clara.'

Horrified, she frowned, searching his stare for the truth as ice shifted through her veins.

Andreas's beautiful mouth flattened into a grim line. 'No one works for my family without a police check and a background check.'

He'd known...all this time? For all his talk of equality...

'You consented to be vetted when you landed the job,' he explained. 'Palace security investigate everyone who works here: their past, their family and their employment history. It's all thoroughly scrutinised.' His lip curled with the barest hint of distaste. 'The price you pay for any association with me, I'm afraid. I wish it wasn't necessary, just like I wish I could spare you the paparazzi.'

He shrugged with sad inevitability.

Clara shrivelled inside, as if what they'd just done had left her dirty. She looked away from him, their differences neon-bright, and the trust she'd foolishly imagined shattered on the floor like shards of glass.

'Why didn't you say anything?' Humiliation burned her eyes as she forced herself to look at him.

All this time she'd thought that on some level they were equals, just Clara and Andreas enjoying their chemistry, but in reality he'd always held all of the power in the relationship.

'It didn't matter to me,' he said flatly. '*You* did nothing wrong. It's like you said the first time we met—our scars don't define us.'

The lump in her throat expanded. How could she have been so naïve?

Andreas raised her chin. 'If you care for me at all, please don't let them come between us. We know who we are, what we value, and we know each other. You know me, Clara. If I say it doesn't matter to me, it doesn't matter.'

Numb, Clara nodded. She *did* know this man. She knew her feelings for him were reckless. She knew he'd seen the deeply vulnerable part of her that she'd always kept guarded. She knew that, if she wasn't careful with her heart, she could fall for him and he could destroy her.

I'll let you go soon...

She winced, hating the words she'd been too pleasure-drunk to analyse when he'd spoken them earlier. She didn't want to be *this* Clara: uncertain, emotionally exposed, scared. She wanted to be her old self, the woman who could take care of herself, needed no one and had her life all figured out.

'I need to go,' she said, clearing her throat. 'I have to drive home and change and head to Nordic Care. I'm doing a late shift.'

He cupped her face. 'I'll take care of the press. Trust me.'

She nodded numbly, kissing him and then moving to the door. She *did* trust him, but it changed nothing. She'd let Andreas too close. She'd wanted him and he'd wanted her and their fling had seemed harmless. But danger was everywhere, overwhelming.

At the door, she turned to look at him one last time. His back was to her. He checked his watch, tugging on his cuffs, and pressed a buzzer on the desk, presumably summoning the valet once more.

He was unspeakably beautiful. The demands on him were staggering. She'd wanted to ease his burdens, not add to them. She'd wanted to be there for him, not rely on him. She'd wanted to enjoy their affair and then walk away unscathed.

But it was like he'd once said: 'you don't always get what you want'.

CHAPTER FOURTEEN

ANDREAS'S FINAL SHIFT at Nordic Care arrived two days later, much sooner than planned. With a heavy, grieving heart, he strode onto Clara's ward, his eyes scanning for sight of her. Even now, when tension seemed to colour their every interaction, he selfishly craved her like a drug.

Curtains were drawn around the bed of one of his patients. From the urgent comings and goings, Andreas surmised some sort of emergency was taking place. Curious, he entered the bay. Clara, the ward sister and the new registrar, Dr Nilsen, attended to an elderly man, who was breathless.

'Hello, Mr Hagen.' He addressed the patient he'd admitted a week earlier with uncontrolled diabetes and infected venous ulceration of the lower leg, and looked to Clara for guidance as to the nature of the emergency.

Their eyes met. Pressure built in his chest. He'd missed her so much. Her obvious concern for their patient triggered his protective urges. How he ached to comfort her, to spirit them both away—maybe to the hunting lodge so they could be alone, and work out everything that felt tense between them since she'd panicked about her father, and go to bed until the pieces of his world slotted back into place.

But there was no time for any of that.

'What's the situation?' he asked, scanning the monitors. The patient was clearly in respiratory distress, his respiratory rate elevated and his blood oxygen saturations ninety-four percent.

Clara frowned, as if he had no right to be there. 'Acute shortness of breath. Dr Nilsen was on the ward.' She looked away.

'Good, but I know this patient well.' Stifling an irrational flinch of rejection, Andreas took the man's pulse, which was fast but regular, noting the fine beads of sweat on his brow. That Clara had bypassed him and gone straight to another doctor irked. It shouldn't matter, but it was another sign of her dwindling trust. Not that he could blame her; after today, he wouldn't even work at Nordic Care.

'I think it's acute left ventricular failure,' the registrar said while Clara silently passed Andreas an ECG tracing.

'Any chest pain?' Andreas asked, reaching for his stethoscope to listen to Mr Hagen's lungs.

'No,' Clara answered, while the registrar set about siting an intravenous cannula in the man's antecubital fossa.

Andreas listened to the patient's chest, hearing the unmistakeable crackle of pulmonary oedema, or fluid in the lower lobes of the lungs.

'Let's get some intravenous diuretic and morphine, please, Nurse Lund,' he said, taking control of the situation while trying not to draw parallels with his first day there a few short weeks ago.

So much had happened since they'd met, kissed and faced their first emergency together. He felt as if he'd known Clara a lifetime. But how did *she* feel? Did she still relate to the real him, or was she too overwhelmed by the inconveniences of his public life to keep sight of what they'd shared?

Clara left the bay to fetch the medication, returning with two vials and a syringe, which she handed to the registrar, who quickly drew up the drugs and injected them through the IV cannula.

She couldn't even look at him. It was as if she'd already made up her mind and deemed him too much trouble. Andreas concealed his sigh. He might want to protect her, but he couldn't make any guarantees. He didn't want to let her down or fail her in any way.

'Have you listened to Mr Hagen's chest?' he asked, handing over his stethoscope.

The patient's distress eased as the drugs worked. 'Nurse Lund is going to have a listen, Mr Hagen.'

They'd always collaborated on cases and trusted each other's clinical skills and diligence, regardless of the traditional role demarcations of doctor and nurse. They were a team. He wasn't about to act differently now that his personal circumstances dictated that his other job, the one he would inherit, demanded more of his time.

'We need a chest X-ray, bloods and an echo.' He addressed the team. 'He also needs a catheter to monitor urine output. I'll speak to cardiology, make an urgent referral. We need to exclude a silent myocardial infarction.'

There was a flurry of activity, a dividing up of the tasks. Andreas explained the diagnosis and the tests he's ordered to Mr Hagen, and then sat at a computer station to write in the patient's notes.

He kept one eye on Clara while she went about her duties but she wouldn't meet his eye. He'd just finished speaking to his cardiology colleagues when he spied her heading for the ward exit with her bag slung over her shoulder.

He caught up with her just as she left the ward. 'Clara, can we talk?'

She cast a wary glance around the foyer before pushing through the door to the stairwell, a place of relative privacy.

'Why didn't you call me about Mr Hagen?' he asked when the door closed, unable to keep the hurt or accusation from his voice. He stood as close as he dared, desperate to reach for her. But she was rigid and remote.

'I assumed you were busy,' she said, her expression hurt. 'I understand that today is your last day at Nordic Care.' She shrugged, resigned. 'Hospital rumour mill.'

Andreas winced, reaching for her bare arm, the feel of her skin a jolt of desire to his system. 'I'm sorry. I meant to tell you. I've been stuck in A and E most of the morning. The seasonal flu rush has started.'

'It's fine.' She shook her head, her cheeks flushed, as if she was embarrassed by her hurt feelings.

Despair gripped his throat. He stepped closer, dropping his voice. 'You know how I've struggled with giving up work. I've tried to delay the inevitable as long as possible.'

She nodded. 'I understand. You don't have to explain.'

'Yes, I *do*,' he muttered, willing her to look at him properly. She was slipping through his fingers.

'Everything came to a head this morning,' he said, desperate to downplay the matter so she didn't get too spooked and end this right now. 'More leaks to the press about Father's radiotherapy, speculation about how long he has left. The palace communication team are scrambling to control the flow of information, but tensions are high.'

Sometimes he felt as if his entire world was crumbling. He swallowed, relieved to see the compassion in her stare. 'It's finally forced me to face facts.' He took her hand, needing to touch her. 'I can no longer spread myself so thinly.'

'Of course you can't.' Clara tilted her head in understanding and concern. 'And the demands on you are only going to increase.'

Andreas clenched his jaw in frustration. He wished they were anywhere but there, where they could barely look at each other for fear of discovery, let alone have a meaningful conversation.

'Can you come over tonight?' he asked with a desperate edge to his voice that he hoped she wouldn't hear. 'We can talk, in private.'

'I finish at six…' She hesitated, glancing down at her feet. 'But perhaps we should…cool it off for a while.'

'This again…?' With his pulse pounding in panic, he rested his hand on her waist, as if he could physically stop her withdrawing. But lately every time they were together felt as if it might be the last time.

'Look, all this media fuss will die down,' he said, willing her to trust him enough to overlook the gossip. 'I know you're nervous about exposure, but I'm dealing with it. I won't let you down.'

Her trust had been badly damaged in the past, so it was no wonder she struggled to completely trust a man like him: a man with baggage. A man whose life was public property.

But couldn't she see that he'd move mountains to protect her?

She sighed, her eyes on their clasped together hands. 'There have been…whisperings on the ward. I think people recognised me from that photo.' She looked up, her fear and uncertainty etched into her face. 'I still need to work here after you've gone, Andreas.'

Nausea rolled through his gut. She was right—after today, he wouldn't be at work to collaborate with her or to be there for her. He didn't want to leave Nordic Care and leave Clara to the wolves. He wanted to look after her. That was what people did when they cared about someone. That was what Clara herself did all the time: with her patients, her family, even with Andreas.

Except, just like the rest of his life, her trust in him, the connection they'd shared, seemed to be crumbling before his eyes. Without even trying, he was failing her.

'I'm sorry,' he said simply, because he couldn't make her

any promises. He had to leave his career. 'I know it's a lot to take on. Of course you must protect yourself.'

With Prince Henrik's diagnosis, with a change of ruler imminent, the media heat on Andreas was only likely to increase. No matter how much he wanted to protect Clara, he was sickeningly aware that, unless she was part of his life, what he could do to keep her family and her safe and safeguard their privacy was limited.

Maybe that was the solution… But she didn't *want* his help.

Fear laced his blood. He'd dated women in the past who'd ended the relationship because they wanted no part of life in the public eye. He'd hoped Clara was different—that she understood him, saw the role, the stage, the act, for what it was: something he did, not something he was. Desperation for her raced through his blood. He didn't want to lose her over this.

'You know all that stuff,' he said, his voice close to begging, 'The media, the photos, the PR moves—that's not the real me. It's just a role I put on, the same way we put on our roles as doctor and nurse when we put on our white coat and uniform.'

'I know.' She inclined her head, regarding him with sad eyes. 'And I've always understood that you have other priorities beyond me.' Her hand rested on his arm. 'I walked willingly into this affair. This isn't a bid for my share of your attention.'

'And just because I'm leaving here sooner than I planned,' he argued, 'Doesn't mean that I'm walking away from *us*. We can still see each other.'

His teeth ground together with frustration. He was already failing at his career and his royal role. And, by selfishly craving Clara, he'd exposed her to speculation, letting her down too.

His stomach dropped. Maybe he should do the right thing and let her go…

He would hate to drag her name into the press and then have

her snubbed or criticised for not fitting some arbitrary mould. In his eyes, she was perfect just as she was.

'I'm just trying to be realistic,' she said. 'We agreed it was temporary.'

'Damn realistic,' he snapped, dragging her into his arms and kissing her, his misery finally spilling over. 'Give me a little longer, *sötnos*.'

He was full-blown begging now, his heart pounding against hers as she looked up at him with uncertainty.

A door below them opened, footsteps echoing on the stairs.

Clara stepped out of his embrace, a guilty look on her face. 'I'll try.'

Casting him one last inscrutable look, she descended the stairs and disappeared. Andreas curled his fingers into fists. He'd always known it would take a special woman to tolerate his life. Since they'd begun their affair, he'd experienced brief flashes of inspiration when he'd wondered if Clara might be that very woman.

But now… Was he failing her? Did he risk hurting her by asking her to stay? A man in his position, with the eyes of the world watching and the weight of a nation on his shoulders— not to mention the self-imposed burden of honouring both his father and his brother as the future of Varborg's monarchy— couldn't afford to be wrong about anything, including Clara.

He couldn't bear to make a mistake. If he wasn't careful, he'd let Clara down. He'd let himself down. And he'd let Oscar down.

None of that was an option.

CHAPTER FIFTEEN

LATER THAT EVENING, shaken from the power of her orgasm, Clara clung to Andreas, certain that she'd never let him go. His groan died against her neck where he'd pressed so many passionate kisses she felt sure he'd leave a mark on her skin.

Not that she cared. The reckless part that was wild for him welcomed a sign of his possession. A reminder that, for a brief time, this connection she'd never felt with anyone else had been real.

He pulled back, slipping from her body, looking down to where she was sprawled on the sofa. This time, they hadn't even made it to the bedroom. Even when they were about to discuss the end of their fling, they couldn't keep their hands off each other.

But Clara was a realist. Their time together was coming to an end. Despite the ache in her heart, and the confusion slashed across Andreas's beautiful face, she smiled up at him sadly.

'It's not over, Clara,' he said defiantly, his breaths gusting. 'Not by a long shot.'

He tucked himself back into his jeans and zipped up.

Close to tears, her blood still thick with endorphins, Clara scooped up her underwear from the floor and wordlessly replaced the garment. She needed to be fully clothed for this talk.

'Maybe not.' She stood and moved away, desperate to escape him and the scent of sex, the cloud of pheromones urging her to keep her mouth shut and get lost in his arms once more. 'But we knew it wasn't going to last for ever. We *agreed*.'

'I understand you're scared for your family's reputation,' he said, his tone that of a coaxing parent for a frightened child, 'But I could protect you, all of you.'

'How?' she asked, incredulous. 'Because, of course I'm scared. My family have been through enough and so have yours. I work here. I still have to face Prince Henrik, and I don't want Mum to have to relive the shame of my father's conviction. But it feels as if it's only a matter of time before it's all dredged up in public.'

'There are vacant properties on the estate.' He reached for her, gripping her upper arms. 'You could all move in until interest in my personal life dies down. The press couldn't get to you there.'

Clara frowned, horrified, her heart cracking that he understood her so little. 'Listen to what you're suggesting. Us moving into a palace property would be confirmation that you and I are involved in some sort of seedy tryst. And my mother and I would still need to leave to go to work and my sister to college.'

'Clara…' He cupped her face and stared into her eyes. 'I have more money than I'll ever know what to do with. I can support you and your family, indefinitely.'

Clara yanked herself free. 'Are you suggesting that I give up my job too? And what—be a kept woman, waiting in some hidden away cottage for your clandestine visits when you have a break in your important schedule or when the royal itch requires scratching?'

'Stop.' His voice was low but authoritative, his scowl the only sign of his fury. 'It wouldn't be like that. I'm not suggesting for ever. I'm just trying to help, because I care about you.'

'I care about you too.' Clara paced out of his reach, suddenly too hot *and* too cold. 'But I told you from the start—I need my independence.'

She levelled him with a defiant stare. 'I watched Mum take second place to my father, quietly toiling away to put food on the table while he chased dream after dream, scheme after scheme, only to put us more and more in debt. I never understood how she could forgive him, time and again. How nothing he did seemed to destroy her love.'

'I'm not your father.' He scrubbed a hand through his already dishevelled hair. 'I'm not trying to steal your independence. I just don't want this to end over one grainy photo online. I thought you understood me, my life, my dreams, the part of me the public don't get to see. I showed you all of me.'

'I *do* understand you.' She rushed back to him because she just couldn't stay away. 'I don't want this to end either.' Hot tears pricked the back of her eyes. The situation was impossible and always had been—a hopeless fantasy.

But, for Clara, it wasn't just fear of exposure. There were other more terrifying feelings making her irrational and confused. She'd opened up to Andreas and become vulnerable in a way she'd never been with another person. She'd told him her most shameful family secrets. She'd worked with him, laid in his arms and held him through his struggles and grief.

Despite all her tough self-talk and caution, all her warnings about holding something back, she'd somehow fallen in love with him. And she was scared, so scared.

As if he knew the tender contents of her heart, he reached for her, roughly tugging her into his arms, pressing his mouth to hers with fierce and desperate possession. Clara embraced the kiss, her tongue surging to meet his, squeezing her eyes tightly shut as if she could block out the rest of the world and just be with him like this: just the two of them, no intrusions, no expectations, no fear.

When they were intimate, everything seemed to make

sense. But the minute it was over she couldn't help but see how strongly she was kidding herself. She wasn't the woman for him, not long term. Having him would mean losing her independence. She wouldn't become like her mother, loving a man on whom she couldn't depend. Abandoning the hard-working provider Clara had become out of necessity would not only make her reliant, it would shatter any hope of Andreas and her being equals. She might love him, but if she let go of that hope she would struggle to love and respect herself.

And the longer she stayed, the greater the risk that she'd break when this ended. Wasn't it better to go now, on *her* terms?

They broke apart, panting.

Clara shook her head. 'I can't do it,' she whispered. 'I can't be this needy, frightened version of myself. I can't rely on you, or anyone, don't you see that?' Not when he could never love her in return. It would be too great a sacrifice.

Pain shifted through his eyes. 'Can't or won't? All I'm hearing are excuses. You can still be yourself and want me as I am. I'm not trying to change you, or contain you, or clip your wings. You said you wanted us to be equals, but maybe it's *me* you find wanting.'

Clara shook her head, hot licks of shame flooding her face. He was right: they were similar, both broken, damaged and scarred. Her fear was compounding his because he was scared to embrace the role he'd been born for: scared to fail his nation, his dying father and maybe even his beloved Oscar.

Just then, the room's intercom connected.

'Your Highness, there's been an accident in the Banquet Hall. Someone fell from a ladder while decorating for the Christmas party. Can you come?'

Without hesitation, Andreas marched to the intercom, pressed the connection button and spoke. 'I'll be there. Call an ambulance.'

He rushed to the bedroom and returned seconds later with his medical bag.

'I'll come with you,' Clara said. No matter what their personal issues, they were still a team.

He paused at the door, as if about to point out that her presence at the palace when she was off duty would expose their secret affair, but he said nothing.

Clara shoved aside her fears. She loved him and she couldn't have him. What was a little workplace humiliation compared to that?

The Banquet Hall had been transformed by two enormous Christmas trees, and twinkling festive garlands hung from every column and doorway. The casualty, a woman in her fifties, was surrounded by a small group of concerned staff members.

Clara and Andreas kneeled at her side.

'She's unconscious,' Clara said, feeling for breath.

'There's a pulse,' Andreas replied.

'She's barely breathing,' Clara added, seeing an obvious compound fracture of her lower leg.

Andreas produced a bag and mask from his medical case, which he placed over the woman's mouth and nose, and began rhythmically inflating her lungs with air.

'Can you stabilise her neck?' He glanced at Clara. 'She might have a spinal fracture.'

Clara held the woman's head steady while Andreas continued to inflate her lungs. Their eyes met, their concerns shared. Any movement could destabilise a fractured vertebra. But, until the paramedics arrived with a neck splint, all they had was each other.

'Has an ambulance been called?' Andreas asked the nearby staff in a choked voice.

Several of them nodded.

'Can someone get a clean towel from housekeeping?' he

instructed, his face pale and slashed with worry. 'And cover that leg wound, please.'

Clara's throat tightened. Andreas seemed frantic.

'Do you know her name?' Clara whispered, her bruised and battered heart going out to him.

'Kari. She's worked here over twenty years. She's always in charge of the staff Christmas party. I... I've met her grand-children.'

He clearly felt responsible for this woman.

Clara stared at his anguished face, trying to communicate her support without words. Personally, things between them were horribly uncertain, the emotional divide widening with their mismatched expectations and the things holding them back, but she was still there for him.

'Can we have some privacy, please?' Andreas spoke with authority to the onlookers. 'Jens and Magda, you stay. The rest of you, thank you for your help, but we'll take it from here.'

When they were alone, the two remaining staff members having moved a short distance away, Andreas swallowed, his expression pained. 'Thank you for being here. I appreciate your support.'

'It was an accident,' Clara whispered, knowing that he would torture himself if something serious happened to this member of his staff, a woman he'd known most of his life. She knew him so well, this Viking of hers. And the last thing Clara wanted was to add to his burdens. Maybe she could hold on a little longer—lock up her heart and give their re-lationship some more time until he'd come to terms with the changes in his life.

But, oh, the risk was massive...

Kari stirred, regaining consciousness. She groaned in pain, trying to swipe away the mask covering her face.

'Kari, hold still,' Andreas said. 'You've had a fall, bumped your head.'

While Clara tried to keep the casualty immobilised, someone returned with a clean towel and Andreas set aside the Ambu bag to cover the lower leg fracture, which had punctured the skin and would be prone to infection if left exposed.

The paramedics arrived with oxygen, a hard collar and back board. While Clara fitted a nasal oxygen catheter in place, Andreas explained what had happened to the paramedics. The ambulance crew fitted the neck brace and back board, and administered some painkillers. Andreas and Clara helped out by splinting Kari's fractured leg so she could be transported to hospital.

'I'm going with her in the ambulance,' Andreas said distractedly as the paramedics lifted Kari onto a stretcher.

Clara nodded, their break-up set aside for now. 'Will you call me later? Let me know how she is?'

He nodded and met her stare, the things they'd left unsaid hovering between them. His accusation from earlier reverberated in her head.

Maybe it's me you find wanting...

Clara swallowed, desperate to hold him. There was nothing lacking in him; the deficiency lay with *her*. She'd never been in love before and she was terrified to love him openly, freely, honestly because of how vulnerable she'd be.

But they weren't alone and he had enough to deal with.

As the paramedics wheeled Kari away, Clara watched Andreas leave, every part of her aching with love for him. She made her way back to the guest wing, her resolve strengthening. She would give him a little more time, perhaps until Christmas, but then she *would* walk away. She would bury her feelings, because loving him changed nothing. If she became the person making all of the sacrifices, her love would never survive. Better to be alone and heartbroken than be on the wrong side of an unequal relationship.

After all, being self-sufficient was second nature.

CHAPTER SIXTEEN

A WEEK LATER, after a night shift at the palace, Clara returned home, her plan to indulge in some well-earned self-care—a long soak in the bath, painting her fingernails and styling her hair in an elegant up-do.

Tonight was the staff Christmas party and she wanted to look her best for Andreas. They'd only managed to see each other twice since Kari's accident. Both times, he'd sneaked Clara into the palace and they'd made love as if it was the last time, and had carefully avoided any talk of breaking up. The cracks in Clara's heart had deepened each time, but Christmas was only two weeks away.

In the bathroom, Clara removed the contents of a brown paper bag from the pharmacy, a flutter of nervous anticipation in her stomach: gold nail polish, volumising hairspray… and a pregnancy test. She could no longer ignore the fact that her period was three days late when she was unfailingly regular; her breasts were sore and she was more tired than usual. She took the test and filled the bath, pouring in some scented bubble bath to take her mind off the little white plastic stick.

What would she do if it turned positive? More importantly, how would Andreas react?

She stripped off her clothes, her gaze drawn to the test, which already boasted two pink lines: positive. Her hand fell protectively to her abdomen, her heart thumping wildly. Those two pink lines changed *everything*. She was pregnant with Andreas's baby.

After her bath, she dressed in the green vintage dress she'd borrowed from Alma, fitting matching glass earrings with trembling hands. She stared at her reflection, half in awe of the woman staring back, half panic-stricken. The dress complemented her skin tone, so she appeared radiant, and there was a new strength to the set of her posture, as if she was already inhabiting her new role as a mother.

She was adamant—the baby's happiness would be paramount.

Her phone pinged with an incoming text from Andreas.

Can't wait to see you tonight.

Clara blinked back tears, refusing to ruin her mascara. Now she had bigger issues than when to walk away from the man she loved but could never have. Now she'd have to tell him about the pregnancy—tonight.

She sat on the bed and typed a reply.

Me too.

Then she deleted it and threw down her phone. That wasn't entirely true. Part of her was dreading their conversation. What would Andreas expect of her now? Would he want shared custody of their child or would he be forced constitutionally to disown the baby? After all, they weren't married.

Nauseated, Clara slipped her feet into her heels and fastened the buckles, her mind racing with the many implications. She'd have to pull back on the hours she worked as her pregnancy progressed. She'd need to take maternity leave, and then what? There was an excellent state-run crèche near

Nordic Care that her colleagues talked about but would Andreas approve? Would he demand a private facility beyond Clara's budget?

And what about their child's privacy? Would simply being related to Andreas make the baby a target? How would Clara keep their child safe and keep her independence? What if, as a prince, Andreas's custodial rights to their child surpassed her own? What if he wanted to raise their child as a prince or princess without Clara? What if he made all the decisions and she was powerless?

Standing, she smoothed her palms over the silky fabric of the dress. She wouldn't allow any harm befall her child. Her mother had raised two daughters as good as alone, and Clara could do the same. She would protect this baby with her life and provide for its every need, with Andreas's input or without it.

'I'm glad you're feeling better,' Andreas said to Kari at the Christmas party. 'Thank you for the festive transformation. The hall looks magical.'

The room glittered with a thousand lights and was bedecked with two enormous Christmas trees. That Kari was there after all her hard work, albeit on crutches, her broken leg in plaster, raised his dampened spirits.

Why hadn't Clara replied to his text?

They hadn't raised the subject of ending their fling since the night of Kari's accident. The past week had passed in a busy blur. Clara had taken extra shifts at the hospital to cover staff illness and Andreas had been occupied with a state visit to Finland and with preparations for this evening's festivities. He'd even supervised the renovation of his new suite of rooms. He was determined to stamp his own mark on ruling the principality, and the first step was feeling comfortable enough to make the role his own.

His stomach twisted in recognition of how he'd decorated with Clara in mind. Foolish, given his inability to see beyond the life-changing events of the next few months. But, if he could just hold onto her and protect her a little longer until the intense media interest died down, then he could think straight.

Andreas moved on to welcome another group, glancing at Prince Henrik, who was doing the same thing on the other side of the hall. His father had insisted on being present, and for now showed good energy levels, but Andreas was determined to keep an eye on him.

The Cronstedt family couldn't exist without the hundreds of people filling the ballroom, their tireless work behind the scenes as vital as the prince's ribbon-cutting ceremonies, diplomatic speeches and weekly audiences with Varborg's Prime Minister.

Speaking of vital…was Clara there?

Discreetly, he scanned the room before asking after the palace administration manager's small children. His jaw ached from smiling, his reserves of small talk running low. He needed to see Clara, to know that he could convince her to stay his for a little while longer.

He'd just moved on from a conversation with the housekeeping team when he spied Clara talking to her fellow nurses and the prince's personal physician. Even though the other doctor was in his fifties and happily married, a white-hot shaft of jealousy pierced Andreas's chest as he watched her smile up at the man.

She looked radiant and seemed so carefree, so Clara.

When was the last time she'd smiled at him that carefree way? Was his desperation for her hurting her, crushing her sense of independence? Would he fail her if he didn't let her go soon? But every time he tried to imagine being without her he rushed the other way, clinging tighter.

With everything going on in his life, they seemed to have

lurched from one crisis to another, the only highlights the blissful moments of intimacy they managed to snatch.

Something jolted in his chest as he watched her. Were those moments of intimacy enough? Clara deserved more. She deserved peace of mind, security and privacy. She deserved a man who was focussed only on her, a man who'd protect her and never fail her. These were all things Andreas longed to give her but, because of his position, couldn't guarantee.

At his side, Nils spoke. 'Your Highness...'

Andreas came to. He'd been staring, mesmerised by her, as he'd been from the start. Deviating from the planned route around the room, Andreas walked her way.

'I wanted to thank you all personally,' he said to the entire group, 'For taking such good care of Prince Henrik. As you can see—' he tilted his head in his father's direction '—he's feeling much restored tonight, and that's down to all of you.'

Clara hadn't yet met his eye, and he couldn't be seen to favour one staff member over any other, not when gossip had already spread since the night she'd attended Kari's accident by his side.

If it were down to him, he'd whisk her away to his new bedroom and make love to her all night until he convinced her that she wanted him, the real Andreas, more than she wanted her career, her independence and her anonymity.

At last, he allowed his gaze briefly to settle on Clara. It hurt to look at her beauty and not touch her. But, on closer inspection, she appeared pale. Was she unwell, or had she reached her decision and would soon tell him it was over?

Sensing Nils's discomfort, because Andreas was on a tight schedule to talk to at least half of the staff, he prepared to walk away, panic surging through him. Then, at the last second, she looked up, looked right at him and the party around him seemed to stutter to a stop.

He stared hard, pouring all his feelings for this woman into his eye contact so she would see how much he cared, how much he wanted her, how he wished he could be just a man she was free to care for in return, without risk.

She looked away.

Crestfallen, Andreas was spurred into action. He plastered on his smile and moved on to greet the next group, but not before he instructed Nils, 'Bring her to me at the end of the festivities—the Blue Room.'

All he had to do was make it through the party. It was going to be a very long night.

For the rest of the evening, Clara watched Andreas from afar, a sense of déjà vu chilling her to the bone. The first time they'd danced in that very hall, she'd known that he was a natural born leader. He'd been torn between the role he'd trained for and the role that was his birth right, because he lived with deep unresolved guilt over his brother's death.

But his royal status shone as people vied for his attention. He was a prince. He had it all—charisma, kindness and empathy. How could she avoid falling head over heels in love with a man like him?

Swallowing the lump in her throat, Clara paced to the window of the Blue Room, the place where she'd been instructed by Nils to meet Andreas. This was the room where they'd negotiated their fling. How fitting that this would also be the scene of the conversation to come.

Clara stared out at the illuminated balcony and beyond to the vast, snow-capped mountain range that separated Varborg from the rest of Scandinavia. It was a stunning night. Crisp, cloudless skies were an inky blank canvas for the multitude of stars.

Clara's vision blurred, fear a metallic taste in her mouth. How would he take her news? How would she tell him that she was carrying his baby and still hold on to her heart? How would she find the strength to walk away? Because she must, and sooner than she'd promised. Now that there was the baby's happiness and safety to consider, she needed to be stronger than ever.

Just then, the sky above the mountain tops began to dance with the magical wonder of the Aurora Borealis, or northern lights, the green light streaking the blackness. Clara watched, mesmerised. There was magic here, in Andreas's world. But the clock was about to strike midnight and she couldn't stay.

A sound in the room behind Clara drew her attention. She spun to find Andreas observing her, his face dark with repressed need.

'You look breath-taking tonight,' he said.

Clara swallowed, her pulse a painful thud in her throat.

'More so than nature's display outside, even.' His stare latched to hers, but he didn't step closer or try to touch her. 'Green suits you, *sötnos*. You should wear it more often.'

'Thank you. This dress belonged to my mother.' She glanced down at the simple silky sheath. 'I'm recycling.'

She looked up and swept her gaze over him from head to toe, the ache in her chest sharpening at his refined splendour. 'You look very regal, every inch the prince you were born to be.'

A small frown pinched his eyebrows together. 'And yet here, with you, I'm just Andreas.'

Clara nodded, her heart cracking open a little wider. Just because she'd fallen in love with him didn't mean that she could have him as her own. He needed a woman content to exist in his shadow and, while Clara might tolerate that in public for appearances' sake, it would destroy her to know that they weren't equals in their private lives—to know that she loved him desperately, but that he didn't love her.

But how could they ever be true equals? He was a prince, a ruler, and she was a penniless nobody in a borrowed dress.

'I need to tell you something,' she said, cautiously stepping closer, because even when she was ready to walk away she wanted him with terrifying desperation.

'Okay.' His frown deepened.

Clara raised her chin, resolute. 'I'm pregnant.'

His body seemed to sag with relief, excitement in his eyes. He almost stumbled as he lurched for her, gripping her arms.

'Are you sure?' His pulse ticked furiously in his neck.

Clara nodded. 'My period was three days late so I did a test this afternoon. It was positive, but obviously it's very early days.'

She shrugged, her own joy at the news diminished, because in the deepest part of her soul she'd dared to imagine that, if she ever had a child, it would be with a man who loved her and who she could love freely in return.

But this wasn't a fairy tale. This was reality. Ahead lay confusion and doubt for the future and fear that her parental rights would be restrained because of her baby's paternity.

With his face wreathed in delight, Andreas hauled her into his arms. Clara rested her head against his crisp white shirt, against the soothing thud of his heart. She closed her eyes, dragging in the scent of him, fighting tears.

'That's wonderful news.' He pulled back, his stare swooping to her flat stomach. 'Are you feeling okay?'

She nodded numbly. 'I'm fine, Andreas. A little tired, perhaps.'

'Do you want to sit while we talk?' he asked, clearly still dazed.

Clara shook her head. 'I wanted you to know straight away, but we don't have to sort everything out right now.' She needed more time to think things through.

Doubt flashed in his sparking eyes for a split second before he rallied. 'What's there to sort out? You're carrying a Cronstedt prince or princess. I'm going to be a father.'

His awestruck grin made her vision blur. She hated being

the one to burst his bubble. 'I'm glad that you're happy.' She winced and ducked her head. 'But the prince-princess thing doesn't count. We're not married. I'm just an ordinary woman.'

Andreas laughed, clutching her back to his chest. 'A hundred years ago that might have mattered, but today my heir is my heir. Besides,' he said, 'We'll *get* married.'

Clara swallowed, dread sliding through her veins. 'Just like that—you decide and I have no say or rights? Don't you think you should ask me what *I* want?'

She might as well be a brood mare.

All her greatest fears rolled in like storm clouds in the sky. *He* was the important one in this relationship. *He* had all the power. Was she meekly to agree to his sterile marriage proposal, give up her career and simply exist as a royal appendage, too lovesick to question the arrangement?

'I'm sorry.' He gripped her shoulders, peering at her with confusion. 'What *do* you want? I assumed that you'd be overjoyed by this news, but you must also be in shock.'

'I *am* happy,' Clara said, a massive part of her, the part that loved him and ached for a ridiculous fantasy, feeling anything but. 'But…there's so much to think about. I want us to raise this child together, but we shouldn't rush this conversation. Let's take a few days to come to terms with the news and then we can discuss a way forward.'

Once her shock wore off, maybe she'd have the strength to tell him how she felt about him.

Andreas's expression darkened. 'There is only *one* way forward, Clara. I'm a Cronstedt. My child, *our* child, will one day rule Varborg. I'm sorry, but there's no getting around that.'

'I understand.' Clara shook her head, which was fuzzy with confusion, her heart sore with grief. 'But that's a separate issue. I don't want some sort of pragmatic royal marriage.'

She might have felt differently about the institution if he'd loved her, if he'd proposed in some romantic way rather than with ruthless practicality. But she'd never once envisioned being trapped in a loveless marriage, a relationship in name only, for show when the cameras were rolling or to give their child a sense of legitimacy.

'Then we'll live together,' he stated, adamant. 'Raise our child together. It's unconventional for my family, but I'll make it all right. After all, I plan on modernisation. What's more modern than co-habitation and co-parenting?'

'You're not hearing me, Andreas,' she said, her stomach twisted into knots with grief. 'I can't live like this, the way you do.'

Not if she couldn't have all of him, including his heart. The civilised, unconventional relationship he proposed would be doomed from the start. She'd be the one making all the sacrifices, without even gaining the reward of his love in return. She'd be just like her mother: loving a man who couldn't possibly care as deeply for her; forced to sacrifice her career, her independence, to put his needs first; vulnerable, her options limited because they'd made a child together, a child she would always prioritise above herself.

'I can't lose everything that I am,' she continued, trying to keep her voice even. 'My job, my independence, my autonomy.'

'You can still have those things and be with me, Clara. I'll take care of you and our child. Protect you both. Support you always. I won't let either of you down.' He frowned, disbelief entering his eyes. 'Unless it's *me* you don't want...'

His voice was flat, but there was a question in the last word, a question that split Clara's heart in two. She held her hand over her mouth to hold in a sob. She wanted him so badly she was crushed by the weight of her desire. But this was no longer about what *she* wanted. It was time to be realistic. To set aside this fantasy and focus on making a secure life for their child, who would never have to grow up too quickly, the way they'd both had to.

'You once said that we don't always get what we want,' she whispered, wishing she believed in dreams, wishing she could escape into his magical world, wishing he could love her as deeply as she loved him. 'That sometimes we must be something others need us to be.'

He frowned, staring as if carved from stone.

She faltered. But she needed to be strong for all of them—herself, Andreas and the baby.

'You need to be Prince Andreas Cronstedt,' she said, sweeping her eyes over his immaculate suit, and his tie bearing the royal crest. 'You need to rule Varborg, because that's who you were born to be.'

'How two-dimensional I sound—a cardboard cut-out.' Disappointment dimmed his stare. He clenched his jaw and stood a little taller. 'And what do *you* need?'

Desperately trying to hold in her tears, to stand her ground and not reach for him, Clara exhaled a shuddering breath. 'I need to be a mother.'

He nodded once. 'And us?'

'I'm sorry,' Clara said, tears finally spilling over her eyelids to land on her cheeks. 'I'm so sorry. I can't.'

Clara fled, finally giving herself over to the body-racking sobs once she was safely ensconced in the back of a taxi and speeding into the night.

CHAPTER SEVENTEEN

THREE DAYS LATER, Andreas ducked his head as he alighted from the House of Cronstedt jet, the bitterly cold wind stinging his face. He descended the plane's metal staircase and slid into the back seat of his car beside Nils.

He'd been forced to keep his engagement, a visit to Oslo, but now that he was home, now that he'd given her as much space as he could tolerate, he wanted only one thing: Clara.

But she didn't want him.

He scowled at his reflection in the car's window. It was dark out, after eleven p.m., and his mood was as black as the landscape. Clara's dismissal and lack of faith in him the night of the Christmas party had stung worse than any pain he'd ever known. Nothing had felt right since he'd allowed her to run away, as if all the colour had leached out of the world.

He balled his hands into fists, failure choking him. His baby was smaller than a pea, but he'd already broken his word and let his child and Clara down. He'd been so wary of failing her as he'd failed Oscar that he'd said the wrong things and pushed her further away, given up too easily. Just as he hadn't fought hard enough for Oscar, he hadn't fought hard enough for Clara; hadn't told her that he loved her and begged her to stay.

And the price of those mistakes crushed him. He missed the sound of her laughter, the scent of her skin and the tiny gem twinkling in her nose, like her own personal star. He missed her passion, her massive heart and the way she made him twice the man he was alone.

The car pulled up at the palace and Andreas stalked inside. He would go for a swim, do length after length after length until he collapsed with exhaustion. Maybe then he'd know what to do, how to change her mind and fix this.

'Your Highness,' Møller said, appearing from the shadows. 'Prince Henrik requests an audience, sir.'

'Is the prince unwell, Møller?'

'No, sir.'

'Very well.'

Andreas found his father in his library, behind the great slab of a desk that had once seemed vast and intimidating to Andreas the boy. But now he saw it for what it was—just a functional piece of furniture.

'You wanted to see me, Pappa.'

Prince Henrik stood and joined Andreas near the fire, a sheaf of documents in his hand.

'Take a seat, son.'

Andreas folded himself onto an arm chair opposite his father.

'Everything is finalised.' The prince tapped the folder that contained the state funeral plans for Prince Henrik: Operation Aurora. 'A copy for your final approval.'

Andreas nodded, taking the folder and then staring into the flames. He respected his father's wishes for the funeral. That didn't make his dying any easier to bear.

'You are an inspiration, Pappa,' he said, his voice strangled with emotion. 'I'll try to do you proud. You have my word on that.'

Especially when, despite being a doctor, he could do so little for his father now. But, when he thought of the future, Clara was always at his side. What if, without her, he would never be whole?

'I did things my way, just as you will do things yours,' the prince said, walking to his drinks cabinet and pouring two tumblers of Torv, Varborg's finest whisky. 'Varborg will be lucky to have you as its ruler.'

Startled by his father's declaration, Andreas took the offered glass. He'd always seen his father as a proud, emotionally distant but otherwise honourable man. Could Clara have been right? Had Andreas's guilt and grief over Oscar blinded him to the truth? Should he have confronted his demons and spoken to his father sooner?

The prince took a seat. 'My decisions weren't always the right ones. We are all human, after all. After your mother died, I worried that I gave you too much freedom. I missed her so terribly, and she'd made me promise I would try to give both our boys as normal an upbringing as possible. It wasn't always feasible with Oscar,' his father said, sipping his drink. 'I had to prepare him for the reality of his situation, but with you... I tried my best. And look what you've achieved.'

Prince Henrik glanced his way. 'I am incredibly proud of you, Doctor Cronstedt.'

Andreas held his breath. 'Even when it should have been Oscar sitting here with you today, discussing the succession?'

Prince Henrik frowned. 'Life doesn't work like that. There are no guarantees. We play with the hand we've been dealt.'

Andreas looked down at his hand wrapped around the crystal tumbler, his knuckles white. He was going to be a father— time to be the man his child would need. 'I want you to know that I fought with everything I had to save Oscar. I just wish I could have done more.'

The panic flared in his chest, as if he was back inside that crushed vehicle.

'Of course you did. You're a doctor,' the prince said. 'You've saved countless lives.'

Andreas faced his father. 'Except I couldn't save the most important person to me, to our family, to Varborg.'

The older man stared, a rare display of emotion shifting over his expression. 'I could have lost you both that day. I've read the official inquiry into the accident. I know what you did to try and save your brother. You were incredibly brave and fearless and determined. *No one* could have done more.'

Andreas swallowed, his throat too tight to take a sip of whisky. 'I blamed myself for a long time.'

'I'm sure, but no one else blames you,' his father said. 'You are a credit to me and to Varborg. I should have told you that before today. Time to lay Oscar to rest, perhaps, and live *your* life.'

'How…?' Andreas's voice broke.

Prince Henrik tilted his head, compassion in his eyes. 'The mark of a life well-lived is that you have far fewer regrets than blessings. I was blessed with a meaningful role, marrying the love of my life and with my two sons. What more can a man ask?'

Andreas stared ahead, wondering if it could be as simple as minimising regret. Could he honour his brother, his family, his nation, by chasing what he needed to be happy?

'Pappa,' Andreas said eventually, 'I have something to tell you. Another blessing for the tally—you're going to be a grandfather.'

Prince Henrik smiled, nodding his head sagely. 'Indeed, another blessing. Congratulations.'

Andreas's heart skipped a beat, the expectant flutter of excitement, a certainty that if he could win back Clara anything was possible. 'Don't you want to know who the mother is?' he asked, wishing he would one day be able to count as many blessings as his father.

Prince Henrik shrugged. 'Does it matter? If you've found love, that's all I care about. Because this job—and it's best to think of it that way if you can—will be so much easier if you have someone you love at your side.'

Andreas knocked back the whisky in a single swallow, pulled out his phone and checked his schedule for the next day. He had a visit to the local army barracks that he couldn't reschedule, but then he would find Clara and tell her that he loved her.

Because he *had* found love with a woman who was his equal in every way that mattered. He didn't want to spend another day without her, so he'd have to persuade her that their fears—his that he'd let her down and hers that she couldn't be independent—weren't good enough reasons for them to be apart.

Clara opened the door of her family's home, kicked off her shoes and barely made it to the sofa before she collapsed in a wretched heap of exhaustion. She should head up to the shower, peel off her creased Nordic Care uniform and hide under the spray until she'd cried out, but she couldn't seem to move.

Was it possible to feel so broken, but still have her heart beat? Was it because it beat for him, Andreas? Did it know better than her head what was right for her?

Reaching for a beautiful, hand-made crocheted throw her mother had made while recovering from her cancer treatment, Clara pulled it over herself and curled into a foetal ball. Would she ever feel warm again?

Alma appeared from the kitchen with two mugs of hot chocolate. 'You look frozen. They say there's more snow due tonight.'

She placed the mugs on a side table, sat on the sofa and reached for Clara's foot, tugging it into her lap so she could massage Clara's aching instep.

'My first job was waitressing,' Alma said, telling the story

Clara had heard before. 'I would come home from work in tears, my feet were so sore.'

'You're so strong, Mama,' Clara whispered, trying not to cry. 'What's your secret?'

Alma made a dismissive sound. 'I'm a woman. We're born strong. Look at you, for instance.'

Clara smiled, but her eyes burned with unshed tears. If only she'd been strong enough to resist Andreas. But no, she would never wish away meeting him. Falling in love had given her the most precious of gifts: her baby. *Their* baby.

'But strength comes from being yourself and being happy,' Alma continued. 'I've always taught you and Freja to unapologetically love yourselves.'

Clara sighed. 'Being happy is…complicated. And what happens if you love someone else, if their happiness feels more important than your own?'

She'd seen Alma's love for Lars, how one-sided it had been. How soul-destroying it must have felt to be so let down by him.

Alma released Clara's foot and took a good look at her daughter, understanding dawning. 'Then the key is finding someone who loves you like that in return.'

'Exactly.' Clara offered up her other foot for a rub, bombarded by the image of Andreas's expression when she'd rejected him. 'Complicated.'

'Is this about your father?' Alma asked, working her magic on Clara's foot. 'You know he wasn't always the man he became in the end. We were crazy about each other, loved each other passionately for many years. We made two beautiful and kind daughters before we lost our way as a couple.'

Clara stilled, her heart pounding rapidly. It was hard to imagine her parents young and madly in love. 'So you don't regret loving him, despite the way it turned out in the end?'

Alma frowned. 'I know Lars let you down when he left. I wish he'd been there for you and Freja. What *I* regret is that you took on too much responsibility when I got sick,' Alma continued, peering at Clara a little too closely for comfort. 'You were barely an adult. Lars and I should have protected you better. But I'm fine now. You don't need to worry about me. You have to live your own life.'

Clara smiled sadly certain that, by leaving Andreas the night of the Christmas party when she'd been too overwhelmed to think straight, she'd walked away from her only chance to feel happy.

'I made my choices, as did Lars,' Alma Lund continued, as if sensing the depth of Clara's despair. 'I've lived with them, made more choices. That's all any of us can do. We can't hold ourselves back from love in case it fades or turns sour or dies. And you shouldn't let my choices, your father's choices, stop you from making your own. That's not the independent woman I know.'

Tears seeped from the corners of Clara's eyes and tracked into her hair at her temples. She was so sick of crying, so tired of feeling empty. She wanted to live, to feel young and vibrantly alive, the way she did with Andreas.

'I *am* in love, Mama,' she whispered. 'And I'm having his baby.'

Alma gasped, tears of joy glittering in her eyes. 'And does he love you?'

Clara shrugged, her heart a rock. 'I don't know. I couldn't tell him how I feel and he's…kind of preoccupied with important stuff.'

Alma snorted. 'Nothing is more important than love, Clara. You will soon know that when my grandbaby is born.'

Clara smiled indulgently, thinking about Andreas. Ruling Varborg *was* pretty important.

'You must tell him how you feel,' Alma said. 'You are so much stronger than me. There's nothing you can't do, including being honest with this man. If he's worthy of your love, then tell him, see where love takes you. It will be an adventure you'll never regret, even if it isn't perfect or doesn't last for ever.'

'You're right.' Clara sniffed, her tears drying up. 'I *should* tell him. He likes my outspoken streak.'

'See? I like this man already.' Alma smiled. 'Let's have him over for dinner.'

Clara laughed. She couldn't wait to see the look on Alma's face when Prince Andreas walked through the door.

Except he was just Andreas, and if she ever met him Alma Lund would see that. But only if Clara stopped feeling sorry for herself and told him that she loved him—the *real* him.

'A grandbaby.' Alma clapped her hands excitedly and reached for her knitting bag. 'I can't believe it.'

'Are you staying up?' Clara said, shrugging off the throw and heading for the shower. 'I might head to bed. I'm exhausted.'

'You get some rest. I'll be up in a while. I just want to make a start on baby clothes.'

Clara smiled fondly as she plodded upstairs. She didn't have the heart to tell her mother that her grandbaby was going to be a prince or princess. It wouldn't make a blind bit of difference to the home knits.

As she lay in bed, she made the baby a promise. Andreas deserved to know that she loved him, that he was her first and only choice; that, for her and for their baby, he was the best man possible.

CHAPTER EIGHTEEN

THE METAL BARRIER was icy-cold. Clara clung tightly, refusing to relinquish her spot at the front of the waiting crowd. Varborg's dashing heir to the throne was a popular man. If one more onlooker screamed his name in Clara's ear, she was going to lose it.

None of these people knew the real him. They only saw the two-dimensional version, the sexy Viking who lived in a palace, whereas Clara knew his passions and his dreams. She knew the feel of his skin and the shape of his smile. She knew the rhythm of his heart and the deepest regrets of his soul.

She loved him, pure and simple, and she needed him to know.

But maybe she'd left it too late…

The doors at the front of the army barracks opened and the waiting crown roared, even before Andreas appeared. Clara held her hands over her ears, scared that the noise would somehow hurt their baby, but her eyes were glued to Andreas as he emerged.

Her legs trembled with desire. He was wearing his dress uniform, the navy-blue coat trimmed with white epaulettes making his broad shoulders appear wider, the row of medals on his chest testament to the calibre of man he was. He smiled a movie-star smile, waving at the crowd before shaking the hands of the officials lined up between the exit and his car idling a short distance away.

The people sharing Clara's section of barrier screamed his name and waved Varborg's flag, clamouring for a closer glimpse of him, perhaps a wave, a direct smile.

Clara knew exactly what they wanted because she clamoured too. Those things were just as precious to her, perhaps more so, because she loved Andreas the man, and the fans out there in the cold only admired and respected Andreas the prince.

Leaning over the barrier, she willed him to look her way. One look in his eyes and she'd know if he'd already moved on and made practical arrangements for their baby, but forgotten Clara. The woman beside her screamed his name in earnest. For a moment, it looked as if he might head straight to his car after passing along the military line-up, but then he spied a little girl holding a small posy of flowers and he approached the crowd-control barrier, stooping to share a few words with the lucky child.

Clara held her breath, tears prickling the backs of her eyes. He was going to make such a wonderful father and she hadn't given him a chance to be ecstatic about her news. She'd ruined it with her fear that he could never love her back. But loving someone didn't make a person weak, it made them strong. Love was the most powerful force in the universe. It made humans do extraordinary things, such as Andreas fighting to save the brother he loved. She didn't have to fear her love for him, she just had to embrace it and let it work its magic.

'Prince Andreas!' Clara's neighbour cried as he worked his way along the row, shaking hands, answering questions, smiling for his admirers.

Clara froze, her stare tracing every inch of him. He had shadows under his eyes, as if he hadn't slept. She wanted to hold him so badly, she hooked her feet up on the edge of the barrier and leaned closer as he approached.

Andreas reached for the hand of the woman at Clara's side, his stare flitting over the crowd behind as he tried to acknowledge as many onlookers as possible. The woman began to gush, telling him how much she admired him, how handsome he looked in his uniform, how sorry she was to hear that his father was terminal...

The noise around Clara dimmed to silence. He was close enough to touch now. If she just reached out...

He turned his head, saw her and froze. 'Clara...'

Clara blinked, her eyes hot with tears. She stared, seeing in his beautiful eyes that she still had a chance to tell him how she felt. That it wasn't too late.

Snapped from his shock at seeing her, Andreas removed his hand from Clara's persistent neighbour's grasp. He gave Nils some instructions, his eyes never leaving Clara's.

Her heart soared with excitement. She would go to him, tell him that she loved the real him, and all his other versions, and ask him to give her another chance. Tell him that with her he would always be safe to be himself. Just then, Clara felt a weight slumping against her shoulder, sliding down, shoving her sideways.

She dragged her eyes from Andreas and watched with horror as the frantic fan next to her slid to the floor in a faint. Clara spread her arms wide, trying to push back the crowd, to stop them from trampling the poor woman to death. But it was like trying to hold back the tide with her bare hands. Trying not to panic for her own safety and that of the baby, Clara stooped at her neighbour's side and held her head to protect it from hitting the ground.

There was a rush of movement, the barrier parting, soldiers shouting, the crowd around her clearing. Andreas appeared, kneeling opposite her, his expression one of frenzied concern.

'Are you okay?' he asked, his arms spread wide to protect Clara and the fan from any stray onlookers.

Clara nodded, desperate to touch him, to kiss him and beg him to hear her out. 'She's fainted.'

Clara removed her scarf and propped it between the woman's head and the cold, hard ground. Andreas felt for a pulse and instructed one of the nearby soldiers to lift the woman's legs to return the blood back to her head. Within seconds, Nils had organised a circle of soldiers, a human barrier to stand guard around her, the casualty and Andreas.

The woman stirred, coming to. 'Prince Andreas...' she said, sounding delirious that her rescuer was the man she'd come there to see.

'You're okay,' he said. 'You just fainted. We're going to get you some help. Just relax.'

The woman tried to sit up, sliding a hand through her hair to ensure she looked her best. Clara smiled up at him; she could relate.

'You're here,' he said to Clara, as if dazed.

Clara nodded. 'We need to finish that conversation.'

As paramedics arrived and began tending to the woman, Andreas took Clara's hand, his grip determined. 'Come with me, *sötnos*.'

He stood, helping Clara to her feet, and Nils urged them towards the car.

Hope surged in Clara's chest as she climbed into the black car with the tinted windows, her head light, as if she too might pass out.

Andreas dragged Clara into the back of the car, his adrenaline so high, his head spun.

'Tell me you're okay,' he pleaded, his hands on her shoulders, holding her distant so he could scour every inch of her for evidence of trauma.

'I'm fine.' She smiled. 'A little jealous at the effect you have on women, but apart from that, I'm good.'

Andreas crushed her in his arms, his sense of humour abandoned. He pressed his lips to her temple and breathed in the scent of her hair. 'I've never been more scared than when I saw you go down in the middle of that crowd. I almost ripped apart that barrier with my bare hands to get to you.'

He pulled back, his stare flitting over her face to make sure she was real. 'And the baby's okay?' He glanced down at her stomach, as if he had X-ray vision.

Clara rested her hand there. 'I think so.'

'Clara…' His voice broke, his face crumpling with anguish. 'I love you.'

She'd come to him. That had to mean something. Perhaps she was ready to give him another chance. He slid his hands from her shoulders to cup her face. 'I love you, and I need you, and I want you.'

Speechless, she blinked, her eyes shining with tears.

'I've tried to give you some time. But I can't take it any more. I need you to understand how deeply I've fallen in love with you and how I'll do anything, *anything*, to have you in my life.'

She gripped his wrists, and for a panicked second he thought she would tug his hands away, but she didn't. The move reminded him of their first meeting, their first kiss.

But he had to say everything he needed to say.

'I know the idea of my life is hard for you, but I'll abdicate if I have to. You don't have to give up your career. I wouldn't change a single wonderful thing about you. Or we can work together,' he rushed on. 'I want to build a dedicated rehabilitation hospital for wounded veterans. You can help me. We can build something to be proud of together—equals.'

'Andreas…' she whispered, tears spilling over her eyelids.

'We can raise our baby together,' he said, brushing the tears away with his thumbs and pressing kisses to her damp cheeks. 'We don't have to marry if it's not what you want, but I'll spend every day of my life being there for you, as you deserve. You and our child will always be my first priority. You'll always be able to rely on me.'

'Andreas, I love you too,' she said.

Andreas did a double-take, staring at her mouth in case he'd misheard.

She smiled and his heart soared with hope. 'I love you. I came today to see you, to tell you. I should have told you the night of the Christmas party.'

Still a little confused, he shook his head. 'You do?'

'Of course. I love you.' She laughed with joy. 'The real you and all your other amazing versions—doctor, ruler, prince. I've known for ages, but I just got scared. I've never been in love before. I couldn't handle how vulnerable it made me feel. But it also makes me strong. Loving you means I can face anything life might throw at us.'

She cupped his face, her fingers curling into his hair. 'I'm sorry about the things I said. How I made you feel inadequate. But my fear was about *me*, about *my* hang-ups, not about you. You're everything I want. You're not my father, you're *you*. That will always be enough for me. I choose *you*. Even if there was no baby, no throne, no palace—'

'Palaces,' he interrupted, his heart as light as a feather. But she needed to know what she was entering into.

'Palaces,' she continued, completely unfazed, 'I would still choose you. Because I know *you*. You're a man of passion and integrity. Varborg is lucky to have you. *I* would be lucky to have you.'

Andreas dragged her close and kissed her. Joy spread through his body as their lips met, melded together then parted.

'Clara,' he said, pulling back to stare into her beautiful eyes, eyes that shone with love for him. 'I want you to know that you can trust me. I won't hurt you. I'll love you and respect you and cherish you every day. Even if our relationship fails for some reason—and I'll devote my life to ensuring that it doesn't—I'll still love you, still respect you, still take care of you.'

She laughed, pressed her lips to his, pushed him back against the seat and sat astride his lap. 'No, *I'll* take care of *you*.'

Andreas grinned up at her, his hands gripping her hips. 'We can settle the details later, *sötnos*. All that matters to me is that you're mine.'

She nodded, her stare bright with resolve, with her signature passion, with love. This time when they kissed Andreas held onto her for all he was worth. He would never stifle or try to change this incredible woman. He would worship her, subtly care for her behind her back and love her.

'Where are we going?' she asked, pulling back from their kiss to glance out of the window.

Andreas unbuttoned her coat and slid his hands inside her jumper. He needed the feel of her soft skin under his palms, telling him she was real, she was *his*.

'Bed, I hope,' he said, tugging her mouth back to his. 'Or, if you prefer, my giant bath tub, or wherever you fancy... As long as I'm inside you, I don't care.'

She pressed kisses down the side of his neck while her fingers tackled the metal buttons of his uniform coat. 'In that case, I have a request—a negotiation, even.'

He grinned, loving the way this conversation was going. 'I'm all yours, *sötnos*.'

Andreas lay back against the seat and spread his thighs under her backside, shunting their hips closer so the heat between her legs burned through his trousers where he was hard for her.

'Can we go to the cabin?' She loosened his tie, using it to pull his mouth closer. 'I thought we could try out those fur pelts before the fire in true Viking style.'

Andreas closed his eyes as her lips caressed his earlobe,

overcome with the passion and love for his sweet nose, his *sötnos*, his equal in every way.

His hand reached for the intercom to speak to the driver behind the tinted-glass partition. 'The hunting lodge, please, Tor. And call the housekeeper.' His speech was slurred with desire as Clara rocked her hips against his. 'Have him light the fires. Tell him I'm bringing my princess.'

'Yes, Your Royal Highness,' Tor said.

Clara took off his tie, her expression approving and serious with concentration as she exposed his chest and pressed her lips to his skin.

He pressed the button again. 'And, Tor?' he mumbled, dragging his lips free of Clara's wild kisses while he popped the clasp of her bra with his other hand. 'Put your foot down.'

EPILOGUE

Five months later...

CLARA LAZILY CURLED her toes into the padded seat of the sun lounger as desire, thick and drugging, pooled in her belly. From under the wide brim of her sun hat, she watched with almost fanatical concentration as Andreas swam lengths of the pool at Varborg's summer palace near the capital.

Her husband's lean and powerful body barely caused a ripple on the azure blue surface as his muscular arms sliced through the water, his back flexing and clenching with every stroke.

What was it about him and water? Clara's palms itched to get hold of him; to trace every muscle; to feel his skin and the springy golden hair of his magnificent chest; to sink her nails into those broad shoulders of his, while she cried out his name with the passion that was never far away when they were together.

Or when they were apart, come to think of it. Desperate to have him finish his swim and pay her some much-needed attention, Clara forced herself to look away from Europe's hottest, but no longer most eligible, prince. Just because she loved the security of being held in those strong arms didn't mean it was seemly to drool.

After all, she was a princess. They'd married in a small private ceremony on Christmas Eve, with only Prince Henrik, Alma and Freja as guests.

Now what had she been doing before she'd become so thoroughly distracted...?

Clara glanced at the paperwork on her lap, closing the folder and setting it aside. Building work was well under way on their veterans' rehabilitation centre, which was due to open in three months' time. With any luck, Clara would make the opening ceremony, having safely delivered their baby. But there were other projects in the pipeline: a grief counselling centre; a charity hospital in honour of Oscar; a state-of-the-art hospice facility in memory of Prince Henrik, who'd sadly lost his battle with cancer just after Christmas. Clara and Andreas had found endless ways to use their medical training to help others. That they could continue to work alongside each other was the icing on the cake.

Clara heard a splash. Andreas finished his swim and hauled his golden, tanned, athletic body from the pool using his considerable upper-body strength, all those gorgeous muscles she now knew by heart rippling.

Pretending to be asleep under her sunglasses, Clara watched him shuck off his swimming trunks, attach his prosthesis and wrap a towel around his hips, concealing his magnificent manhood from her greedy gaze.

Her core clenched as he carelessly slicked back his hair from his handsome face. She lay frozen so she could enjoy the hungry look on his face as he glanced her way. Mesmerised by his wild, Viking beauty, she watched him skirt the pool and walk her way. The water droplets on his chest glistened in the sunlight.

The molten heat between Clara's legs built to an inferno as he paced closer.

'I know you're awake, *sötnos*. I felt you watching me.'

He paused beside her lounger and looked down at her with predatory intent, his stare raking every part of her bikini-clad body, pausing at her breasts—which were almost spilling free of the tiny bikini top—the mound of her pregnant belly and lower, to where a triangle of fabric was all that concealed how much she wanted him.

But of course he knew. They were constantly wild for each other. Clara scraped her teeth over her bottom lip, her eyes tracing one particular droplet of water that slid down his bronzed chest and the ladder of his abs into the gold-tinged trail of hair that began below his navel.

'Can I help it if I like you all wet?' She sighed with longing.

Before he could answer, she swung her legs over the side of the lounger and stood before him, her fingertip tracing another droplet intent on a similar path.

Quick as lightning, his fingers encircled her wrist, guiding her hand lower to press against his hardness under the towel.

'Careful, *sötnos*.' His eyes blazed with arousal. 'I don't want to tire you out and we've already made love twice today.'

Clara scooped her arms around his waist and pressed her still needy body against his, her baby bump getting in the way.

'You know what they say…' She raised her face to his and melted into his strong arms as he kissed her, the passionate surges of his tongue against hers spreading flames along her every nerve. 'Third time lucky.' She pulled back, aware that his towel had slipped, and he stood naked, proud and beautiful in the sunlight.

He cupped her face, his stare full of desire, promise and love. 'I'm the lucky one,' he said, tilting up her chin to press another kiss to her lips. 'But whatever my princess wants, she shall have.'

His hands skimmed her breasts, her waist and her hips until he filled them with the cheeks of her backside, pressing her close.

Clara sighed, her heart full to bursting with love for the only man who could make her fairy-tale ending come true. 'I want *you*, Andreas. Always.'

* * * * *

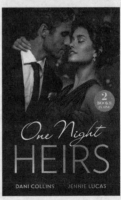

COMING SOON!

We really hope you enjoyed reading this book.
If you're looking for more romance
be sure to head to the shops when
new books are available on

Thursday 20th
June

MILLS & BOON

MILLS & BOON®

Coming next month

ER DOC'S MIRACLE TRIPLETS
Tina Beckett

'There's something I need you to know.'

Seb sat in silence, staring at her face as if he didn't want her to say another word. But she had to. He deserved to hear the words so that he could make whatever decision he felt he needed to. So she pushed forward. 'I'm pregnant.'

'Pregnant.' A series of emotions crossed his face. Emotions that she couldn't read. Or maybe she was too afraid of trying to figure them out. 'But the last attempt failed.'

Even as his words faded away, an awful twist of his mouth gave evidence to what he was thinking. That the babies weren't his. She hurried to correct him. 'But it didn't. I assumed when I started spotting that I'd lost the pregnancy, because it was the pattern with the other IVF attempts. And I didn't go to have it checked out right away because of all the stress. I waited until you were gone to try to sort through things.'

'So you didn't lose the baby?'

His words were tentative, as if he was afraid that even saying them out loud might jinx everything. She got it. She'd felt the same way when they'd done the ultrasound on her and told her the wonderful news.

'Babies. I didn't lose the babies…plural.'

He sat up in his chair. He was shocked. Obviously. But was he also happy? Dismayed? Angry? She could no longer read him the way she'd once been able to.

'You're carrying twins?'

She slowly shook her head, unable to prevent a smile from reaching her lips. 'There are three of them.'

Continue reading
ER DOC'S MIRACLE TRIPLETS
Tina Beckett

Available next month
millsandboon.co.uk

afterglow BOOKS

Afterglow Books are trend-led, trope-filled books with diverse, authentic and relatable characters and a wide array of voices and representations.

Experience real world trials and tribulations, all the tropes you could possibly want (think small-town settings, fake relationships, grumpy vs sunshine, enemies to lovers).

All with a generous dose of spice in every story!

OUT NOW

Two stories published every month.
To discover more visit:
Afterglowbooks.co.uk

LET'S TALK
Romance

For exclusive extracts, competitions and special offers, find us online:

- **f** MillsandBoon
- **X** @MillsandBoon
- **⊙** @MillsandBoonUK
- **♪** @MillsandBoonUK

Get in touch on 01413 063 232

MILLS & BOON

THE HEART OF ROMANCE

A ROMANCE FOR EVERY READER

MODERN

Prepare to be swept off your feet by sophisticated, sexy and seductive heroes, in some of the world's most glamourous and romantic locations, where power and passion collide.

HISTORICAL

Escape with historical heroes from time gone by. Whether your passion is for wicked Regency Rakes, muscled Vikings or rugged Highlanders, awaken the romance of the past.

MEDICAL

Set your pulse racing with dedicated, delectable doctors in the high-pressure world of medicine, where emotions run high and passion, comfort and love are the best medicine.

True Love

Celebrate true love with tender stories of heartfelt romance, from the rush of falling in love to the joy a new baby can bring, and a focus on the emotional heart of a relationship.

HEROES

The excitement of a gripping thriller, with intense romance at its heart. Resourceful, true-to-life women and strong, fearless men face danger and desire - a killer combination!

From showing up to glowing up, these characters are on the path to leading their best lives and finding romance along the way – with plenty of sizzling spice!

To see which titles are coming soon, please visit

millsandboon.co.uk/nextmonth